The Forger

by the same author

fiction

NIGHT OVER DAY OVER NIGHT

CALM AT SUNSET, CALM AT DAWN

IN THE BLUE LIGHT OF AFRICAN DREAMS

THE PROMISE OF LIGHT

ARCHANGEL

THE STORY OF MY DISAPPEARANCE

non-fiction

STAND BEFORE YOUR GOD

The Forger

PAUL WATKINS

faber and faber

First published in 2000
by Faber and Faber Limited
3 Queen Square London WC1N 3AU

Typeset by Faber and Faber Ltd
Printed in England by Clays Ltd, St Ives plc

A CIP record for this book
is available from the British Library

ISBN 0–571–20194–6

2 4 6 8 10 9 7 5 3 1

The Forger

1

I reached Paris in the summer of 1939, at the age of twenty-one.

All my life I'd dreamed of coming here. A thousand times I had pictured myself as I was then, getting off the train at the Gare St Lazare. Now that the moment was finally here, it seemed to me even more glorious than anything I had imagined.

This lasted about ten seconds.

Halfway down the platform, one of my suitcases fell open. Tubes of paint, brushes and palette knives scattered on the ground. I swore quietly, got down on my hands and knees and began to gather them up. Travellers stepped past, shuffling to get around. Then a pair of boots appeared in front of me. They were black and mirror-polished. Slowly I raised my head, squinting in the sunlight that beamed down through the glass roof of the station.

It was a policeman. He wore a black uniform with a row of silver buttons down the front and a stiff-brimmed cap set squarely on his head. He had a short moustache and eyes as dark as his boots. The man held his hands behind his back. He was not smiling.

Someone had trodden on a tube of crimson paint, tracking red footprints across the platform.

'You're a painter?' he asked.

'Yes, sir,' I told him.

'Just what we need,' he said. 'Another artist.'

The month before, I had received a letter notifying me that I'd been awarded a scholarship by the Levasseur Committee for Fine Arts. After a show of my paintings in New York City, I'd been interviewed by a French art magazine called *Le Dessin*.

Not long afterwards, I heard from the Levasseur Committee. The scholarship entitled me to three months' study at the Atelier Alexander Pankratov, 21 rue Descalzi. A stipend was included for living expenses and an apartment would be rented for me. I hadn't applied for any scholarships and I'd never heard of the Levasseur Committee, but no one had to talk me into going.

My ship was late arriving in Cherbourg. By the time I got to Paris, classes had already begun.

I took a taxi straight to the atelier. It was five flights up a set of wide and worn-down stairs. No elevator. Outside the atelier I stopped to catch my breath and set down my suitcases. I wiped sweat off my face with a handkerchief, then opened the door.

The atelier was one huge room. An entire wall was filled by a window that overlooked the city. The panes were old and gave a rippled view of houses, trees and roads, making them seem drunk and crooked, like a hundred-piece puzzle that had been forced together even though the pieces didn't fit. The rest of the room was panelled with dark wood and patched with cork board, which had been nailed up haphazardly for the display of student sketches.

In the middle of the room was a platform. On it was a naked woman. She was sitting on a chair with her back to me, so all I could see was the slightly freckled sweep of her shoulders and dark hair ponytailed down the middle of her back. It was about the most beautiful hair I'd ever seen. Dark and shining as oriental hair, but glimmering deep lacquer-red among the silk-fine strands, like wine held up to sunlight. Perched around her on high-legged stools were the other students in the atelier. But only two of them: a woman and a man. They were both sketching at their easels but stopped to look up when I appeared. I wondered where the others were. Surely there have to be more, I thought.

'Change!' boomed a voice. 'Begin again!'

The noise sent me stumbling backwards. I peered into the gloom, trying to see who had shouted.

There was a shuffling of paper. The naked woman shifted her position. A new round of sketching began.

It took me a second to pinpoint the source of the voice. Now I saw a man sitting in the shadows. He was short and broad-shouldered, with a tattered fluff of grey hair that made him look like someone emerging from the smoke of an explosion. His eyes were slightly narrowed, as if waiting for another detonation. He had the slightly jutting chin and crumpled lips of a man about to spit.

The man slouched in a flimsy chair made of wood and canvas. The armrests were leather straps and the canvas seat and back were held in place by a rope that threaded through a series of brass grommets. It all looked as if it might at any moment dump its owner on the floor. My first thought, however, was that the chair, like everything and everyone else in the room, was so terrified that it would never dare to fail him.

I stood in the doorway, waiting to be asked in.

The man appeared to be ignoring me. He rested his elbows on the straps of his chair and touched the tips of his fingers together, just in front of his face. His eyes stayed closed and his mouth twitched as if he were counting to himself.

I lugged my suitcases over to an empty stool, smelling the sharp sap reek of turpentine, which knifed through first one and then all of my senses. I felt the closed-off trance that came when I was painting. I looked up at the shelves along the walls and saw the dirty bottles filled with linseed oil the colour of tea. Their tops were stuffed with dirty rags, like an arsenal of gasoline bombs.

I got hold of a piece of charcoal and some paper from my suitcase and squinted at the model, ready to draw.

She was staring right at me, sitting slightly bent forward with her hands pressed together between her knees. Her feet were set apart, resting on her curled toes like a ballerina. She had a very round face. There was something almost Asiatic about her eyes and the height of her cheekbones, but her skin was pale and she was tall and full in her body and seemed so completely at ease with her nakedness before us that she gave the impression of someone who did not understand the point of clothing.

I had drawn precisely one line when the man's eyes popped open. He launched himself out of his chair and shouted 'Stop!'

A sigh passed through the room. The two students sat back from their work and laid down their pencils.

From far below in the street came the sound of cars shifting through their gears as they gathered speed down the Rue Descalzi.

The model stood up from her bench and stretched, raising her arms above her head and locking her fingers together, bending them back on themselves. The whole sweep of her body stretched in one unbroken smoothness from the muscles of her thighs up to the tendons of her neck.

The man paced behind us, saying nothing. Now that he was on his feet, I saw he was shorter than he'd first appeared. When he reached me, he stopped. I heard him stirring his toe in my open suitcase, shifting the jumble of paint tubes. Then his head appeared over my shoulder.

'You are Monsieur Halifax,' he said. He pronounced it 'Alley-fax'.

'Yes, sir,' I replied, not turning my head to face him because he was too close.

He nodded slowly, looking at the single smoky line that I had drawn. 'Alexander Pankratov,' he said, as if that were not his name but an elevated state of mind, which I would never fully grasp. 'You speak French,' he told me.

'Yes, sir,' I said, wondering how he could judge that from only two words. My mother was French-Canadian and had taught me French at the same time as she had taught me English. Some of my Québecois phrases might have sounded old-fashioned to the French, but I could make myself understood.

'You have come a long way,' he told me.

'Yes, sir. From America.' I rummaged in my jacket for the acceptance form that carried his signature. 'I have the Levasseur scholarship. I'm signed up for . . .'

'I know you are signed up,' he snapped.

Slowly, I let my hand slip down from my inside pocket.

Pankratov moved on to the others.

It was only now that I had time to study them. My first instinct was to look at their work, even before I looked at them, but the easels had been arranged in such a way that I couldn't see what they'd drawn. Both had been issued white smocks, which made them look like hospital patients.

The woman looked to be in her mid-forties. She kept her chin raised in a gesture of dignity and defiance, but the way her eyes followed Pankratov's every move showed what lay behind her barricade of confidence.

The young man had dark and bushy hair, a broad nose and heavy lips. His complexion was rough and red, as if maybe he drank a lot. He had two pencils in his mouth. He ground his jaw and the pencils waggled like antennae. The ends were chewed to splinters. He seemed very pleased with his work, tilting his head from side to side in admiration of the drawing and brushing at the charcoal lines with the side of his thumb to blur the edges. When he stood to take off his apron, I noticed he was heavy in the chest without being overweight. His hands were strong and muscular. He dragged his fingers down the stubbly shadows of his chin, which made a gentle tearing sound and left a dull grey smudge.

He had taken off his smock and left the cord around his neck, so that the white sheet trailed down his back like a circus ringmaster's cape. The young man realized I was looking at him. He turned his head and smiled at me. He held his charcoal pencil as if it were a dart he was preparing to throw at me. 'Pankratov likes you,' he whispered. 'He didn't give you his withering stare.' He hardened his gaze into an evil squint to imitate Pankratov. 'He's quite mad, you know. I mean, a genius, of course, but quite mad.' The man leaned forward and murmured, conspiratorially, 'He drinks turpentine while he's painting.'

I had heard about some artists who did that. Sometimes I felt the same temptation. When the clean burn of it is pinching in your lungs and nose and its vapours are washing cold through your blood, it is hard not to want to feel it even stronger inside you, to have the essence of your own painting suicidally pumped by your heart.

'We're all going down to the café afterwards,' he said. 'You ought to come.'

'Monsieur Balard!' barked Pankratov from the other side of the room.

'Yes, sir!' answered the man.

'You are always talking about what will happen after the class.'

'Yes, sir!' said Balard again.

Pankratov mumbled something unintelligible, which made him sound like a clockwork machine running down. He turned away to face the window.

Balard rolled his eyes at us.

I realized that Pankratov was watching Balard's reflection in the window. I winced, waited for him to explode; but he pretended not to notice. It occurred to me that Pankratov might be fond of Balard, despite his tone of voice. Maybe he was glad to have found someone who would stand up to him.

I, however, joined the ranks of the intimidated, unable to shake from my mind the bowel-cramping memories of schoolmasters with their cannon-fire voices and chalk-throwing, head-slapping, hair-pulling punishments.

The day continued in this fashion, with Pankratov ordering us to sketch the woman on the platform and then to stop and sketch her again. It was all sketching, interrupted by his pacing round the room to inspect our work. He made only one comment to me. After one series of sketches, he took the paper from my easel and held it up in front of him, as if he were holding up a banknote to see its watermark. 'You have come a long way,' he said, 'to be here.'

'Yes, sir.'

He handed me back the paper. 'And if you cannot be here on time and do better than this, you will have come a long way for nothing.'

I jerked my head around. That was too much for me.

He was right there, inches away. Come on, he seemed to be thinking. Talk back to me. Talk back and see what happens.

I didn't talk back. My face grew hot with frustration and shame.

There was a knock at the blurred glass window of the door.

We all turned to see who it was.

I saw the pink smudge of a face and then a hand, tap-tapping a ring against the glass.

'Fleury,' said Pankratov. 'What the hell does he want now?'

The door opened slowly and a frail, well-dressed man poked his head cautiously into the room.

'Well, Fleury?' demanded Pankratov. 'What is it?'

Fleury cracked a smile. He held out a fan of little cards. 'Tickets!' he said. He stepped into the room. 'Tickets to an opening tonight at my gallery. Everyone will be there. Free champagne. Little cheesy things. It will be grand. You'll see.'

Now I got a better look at Fleury.

He was my age, but his clothes made him seem older. He wore thick, black-rimmed glasses and an expensive-looking navy double-breasted suit, which nevertheless did not fit him. His wrists and hands hung down so far below the sleeves that it looked as if he had dislocated his arms. He was tall and gaunt, and his hair was short but studiously unkempt, as if designed to clash with his otherwise impeccable appearance. He still held the tickets, like someone about to perform a magic trick with cards.

'I won't prevent it,' said Pankratov, 'but I certainly don't recommend it.'

Fleury didn't seem to hear. He was staring at the woman on the stage.

She was half-turned in her chair, not shy about her nakedness. She smiled at Fleury. 'Hello, Guillaume,' she said.

'Oh, hello, Valya,' he replied quietly. 'Will you come to the show?'

'I might,' she told him. 'The free champagne sounds nice.'

'It is,' said Fleury, nodding and looking vaguely stunned. 'It will be. Valya.' He said her name softly, by itself.

I thought, There stands a man in love.

'Come along, then!' Pankratov snapped his fingers, as if to wake Fleury from his trance. 'Give me the tickets and push off.'

Fleury held out the tickets and Pankratov snatched them away.

'You have a new pupil,' said Fleury, jerking his chin in my direction.

'Yes,' said Pankratov. 'All the way from America.'

'Oh, this is the American?' asked Fleury. 'The one . . .'

'Yes, the one I told you about,' snapped Pankratov. 'Now, if you don't mind, I'm running my class.'

Fleury made his retreat. 'I hope to see you all there,' he announced to the room. 'And you, Valya. I hope you'll come tonight.'

'We'll see,' she said.

When Fleury had gone, Pankratov sighed violently. 'Stay away from that man,' he muttered.

I wondered if he was telling all of us or only Valya.

'Why don't you want us to go to the show?' I asked.

The man and the woman stared at me, surprised that I would dare to open my mouth.

Seeing their expressions, I immediately wished I hadn't.

'You be careful around Monsieur Fleury.' Pankratov wagged one finger slowly in the air, as if it were too heavy for his hand. 'You might think you are an artist, Monsieur Halifax. You might actually be an artist. But Monsieur Fleury, he is something quite different. Monsieur Fleury is a *dealer*.'

Before I had a chance to reply, Pankratov wheeled around and clapped his hands. 'Begin again!' he thundered.

I returned to my drawing, blind with obedience, forgetting everything else.

Outside, the summer day filed past in brassy sunlight and only when the brass had turned to copper, warped through each distorted pane of glass on the great window of the atelier, did Pankratov allow us to leave. He smashed his palms together in the dusty air and told us all to be on time tomorrow. Then he hooked his thumbs into the thick leather belt around his middle. The buckle of this belt was a large slab of brass, on which I could make out an ornate spread-winged eagle with two heads. The eagle was holding a sceptre in one claw and a crown in the other, and there was some kind of royal crest on the eagle's front.

I tried to get a better look at it as I walked up to Pankratov, holding out the papers of my scholarship. 'I wanted to ask you,' I said.

He raised his eyebrows. 'Ask me what?'

'About the Levasseur Committee.'

'What about them?' he asked.

'Well, I wanted to thank the committee. There's no address on their letter. I wondered if you knew where they are.'

He shrugged his shoulders. 'Perhaps they like to remain anonymous. I'm sure if they want to talk, they'll come and find you.'

Slowly I folded the papers and put them back in my coat pocket.

Pankratov busied himself with a broom, sweeping with wide and violent strokes across the bare wood floor.

On the way downstairs, I felt the relief of having been set free from Pankratov's pacing behind our backs.

So did the others. The nervous woman seemed to have grown a decade younger on her walk down to the street. She introduced herself as Marie-Claire de Boinville. Her features were fine, her nose aquiline and dignified. The dark and narrow chevrons of her eyebrows stood out against her cedar-blonde hair. She had kept the beauty of her much younger years and she knew she was still beautiful. She carried herself that way, without arrogance or effort. Her clothes were dark and conservative, but there was a sultriness about her short-cut jacket draping across her shoulders and the way her footsteps seemed to trace a line from stair to stair, as if she were walking a tightrope. 'This was one of Pankratov's good days,' she said, 'if you can believe it.'

'I was wondering how he would be.'

'Oh, he can be worse. Much worse. He's so moody.' She waved one hand dismissively. On her ring finger was a large diamond engagement ring flanked by two rubies, and a heavy gold wedding band. 'He just has to be endured.'

'Where are the other students?' I asked. 'I mean, *are* there any others?'

She shook her head. 'So few people can stand him.'

'What does he have against dealers?' I asked.

'Oh, Pankratov has something against everybody.'

The man with the black curly hair spoke up behind us. 'Pankratov is a genius. Even people who hate him agree.'

'How many do you think there are who hate him?' asked Marie-Claire. 'Do you suppose it runs into the thousands?'

The black-haired man set his hand upon my shoulder. 'My name is Artemis Balard.'

'David Halifax,' I said. We shook hands awkwardly, as he reached down from the step above.

'You mustn't take it badly,' he said, 'if Pankratov comes down hard on you. He's a good judge of art. You just have to accept that. He criticized me once, back when we first started.' Then he slapped me on the back. 'Good to have you along.' Artemis Balard galloped past me down the stairs, pom-pomming some tune of his own invention.

Then it was just Madame de Boinville and me. She smiled

faintly. 'Artemis is very sweet, but sometimes he doesn't think before he speaks. He's right about Pankratov, though. The man may be a genius, but the truth is I don't know how much more of him I can take. Do you suppose all geniuses are like that? I mean, I don't think I've ever met a genius before. Not a real one, anyway. Unless of course, you're a genius,' she added after a moment. 'In which case I've met two.'

I shook my head and smiled.

'Well, I'm glad,' she whispered, and rested her hand for a moment on my arm. 'One is about all I could stand.'

I didn't go to the café that first day, despite Balard's invitation. I had promised myself only work while I was here. No lounging in coffee shops. For as long as I could take it. Only work. I'd set myself the goal of twelve finished paintings within the first two months. I'd brought no pieces with me. Nor had I arranged to have a gallery represent me. Once I had the paintings, I'd set about finding one. There was something about starting out fresh in this new city that had appealed to me before I left.

My apartment building was number 50 on the Rue Descalzi. I rode to the top floor, three flights up in a cage of an elevator whose suspension cord creaked and grumbled as it hauled its cargo of the old landlady and me. Her name was Madame LaRoche. She had tightly curled grey hair, and wore a flower-patterned housedress with clumpy black shoes. The first thing she did after shaking my hand was to point at a large and gaudy coat of arms, carved out of wood and painted, which hung in the main entranceway. 'My family,' she said. 'Very noble.'

'Yes,' I said.

'And your family?' she asked, her voice rising.

'Not very noble, I guess.'

She nodded severely, to show it was a problem that could neither be helped nor overlooked.

The apartment was a one-room studio divided into kitchen, bathroom and bedroom by three heavy velvet curtains, which hung from brass rings on wooden rails. It had a window at the front and a window at the back. Slowly I set down my cases. Then I straightened up and clenched and unclenched my hands to get the blood flowing again. I went to the front window. It looked out at a large advertisement that had been painted on the wall of a building across the road, which was some kind of warehouse. The advertisement was bone-white with a wineglass in the middle. The glass was half full of red wine. Below it, in black letters, was: *'Buvez les vins du Postillon.'*

'Beautiful,' she said, and gestured out of the window. 'The view.' She didn't sound very convincing.

'When does the sun come in?' I asked. 'For how many hours a day?' I wanted to know if I could get any painting done here.

'It depends,' she said suspiciously. 'The clouds. The time of year. Most of the day you will get sun. You don't want to see the kitchen?'

'That's all right,' I told her.

Madame LaRoche squinted with suspicion. She held out the keys, pinched between her thumb and index finger. 'You are an artist,' she said.

'That's right,' I replied.

'If this committee weren't paying your rent, and paying for it in advance, I wouldn't let an artist stay here.'

'Yes, ma'am,' I said, wearily. I'd heard talk like that before.

'The only other exception I have made is for Monsieur Fleury. He lives here, you know, in one of the luxury suites downstairs.' She emphasized the word 'luxury', letting it roll off her tongue in slow motion. 'I expect you have met Monsieur Fleury. Everybody has. Everybody here likes Monsieur Fleury. He is a very charming artist.'

'I did meet him,' I told her. 'I think he's a dealer. Not an artist.'

She looked me up and down. 'You are an artist at making paintings. *He* is an artist at selling them.'

'I guess you could see it that way,' I said.

'I see it,' she told me, 'just the way it is. And I tell you one other thing I see: I see people who come to Paris because they think that the city will make them into what they want to be. Actors. Painters. Musicians. But it doesn't, you know. It doesn't work that way.' Having made this pronouncement, she went out into the hall and pressed the button for the elevator to take her back down.

I walked over to the window and hauled it open, hearing the iron counter-balance weights rattle inside the frame. Warm air coming off the sun-heated slates on the rooftops brushed against my face. I leaned on the lead sheeting that plated the narrow sloping rim of the building, and looked out across what little of Paris I could see. I listened to the noises of the city, squinting in the glare of sun off the Postillon wine advertisement.

Already, I was starting to feel lonely. I looked down and was surprised to see Fleury standing in the middle of the street.

He was looking up at me, his hands tucked into the pockets of his jacket. The whites of his teeth showed when he smiled and the sun winked off his glasses. 'I see we're going to be neighbours,' he called out.

Madame LaRoche heard his voice. She came in from the hall, pushed me aside and wedged herself half out of the window. 'Hello, Monsieur Fleury! Have you been working hard?'

'Madame LaRoche!' Fleury filled the air with her name. 'You look lovely today!'

'Oh,' said Madam LaRoche very quietly, then glanced about the street to gauge how many people might have heard him call her lovely. She waved and then stepped back into the room. 'You see,' she said to me. 'He is so charming. A gentleman of the old days.'

'You should come to the show,' Fleury shouted to me.

'I ought to work,' I told him.

'But it *would* be work,' he said. 'Now that you're here, you'd better start making connections.'

I held up the ticket, to show I hadn't thrown it away, and gave him a non-committal smile.

He gave a short wave and walked towards the café at the far end of the street.

I set up my easel in the corner of the room and then, from my suitcase, I brought out a little pyramid-shaped box. Inside it was a metronome, the kind that people use when they are learning to play the piano. I started it ticking on the table in the kitchen, very slowly, with the easy swing of a grandfather clock pendulum. Whenever I came to a new place, unfamiliar sounds always got in the way of my concentration.

With this apartment, the noises were mostly from the warehouse across the road. I spent a few minutes observing the nearly constant line of trucks that pulled up outside the front gate. They were loaded with crates of wine, the bottles packed in straw. The bottles clinked as they slid on to the flatbed of the truck. Each shipment was checked by a man with a long moustache and hobnailed boots. The sound of his footsteps echoed up and down the street. After inspecting each truck, he banged the flat of his hand against its side, to signal that it could drive off. I found myself waiting for the next thump of the foreman's hand, or wondering why the hobnails had momentarily stopped crashing on the cobblestones. And later, at closing time, I was startled by the thundery rumble of large rolling metal doors with *Défense de Stationner* painted on them as they were pulled down and locked in front of the Postillon warehouse. There were indoor sounds as well. Water dripping. Muffled conversation in the room across the hall. Someone sloshing in a bath downstairs. The metronome helped to clear these distractions from my head.

It was dark outside now. From down in the street came sounds of laughter. Breaths of music reached me high up in my dingy apartment, which smelled of old cooked meat and coal-tar soap and the faint sourness of milk. In my newness here, I could pick out each individual odour of the place. I wondered how long it would be before they merged together in my senses and I would find them comforting. I brushed aside the red velvet curtains. The way they partitioned the space gave me the impression that I was living in the chambers of a heart. I lay down on the bed, too exhausted even to take off my clothes or roll back the sheets or care that the bed was too short.

I thought about the people I had left behind, my mother and my brother. I wondered what they would be doing now. After my father had been killed in the Great War, she had used her widow's pension from the army to buy a small boarding house in Narragansett. Her days were caught up in the flow of visitors from Boston, New York and Philadelphia. They came to walk the beaches and maybe catch a glimpse of Newport high society, like children staring through the window of a pastry shop. My brother was a trawlerman, a job for which I alternately admired him because of the risks he took, and pitied him, because of those same risks. The hurricane season was approaching fast, and soon there would be news of boats going down, as they always did, under the greybeard rollers off Cape Cod. I remembered being disappointed at how easily they took the news that I'd be leaving for France. It wasn't that I wanted them to talk me out of it. If I was honest with myself, it was more that I had wanted them to try, the same way they had once tried to talk me out of my career as an artist. I realized that, for them, Paris was so far away it was as if I'd slipped into a world of dreams and was unreachable. In their minds, I had become as distant as my father.

The days spent on the ship on my way here had left the faintest rocking in my skull, the slow pendulum swing of the Atlantic's deep-sea swells. I dropped away into sleep with the vertigo rush of falling off a cliff.

2

One hour later I woke with a start when a car backfired down in the street. I raised one hand to rub the sleep-creases from my face and realized I was still holding the ticket to Fleury's gallery show.

I decided I would go. I had to get something to eat, anyway, and I didn't feel like spending my first evening stuck by myself in the apartment.

The gallery was on the Rue des Archives. I asked directions from Madame LaRoche, who was sitting on a collapsible metal chair in front of the apartment building, smoking a little pipe.

The streets were busy. I passed dozens of restaurants whose awnings sheltered the pavement. Hand-holding couples stopped to check menus. They leaned towards the chalkboards on which the specials were written. Soft light pooled on their faces. Diners were jammed elbow to elbow at small tables. Waiters with long white aprons and slicked-back hair navigated through them, trays raised above their heads. Smells of garlic and wine wafted into the street. Some places had beds of ice on which oysters and sea urchins and shrimp were laid out. I could smell the faint salty sweetness of fresh seafood. My stomach cramped with hunger. But I didn't want to sit in a restaurant by myself. Not tonight, anyway. I figured I would wait until after I'd gone to the gallery show, then buy some bread and cheese and maybe some wine and head back to the Rue Descalzi. The brightness of restaurant lights and streetlamps and the dark emptiness of shops that had closed down gave me the sensation of everything drifting about, unattached, rushing by in a flickering hallucination. Hunger and my tiredness and, it seemed, the boom of Pankratov's voice still an echo someplace in my head all piled together to make my walking in the streets like walking in a dream. I'm finally here, I thought, and at the same time I expected to wake up at any minute and find myself back home, in the summer heat, my old dust-greasy table fan creaking around on the window sill and blowing a feeble breeze over the block of ice I went out and bought each August night. I would take the ice back to my apartment wrapped in brown paper and set it in a large pasta bowl. I put the fan behind the bowl and turned it on. In the mornings, I would wash my face in the cold water from the melted ice. I waited for the sound of the fan to work its way into my sleep. I listened past the rumble of the city for that faint persistent sound, which would be proof this was a dream. When it didn't happen, I breathed out a sigh from the bottom of my lungs.

The closer I got to the gallery, the more nervous I became. Fleury was right about these openings being work. I never did well at them, even though I knew they were a necessary part of the business. I felt a sickening sharpness in my guts, as if I had swallowed broken glass, whenever I thought about the fancy-dress slaughterhouse of art openings. At the last show of my own work, I had arrived late, walked once around the room and then ducked out the back door. I was halfway to the train station before the gallery owner had caught up with me and persuaded me to come back.

Ten minutes, I thought to myself. Give it ten minutes and then leave, even if Fleury asks you to stay. Or five, even. Five minutes. I was locked in a reverse bidding war with an auctioneer inside my head.

I saw where the gallery was half a block before I came to it. People spilled out into the little side street, hugging glasses of champagne in one hand and cigarettes in the other. I listened to the hum of party talk. Everyone was smoking. A blue-grey cloud of tobacco hung in the still air of the street.

Five minutes, I thought. Two minutes. One minute.

Inside, the place was so dense with people and smoke that

the paintings were almost impossible to see. The artist stood against the far wall, wedged in by two women and a man. They were talking with their faces so close to his that he could not raise his glass to his lips to take a drink. They waved their cigarettes dangerously close to him and his nervous smile twitched as he flinched back from the burning tips.

I saw Fleury. He dodged from group to group like a humming-bird gathering pollen. People who clearly did not know him were grasped by the hand or shoulder or sleeve and made to feel, somewhere in the barrage of niceties, that they ought to know to whom they were talking. He caught my eye and waved me over as if he were hailing a cab.

Grimly, I made my way towards him.

'I want you to meet someone very important,' said Fleury, in a voice too loud to go unnoticed by everyone who stood nearby. 'This is Madame Pontier. Of the Musée Duarte.'

Madame Pontier was wearing a loden coat with big buttons down the front, as big as silver dollars. She was thin and distinguished-looking. The age lines in her face were scowling lines, cut deep into the angles of her cheeks.

Judging from the small crowd that had gathered around her, she was obviously a person of some importance and Fleury was making the most of her presence at his gallery. She had a look on her face as if she had already been introduced to too many people this evening and could not stand it any more. Fleury kept her strategically placed in the centre of the room, at the foot of three small steps that separated the front half of the gallery from the rear. Everyone who came to see the exhibition would either have to shake her hand or ignore her, and she did not look like the kind of person who got ignored very often.

I offered her the same Egyptian-mummy grin that she gave me.

'Madame Pontier,' said Fleury, 'is what is called *un expert auprès du tribunal*. This means she can authenticate any painting and, if she puts her stamp on it, her word is law. Show him the stamp.'

'Do you really think this is necessary?' Madame Pontier's voice made her seem at the point of total exhaustion.

'Make me happy!' said Fleury.

Madame Pontier reached into her pocket. Her hand was clenched into a fist when she pulled it out. Then she uncurled her fingers, revealing a small gold stamp with a base of jade-like stone. It was carved with some kind of seal and attached by a fine gold chain to a buttonhole of her jacket.

'Oh, is that really it?' asked a man in the group. He was tall and gaunt, with wavy hair plastered flat on his head with pomade. Sweat dappled the chest of his starched white shirt.

'It is.' Madame Pontier's fist closed again around the seal.

'This is Monsieur Lebel' – Fleury introduced the man to me – 'a connoisseur of important works of art, and owner of the Metropole Cabaret.'

'Yes. Oh.' Lebel grabbed my hand, stared right through me and immediately went back to ogling Madame Pontier.

The group of people seemed to close even more tightly around her, and I took the opportunity to step back. I was turning to leave, when I found Fleury standing right beside me.

'Taking off?' he asked.

'Well, I think so. Yes.' I looked at my wrist, as if to check the time, but realized I had left my watch back at the apartment.

'Have you had anything to eat?' he asked.

'No, actually,' I replied.

'Come,' said Fleury. 'Let me buy us dinner.'

'What about the show?' I asked.

He waved his hand dismissively. 'It's winding down. I have an assistant who'll take care of it. I always hate to be the last one to leave a party, even when it is my own.'

I was too tired and hungry to refuse.

'You didn't happen to see Valya on your way over here, did you?' he asked.

I shook my head. 'I'm sorry. No.'

'No matter,' he said quickly.

We walked out through the veils of smoke into the street.

As we moved down the Rue des Archives, Fleury took out a small handkerchief, folded it up and pressed it once against his forehead. This was the only sign that he had exerted himself physically. 'How did you like the show?' he asked.

I admitted that I never felt comfortable at openings.

'It's just as well,' he said. 'Do you know what happens when I go from one gallery party to another, one café to the next, parading up and down the street to all the different openings and making sure I get in all the hellos that need to be said? What happens is that everybody starts to look the same. Everybody is afraid of the same things. They're all identically insecure. Me included. It all just starts to merge together. If I focus on people or things, they just blur. It's as if things exist only in fast motion. Everything rushing around. Everything new. And loud. And quite drunk most of the time.'

'That's a different world from the one I'm used to,' I told him.

'You might think you're not a part of the same world, but you are. You do the work that keeps it in motion. Without the work – the *doing* – all this just disappears. Am I right?'

'I guess,' I said.

'No guessing. That's a fact.' Then a look came over his face as if he had said more than he wanted to. 'What did you think of the paintings?' he asked, to change the subject.

I shrugged awkwardly. 'I didn't really get the chance, to be honest.' I was afraid he would turn us around and make us go back to the gallery.

Fleury shook his head wearily. 'They were *awful*. The artist is the stepson of a gallery owner across town. A man to whom I owe some favours. He was the one who persuaded Madame Pontier to come. She is a big fish in these waters. That's why I got the crowd. That and the fact that I was serving proper champagne, for a change. The work won't sell, you know. None of it.' Fleury spoke as if he were making a decree. 'Except perhaps to his relatives.'

I felt a pinch in my side when Fleury said this. Before my own work had started to sell, I had refused to let any of my relatives buy it. This, of course, made no sense to them and they took it to mean that I didn't think they had any taste. They got annoyed about it and said that their money was as good as anybody else's, so I was made to explain that I couldn't stand the thought of them subsidizing me. Even when they complained that subsidizing had nothing to do with it, I didn't believe them and still wouldn't sell them the work. Instead I just gave it away.

It had started to rain in mist so fine that I could barely feel it. The greyness that swirled through this watery air was like a failing of my sight, as if cataracts were gathering like smoke behind my eyes. I turned up the collar of my jacket and hugged it to my throat.

Fleury brought us to a restaurant called the Polidor on a street named Monsieur-Le-Prince. Inside, the place was warm and crowded, with tables set together in rows and heavy pale-green pillars holding up the roof.

Fleury waved at the waitress, who nodded hello. She was a large woman with long blonde hair and a red velvet dress. Her face was tough and beautiful. She was big all over, with the kind of body that Rubens might have painted.

Fleury and I squashed ourselves into a table by the wall. Fleury whispered to the waitress. She bowed down next to him to hear, her thick blonde hair falling over his shoulders, and her chest close to his face. When Fleury had finished whispering, the waitress laughed loudly and raked her nails gently down the back of his neck.

I didn't ask what he had said to her.

A pitcher of red wine was brought. Its clay sides were cold and beaded with moisture. The tendons strained in Fleury's wrists as he lifted the pitcher and filled our glasses.

'This is very kind of you,' I said, but I made sure that he understood from the tone of my voice that I needed some kind of explanation about what he wanted.

Fleury set down the pitcher and gave me a smile, to show he didn't mind my curiosity. 'Pankratov speaks very highly of you,' he explained. 'And I expect you know by now that he doesn't speak highly of many people. Any man who is of interest to Pankratov is of interest to me.'

It occurred to me that one person Pankratov did not seem to be interested in was Fleury himself. 'But Pankratov doesn't know me,' I said.

Fleury shook his head. 'He seems to know your work, at any rate.'

I explained to him about the Levasseur scholarship. I told him how much I had always wanted to come here.

He nodded slowly while I talked, at one point taking off his glasses and polishing them on his tie.

'And I don't even know who these Levasseur people are,' I told him, when I had finished the story.

'Nor I.' Fleury shook his head. 'But who cares, as long as they're paying, eh?'

'What should we order?' I asked, to change the subject.

'Whatever's the special,' Fleury told me. He drained his glass and let his head fall back. I saw the wine pulse down his throat. He sighed noisily. Slowly, almost mechanically, he lowered his head until he was facing me again. 'Now you must admit,' he said, 'that this is more fun than working at home.'

'I admit it,' I said. 'But I didn't come to Paris just to have fun.'

'And let me guess. You feel shitty about enjoying it now.'

'Maybe later,' I said. I drank some wine. It was sharp in the corners of my mouth.

'So,' said Fleury, laying his hands flat on the table, 'did you bring any work with you?'

I shook my head. 'I wanted to start out fresh when I got here.'

The smile slipped lopsidedly from his face, like a fried egg sliding off a plate. 'And do you have a dealer here is Paris?'

'Not yet,' I told him.

He raised his eyebrows, smile returning. 'Well, that's easily remedied.'

'I'd better get some work done first,' I said. I had planned out a series of a dozen paintings, to be based on my memories of Narragansett Bay in Rhode Island, where I'd lived all my life. I would give them the unreliability that memories take on. Objects would be painted deliberately out of scale – waves too big, houses too small, the colours strong and glaring, with some things left only as outlines. I didn't want to tell Fleury any of this yet. 'How long have you had your own gallery?' I asked him.

'Less than a year,' he replied. 'Before that, I worked for the Gallery St Edouard over on the Avenue Matignon. I had in mind that I would work as an apprentice for a few years, just to learn the ropes, then start up a gallery on my own. What I learned instead was that it would take a lot longer than my patience would endure.' He rummaged in his pocket for a cigarette and lit it with a wooden match, which he struck against the heel of his shoe. He jammed the still-flaring match head against the end of his cigarette and puffed. 'I was accused of being ambitious, although God knows why that should count against me. I remember the owner of the St Edouard gallery saying to me that I was a young man with "ideas above my station". Do you know, that's the worst thing anybody ever said to me. But I tell you, they were doing me a favour.' He spoke quickly, his words almost running together. 'So I said to hell with it, and opened up my own gallery anyway. Borrowed from every friend and relative I could find. Found a place. Haven't had a day off in months.' He sucked in a lungful of smoke, his lips popping quietly together as he pulled the cigarette from his mouth. 'Don't regret it. Not for a minute. Even if I have to listen to those people tell me they were right that I had "ideas above my station". At least I gave it a try.'

I knew those words must have kept him up nights, fuming at the insult. It reminded me of the time I had overheard one of my old college friends joking that I could come and live in his basement any time I wanted to, to save me from freezing to death as a penniless artist. But from then on, I *would* have frozen to death rather than go and live in that man's basement. So I knew what Fleury was talking about. I didn't doubt he would succeed. You can tell this about some people, that they will get what they want and are not just fooling themselves or anybody else. They have an instinctive sense of the balance of luck and skill and specificity of purpose that's required. I hadn't expected to like Fleury, and was surprised to find that I did. I was equally surprised that he seemed to like me as well.

'When you get some art together,' he told me, 'you let me know. Maybe we'll work together some day soon.'

'If Pankratov gives me any time to paint,' I said.

At the mention of Pankratov's name, Fleury sighed and patted his hand against the back of his neck, as if the joints of his spine had come loose and he was tapping them back into place.

'What do you know about him?' I asked.

Fleury shrugged. 'Not enough.' He stubbed out his cigarette, jabbing the butt into the ashtray until it crumbled apart. 'Everybody in Paris has heard of the man. People are always talking about him at gallery functions precisely because he never comes to them. They've all got Pankratov stories of their own, most of them completely untrue, I suspect, but it gives us something to talk about. Look,' he said, 'I don't know what he said about me after I left the atelier today, but I rather doubt it was flattering. You make your own judgement. Will you do that? If we're going to work together some day, and I hope we will, I'd rather you based your opinion on what you see rather than on what you hear. It is a question of trust, and should not be left up to strangers.'

As he spoke, I felt that never-trusting part of me peer out cautiously from behind its barricade of ribs and the tangled barbed wire of veins.

'You know,' said Fleury, 'I have a hunch that now you're here, you might decide to stay.'

'Why do you say that?' I asked.

'I can tell from the way you talk about Paris. You loved this city before you ever saw it. We all have dreams of how a place will be before we get there, and usually the dreams are much more lavish than the reality. You can't help but end up disappointed. But Paris is the only place on earth where the reality is even more beautiful than the dream.' He nodded to show he was serious.

'I might fall in love with it if I had the time,' I told him, 'but after the grant runs out, I can't afford to stay here. I don't have work papers, so the only kind of job I could get wouldn't pay me enough to live off and get any painting done at the same time.'

'You might find a way,' he said. 'You never know.'

Before Fleury mentioned the idea of staying, going home had seemed inevitable to me. Now the image of remaining here began to burn itself into my thoughts.

'Welcome to Paris,' said Fleury, pouring out more wine. 'I think you have finally arrived.'

Heaven on earth. That was how my father had described Paris in his letters home. He had come here as a soldier in 1918 and been killed at Belleau Wood. He died when I was only a few months old. My acquaintance with him began and ended with those letters, and the occasional anecdote told by my mother when some sound or smell catapulted her back into the past.

I also had an uncle Charlie, who had come to France before America entered the war and was a pilot for the French air corps. My uncle Charlie never came home after the armistice. He disappeared in 1926, in an attempt to fly the first non-stop flight across the Atlantic. I had pictures of my father and my uncle in their wool coats and puttee-wrapped legs, side by side in the city of heaven on earth. Ever since I was a child, their sepia-tinted ghosts had drawn me to this place.

For me, Paris became the only tangible link between my father and myself. It was not enough to hold on to the flimsy blades of paper that were his letters and to think that he had once held them in his own hands. And the blurred and fading picture was not enough. But if I could only get to Paris, I used to think, and be in the place where he had been and fall in love with it the way he had fallen in love with it, then I might understand who he had been. Might know him in myself.

When people would say to me, 'You look like your father,' or 'Your father used to do that,' or 'Your father would have liked that,' it was like being haunted. What troubled me wasn't so much the physical resemblance: it was the traits of character, which I could not call my own because they had been his before me, even if I had never learned them from him. Instead, they had reached me like some echo of his voice inside my blood.

I looked to Paris for the answers. It would be my bridge between the present and the past. It would give me peace of mind, just as the painting did when it was going well. Sometimes I think I started painting precisely because I knew that my father had not been a painter. So I could call it my own.

That may have been what got me started, but what kept me at it all these years was beyond me. It wasn't until I had given up trying to figure it out that I realized I wasn't supposed to know. If the answer had been clear, I would never have needed to paint. And if I ever did figure it out, I might never need to paint again. I decided it was not my job to know. It was only my job to do the painting.

During my first days in the city, I found myself wondering again and again if my father and my uncle Charlie had seen what I was seeing now. Not the great monuments or famous buildings but the small anonymous things: a crack in the sidewalk that was shaped like a crescent moon on the Rue de Rivoli. A certain dapple-trunked tree growing in the Tuileries gardens. A chip in the blue enamel of a street sign on the Rue Solferino. It chased away the loneliness, as I grew used to my new surroundings.

I learned the precise stab of the key into the lock of my apartment, the setting of my shoe against the door and the flick of the brass knob to open it. The musty smell of the place that rushed into my lungs soon became familiar. The noises of people living on my floor – pots clunking in sinks, the swish of flushing toilets, softly played gramophone music – all merged into a different kind of silence. I put away the metronome.

There was something hypnotic about the idea of working at the atelier. Never far from my thoughts was the knowledge that, outside Pankratov's studio, we were regarded with suspicion and sarcasm by those who saw no future in painting. It was a relief to find myself in the company of people who shared the same necessary stubbornness of vision. Even if painting was the only thing we had in common, that was enough.

By the end of the first week, I had become not only a student of the atelier, but a student of Balard and Marie-Claire as well. I watched the way they worked.

Balard never sat on his stool while he drew. Instead, he stood back from his easel, drawing with his arm outstretched. He used thick wedges of compressed charcoal, pressing hard against the paper and drawing quickly, with great flourishes of his free hand and strange whistling and grunting sounds. Over the course of the day, he would get charcoal smudges halfway up his arms and all over his face, so that he looked like a man who had been in a fire.

Marie-Claire used delicate strands of vine charcoal. In contrast to Balard, she moved slowly and carefully around the paper, often closing one eye and measuring distances with her thumb, rather than trusting her instincts. She tilted back and forth on her stool, looking at her work from different angles. Sometimes she just sat there, staring at it, hands resting in her lap, as if overcome by daydreams. I liked her drawings. They were deceptively simple: as much about what she left out as what she put on the page. She worked so close to her easel that she seemed to be trying to hide her drawing from anyone who might be looking on. Pankratov often scolded her for overemphasizing the faces in her sketching. She would listen patiently to Pankratov, and then go right back to working on the face, as if she couldn't help herself. She stuck to the middle of the page, leaving huge white borders, and drew dozens of lines where one would have been enough. The lines were all of equal pressure, fuzzy like the contrails of high-flying aeroplanes.

I could tell I'd had more formal training than Balard or Marie-Claire, but this didn't mean that Pankratov was any easier on me. I worked hard to gain his approval, which he gave in such small and obscure doses that it took me a while before I could tell when he was pleased and when he wasn't. When he gave his critiques, he would speak for a long time, often in raging monologues, using strange imagery, which he apparently translated directly out of Russian. It was as if he were trying to read words that scrolled before his eyes too quickly for him to decipher or to understand what he was saying. It had been a long time since I let anyone rule my days the way this man did now.

So far, I'd seen nothing to convince me of his genius. I found none of his paintings at the galleries or museums. I'd even rummaged through old auction catalogues at the *bouquainistes*, the little green book stands bolted to the stone walls bordering the Seine. There was no trace of the art of Alexander Pankratov.

Pankratov required us to be at the atelier by 7.30 a.m., but as that time came and went Pankratov himself would be sitting across the street in a café called the Dimitri. It was like a thousand other cafés in Paris, each one chosen as a regular haunt by a group that never amounted to more than fifty or sixty. The café was too small to hold even half this number, so they came at different times, some to talk and some with the need to stay silent and apart but not alone. The Dimitri had a small blue awning that ran the length of the café front. Unlike most others, which would say Café this-or-that, this awning just said 'Dimitri'. Four frosted panes of glass made up the front window. The menu of the day was written in soap on the window nearest the door. Out on the sidewalk, there was room for only one table. Pedestrians had to step into the gutter to pass by. The sidewalk was on a slope, so the owner had built a large wooden wedge on which to set the table and make it level. The chairs were flimsy metal with slatted wooden seats and backs.

I quickly learned that you couldn't underestimate the importance of a neighbourhood café in the lives of the people who used it. The choosing of the café was a delicate and personal affair, and it was very important for the café not to appear to be trying too hard to attract its customers. This was not like back in America, where the more lights and flashy signs you put out, the more likely it was that people would stop to see what all the fuss was about. There was a big diner that opened up near where I lived. It was called the Liberty Diner. It had a sign out front with an eagle on it and the eagle was carrying a menu in its claws. Under the eagle was a big clock with the numbers done in the popular chunky style, with the fake shadow of each letter painted just behind it. The owners put a slogan under the clock which lit up at night. It said TIME TO DINE. Local kids were always shooting out the letter N with slingshots, so it usually read TIME TO DIE. I got superstitious about it and wouldn't go in there.

Even as 7.30 became 8 o'clock, Pankratov would be sitting at his corner table in the Dimitri. He would be smoking exactly half a cigarette, having sliced it in two with a wooden-handled Opinel knife and struck a blue-tipped match on the buckle of his belt. He ordered a coffee, which was served in a cup so small it looked as if it had been stolen from a doll's house. Before he drank it, he would set a sugar lump between his cheek and gum, the way people used chewing tobacco back home. The coffee was followed by a cup of steamed milk. While Pankratov drank the milk, he chewed on a single date that the café owner placed by itself on a small white plate beside him. When he had smoked his half-cigarette down to the point at which it might burn the prints off his fingers, he would raise an ashtray up to his face and quietly spit into it. Then he would roll the end of the cigarette in the spit until it was extinguished. Either this little gesture continually went unnoticed by the others in the café, or they had seen it so many times that they no longer cared to watch. I wondered why he did this, rather than simply squashing the butt dead among the ashes. I couldn't just go up and ask him. It seemed to me you couldn't do a thing like that with Pankratov. It was his private world, and not to be visited by anyone but him. He seemed to possess some mighty secret, the knowledge of which had absolved him from participating in the life the rest of us were living.

I knew this much about his habits because one morning I went to the Dimitri before he got there and sat at the far end of the café. I hid behind a newspaper, waiting for him.

The Dimitri was larger on the inside than the four skinny windows made it seem. The furnishings were a strange mixture of Arab rugs, Russian samovars, crossed Cossack swords on the walls and a single white kepi, hung above the oval mirror at the bar. Here, you could buy a drink made from mint that had been packed into a glass and doused with sweet green tea; or coffee made with goat's milk. There were few other concessions to the outside world: no music of the kind that filled other cafés, the endless warbled croonings of Edith Piaf. At the Dimitri, there was only the rustle of papers kept on wooden rods and stored each day on a rack. No special furniture. Plain, zinc-topped tables with iron legs and chairs with tightly woven wicker seats. The bar was plated with copper, scrubbed clean with lemon juice and bicarbonate of soda, which added to the smell of the café.

The owner was named Ivan Konovalchik. He ran the Dimitri from 6.30 in the morning until midnight and then slept on the top of the bar, laid out like a corpse at a wake, hands folded on his chest. He wasn't a large man, but he was formidable. He wore the uniform of most Paris waiters, a short black coat with wide lapels, almost like a chopped-down tuxedo, and a low-cut waistcoat with big pockets in which he kept his change. Around his waist, he wore a long white apron that stretched to the top of his shoes. His short-spiked hair had gone grey, but his eyebrows were still dark. His hands were thick and it was clear from the white flecks of scarring that a long time ago he had worked with them in jobs that gouged and pinched and cut. He had been, he told me, a Foreign Legionnaire in the Moroccan Sahara in the 1920s, and before that he had been an officer in the Imperial Russian cavalry. Just like Pankratov, he said. The Dimitri was named after a famous café in Morocco, a legionnaires' café in a place called Mogador. This explained the trappings of the place, and the Arabs who spent their mornings at the bar and the old legionnaires with their elephant-hide skin burned permanently red from sun and drink and fear, as if the red dust of the Sahara lay in a fine and gritty layer just beneath its surface. Even though the Arabs and these legionnaires had been at war, both sides clung to this place. They didn't speak much. They greeted each other with the words 'Leh Bess', which Ivan told me was Moroccan for 'No harm', or 'I mean you no harm'. Considering how much harm they had once done each other, Ivan explained to me, it seemed like the right thing to say. The Arabs and the legionnaires kept to their separate tables but seemed to need each other's company. There was something here, in the name and the particular date-sweetened bitterness of the coffee and the mint tea, that made more sense to them than the life of Paris thundering past outside the door.

There were many rumours about Ivan Konovalchik. He had acquired them like limpets on the hull of a boat. The relics he hung upon his walls were only talismans that let you know how much it was you would never know about him. One story was that he had been to America, but when I asked him about this, he gave a curious reply.

'If I went there,' he said dreamily, 'I don't remember it.'

'Do you mean you went there as a child?' I asked.

'No,' he shook his head.

It occurred to me that Ivan probably was the kind of man who could forget such a thing.

'Halifax.' He said the word as if to feel it in his mouth.

'Yes?' I replied.

'Halifax,' he said again. 'That is a common name in America?'

'Not too common, I guess.' I shrugged. 'I don't know.'

'And perhaps you have a relative named Charles. Charlie. Perhaps.'

My head jerked up. 'That's my uncle!' My voice was loud with surprise. 'Do you know him?'

'I met him a long time ago.' Ivan began polishing a glass, holding it up to the light. 'Probably not the same person.'

'My uncle was a pilot. An American who flew for the French.'

'Ah, well,' said Ivan. 'Then it is him after all.'

'He disappeared after the war,' I said.

'Yes' – he spoke as if he were talking in his sleep – 'I think we all disappeared around that time.'

I could get no more out of him and felt the frustration of having come very close to something, then suddenly found myself as far away as ever.

At last Pankratov arrived, dressed in the thigh-length canvas coat he always wore. It was a grey-green colour, with two flapped pockets at the waist and dull grey buttons up the front. The buttonholes had worn out and were clumsily restitched in black thread. The collar had frayed, as had the cuffs. It was a garment that should long ago have been put out of its misery, but Pankratov seemed determined to wear the thing until it turned to vapour and drifted away from his body, leaving the buttons to rattle across the floor. He didn't take the coat off, as if he feared someone would steal it. He smoked his half-cigarette, which he took from a black and orange box labelled 'Imperiale'. He drank his doll's portion of coffee, strained through the whiteness of his teeth and the dissolving sugar cube. He ate one fat and crinkled date, then spat and extinguished his cigarette. Finally, he set two coins on the table and lifted his chair as he stood, so that it would not drag across the floor. 'Shokran,' he said to Ivan.

'Shokran, effendi,' replied Ivan Konovalchik, without looking up.

Pankratov started out across the road towards his atelier.

I left a moment later, and raced up the stairs, not catching up with him until just before he reached the open door of the studio. Inside, it was completely silent. Everyone was watching us. Valya turned in her chair, breaking from her naked statue pose, and surveyed us critically.

'I'm sorry I'm late,' I mumbled as I tried to move past him into the room.

'Monsieur Halifax,' he said, not letting me go by.

'Yes, sir,' I answered, breathing hard from the climb.

'You would make an incompetent spy.'

I was quiet for a moment. 'All good spies appear incompetent,' I said.

Pankratov's eyes opened for a moment, raising the thick visor of his eyebrows. 'Ye-e-es,' he said quietly, 'and if someone would employ you as a spy, you might have an excuse for your incompetence.' He jerked his head, ordering me inside.

I sat down at my easel.

'Begin to draw!' His voice had the power to jolt all other thoughts from my head.

I set up my paper and began to draw Valya.

She came only in the mornings and left as soon as she could. She was always on time, striding in, eyes fixed on the platform where she would take her place. She walked across to a set of brass coat pegs that were screwed haphazardly into the wall and began to undress. She shed her clothing with an angry sensuality, letting the coat slide from her shoulders and catching it before it hit the floor. She kicked off her rope-soled shoes, heel against toe, heel against toe, then undid the fiddly buttons on her shirt with less patience than the job required. Her hips swung slightly as she let her skirt fall to the floor, then bent her legs down to pick it up, holding her upper body straight.

Valya was harshly beautiful. She had an intolerant crookedness to her lips, and usually wore her hair tied back severely in a ponytail. I watched the way her skin pressed against the wooden seat and the way she drew her legs together, covering one set of toes with the other. The pale curve of her hips and the way they slid into the narrows of her waist sometimes forced me to lower my head, in case she read the thoughts inside my eyes.

Pankratov never brought the thunder of his voice to bear on her. She seemed beyond any words that he could muster.

I found I could not distil Valya into the lines and shadows and planes of light that would allow me to draw her correctly. I could see her only as a whole, and it was as if my pencil could find no place to start on the snowfield of the sketching page. I was always relieved when we turned to other subjects, hauling out the paints and mixing boards, brushes stuck in the belt of my smock like the knives of a Japanese chef.

We would begin our sketches of the shivering Valya the moment she sat down in her chair on the stage. Mornings were always cold in the atelier, before the sun had reached into the room. We kept our coats on, long scarves looped around our necks. The undersides of my coat sleeves were shiny black like a tramp's from wearing it as I drew with charcoal in those early mornings.

The moment Pankratov arrived, he would tell Valya to sit or stand a certain way, or he would walk over to his junk pile of props: broken umbrellas with the silk domes in shreds like the tattered wings of ravens, baskets of eggshells and various animal bones. They were bleached and dry and drank the moisture from my fingers when I picked them up. He would hand one of these to Valya and make her pose with it. Like a marionette without strings, she obeyed.

After a while, we gave up sketching before Pankratov's arrival. Whatever work we were doing at the time he walked in would be brushed aside and ignored, the paper wasted, and a few more centimes lost from my too-small bank account. Even though we weren't drawing, Valya still undressed and sat down on the chair. She rarely joined in our conversations. Sometimes she smiled at one of Balard's one-liner jokes. Or she would groan in agreement if Marie-Claire did one of her imitations of the way Pankratov critiqued her paintings. Mostly Valya just sat there, as if the two-foot height of the stage had placed her out of the range of any friendship she could find at lower elevations.

Valya offered no explanation as to why she sat there naked when she didn't have to. It seemed to be some kind of punishment she'd chosen for herself. One day, I went ahead and asked why she undressed before Pankratov arrived. Immediately the room went silent, as if I had just rolled a hand grenade across the floor. Slowly, almost wearily, Valya turned to face me. 'Did you say something?' she asked.

'We're not drawing,' I said, as if that would explain everything.

'No,' she said slowly, as if talking to an idiot who could at any moment become violent.

'And we don't draw until he shows up,' I said, my courage beginning to fail me.

She let her head fall back a little, without releasing me from her gaze. 'I'm paid by the hour,' she said.

'But why do you have to take your clothes off now?' I asked.

'Do you mind that my clothes are off?'

Balard laughed behind his easel. I heard the clunk and switch of his lighter as he lit himself a cigarette.

'It's not that,' I said.

'If I just come in here and sit down,' she explained, 'Pankratov can say I'm not working. That I haven't started yet. But if I strip like this, it's work. And my work starts when I get here, not when he gets here.' The wind batted up against the windows and Valya shivered. She folded her arms across her chest.

I raised my hands and let them fall again in a gesture of surrender. 'Fine,' I said.

'No,' she snapped. 'It is not fine. To hell with all artists and to hell with me for spending time with them.'

I opened my mouth, ready to ask, So why are you here? What power does that crazy Russian have over you?

But there was no more talk between us, because Pankratov had arrived. He stood in the doorway, nostrils flared from the effort of climbing the stairs. His bright eyes swept across us like the beacon of a lighthouse. 'Begin to draw!' he shouted, with a voice of such authority that it was as if he held in his command the actual rotation of the earth.

3

It wasn't long before Balard began to take exception to me.

Even though I had no designs on Marie-Claire, my arrival had thrown out Balard's monopoly of charm. Now he was trying too hard. He spoke at great length about artists he'd studied and exhibitions he had seen. Then he would express concern that we hadn't been to the exhibitions, even though they might have taken place years before any of us had come to Paris. Balard was the only native Parisian among us. The fact that Marie-Claire knew very little about artists like Elisabetta Sirani, Luca Giordano and Andreas Benedetti didn't bother Balard. He seemed to find it charming. But my ignorance he would not tolerate.

When I said I wasn't familiar with Sirani, he sat back on his stool, feet hooked into the rung at the bottom. 'Not familiar?' he asked. 'You're not *familiar* with Elisabetta Sirani?'

'That's what I said.'

'I can't believe you're not familiar with her work.'

'Why do you keep using that word?' I asked him.

'What word?'

'Familiar.'

'I'm not *using* it at all!' He gave a forced-out deep-voice laugh. 'You said it first. I am just surprised.'

Marie-Claire watched, saying nothing. Perhaps she was even a little flattered that Balard would go to all this trouble over her. The bottom line was that if Balard did succeed in making a fool of me, she would like him for it. It was a primitive thing, but it was there nonetheless.

'You are not very educated in the arts, are you?' Balard asked me.

I felt myself sighing. All right, I thought. Let's get this

over with. 'I am,' I said, 'too busy painting to talk about painting. There's always the danger,' I told him, 'of becoming an artist who doesn't do any art.'

Balard folded his arms and then unfolded them again. 'Are you saying I'm not an artist? Are you saying that you are the only artist here?' He tried to make it seem as if my insulting him was an insult to Marie-Claire, as well, but already Marie-Claire was watching him with different eyes. Balard held up his sketch. 'I am an artist! What do you call this?'

Both Marie-Claire and I looked at his half-done sketch of Valya and knew exactly what to call it. The room filled chokingly with silence, like a jar filling with milk.

'I *am* an artist,' said Balard, his face gone fiery with blushing.

Marie-Claire reached her hand across and rested it comfortingly on his knee.

He looked at her. His gaze was bright and pleading.

'You're a very good artist,' she said.

What I didn't admit, of course, was that Balard had been right. Given the choice between painting and looking at other painters, I would always paint. There was never enough time to do both, so I was always painting.

After the class, Balard came up to me while I was packing away my pencils and paper into the leather portfolio that I had brought with me from home. He hovered there for a while, casting his gloomy shadow. 'We got off on the wrong foot,' he said.

I looked across at Marie-Claire. She had packed up her kit and was standing by the brass pegs, ready to put on her coat. She glanced alternately at Balard and at me and then fussed with the buttons of her coat.

'It's just a crazy day,' I said to Balard, as we headed out.

'Crazy!' said Balard loudly. 'A crazy day! Oh, yes. Perhaps I can buy you a beer.'

We made our peace and there was no more jousting between Balard and me across the worn-out floorboards of the atelier Pankratov.

The next day, at the end of our sketching, Valya stood up from her perch, stepped down from the platform and padded barefoot across the dirty floor to where her clothes hung on the brass coat pegs. She began to dress.

I noticed that Pankratov turned away, even though his chair was facing where she stood. Still looking away, as if distracted by something in the dingy rafters of the room, he said, 'Valya, I was thinking you could help me tidy up the place once the students are gone.' He reserved for her a softness of voice that he shared with no one else. I knew immediately he was in love with her and that she knew it and despised every measure of his devotion. He seemed humbled by her. She always got her way; whether it was refusing to stand naked up on the stage any more because she said she was cold, in which case we drew her wearing her fur coat and nothing else, or if she wanted to leave an hour early, Pankratov always gave in.

The rest of us were packing away our things, untying the knots that belted our smocks to our bodies, washing out brushes. There was a general clatter of furniture being shifted and the hiss of the tap in the paint-splattered aluminium sink. We gave every appearance of not listening, but we were. Not one word passed between us as we strained our ears to catch each subtlety of breath.

'You're not paying me to clean up,' said Valya. She stepped into her shoes, jamming her heels into place.

'I shouldn't have to pay you at all,' replied Pankratov.

'Then don't,' snapped Valya. After that, there was only the sound of her footsteps fading away down the flights of stairs and at last the thump of the front door closing, which startled us back into motion.

'What is it,' I asked Marie-Claire, as we poured out into the Rue Descalzi, 'with Pankratov and the girl?'

We were out in the street, taking our first breaths of air not tinted with the reek of paint and thinners.

'I'll tell you,' she replied, 'but let's go to the café.' When I hesitated, thinking that today I might go home and try to work on my own paintings, she set the flat of her hand between my shoulder blades and pushed me gently toward the café door. 'It's *Friday*,' she said again, 'and sometimes it's as important to stop working as it is to start.'

I hadn't been thinking about it like that. 'You're right,' I told her.

'Of course I am,' she said.

I thought of letting the hours trail by in a fog of coffee and tobacco and the banana-yellow brain-fuzzing liquorice of pastis. The idea was sweet and intoxicating, as if I had already drunk the pastis and breathed in the nerve-smoothing Caporal smoke.

The tables at the Dimitri were filling rapidly. Behind the bar, Ivan worked the coffee machine with movements like an orchestra leader. He smacked the coffee grounds from each espresso shot into a garbage can the size of an oil drum. The sound made a dull boom in the crowded space of the café, as if Ivan were conducting his own version of the '1812 Overture'.

Balard was waiting for Marie-Claire at a table in the corner. He did not look particularly pleased to see me.

'We could make it another time,' I said quietly to Marie-Claire.

'No,' she replied. 'Not another time.'

I wondered if she had asked me along so that it would not just be the two of them. I knew she was very fond of Balard. Maybe even falling in love with him. But it was clear to me that Balard had fallen much harder and faster. Perhaps she didn't like things to be going quite so fast. I didn't much want to be getting in Balard's way again, but there didn't seem to be any way of escaping it now.

'So what is it about Pankratov and Valya?' I asked again, once we had sat down.

'What you have been witnessing,' said Marie-Claire, 'is the torment of a man who makes this woman stand there naked before him and yet who cannot possess her. He is so infatuated that he doesn't even know how to talk to her, let alone make love.'

'Valya is the one weak spot in the hide of an otherwise bulletproof man,' announced Balard, then ordered his usual drink. He called it a French 75, and said it was named after the French 75 mm artillery gun of the Great War.

Daylight trailed away over the rooftops. Marie-Claire, Balard and I sifted through our theories of Pankratov and life inside the tiny universe of the atelier. I gave myself up to the Great God Pastis, adding water from a white jug into the glasses of sharp, honey-coloured liquid, seeing it turn powdery yellow. I felt the soft absinthe explosions in my head, one after the other, until it seemed as if my blood were no longer contained inside the anchor of my body.

On my way home that night, I decided not to be stingy with my free time. What good was being in Paris, I asked myself, if I didn't live some of the life I had dreamed so long of living? I had to make a balance between working and not working.

In the days that followed, I became a regular at the Dimitri, whiling away my afternoons and evenings with Marie-Claire and Balard in the happy thrum of café life. Balard soon grew used to my presence. I always left before they did and from some of the things they said, I had the feeling they usually went back to his place afterwards. I spent a great deal of time politely ignoring the way they held hands under the table and the way their knees touched, a way that could be mistaken for accidental, except it wasn't.

We often talked about how hard it was to make a living as a painter.

'We'll have to live in a commune,' said Balard. 'All of us together.'

'Wouldn't that be fine?' asked Marie-Claire. She put her arms around Balard's neck and hugged him.

I wanted to ask what her husband would think of living in

a commune, but Marie-Claire seemed to have forgotten all about her husband in these past few days.

One night, more than a week later, I came home from the Dimitri and found Madame LaRoche sitting on a chair on the sidewalk outside our building. When I stopped to wish her a good evening, she took the pipe from her mouth and looked at it sternly, as if it had just caused her some offence. 'Monsieur Halifax,' she said.

'Good evening, Madame LaRoche.'

'Your Levasseur people paid their rent today. On time. I thought you'd like to know. I see you have chosen your café.' She was still looking at the pipe and not at me.

'Yes, ma'am. The Dimitri.'

She nodded. 'And how is your painting?'

'Very fine,' I told her.

Her eyes flicked up to me and then away. 'Ah ha,' she said. Then she tapped the old tobacco out of her pipe on the heel of her clumpy black shoe.

It didn't hit me until I was riding up to my room in the elevator, the gloss-black paint on the bars glimmering with the light of each passing floor. 'Oh no,' I said quietly.

When I reached my apartment, the first thing I saw was my easel in the corner, untouched for many days.

'Oh no,' I said again. I walked in circles around the room. All my promises to work. The twelve paintings I was going to do. I hadn't made a balance between working and not working. I hadn't done any damned work at all. Instead of that, I'd grown numb to the passing of time. It had been too easy to follow everyone else into the café. My time at the Dimitri was like being addicted to alcohol or cigarettes. There were times when I had said to myself that this would be the day I'd start my paintings, but when the time came, the whole idea of the work would suddenly stop making sense. I told myself I was just too tired to paint, that I'd already done enough work that day, sketching for Pankratov – told myself I didn't feel inspired. The excuses lined up so far back in my head it seemed to me I could use a new one every time and still never run out. I understood now that none of these was the real reason. I was afraid of working here. Better never to have tried to make my way as an artist in this city than to try and fail and have to carry that home with me like some cancer spreading in my guts.

Now staring me in the face was the fact that I did not have a single painting. All I had were the endless sketches from Pankratov's class, and a few attempts at my Narragansett series; and they were worth nothing to a gallery.

I opened my black metal money box and looked inside. Even with the money from the stipend, my cash was already running low. It wasn't as if I could just cable my bank at home and have money sent over, either. What I had now was all I had. I shut the lid and shoved the box away.

There was no point making more brave promises. I had already made vows and broken them. The only thing left now was to shut up and work and try to make up for lost time.

I swept the breadcrumbs of that morning's breakfast into my cupped hand and threw them out on the window ledge for the pigeons. Then I opened up my supply box and mixed paints. I arranged my materials, and started painting. I worked until deep into the night, knowing that I worked too hastily – that I would have to go back over this and correct the mistakes I was making. But what mattered now was to be working.

I felt an easing of unfamiliar muscles, cramped so long inside me that I'd mistaken them for bones. The feeling of working after a long time of not working was unlike anything else. I knew I would sleep deeply that night. The only times I ever slept well were after I had been painting.

Deep into the night hours, the city seemed to rumble, as if thunder were gathering beneath it. The deep-sleep breathing of a hundred thousand people.

I rubbed my hands across my face, smelling the dust of charcoal and paint powder ground into each swirl of my fingerprints. Then I went over to the sink and splashed water in my eyes. I looked at the time. It was too late to go to bed, but too early to go out and buy breakfast. I was too tired to work any more. I set my chair in front of the window and watched the dawn. The pigeons dozed on the ledge, heads tucked under their smoky-violet wings. I smelled baking bread from the bakery down the street; heard the whisper-whisper of the street-sweepers with their witches' brooms, tramcars starting their rounds, the first clip-clop of footsteps, the coo and flutter of the pigeons as they set off in search of food; then saw the sun exploding on the dewy rooftops. I felt at home in Paris now, as if each pull of air into my lungs had matched itself against the breathing of those hundred thousand dreamers in the dark.

I went to class as usual the next day, but that afternoon I didn't go to the Dimitri. Instead I went home and worked. Marie-Claire and Balard understood. Balard even sounded genuine when he said he hoped I'd come with them tomorrow. They disappeared into the café. The frosted glass door swallowed them up like a mist.

After that, whenever I was up in my room, the sound of laughter or music from down in the street would tempt me away from my easel. But I was working well now and the temptations were easier to resist.

When I worked, I slipped away from Paris and felt again the pull of tides in Narragansett Bay, and streams running to the sea through marshes of spartina grass. It seemed to me that I could sense the storms coming down from the north, as they would this time of year; red hurricane warning flags blown to shreds on the splintering flag poles; Indian summer, which would be coming soon; chevrons of Canada geese overhead, waking me each morning with their muttered honking. I saw the white birch trees bowed down in sheaths of ice, the winter waves frozen glacier-green on the empty beaches and the grim faces of the lobstermen, sweeping the snow from their decks as they moved out into the bay, to haul up their pots until their hands froze around the weed-slick ropes. The visions that reached me were astonishing in their clarity. I thought how strange it was that I had had to cross an ocean before I could be made to understand the value of that place I'd left behind.

When I painted, I moved through many stages of sketching and preliminary studies. I worked at the forms until they stopped being drawings of things. The figures in the sketch slowly evolved in relation to each other, separate from the world from which they had come. Only then, when the picture had detached itself from its source, would I begin to paint.

I usually made a lot of false starts, but eventually the image that appeared among the smoky charcoal trails of sketches tacked to each flat surface around me, walling me in, blocking out the light, would become the image I wanted on the canvas.

I didn't use paint generously. I didn't slap it on the canvas and paint over it if I didn't like what I saw. I scraped it back down to the undercoat and started again. I liked the undercoat to be thin as well, so you could see the fabric of the canvas and so that even when the painting was done, you could still make out the texture, but only if you brought your eyes very close. I liked the way it drew the eye towards the picture, made you look at the minutest detail, so that it would stop being the whole picture and would break down into its individual parts, which were different from what the parts had been in reality. Now they were the fragments of a different thing, a thing all by itself. But the ghost of the canvas underneath, the reminder of it, would always bring you back into the world from which the painting had emerged, many incarnations ago.

As the days went by, I grew more and more frustrated with the endless sketching at Pankratov's. Once, as he checked my work and breathed a gloomy sigh over my shoulder, I turned to face him. 'What's wrong?' I asked.

Pankratov looked vaguely confused, as if I could not possibly have spoken to him in that way and he must have misunderstood.

'What's wrong with it?' I asked again.

'Did I say there was something wrong?' asked Pankratov. Then he looked over my head, taking in the whole class with his gaze. 'No more sketching today!' he shouted. He strode back to his chair and sat down heavily into its canvas seat. 'This weekend, you three will do studies for me. You will go to the Musée Duarte and choose sixteen of the works there, and I expect you to have studies of these works by the time I walk into the classroom on Monday morning. Good!' He clapped his hands. 'You are dismissed!'

For a moment, I thought I saw relief drift like a scattering of dust across his face. I wondered if this was part of his teaching: that he would make us sketch and sketch until we rebelled against it and only then would we be ready to move on. Is that it? I wanted to ask him, How in God's name does your mind work?

There was a silence that followed his announcement. Balard and Marie-Claire glanced at each other, looking for reassurance that their weekends were not shot to bits.

But I knew exactly what would be left of our free time. Absolutely nothing. I'd had assignments like this before. In my head I drew a neat line through Saturday, when I had planned to go to the open-air markets at Clignancourt and buy some cheap art supplies, since I'd run out of everything I'd brought with me and couldn't afford high-quality materials from the shops on the Rue de Charonne. I had to force myself to calm down. I couldn't get out of doing the assignment. I would just have to get it over with and then there would be time for my own work.

I was too annoyed to paint, so I took a walk down Avenue Matignon in the Faubourg St Honoré. Most of the galleries were here. I scouted out the neat little shops, with all manner of paintings set on easels in the front window. They looked so clean and well lit and so unlike the chaos of Pankratov's atelier that I found it hard to imagine that the paintings on display had come from any paint-splattered artist's studio. These works seemed to have been transported into a different dimension, where I could neither purchase them nor bring my own work to be sold. I walked home along the Quai du Louvre. I stopped to look at the bronze statue of a lion fighting a wild boar. The bronze was pale green with age. In the fading light, the metal seemed to glow from inside. It was as if the bronze were only a shell, under which the beasts were waiting for the moment when they could cast off their cocoons, thin and shattering upon the road. Then they would roam snarling through the streets, forgetting their centuries of patience.

At 10 o'clock on Saturday morning I showed up at the Musée Duarte. It was an intimidating yellow stone building on the Rue Louis Blanc. In the courtyard was a fountain made of the same yellow stone but streaked arsenic green from decades of water trickling over the side. The fountain was turned off and empty. The main entrance was barred with iron railings. The tip of each rail was formed into a spike. The gates had been locked and the main doors were shut.

I walked across the road to a bench and sat down, waiting for the place to open. I set my portfolio on the bench beside me. One hour later I was still sitting there. I walked down the road and bought a crêpe filled with hazelnut paste from a street vendor. Then I went back to the bench and was there another half-hour before an old woman sat down beside me with her shopping in a little basket with wheels on the bottom.

We both stared straight ahead for a minute or two.

Out of her wheely basket baguettes jutted up like clumsy replicas of the museum gates. 'Are you an artist?' she asked.

'I'm working at it,' I replied.

'Oh, you're Canadian,' she said, having noticed my accent.

'American. My mother was Canadian.'

'American,' she corrected herself. 'You aren't waiting for the museum to open, are you?'

'Actually, yes, I am.'

'Well, you will have to wait a long time. At the weekend, it is only open on Sundays.'

I stood up suddenly. 'What?' I marched out into the street. 'Well, why the hell don't they have a sign posted?' I shouted at the gloomy building. The locked doors and shuttered windows made it look pug-faced and asleep.

'I don't think they've ever had a sign,' said the old woman. 'It is just a thing one is expected to know.'

I spun around. 'This whole city is making me crazy!' I shouted. I marched back to pick up my portfolio and tried to calm myself. 'Thank you,' I said to the old woman. 'I apologize for shouting.'

'Not at all,' she said. 'One expects this sort of thing from foreigners.'

I rode the streetcar out to Clignancourt. I was thinking I might get those art supplies after all and still salvage something of the day. I knew this was some joke of Pankratov's to send us to the Musée Duarte when he knew it would be closed. Some test that had nothing to do with how well we could draw or paint. And only I had failed it.

I jumped off the streetcar at the Porte de Clignancourt and disappeared into the swirl of alleyways that made up the Clignancourt fleamarket. Tables were laid out on the uneven cobblestones, piled with old clothes, shoes, china, boxes of spoons, camera parts. Vendors cooked peanuts in sugar, stirring them in steel bowls with wooden spoons. In other stalls, Arabs carved huge roasts of lamb on vertical spits over charcoal fires. The smell of roasting meat salted the air.

I sat on the kerb and drank wine from an earthenware mug at a café whose tables were already full. I buried my face in the mug and felt the wine splash down inside me. All right, I thought. So I wasted a morning sitting on a bench. So maybe I'll learn to be more careful next time. That's what Pankratov was teaching me. I'll do those sketches later on today when the museum opens up. I eased myself up off the pavement, set my empty mug on a table and went looking for art supplies.

I found a shop at the end of a cobblestoned alleyway, somewhere in the labyrinth of market stalls. It had a sign on the front that said: *'Fournisseur des Matériaux Artistiques. R. Quattrocci. Prop.'* It was done in swirly letters and borders of painted ivy. The sign stuck out about a foot into the alleyways on either side of the shop.

Everything in the shop was coated with dust. The place was crammed with stacks of artists' paper and jars of pencils and half-used tubes of paint. Old artists' paintboxes and portable easels hung from the ceiling. The owner, a large man with deep-set, sleepy eyes, had to keep moving things aside whenever he moved about in the shop. He wore a painter's smock that was dirty from the constant wiping of his hands across his chest. When I walked in, his big hands were in mid-wipe over his chest, like a woman trying to hide her naked breasts.

'I need some paper, please,' I said, 'and charcoal pencils, too.'

'Bof,' he said and puffed up his cheeks. 'This whole place is made of paper. What type of paper do you want?'

'I need it for sketching,' I said.

Just then, a man stuck his head in and shouted, 'Rocco!'

I couldn't see who it was and nor could the owner. Our view of the entrance was blocked by a large gilded frame that held the shredded remains of a painting. It hung from the ceiling on two old leather belts.

'Rocco Quatrocci!' said the man, with the voice of a ringmaster introducing his prize act to the crowd. 'Quatrocci, the King of the World!'

Rocco waved uncertainly and smiled.

'Rocco!' said the man again, as if the word felt good in his mouth and he could not help saying it again. Then he was gone, whistling, the echo calling back to him from the overhanging rooftops of the alleyway, where dandelions grew in the leaf-clogged gutters.

'I have no idea who that was,' said Rocco. 'Paper. Let me see.' He walked his fingertips up and down his lips, which popped against each other with a sound like water dripping. 'There,' he said, pointing to a stack that lay beneath a shelf of brushes, divided up by size and stacked in old jam jars. 'But it is very old.'

I hauled down one of the sketchbook pads. I could tell by the print-style of the manufacturer's name on the front that the pads were from the turn of the century or perhaps even before. The paper in them had browned at the edges. It was brittle. In some places it had started to come apart like dead leaves crumbling. I asked him how much they were.

'I am thinking,' said Rocco, the King of the World. He flippered his lips again. Plip plop plip. 'Will you buy all of them?' His voice sounded breathlessly hopeful, as if he carried the weight of all this dusted junk not only in his shop but in his mind.

I didn't buy all of it, but I bought more than I'd planned to.

I liked it there at Clignancourt, being around all the old books and clothes and china and cigarette cases and wallets picked from pockets years ago and dusted with mould the colour of weathered bronze and sold now in heaps on collapsible tables. I liked the way the present and the past collided in the relics that had made their way here, whose stories you could read like Braille in each chipped cup and crease of leather.

I rode the streetcar home, feeling the sweat cool on my back from the effort of carrying the heavy paper to the tram stop. My pockets were filled with old charcoal pencils and pastels, mostly broken but still good. I had three sable brushes tucked into my socks because I had no other way to carry them. Their quality had once been good. I didn't think Pankratov would mind me working on this stuff. I smelled the mustiness of Rocco's shop in the paper. Rocco. King of the World. I even said it to myself a few times, under my breath, my voice lost in the jangle and clatter of the streetcar.

I made calculations, mumbling the sums, figuring how many more days it would buy me in Paris to work with cheap supplies.

The conductor made his way up and down the car with his metal ticket machine slung across his chest, flipping the red, blue and yellow plastic buttons, then striking a lever that spat out a thin yellow slip with a rapid zipping sound.

There was a breeze blowing in from the west. 'It's blowing in from Normandy,' said one old lady. 'You can smell the apple blossoms from the fields outside Bayeux.' People smiled and filled their lungs. I didn't smell any apples. Bayeux was a long way off. It was just a thing to say, but still it made everybody smile with the pleasure of remembering the smell. The breeze filled the space of the streetcar, and people turned their faces to it, closing their eyes. I did the same. I felt the dizziness of clean air deep inside me and knew a part of me belonged here now, in the flow of people and machines.

4

'See me afterwards,' said Pankratov. He had collected our Musée Duarte sketches at the end of the previous day. Now he was handing them back.

I stared at the folder, unable to hide my dread. Pankratov's words reminded me too much of what my old Latin teacher used to say when I had failed a test.

After class, when the others had cleared out, I remained at my stool. I hadn't touched the sketches.

Pankratov sat down in his chair. 'Come over here,' he said.

I slipped off the stool and walked towards him.

'Bring the sketches,' he told me.

I turned around, returned to the easel and fetched the damned sketches.

Pankratov held out his hand for the folder.

I handed it over.

He opened the folder and looked through the sketches again. 'These are very good, you know,' he said.

For a moment, I was too surprised to reply. I'd had no idea what he would think of my work, but had just assumed the worst.

'Did you hear what I told you?' asked Pankratov.

'Yes,' I replied faintly. 'Thank you.'

'They're very good. Do you understand what I'm saying?'

'I think so,' I told him.

'I'm impressed,' he said, looking around the room as if unwilling to look me in the eye when making such a statement. Then his head snapped back to face me. 'All right,' he announced. 'You can go now.'

As I walked down to the Rue Descalzi, I replayed his words over and over in my head, not trusting their meaning – sure that he had intended something else. I had never expected any kind of compliment from him. I didn't think him capable of it. Slowly, as I began to relax, I realized what a hold this man had on me, and how badly I needed his approval.

The next morning I woke, as usual, to the sound of muttering voices in the Rue Descalzi. I could smell the particularly sour, perfumy reek of Matelot tobacco, which was the cheapest brand. When I looked from my window, I saw a line of men outside the gates of the Postillon warehouse. They were shabbily dressed, with floppy caps that hid their faces in the shadows of the morning. They stood with the bowed heads of men down on their luck.

When the foreman arrived with his hobnailed boots echoing in the street, his dragoon moustache was always freshly waxed. Brass buttons gleamed on his double-breasted tunic. He picked out a few of the men, selecting each one with a jerk of his chin. He didn't make his choices by who was first in line, but the other men offered no protest. Either they were too tired or they knew they would never be picked if they kicked up a fuss. They shambled away down the street with their hands in their pockets. The chosen men followed the foreman into the warehouse. A few minutes later, they rode out of the warehouse on rickety bicycles. They carried wooden placards on their backs. On the placards was the wine company's motto: 'BUVEZ LES VINS DU POSTILLON'.

Ever since Fleury had brought up the idea of staying in Paris, I had tried to push the idea to the back of my mind. I still had a month to go before the Levasseur grant ran out. But every morning when I saw those men outside the warehouse, waiting for work, I tried to imagine myself down there with them. Even if I did decide to stay, I had no idea where the money would come from. At this rate, it certainly wasn't going to come from the paintings. And then there was the threat of war, which was on everyone's minds these days. The whole idea of remaining here seemed hopeless to me. I kept seeing those men lined up outside the warehouse. I could practically feel the weight of the placard on my back as I bicycled around town. *Buvez les vins du Postillon*. It had become an ugly little chant in my head, like a meaningless taunt shouted across a playground at some unpopular child.

I sat down at my the three-legged kitchen table, which was bolted to the wall to stop it falling over, and pawed through the strange blues and browns of the French notes in my money box, wondering how long I could make it all last.

'You know the war is coming, Monsieur Alley-fax.'

Pankratov, Valya and I were alone in the atelier. Balard and Marie-Claire had been sent out on assignments, the result of Pankratov's pinning a giant map of Paris up on a wall and making each of us in turn throw a dart at the map at a distance of ten paces. Wherever the dart landed, the person had to go and paint that place. Since my dart missed the map entirely, and stuck itself in the door, Pankratov said he would take pity on me. He decided that since I could not even throw a dart, I would mostly likely just get lost trying to find any location on the map. I would paint Valya instead.

I tried to look suitably humiliated. The truth was, I'd done it on purpose. I didn't like painting in the street. People were always coming up to you and staring over your shoulder and making comments under their breath that they thought you couldn't hear.

The others clattered away down the stairs, hugging their boxes of paints and their collapsible easels. Then it was just me and Pankratov and Valya.

'How do you want me to be?' Valya asked Pankratov, to show she didn't care what I did with her body on my canvas.

Pankratov shrugged. 'Ask the American. I'm not painting you.'

She turned to me. 'Well?' she asked, holding out her arms.

I asked her to stand by the large window. I said she should keep her clothes on.

She obeyed without a word, as if this was what every artist asked her to do when given the chance and it was all very boring and she had done this a hundred times already.

That day, I tried to paint the cold outside. I gave the work a steely look to match the light of the late afternoon. Valya was in silhouette. I painted her as if she were shadows coming to life, the way incense rises to form shapes around the altar of a church. I painted the crumpled light that each window pane allowed into the dark space of the atelier. I allowed it to be warm inside, but just beyond the thin veil of the glass, I made winter settle on the woman by the window.

While I painted, Pankratov sat in his camp chair, fingertips pressed together in front of his face, eyes unfocused. 'The war,' he said again.

I didn't look up. I measured out varnish and paint, then stirred them together with the narrow, rounded blade of my palette knife.

'The war, Monsieur Halifax.'

I didn't want to talk about it. For me, all notions about the safety of France began and ended with the Maginot Line, miles and miles of tunnels built into the French–German border, underground railways, barracks, even cinemas, gunpits arranged to blast anything that tried to cross the frontier. Nothing could get through that. It was the most advanced fortification in the world. The Germans said they didn't want France, anyway. They wanted places that had been German, or at least partly German, like Austria and Czechoslovakia.

It was already a dead topic. Talk like this had been going on for years and people were tired of it. If there was going to be a war, I told myself, I wouldn't be able to do anything to stop it. It seemed to me most people felt that way.

'I wanted to know,' asked Pankratov, 'whether you have made provisions for leaving. For leaving in a hurry, I mean.'

'No, sir,' I said. 'All I've been thinking about lately is staying.'

Pankratov made a growling noise at the back of his throat. He rose up from his chair and walked over to the door. 'I have to go out,' he said. He lifted his faded canvas coat off a brass peg nailed into the wall. The peg had been placed without alignment to anything else in the room. It lay directly in the path of his leaving the room from his chair and at the height required for him to sweep his jacket off the hook without effort. He seemed to have no real sense of order beyond the immediate practicality of things. They were placed where he needed them, without regard to colour or style or the convenience of anyone else.

Pankratov shut the door and from the other side the shape of his body blurred behind the pebbled-glass window. It made him look like a bear standing up on its hind legs. His footsteps clumped down a few paces and then stopped.

He must be lighting a cigarette, I thought. Unconsciously, I found myself waiting for the footsteps to continue. When, after a few seconds, they didn't, I looked up from my work and straight into Valya's eyes.

She was waiting, too.

Eventually, after what seemed a long time, the footsteps continued, fading down and down until there was a distant boom as he closed the front door of the building.

'Pankratov doesn't trust us here alone,' said Valya, whispering, as if he were still listening to each breath that passed between us. She called him Pankratov, just like the rest of us.

'Seems that way,' I said.

'He's afraid he'll come back and find us doing it right on the platform. That would give him a shock he'd never get over.'

I looked up from my painting. 'He wouldn't be the only one in shock.'

She chose to ignore what I had said. 'Do you know what he's really afraid of?'

I peered over the top of my easel. 'What?' I asked.

'He thinks we'll steal his chair and sell it.' She left her pose by the window, walked over to the chair and sat down in it. 'The thing I can't understand is why he holds on to this when it is so damned uncomfortable. This chair was once the only thing he owned, apart from that ridiculous belt buckle of his.'

I was only half listening. I gazed at her hips as she sat in the chair and she knew I was looking at her. She made no move to draw my eyes back to her own. Seeing her now with clothes on, knowing each crease and smoothness of her skin beneath the material, did more to me than seeing her naked. I found I could not freeze into my blood the detachment I needed to paint her properly, to be aware of each part of her and not overwhelmed by all of her at once. I had to snap out of it. I looked at the empty space she'd left behind against the wall and realized I preferred the picture without her in it. With the palette knife, I scraped away the layers of paint that had made up her brooding shape and began to paint over it.

'What are you doing?' she asked. Without waiting for me to reply, she got up and walked over to my easel. 'You just erased me!'

'It's not about you,' I told her. 'Not any more. It started out being about you but now it's only about the painting.'

'Why get me to stand there at all?'

'If you hadn't moved, I wouldn't have known it was better this way. It's nothing personal,' I said.

'It seems personal to me.' She couldn't decide whether to be amused or indignant. 'I only wanted to sit down for a minute. I didn't realize that there would be a penalty.'

Now I smiled at her. 'I didn't know you had a sense of humour.'

'One of several things you don't know, Alley-fax. And now that you know something about me, let me ask you something about yourself.'

I glanced up. Here we go, I thought.

Valya smiled, knowing that we understood each other probably better than we wanted to. 'Why have you ditched all your friends? You used to be such a social butterfly. Now you just hole up and paint as if you're possessed or something.'

I sighed and set down the brush, which was what she had

wanted me to do from the start. I considered giving her some flip answer that would allow us to change the subject, but I decided I would speak plainly instead, to find the honest words as much for myself as for her. 'It's how I make sense of the world,' I said. I took up the brush again. 'I don't always paint because I like it. Sometimes I don't like it. Sometimes it's too hard to like what I'm doing.'

'So why do it at all?'

'Because it isn't on a balance of liking and not liking. I need to do this. And when I am done with it, and I stand back and see what has been made, then I understand why I paint.'

'If it's any good, that is.'

'No. Good or not. When I stand back from the work, I see what pushes me on.'

'A fat lot of good that does your friends,' she said, and shook her head pityingly in my direction.

Just then, I pitied her too. As far as she was concerned, I spent my life being hounded by demons from one frenzy of work to another. But in my mind, I felt as if I were constantly trying to unravel some kind of puzzle that was greater than myself. No one painting would do this. Perhaps even all of the paintings put together would not be able to reveal it. But sometimes, in the midst of the work, I felt myself brush up against the source of some great mystery. Once you have felt that, I wanted to tell her, then you feel sorry for anyone who does not know what they are built to do, and who is not driven on to do it. I wanted to explain this to Valya, but I could tell her mind was closed now, so instead I asked her, 'Why sit in his chair if it's so uncomfortable?'

This got her all worked up again. 'Because he's so damned precious about it! He thinks more of it than of you or me or anyone else. This stupid thing of wood and canvas. When he came to Paris, it was all he brought with him.'

I tried to keep my thoughts far away in the wintry light of the painting, in the thick liquid sweep of the brush across the canvas and the hypnotic reek of linseed oil and varnish.

'Do you know the difference between a White Russian and a Red Russian?' Valya wanted to talk. 'The Reds are the communists,' she explained.

'Yes, I know,' I said.

'And the Whites were against the communist revolution. You know. Fighting for the Tsar. Well, Pankratov was a White Russian. That's what his belt buckle stands for. The royal crest of the Romanovs. It's the only thing left of his old uniform and he's too cheap to go out and buy himself a proper belt.'

'Pankratov doesn't strike me as an aristocrat.'

She shrugged. 'He's not. He just had the bad luck to have been drafted before the Revolution and got sent to some outpost by the side of a lake on the Finnish border. Up in the Arctic. Some place where the sun never set in the summer months. At midnight it used to bounce off the horizon like a ball of cantaloupe melon and then start to climb again. The Revolution was half over before anyone even told them about it. And then, because they had no idea who was winning, they decided to stay with the Tsar, even though the Tsar was dead by then, although they didn't know it. It was the winter of 1921 before a detachment of Red guards came hunting them down. He tries to talk about it but every time he goes into a kind of trance. Something about horses under water. Something about meteors. I don't know. Maybe you can get him to tell you and you'll understand.' She flipped her hand. 'Anyway, when he fled from the communists, he brought that chair with him. You see, you can collapse it into a kind of bundle. He took it with him all the way through Finland, into Sweden, and when he ended up in Paris five years later, he still had it. He has spent more time with that chair than he has with any other thing.' She had been walking around the pedestal as she spoke, as if seeing for the first time how exposed she was when she stood up there alone in front of us.

'You hate it here, don't you?' I asked.

'What?' she snapped.

'You don't seem very happy.'

'What business is it of yours if I'm happy? You have the right to paint me, but not to look inside my head.' She went over to the window, where she had left her handbag. She picked it up and slung its strap across her shoulder. 'Are you finished with me here? Because if I'm not in your painting any more, I can go, can't I?'

'Why do you come here every day if you don't want to be here?'

'Why are you so nosy? Are all Americans like you?'

'A lot of them. Look,' I said, 'you wanted to talk. If you want to talk about nothing, then go ahead and leave. I bet I can draw you from memory. I've been staring at you every day since I got to Paris, sketching you this way and that way every time Pankratov claps his hands. I probably know your body about as well as you do.'

'That's outrageous,' she said, but she made no move to leave.

I realized that, in those weeks of living in her own world up on the pedestal, we who hid behind our easels had stopped being real to her. Perhaps, I thought, it's the only way she can stand to be up there, with each wrinkle of her self exposed.

It grew very quiet in the room.

'Why did you come to Paris?' she asked.

'To paint,' I said.

'You could have stayed home and painted.'

'All right,' I said. 'I came to paint in Paris.' I began to get a headache from the turpentine fumes. Some days they got to me that way. The bitter, slippery vapours drilled through my head like the vice clamp of a hangover – the kind that has you wishing you were dead just to stop the pain from cracking your face like a smashed pottery bowl.

'You should leave while you still can,' she said.

'Are we going to talk about the war again?' I asked.

'No,' she replied. 'This has nothing to do with the war. Take a good look at Pankratov.' She gestured at the chair, as if he were sitting in it, invisible and listening, touching the tips of his fingers as if they formed some kind of radio antenna, transmitting to him signals that no one else could hear. 'That's how you'll be, if you stay in Paris.'

Finally I set down my brush. 'I think he's got things pretty well figured out.' I didn't mind Pankratov's eccentricities. He knew who he was, after all.

'Is that why you all worship him so much?'

'What makes you think we do?'

She clapped her hands together, the sharp sound vanishing into the cork-plated walls. 'It's the one thing I *can* tell from where I sit. I can't see how bad your drawings are, or even if you're drawing me at all.' She flipped her hand at the place where she had lived in my painting until a few moments before. 'But I see how you all bow to him. If you really knew him, you would never have such respect.'

She was missing the point. Of course, we wouldn't hold him up so high if we knew all his faults. We didn't want to know them. We wanted him to be larger than life, so that we could work towards the ideal of who he seemed to be, not who he really was. That was what we needed from him, and he knew it, which was why he kept his distance from us. That much I had figured out.

'He is degenerate,' said Valya, 'just like this whole country.'

'And this from a woman who stands around naked all day,' I blurted without thinking.

Her voice grew viciously calm. 'There are changes coming. You'll see. One good kick and this entire rotten, decadent society will collapse. And you, Mr American, should make sure you are not around when it happens.'

'The war again,' I said.

'Yes,' she told me. 'And for once Pankratov is right. It *is* coming.'

'I think I'll stick around and take my chances,' I said.

She shrugged. 'Pankratov is talking about closing down, so it might not be worth sticking around after all. I watch you all come and go. One group of students after another. And each time, I think this will be the last class. That Pankratov will not do this any more. That he will go back to his own painting again. But each time there are more of you.'

'Where are his paintings, anyway?' I asked, since she had brought it up.

'Don't you know?'

I shook my head. 'Nobody's told me anything.'

'They're all gone. Destroyed. He kept his own studio on the Avenue Beauregard. He was a great star in the late 1920s. He had shows all over the place. He was really quite famous. Everyone was jealous of this man who had walked out of the snow and arrived in Paris with nothing but a chair and then in a couple of years become one of the most promising artists of his generation. He used to have photos on the wall of himself with Picasso, Giacometti and writers like Hemingway and Fitzgerald and one with Cole Porter, too, I think. I don't know who else. But then there was a fire in the building where he kept his studio. It was in 1929. His paintings were there, even the work which had sold and which he had borrowed back to be placed in a show – all of it, you understand – burned to nothing. The whole art world of Paris was in shock. In the weeks that followed they gave Pankratov the one thing he had never received in his life before and the last thing on earth that he wanted. They gave him pity. There were maybe even some who knew what pity would do to him, who wanted him out of the way. They showed him the most pity of all. His reputation as a painter grew far greater after the fire than it had been before. They treated him the way they treat famous people who have died. Forget the faults. Remember only the good. It was as if Pankratov had passed away, too. He hasn't painted since. He is afraid that if he did, people would think he doesn't deserve the reputation he has.'

'Does he deserve it?'

She shrugged. 'Pankratov is a genius. And if I, who am always calling him a shit to his face, say he is that good, then you know you can trust what I say. He is greater than all the people who claim to be great who are still breathing in the world. You could see the relief on their faces when he quit. And the fact that he quit when he did is another act of genius, if you think about it.'

'So why do you hate him,' I asked, 'and then show up every day to work here?'

'I don't hate him. Whatever you see go on between us, it's not hate. Pankratov is one of those people who at first seem so rude you will forgive them nothing. But once you know who they are, you will forgive them anything. Like paying me, for example.'

'He doesn't pay you?'

She shrugged. 'Well, he's supposed to, but he has no money. Most people would starve on what he makes. His principal form of nourishment is *Bouillon Zip* and that one date he eats so carefully each day at the Dimitri.'

Bouillon Zip was what people had in Paris when they were down to their last few centimes. It came in little paper packets that contained a tablespoon of grey-brown powder. I bought *Zip* regularly when I first got here and used it for adding flavor to soups, but since I'd heard about the associations, I'd stopped using it. The jokes I heard made about *Bouillon Zip* were a little too close to the bone.

'So how do you survive?' I asked her.

Her face was lost in the fading light. 'I survive because Pankratov is not the only person in whom I forgive everything.'

Valya was gone by the time Pankratov came back. He returned smelling of cigarettes and coffee. He had been down at the Café Dimitri. 'Where did she go?' he asked.

I explained how I had painted her out.

'About time someone did that.' He showed no trace of amusement. 'So,' he said, unbuttoning his coat and settling himself in the sacred chair, 'in America. You have had some success?'

'Some,' I told him. I waited for him to ask who had been sitting in his chair. I had a feeling he could tell.

'You should . . .' He hesitated. 'You should try to get a show together here. Get someone to represent your work.'

That would have been the time to tell Pankratov about Fleury's offer, but I knew how much he disliked Fleury. So I said nothing.

'Unless Fleury is doing that for you,' mumbled Pankratov, staring off to the other end of the room.

'Oh,' I said. I should have guessed he would already know.

Now Pankratov was grinning.

'What do you have against him?' I asked. 'He seems nice enough.'

Pankratov coughed out a sarcastic laugh. 'It's his job to be nice, when he thinks he can make a profit. You know who makes the money around here? It's the dealers! Not the artists. Do you know how much of a percentage the Parisian art dealers make off what they sell?'

'Well,' I said, 'back home it's twenty-five per cent.'

'In Paris it's *forty* per cent. That's what I have against him. And all the other damned dealers in the city. This boy Fleury – I tell you, he's the slyest of the lot.'

'Fleury?' I asked, my voice rising with disbelief.

'Oh, yes!' Pankratov fitted a cigarette into his mouth. He broke it in half and fitted the spare piece back into the packet. 'Fleury might look like an incompetent fop, but believe me, he knows what he's doing.'

Shadows filled the studio. Out across the rooftops, sun was still shining on the city.

'I heard about the fire,' I said to Pankratov.

'Congratulations. Valya talks too much.' The ragged-tipped cigarette wobbled between his lips. There was the tiny roar of his match flaring. He lit the cigarette and his cheeks bowed in with the smoke.

'I wish I could have seen your paintings,' I told him.

'So do a lot of people, I think. For various reasons.' Pankratov turned to me, and fluttered his hands jokingly around his head, as if to wrap himself in some rippling, magical light. 'Are the rumours true? Was I as good as they say? Now we'll never know.'

'We'd know if you started painting again.'

Pankratov dropped his hands. 'Those days aren't coming back,' he said.

'It gives you more pleasure to spend your days running this atelier?'

'Believe it or not, I do enjoy your company. Balard, Marie-Claire, you, the ones who came before. You remind me of myself. Each of you in one way or another.'

'So what am I to think? That I'll end up not painting anything?'

'I don't paint,' Pankratov said slowly, measuring in his head whether to say the words that were gathering in his throat, 'because I discovered I am better at something else.'

'What?' I asked.

He stood up and buttoned his coat, the roughness of his fingers on the dull grey zinc of the buttons. He narrowed his eyes. He was getting ready to close up like an oyster.

'Tell me,' I asked.

'All right,' he said, after a moment, 'but remember you asked. Let's go. We'll have to move quickly.'

Pankratov walked me across town. There was still some light in the streets that ran east–west. We didn't talk. He didn't say where he was taking me. It was only when we reached the Tuileries gardens that I realized we were heading towards the Louvre. Evening glimmered off the powdery yellow stone walkway that led to the huge building. Pankratov brought us to a door beside the main gates.

There was a guard just inside the little door, which was propped open with a chair to let in the breeze, despite the chill. He sat at a desk, reading a paper. He was a short man with a scrubby black moustache. In a hammered brass ashtray on his desk was a pile of crooked cigarette stubs. The paper of the cigarettes was brown, what the French call *papier maïs*. His blue uniform was rumpled and his cap rested on his foot, which he had up on the desk. When we blocked the light in the entranceway, he took his feet off the desk and crammed his cap back on his head. He squinted at our silhouettes.

'On your feet, Monsieur Sevier!' said Pankratov.

Sevier launched himself upright. Then, recognizing Pankratov, he slapped down his paper. 'I wish you wouldn't do that. Now I have to get comfortable again.'

'That shouldn't take long.' Pankratov signed his name in a book on the desk.

'On the contrary,' said Sevier, 'it is an art form in itself.'

'You see,' Pankratov told me, 'in Paris, everyone is an artist in one thing or another.'

Sevier wore an unsteady grin, not quite getting Pankratov's joke.

At the end of the gloomy corridor was another door, which Pankratov opened. We found ourselves in a gallery with huge paintings bracketed in ornate gold frames. My first impression was not of the artwork, but of how much these paintings must have weighed. Pankratov closed the door behind me.

When I turned, I saw that the door had no handle from this side. It disappeared into the panelling.

Pankratov led us over to one of the great wall-length paintings. It was the *Raft of the Medusa* by Géricault. The canvas was about ten feet high and about fifteen feet wide. It showed a group of people on a raft waving to a ship in the distance. Most of the castaways on the raft were dead or dying. Their skin was grey and their faces contorted like a dozen variations of Christ on the cross. Their clothes had rotted from their bodies. They had been at sea a long time. If this boat did not stop to pick them up, they were finished. Huge, glassy waves rose up jagged between them and the distant ship, its sails full and making speed. I knew a little bit about the story of the *Medusa*. It went down off the coast of Africa and no one stopped to pick up the survivors because the people on board were poor immigrants. It caused a scandal that almost brought down the French government. In places, the paint on the canvas was bubbly and black, the way creosote gets on old railroad ties.

I had barely noticed the grandness of the room in which the painting hung, alongside several other massive canvases. The walls were painted flat hunter green and gilded where they met the ceiling.

The last visitors were being herded out by a guard, who walked with his arms spread, making slow swishing motions with his hands, like a scarecrow come to life. One person stopped to make a note in a tiny book. It was a woman. I was admiring the braiding of her hair, and wondering how one braided hair so exactly, when she turned and I saw that it was Valya.

She hadn't seen me, and it caught me so much by surprise to find her here that I didn't call out her name.

People were shuffling past.

'Il est temps, mesdames et messieurs,' said the guard in a droning voice. 'Messieurs, dames, il est temps.' It is time. It is time.

Valya moved on out of sight, flowing with the crowd.

I turned to Pankratov, to see whether he had noticed Valya, but his eyes were fixed upon the painting of the raft. He was lost in it. 'This,' said Pankratov, 'is my art.'

When he said that, I forgot about Valya.

His art, he had called it. I ran the words around in my head a few times. My teeth slowly clamped together as I hesitated to believe what now seemed obvious – that Pankratov was crazy after all, past the line of eccentricity and the twilight world of genius, having lost track of the boundary between the world of dreams and the less satisfying world that surrounds it. The fact seemed unavoidable. It was as if one of the Louvre guards was walking through my head, swishing his hands, shooing the last reservations from my own mind. *Il est fou, messieurs, dames. Il est fou.*

I glanced uneasily at the painting and then at Pankratov.

He still had his hands raised towards the Géricault, his mouth set hard with pride.

'It's by Géricault,' I said quietly.

'Of course it is.' He dropped his hands. 'Come with me,' he ordered.

We returned to the space in the wall where the door had vanished. He pressed against it and the door clicked open. We returned to the dim passageway that led out to the street.

'Sevier,' said Pankratov, calling to the guard as he strode down the hall, 'I want to see the Géricault pictures.'

'Very good.' Sevier had taken his shoes off and was now massaging his feet. He unclipped a set of keys from his belt and handed them to Pankratov. 'You know where they are.'

Pankratov opened a small door beside the desk. A smell of paper billowed out, musty and faintly sweet. A smell of patience and quiet. Inside, the room was stacked with boxes of documents, which lay on shelves that divided the space.

'Go on' – Pankratov waved me in – 'go on.'

I obeyed.

He walked straight over to a box, hauled it down and let it thump on to the floor.

Coppery light filtered in through the blinds. The air in the room was still and warm. I felt around me the great solidity of the building. The permanence of it. As if it knew somehow that even though it had been built by man to glorify man, it was greater now than the people who had built it. It glorified only itself. I felt that about a lot of the great buildings in Paris. I sensed that they knew what they were.

We crouched down over the box of photos.

'Here.' Pankratov held one out to me.

It was a glossy black-and-white of the Géricault. The entire centre of the painting was gone. It had been replaced by tatters of canvas and the wall behind it, which stood pitted and white beneath its dried-blood-coloured paint. For a few seconds my eyes drifted around the outside of the picture, where the painting was still whole and recognizable, my mind not wanting to admit what it was seeing.

'Last year,' said Pankratov, 'a man named Alphonse Gradovich walked into the building, right down that hallway there' – he gestured to where Sevier was sitting, back at his perch, massaging his feet with tiny groans of pleasure. 'He was carrying a double-barrelled shotgun. Nearly blew Sevier's head off. Sevier!' Pankratov shouted past me, 'Show this man the shotgun marks!'

Obediently, as if he had rehearsed the movements, Sevier stopped rubbing his feet and aimed his finger at various scrapes along the wall where the pellets had ricocheted. The places had been painted over, but they were clear to see now that Sevier had pointed them out. 'This close! With both barrels!' he said and pinched the air in front of him. 'And if I hadn't been so quick . . .' With a broad cutting sweep, he slapped one palm across the other.

'He was asleep,' whispered Pankratov, 'and when Gradovich walked in, Sevier woke up and fell backwards off his chair.'

'If I hadn't been so quick . . .' Sevier said again.

'You'd be only slightly less active than you are at the moment,' Pankratov finished his sentence.

Sevier waved him away. 'Brother, you wait until you have been shot at.'

Pankratov straightened up. 'I *have* been shot at.' He took the picture back from me and looked at it himself. 'Gradovich walked into the room with the Géricault. He went right up to it, reloaded his gun and emptied both barrels into the painting. He blew out the whole centre, as you can see. The guards caught up with him before he made it out to the street.'

'And I can tell you,' said Sevier, 'that Gradovich may be the only man in history to have had his head beaten against the Nike of Samothrace.'

'It took me every night for eight months to repair the damage to the Géricault,' said Pankratov.

'You restored it?' I asked. 'But there isn't a mark on it now! I want to see it again.'

'You don't need to,' he said. 'You are right. There is no trace.'

'Wait a minute,' I said slowly. 'I never heard about any of this. It would have been news all over the world.'

'No,' he said, 'you didn't hear about any of it. The whole thing was kept quiet. The curators here didn't want that painting to become famous for the damage that was done to it. They just wanted it to go on being famous for itself.'

'What happened to the man with the gun?'

'He's in an asylum. He escaped from one to begin with. Now he's back inside and no one believes a word he says, which no one did before.'

'Why did he do it?'

'Ah.' Pankratov nodded, expecting the question. 'Gradovich claimed to be the descendant of someone who died aboard the *Medusa*. He said he hadn't known there was a painting about the shipwreck until he came to Paris and went to the Louvre. Once he'd set eyes on the painting, he couldn't stop thinking about it. It was driving him more mad than he already was. Gradovich said he had to destroy it. I used to think about that when I was working on the Géricault. I believe I understand what he was going through. So you see' – Pankratov flicked the photograph with his fingernails – 'this is what I do best. When there's a call for it. Not every piece is as important as this one. Not every one must be secret. But many of them are. It requires a negation of everything I used to live for. Not to seek fame. Not to require attention.'

'How did you find out you were good at it?'

'Not just good,' Sevier corrected me. 'Pankratov is the best.'

'I discovered it by accident,' explained Pankratov. 'There was some work belonging to another painter that got damaged in the fire at my old studio. My own paintings were too far gone, but in trying to mend this other piece, I suddenly understood that I could do it. I thought I was a painter,' he said, twisting his hand in on itself, as if tracing the path of a wisp of smoke, 'but this is what I really am.'

'You *were* a painter. A great one, from all I hear.'

'All right,' he said. 'Maybe I was good. But I exhausted myself. I got so tired in here' – he bounced the heel of his palm off his forehead. 'Some days, I would set up the canvas and stare at it for an hour and then be so exhausted I'd have to go back to bed. But with restoration, it's different' – he drew his fingers close together, like a man learning to pray. 'It's about the creation of the paint itself. Using only those materials available at the time. Then the lacquer. Then the ageing process. The precision of it. The cheating of time! Do you know that my finest work in that Géricault is the part Géricault got wrong.'

'Got wrong? What do you mean?'

'He was experimenting with different pigments and mediums. Not all of it worked. Did you see those patches on the canvas that look like tar?'

I nodded.

'The pigment corroded after a couple of decades. It is actually eating away through the primer and into the canvas. Or it was, anyway. My job was to recreate the exact look of the experimental pigment, but to make it in such a way that it no longer damaged the canvas underneath it. Now *that* was difficult!'

'People should know about this,' I said, 'about what you have done.'

'No,' said Pankratov, 'they should not. I am not doing this for people. Not even for Géricault. Not even if he came back from the grave to ask me to do it himself. I am doing it for me. Don't you see? If people knew, if they all came to admire the work the way they came to admire my paintings before they were burned, then it would no longer be my art. Then I would be doing it for someone else. There is only one real sacrifice an artist can make, and that is to accept the possibility of being forgotten. Once you have done that, then it is possible no longer to care.'

'He has explained it to me,' said Sevier, rustling the newspaper in front of his face, 'and I still don't get it.'

'But *you* do,' Pankratov told me. He stood, knees crackling as if his legs were filled not with flesh and bone but with tiny pebbles that rearranged themselves each time he moved.

Suddenly I understood why he had brought me here: because even in his world of anonymous brilliance, he still needed someone to understand what he was doing. The only thing I didn't understand was why he had chosen me. Perhaps, I thought, it's because I'm a stranger here, someone just passing through. He needs someone to grasp the enormity of his work – the sacrifice of it. Pankratov needs to see in someone's face the proof he isn't mad, because he is no longer sure himself.

We walked out past Sevier, who had gone back to massaging his feet and was saying, as if someone else were doing it for him, 'There. Oh, there. Magnificent.'

The purple twilight wrapped around us as we headed home along the sidewalks, past the late-working people with their thousand-yard stares of fatigue, trying to switch off the blind-rushing energy of the day so they could sleep that night.

'If it weren't for the fire,' I told him, 'you might never have known.'

He considered this. 'If the Germans take over Europe, it won't matter whether there was a fire or not. I was officially disapproved of by the National Socialist Party,' he said. 'My paintings were declared *entartete Kunst*.'

'What does that mean?' I asked.

'Art whose existence degrades all other art,' he said with a sigh. 'Something like that. Along with Van Gogh, Monet, Manet, Munch, Braque and a few dozen others. Many of them were publicly burned in Berlin last year by the Nazis as a protest, just as many in the Louvre will be, or the Musée d'Orsay or the Jeu de Paumes, if the Germans reach Paris.'

'I saw Valya back there,' I said.

'Back where?'

'At the museum. She was in the next room over. She was looking at some paintings. She was taking notes.'

'No,' said Pankratov. 'That couldn't have been her. She's not interested in any kind of art.'

'It *was* her.'

'Valya would rather spend her afternoons sitting up on the platform at the atelier than wandering around the Louvre and she doesn't much care for that platform, as you well know. Believe me, I may not know my own daughter as well as I should, but I know that much about her.'

I felt as if I had been punched in the stomach. 'Your *daughter*?'

'Yes,' he said, 'she's my daughter.'

'I had no idea! Neither does anyone else!' I was practically shouting in his ear.

'She's not actually my daughter,' said Pankratov, 'but I raised her.'

'I thought you came out of Finland!' I shook my head. 'Just you and that chair of yours!'

He waved the flat of his hand towards the ground to make me lower my voice. 'Me, the chair and Valya. She always leaves herself out of that story.'

'Well, Jesus,' I sighed. I tried to imagine the look on Fleury's face when I told him about this.

'She doesn't like people to know,' said Pankratov.

'Why not?'

Pankratov rolled his shoulders, wincing slowly. 'Here in Paris, she is a refugee, the same as I am,' he said. 'But she is also an orphan. That is too much for her. When you are displaced, you always think about where you come from. It's a question that people who are not displaced never have to ask. You, for example – you know where you come from.'

'Narragansett,' I said. As I spoke the word, some distillate of memory splashed suddenly into my eyes. I went blind from the fast-returning images of the spray off breaking waves across greyish-khaki sand the consistency of granulated sugar.

'But if you don't know,' Pankratov continued, 'your life becomes about not knowing. Some people can stand it. Some people can even profit from the lack of knowing. But she's not one of those. To create a balance of her life, she has made for herself a world of ideals that neither she nor anyone else can maintain. So nobody gets to belong. That is the hard ground on which she lives.'

'But you still work together,' I said, trying to be optimistic.

'She is too idealistic to stay employed anywhere else.'

'If it weren't for you, she'd probably be dead.'

'That's true.' He tilted his head sharply in agreement. 'But it wasn't her choice to live or die. She doesn't owe me for that.'

Now I understood why she hated him. And she *did* hate him. Part of him anyway. And it didn't matter if she loved him as well, because that didn't reduce any of the hate. The two extremes existed side by side in her image of Pankratov. What she hated most was that he didn't love her best. What he loved, more than her or any other living thing, was his work. That was why he stayed alone now.

I wondered if it was inevitable. Maybe you could not be devoted to the work without letting everything else suffer. It was not about how much time you had in each day. It was about the expenditure of passion.

The night crowds were gathering. People walked more slowly, some with broad and careful footsteps, as if they were measuring the number of paces between one place and another. Eventually we reached the place where Pankratov would leave to go to his home, and I would turn down the Rue Descalzi. The city hummed and roared around us, the gears of its great engine winding down.

I was no longer thinking about Valya. I was thinking about what Pankratov had said. About being forgotten and accepting it. I thought how hard Pankratov's knowlege was to come by, and harder still to live it out. The way Pankratov explained things, he had merely adapted to a series of coincidences. But I knew there must be more to it than that. Pankratov was not a man to be swept along by circumstance.

For the rest of the walk, I felt an idea taking shape inside me. It was there, but I couldn't see it clearly. I became afraid it would slip away. I squinted into the murkiness of my own mind and gradually it began to appear. It was as if Pankratov had held out a handful of dust on the flat of his palm and had blown it in my face, and now the dust had settled. 'You set the fire,' I said. 'You burned your own paintings. Is it true?'

He didn't answer.

'But how did you do it?' I demanded. 'Did you pile them all up and cover them in turpentine? What did you do?'

'Much simpler than that,' he said. He took the cigarette from his mouth and almost without thinking he flicked it away. It bounced in the street and glowed, and then blew out.

Now I knew why he spat into his ashtray at the Café Dimitri. 'But what about the ones that had been sold?'

'I got them back. They were all being gathered for a retrospective.'

'Are there no paintings left?' I asked. 'Not one?'

He shook his head. 'The only one I didn't get my hands on was in a German collection and it was burned by the Nazis in that fire I told you about.' He spoke in a low voice that matched the thrum of the city and vanished into it, indecipherable, except in the close space between us.

'Why did you take me to see the Géricault?' I asked. 'Why tell me the secret?'

He smiled. 'You wanted to know who I am. It's why you spied on me at the café. You needed me to earn your trust, so that's what I'm doing now: I'm earning it by telling you the truth. Do you see?'

'Yes,' I said quietly.

He held out his hand.

For the first time, we shook, as if this was our first meeting, and everything that had gone before was just some long illusion.

That night I dreamed of Pankratov setting fire to his paintings. I saw them vanish into an upward-flowing stream of multi-coloured flame as the different paints ignited, the blaze contained for a moment in the wood of the frames, dripping fire, each thread of canvas crumpling brittle into black dust, then the frames collapsing in on themselves, even the nails curling over like fingers drawn into a fist. I saw the tubes of paint exploding and shimmering gargoyles emerging from the floor where old turpentine had soaked into the wood and now ignited. Glass melting out of the windows. The guttural furnace roar of the fire eating through Pankratov's life. It was as if I stood there in the centre of that blazing room, and felt the heat and saw, through the smoke and poppy-red of flames, each object that burned and disintegrated. I felt that if I opened my mouth, smoke might pour from my lungs and boiling the blood in my skull. The sound of it was deafening.

Through all this, the pigeons dreamed on my window ledge. The city grew quiet but not still. The sky that night was filled with meteors, cartwheeling above the chimney pots.

5

I was on the streetcar again, on my way home from seeing Rocco, the King of the World. The pads of paper I'd bought were heavy and dusty on my lap. They gave out a smell like an attic in the summertime.

A man and a young girl got on at Château Rouge. The man was wearing a brown wool suit with a black check pattern woven into it. The little girl, who was about three years old, had a black velvet dress and black patent leather shoes. On one hand she wore a white glove. The other hand was bare. I guessed she had lost the other glove and that her father had not yet noticed. I imagined the slightly exhausted look on his face when he found out, more because of what his wife would say than the cost of a new set of gloves.

'Ocean?' the girl was saying. 'Oceanoceanocean?'

'No, puppy,' said the man, 'we're not going to the ocean today.'

'Ocean coming!' she announced, as if it would be there when she called it.

The father motioned for the little girl to take the seat next to mine. But then he took a closer look at me, and his expression changed. He motioned for his daughter to take the other seat, and sat next to me himself, turning his shoulder away from me.

I looked at my tie, with its paint-splatter at the end and the knot worn at the throat. I looked at my unpolished shoes. My jacket smelled. Worse, it smelled of someone else's sweat because I had bought it at a second-hand shop in Clignancourt. My other jacket had become so filthy from charcoal dust that the cleaner had said he could do nothing for it. I didn't have enough money for a new coat.

No one had ever given me that kind of look before. It was the kind of look you give a tramp when you can't help staring at the filth that burnishes his skin and clothes. I wasn't angry at the man, only ashamed at myself because I was dirty and my clothes were so shabby.

At home, I took a bath and scrubbed my skin raw with coal-tar soap. I put on clean clothes and just sat there, feeling repulsion like an oily shiver around my ribs.

That evening I ran into Fleury outside our building. He liked to chat with Madame LaRoche in the evenings. He would squat down on his haunches and smoke cigarettes while she smoked her pipe.

'Why don't you come out to dinner?' he asked me. 'I'm heading over to the Polidor again.'

I had been on my way to the corner store to get some bread and cheese for dinner and maybe an apple for dessert. I told him I wanted to keep painting. My work had gone badly that day. I needed a break, but it was hard to set myself loose from the canvas when I didn't have anything to show for the hours I'd put in. The other thing was that I didn't want to owe him.

'It's only dinner,' said Fleury. 'Believe me, I want you to be producing work as much as you want to produce it. But you have to eat sometime.'

I couldn't afford to go out to dinner, but I had to get out of that apartment or I thought I would go crazy.

As we set off down the street, I turned to wave goodbye to Madame LaRoche.

She was watching us. She looked old and sad.

It occurred to me that maybe she had wanted Fleury to invite her along, too, but I doubted it had ever crossed his mind.

The Polidor was crowded, warm with the heat of elbow-to-elbow people, each group locked in its own conversation. Outside, the light had faded from the streets. The air that blew in through the open windows carried with it the smell of rain about to fall.

We ate cassoulet and started out with heavy Dordogne wine, an almost blood-thick Château Pineraie. Then we switched to the house red, which tasted acidic and papery in comparison.

I had been waiting for the right moment to let him know about Valya and Pankratov. Now my patience gave way and I told him.

As Fleury listened, he took off his glasses and stared at me across the table. Then he put his glasses back on and stared some more. He gritted his teeth and scratched at his neck as if he had some kind of skin condition. 'Good God,' he said. 'I must admit I did not see this coming.' He squinted at me. 'Are you sure you're not joking?'

'No joke,' I assured him.

'And to think all this time . . .' His voice trailed off. He set his elbow on the table and rubbed his fingers hard across his forehead, leaving red marks.

'But you know, Fleury. Valya . . .' I narrowed my eyes. 'She's a hard case.'

'She certainly is.' Fleury sat back, crossing one leg over the other.

I noticed that, although his brown ankle boots were highly polished, the soles had both worn through and the heels were ground way down. I looked up at his face, in case he saw me staring at those boots.

'Here's the thing, about Valya and me,' he said. 'You know how it is when there are beautiful people all around, but their beauty does nothing to you.'

'I guess,' I said, awkwardly.

'You recognize that they are beautiful,' continued Fleury, 'and charming and intelligent, men and women both, but when you look at them you feel a certain emptiness. It doesn't occur to you that you may never see them again and if it did you wouldn't care. It's as if we each have some kind of coding device inside us. Sometimes our codes partly match with the codes of other people. Mostly they don't match at all. But' – he pinched the air – 'in the rarest moments, the codes will match completely. There is even a feeling of a lock clicking shut. It isn't love or lust. It's something entirely different. It's some unnamed recognition, that makes you want to be near them, no matter what the circumstances. It makes you want to tell them secrets. You don't care what kind of fool you make of yourself. The idea that you might not see this person again sends panic clattering through your head. That is the way I am about Valya. And I tell you, there isn't a damned thing I can do about it.'

'Poor you,' I said.

'Poor me is right.' His face took on a mixture of deviousness and hope. 'But perhaps not as poor as all that, now that I know things are different.' His eyes narrowed as the possibilities took shape in his head.

I felt even more sorry for him than before. Fleury was not a handsome man. Not well built. He seemed to have a certain clumsiness around women, which he hid pretty well behind his sense of humour, but he could only hide it for so long. None of these things should have mattered, and maybe Valya should have loved him from the start because he was kind and intelligent and would have made a good companion – I supposed all that was true – and for a dozen other reasons that didn't matter in the end. They didn't matter because Valya would not have been seen walking out with a man like Fleury. That was a fact.

I figured there wasn't a person in the world who hadn't, at one time or another, sat down with a friend and listened to them go on about loving someone they would never possess. Rather than tell them the truth about their chances, and save them some grief down the road, you just sit there nodding and smiling and feeling bad about it, because that is a thing they'll never believe until they find it out for themselves. So, for the rest of the meal, Fleury talked about Valya and I agreed with every damned thing he said, because he didn't really want to know what I thought. The only thing I could do for Fleury, as a friend, would be not to remind him about all the things he'd said when he got to the point where he wished he'd never said them.

Finally, mercifully, Fleury changed the subject by asking me if I had any paintings for him to sell.

'They're not finished,' I told him. 'They'll be done soon.'

'What about the sketches?' he asked. 'You have some of those, don't you?'

'Yes,' I said. 'I have some studies I did at the Musée Duarte.'

He tapped at his chin with his index finger, thinking. 'Those are the ones Pankratov was raving about.'

'He didn't rave about them,' I said. 'He just said he liked them is all.'

'If Pankratov likes them, that's good enough for me.' Fleury crumpled his napkin and stood. The napkin stayed wrung in his fists like the neck of a small strangled animal.

I looked up, fork still poised over a piece of apple tart. 'What's the matter?'

'I have some calls to make. I'll stop by your place tomorrow,' he said. 'Pick up those sketches, if you don't mind. We can make a start with those.' He was looking over my head and out into the street. A fine rain was falling. His thoughts had already moved on. They raced ahead of his footsteps and out into the dark.

After the meal, I went to the Polidor bar. It was connected to the restaurant through a doorway and down a couple of steps. The wine hummed warmly in my head and I wanted to have a coffee before heading home to work for the rest of the night. A Japanese man in a tuxedo was playing jazz on the piano. His eyes were closed and smiling and his lips moved as if making up words for the songs he was playing.

As I stood in the doorway, watching people at the bar, I realized that one of them was Valya, in the company of a man I'd never seen before. She wore a long black dress and an amber necklace, each marmalade stone held by a silver band and joined with silver links one to another. Her hair was tied up on her head. She looked very beautiful. She was sitting up on the bar with a small thin glass of clear liquid in her hands. Beside her was a bowl of crushed ice with more thin glasses in it, almost like test tubes. She drank the clear liquid in one gulp, her head going back and her neck arching, and the man, momentarily not under her gaze, fixed her with predator's eyes, which had vanished again behind soft-smiling politeness by the time she looked at them again.

I remained almost hidden behind the mounds of coats hanging from the porcelain-tipped brass coat racks that jutted from the wall. Several of them were already broken off from the weight of too many coats. I breathed in the leathery smells of tobacco and strong coffee, mixed with the faint sourness of wine.

'I'll be right back,' said the man. He headed for the bathroom, stepping past me on his way. The man was about six foot two, with brown hair cropped at the sides and longer on the top, which he combed back. He had a broad forehead and deep-set brown eyes the colour of hazelnut shells. His shoes were spit-shined and cross-laced.

Now another man, who was standing at the bar, leaned across to Valya. He was broad-shouldered and round-faced, with his front teeth bunched too close together. 'Why do you like Thomas so much?' he asked, teasing, as if to show he really didn't care.

'I like him,' replied Valya, 'because he doesn't ask stupid questions.'

The man's head rocked back as he laughed, but then he brought his face close to hers and was no longer laughing. His hands gripped the bar on either side of her. 'Why didn't we meet in another life, you and me?'

She rested the heel of her palm on the man's head and gave him a gentle shove backwards. 'He'd kill you if he heard you talk like that.'

The man shrugged to show he didn't care.

'He's coming back,' said Valya.

The man stepped to one side in a quick, fluid movement.

All his brave talk finished, as if perhaps they'd not been joking about the lethal instincts of the brown-eyed man.

I felt suddenly ashamed to be spying on her like this. It was just what she would be expecting of one of her father's pupils. I walked the two steps down into the bar.

From the expression on Valya's face, it was clear she didn't want to start a conversation.

Obligingly, I pretended not to know who she was.

I found a table to myself and drank my coffee. I started thinking about Fleury again. I wondered if I ought to tell him about Valya being here tonight and hoped there might be some way he could find out on his own. Fleury might thank me for bringing him the news, but he would always remember that I was the one who brought it. For now, I tried to push it from my head. I sat on the plush green chairs and felt the music swirl around me as if it were part of the smoky air.

Early the next day Fleury met me outside my apartment, as I was heading to Pankratov's. I had dropped off my sketches the night before. I slid them under his apartment door in a manila folder. He was holding the folder now. His face was serious.

'What's the matter?' I asked him.

'I think I can sell these,' he said.

'But they're just sketches,' I told him.

'I may have a buyer.' His glasses made him owlish. He tilted his head back, as if trying to see out from under the heavy lenses. 'So you'll allow me to represent you?' he asked. 'Just to make it official?'

'Sure,' I told him. 'I'd be glad to.'

'And on your painting series as well, when they're ready. I'd like to have that be a part of the arrangement.'

I thought about it for a second. 'All right,' I said. 'And after the paintings, we can see how it's going.'

'Fair enough,' he said and held out his hand.

I shook it.

Madame LaRoche appeared, carrying her chair. She grunted as she stepped by us and out into the sun. The chair's old hinges creaked as she sat down. She brought out her pipe from her apron and clamped it, unlit, between her teeth. Then she folded her arms and stared into space.

I looked down at the ground, stubbing the toe of my shoe against some imaginary bump in the pavement. 'I saw Valya out with some other guy last night.'

Fleury was silent for a moment. 'Well,' he said, trying to sound nonchalant, 'there was bound to be someone, wasn't there?'

I glanced up. 'Sure, I suppose.'

'Don't count me out yet,' he said. 'Haven't even thrown my hat in the ring yet.'

I couldn't help smiling. 'Good man,' I said.

He raised the manila envelope. 'Let's get these sold, shall we?'

'Lots of luck,' I told him.

'Luck will have nothing to do with it,' he replied. Then he beamed a smile at Madame LaRoche. 'Morning, madame.'

She creased her porridge face into a smile.

When he had gone, I stood for a while in the sun, eyes closed, feeling the warmth on my face. I thought about how things were in motion now, about how there was nothing for me to do but get on with my work. I tried to prepare myself for the fact that the sketches would most likely be rejected. I knew the precise acidic heaviness in my guts from times it had happened before, and how I would try not to let it show.

Madame LaRoche breathed in deeply, which she did whenever she was going to make some pronouncement.

I opened my eyes.

She was watching me. She took the pipe from her mouth and pointed it at me. 'Monsieur Fleury is going to sell your paintings?'

'Yes, ma'am. He's going to try, anyway.'

'It is just as well. We will need some paintings to look at, now that the museums are closing.'

I had been hearing rumours about this for some time. A few days ago, it had become official. Owing to the threat of war, the museums would close on 25 August. I gave a gloomy sigh at the prospect.

'If Monsieur Fleury likes your paintings,' said Madame LaRoche, 'then everyone will like them.'

'Thanks,' I replied.

Madame LaRoche looked down the road after Fleury. 'The compliment is not for you,' she said.

As Marie-Claire, Balard and I poured out into the street at the end of the day's classes, I declined Balard's half-hearted offer to join them at the Dimitri. By now, they were hopelessly in love, beyond all practicality and sense. They were like characters in a pointillist dream, fragmented by late summer's hazy light.

I stepped through the doorway of my apartment building and into the shadows. I was clutching a portfolio to my chest, heading for the elevator at the end of the hall.

There was an explosion.

'Jesus!' I shouted. I dropped to my knees, hard on the tiles of the floor, and then sprawled on to my face. The portfolio flew out of my hands. It slapped on to the floor, spilling paper like a fanned-out deck of cards.

In the silence that followed, I heard laughter.

It was Fleury. He was sitting on one of the benches that lay on either side of the door. No one ever sat on them. It was too gloomy there. He was holding a bottle of champagne and had just fired off the cork, which bounced off the ceiling and came to rest, spinning, right in front of my face. 'Did you think someone was shooting at you?'

'What are you doing there?' I asked, as I gathered up my scattered portfolio.

'I am about to drink this,' he said quietly. 'And then, perhaps, quite a bit more.'

It took a second for this to sink in. 'You sold something?'

He drank some champagne from the bottle, and when he lowered it, the champagne rose up and spilled down over his hand and wrist. From the top pocket of his jacket he took out a wad of money, neatly folded and held with a brass clip. He tossed it on to the floor in front of me.

I looked at the money but didn't touch it yet.

'You doubted me, didn't you?' he said. 'Go on. Admit it. You doubted me.'

'It wasn't you I doubted. It was the work.' I reached over and picked up the bills. I slipped off the paperclip and counted the money. I calculated roughly one month of expenses, including food and rent and painting supplies. This money had come just in time: the Levasseur grant expired in two weeks. 'Did you sell all of them?' I asked.

Fleury set down the champagne bottle, and pushed it gently across the black and white tiled floor so I could reach it. 'Actually, I sold only three of the eight you gave me, to a man who is a private collector.'

'I don't understand. Three pictures?' I held up the wad of bills. 'For all this?'

He sat forward and clasped his hands together. 'What you don't understand is how little work of genuine quality is out there. And you don't know how much quality artwork actually goes for. If you think you're worth very little, so will everyone else.'

'Why didn't you sell all of them?' I asked. 'Didn't he want the others?'

'I didn't even show him the others. I gave out just enough to make him hungry and to keep him that way. He'll get the rest when I'm ready.'

'You can't tell me his name? I mean, I'd like to thank him.'

Fleury ground his heel into the tiles. 'You do your job and let me do mine.' Then he smiled, to hide the force behind his words.

I put the money in my pocket.

You always wonder what you'll do when you get your first break in a new place. The break isn't always about money. It's more about the first vote of confidence. You feel as if everything you have done to get to this place has been worthwhile and that all of the miserable days of doubt will have inverted into something glorious. You wonder what momentous thing you will do to mark the event. Maybe you will climb to the edge of some jagged cliff above the clouds, like a character in a Caspar David Friedrich painting, and watch the sun come up on this new universe of yours. Or maybe you will do a painting to mark the event, the one you will never sell or give away.

Here is what I did instead: I bought a pair of socks. I walked around, aimless but contented, and got lost somewhere between Rue St Dominique and the Avenue Bosquet. I asked an old woman for directions. She had set herself up at a little table, on which she had placed hand-knitted sweaters, socks and gloves. She had made them herself and was knitting a new sweater while she sat there in the street, with a pile of old newspapers for a chair. The wool was thick and nubby and when I pressed it to my face, I smelled the calming fragrance of new wool. She showed me the way to get home.

On the way back, the night cold found its way along my sleeves and down my neck. I strolled down the Rue Racine and the Boulevard St Germain, peering into shop windows at the wistful-looking mannequins. If I sold some more pieces, I might be able to buy myself a few new shirts, maybe even a suit. I peered in at the restaurants, and made a mental note of the ones that looked inviting – places I would go when the money started coming in – to the bar at the Hôtel Meurice and La Crémaillière and Le Boeuf Sur Le Toit.

I went back to thinking about the sketches. I had sold work before. That wasn't what made this so different. What made it different was that this work had been bought in Paris. I realized just how many of my daydreams had been about this moment.

When I got home, I rolled up the money, tied it with string and stashed the bundle at the bottom of a box of oatmeal.

I set some breadcrumbs out for the pigeons, then put on my pyjamas and the new socks. Lying in bed, I wiggled my toes in the socks, which drew a smile across my face. For the first time since I had reached France, I wouldn't wake up with cold feet.

In my dreams that night it seemed to me that all the great paintings of the world filed past behind my closed eyelids. They seemed to have a kind of life in them that I could not identify. These paintings were not alive by themselves, but when I looked at them, it seemed that part of what was living in me passed through them. If I could only keep this vision in my head, I thought. If I could understand it the way I do now in my dream.

When I woke the next morning, the city was rumbling with a smooth even thunder like an engine as it reaches its optimum speed, when everything in the machine suddenly seems to settle and all vibrations stop. I went to class and made no mention of selling the sketches, since I didn't want it to seem like bragging. I didn't want to hear what Pankratov would say about my work and my friendship with Fleury, either.

I liked Fleury, despite Pankratov's railing against him. If Pankratov claimed to see through Fleury and disliked what he saw, I guessed it was only because Fleury could see through him too. The truth was, I admired them both.

About halfway through the day, there was a knock on the door of the atelier. A figure loomed strange and crumble-edged behind the rippled glass. Pankratov launched himself out of his chair and strode across the room. We had all stopped what we were doing. Valya was not there on that day. Instead, Pankratov had built an elaborate still life consisting of the skull of a horse, pottery jugs, old dried-out branches, candlesticks, a bird's nest and a German spiked helmet from the Great War.

Pankratov reached the door, then whirled around and glared at us. 'Did I tell you to stop?'

We went back to work, scribbling or dabbing brushes or mixing paint with dirty palette knives, but as soon as he was at the door and had his back to us, we all stopped working again.

It was a boy at the door, in grey uniform with red piping around the lapels of his jacket and one thin stripe down the side of his trouser leg. He was slightly winded from climbing the stairs, which he appeared to have climbed at the run. He handed Pankratov a yellow envelope and made him sign for it.

Pankratov looked at the envelope, then turned and raised his eyebrows at me.

I felt bad news approaching, like the ground-shake of an avalanche. 'What is it?' I asked.

Pankratov rummaged in the pockets of his baggy corduroys and hauled out a handful of change. Into the boy's hand he dropped a coin, squeezing it as if there were moisture in the metal that had to be pressed out. Then Pankratov walked across to me. 'Telegram,' he said.

The boy stood there a moment longer, peering into the atelier, then jogged away down the stairs, taking them in leaps.

With this news approaching, whatever it was, I suddenly wished I were the boy, and not myself in this paint-smelling room, with this man bearing down on me like a train, his grey hair like chugged-out plumes of steam from an overstoked engine. I wanted to be that boy, with nothing in my life but running and the pleasure and the need of it.

Balard and Marie-Claire had stopped working again. This time Pankratov did not seem to notice.

The sound of me tearing open the envelope was unnaturally loud, all other sounds having vanished. I pulled out the yellow sheet, which was marked with a heavy, blurred stamp showing the time and place of destination. Stuck on the paper were little strips of white ticker tape on which words had been typed:

WAR IMMINENT STOP IMMEDIATE RETURN HOME STOP ARRANGEMENTS TO BE MADE BY THE COMMITTEE STOP LEVASSEUR.

I was no closer to figuring out who the Levasseur people were than I had been when I arrived. Somehow, the fact of their secrecy made me believe for the first time that there might really be a war. I felt a terrible shifting of the air around me, in the entire mottled fabric of the world. There was not supposed to be another war. The last one had been the war to end all wars. I wondered how many people like myself had clung to this idea.

Everyone was looking at me.

'War,' I said.

Nobody spoke.

Three days later, it started.

6

'What do you mean, you're not going?' Pankratov stood in front of me, eyes wide with disbelief.

It had been a month since the outbreak of war.

In the first few days, Paris had been swept up in hysteria. Now, on the surface at least, life seemed to be returning almost to normal. The most noticeable difference on the Rue Descalzi were the black-and-white posters of an *appel immediat*, the calling up of all military reservists. So many had left their civilian jobs that whole sections of France had stopped moving. Trains. Streetcars. Restaurants had to close. Many reservists were released again. The yellow piece of paper on which my telegram arrived had been passed around our little group so many times that it had eventually disintegrated, as if the war itself had disappeared.

Under the surface, however, our lives had become like a fun-house mirror reflection of the way we'd lived before. I realized that I had begun deliberately to ignore certain things that were going on around me: the convoys of military trucks that travelled through the empty streets at night; the stacked rifles and packs of soldiers at the train stations and the soldiers sleeping on the platforms or staring into space, grimly chain-smoking their cigarette rations; the sight of hand-cuffed deserters being dragged through the streets by the white-belted military police. My selective blindness to these things began to disturb me even more than the chaos had earlier.

I lost track of what to call rumours and what to call the truth. I ended up doubting everything I heard. It gave those weeks a dreamlike quality unlike anything I had ever experienced before. Slowly, I grew used to the idea of living in the war. At first I was ashamed of myself. But in time I came to understand that if I didn't adapt, I would go mad in a vortex of anger and sadness and guilt.

In the time it took for the Levasseur people to prepare my travel documents, I decided once and for all that I would stay here as long as I could. I had waited too long to get to Paris. I had visions of myself returning home, only to find that the war had ended by the time I reached New York. I wouldn't have the funds to turn around and go right back to France. I had momentum here. My work was selling. If I gave this up now, I would never forgive myself.

Despite this reasoning of mine, I was bothered by a series of nightmares. They were all about the Maginot Line. I found myself wandering its underground tunnels, trying to wake soldiers who were sleeping in their beds, gunners asleep at their posts, telephone operators heads down and snoring while their switchboard lights flickered with messages.

Pankratov had asked me to stay behind after the day's classes. He held out a bundle of documents – train tickets, boat tickets, a hotel reservation in Cherbourg – his hand shaking almost imperceptibly, as if the papers held an unnatural weight that was too much for him.

That was when I told him I'd be staying. 'I've made up my mind,' I said.

'You're not thinking straight.' He stuffed the papers into the pocket of my coat, then patted the pocket reassuringly and stepped back.

'America isn't in this war. France hasn't been invaded.'

'Not yet, and that isn't going to stop you from getting hurt,' he explained with exaggerated calm. 'The Levasseur Committee doesn't want the responsibility of looking after your safety.'

'Who the hell are they, anyway?' I took the documents from my pocket and tossed them down on to the chair where Valya had been sitting naked only a few minutes before.

'How else do you expect to survive?' he asked.

'I've been selling my work.' I was proud to tell him this. Glad to have the excuse.

Pankratov folded his arms. 'Ah,' he said. 'Fleury.'

'My work is selling,' I told him. 'This is what's supposed to happen.'

Pankratov ignored my words. He took the papers off the chair and waved them in my face. 'The committee is trying to save you!' he shouted. His patience had failed him, as we both knew it would.

'You tell them thank you, but I don't need saving.' My head was filled with brave ideas. I wouldn't leave, I told myself, until the Germans were walking these streets and even then not until they started shooting and even then not until they were actually shooting at me. I could say these things to myself, because I couldn't imagine them happening. I left Pankratov in his atelier and clumped downstairs.

He caught up with me just as I reached the ground floor. He was red-faced from the exertion. 'I have to tell you something,' he said, wheezing faintly through his teeth.

'If it's more of the same,' I told him, 'you can save your breath.'

'No.' He shook his head. 'This you have not heard.' He walked me across the road into the Dimitri, but instead of sitting us down at a table in the main room, he ushered me straight into a windowless chamber at the back, where the waiters hung their street clothes on wooden pegs that lined the walls and changed into their black-and-white outfits. There was a table in the middle of the room. On it was a bottle of wine and a pack of cards dealt out and set down in mid-game. 'Sit,' said Pankratov, and disappeared out of the room.

When he reappeared a moment later, Ivan was with him. Ivan carried a bottle of cognac, a rare commodity these days, and three small Moroccan tea-glasses. He didn't meet my gaze to say hello.

'What's wrong with you two?' I asked.

Without answering, they sat down, one on each side of me. Ivan filled the glasses with cognac.

'What's this all about?' I asked.

'This first,' said Ivan.

We raised the glasses and drank. The alcohol's heat splashed warm and smooth inside me.

Ivan set his fists on the little round table, as if operating the controls to a machine. 'Alexander said this might happen. But I told him you would listen to reason. We were never going to tell you, but now we have to.'

'Tell me what?'

Ivan glanced at Pankratov, indicating that he should be the one.

But Pankratov shrugged and jerked his chin towards me. 'Go on,' he said. 'You do it. Just tell it to him straight.'

Ivan sighed. 'I knew your uncle,' he told me. He was looking at his empty cognac glass. 'Your uncle, Charlie Halifax.'

I remembered the way he had brought up the subject and then dropped it again.

'He and I served in the Foreign Legion together,' Ivan continued. 'Back in the 1920s in Morocco. The circumstances. How we got there.' He steered this imaginary machine, clenching and unclenching his fists. 'None of that matters. We were just two people among thousands who did not want to go home or who had no home to go to when the Great War ended. He was a pilot and I was his mechanic. We both wanted to get out of there and eventually we did. We travelled here to Paris and we bought a plane . . .'

'Tell him the name of the plane,' said Pankratov.

Ivan glanced at me and then away again. 'Levasseur.'

'You!' I shouted. 'You are the Levasseur Committee?'

'We both are.' Ivan jerked his head toward Pankratov. 'He saw an article about you in some magazine . . .'

'Le Dessin,' said Pankratov.

'We got to talking,' continued Ivan, 'and we thought we might do something for you, in memory of your uncle Charlie.'

'Why didn't you tell me?' I asked. 'Why keep it a secret?'

'It was in appreciation of your art,' said Pankratov. 'We saw the pictures. If we'd told you about your uncle, you would have thought it was just about him.'

'I am not so much a connoisseur . . .' Ivan added, 'but I take Pankratov's word for it.'

'Where's my uncle now?' I asked.

'I don't know,' said Ivan, his head tilted to one side, dark eyebrows crooked with concentration. 'In 1926 we flew that plane all the way to America, two years before Lindbergh. We were trying to win the Orteig Prize, which was for the first non-stop flight across the Atlantic. But our plane crashed. We landed in the woods in the state of Maine. The plane was destroyed. The thing was that, by the time we reached America, we had stopped caring about the prize. We no longer wanted the fame it promised us.'

Pankratov slapped his palm against the broad expanse of Ivan's back. 'That's why we understand each other.'

'But what happened to my uncle Charlie? Surely you must know where he went.'

Ivan sat back and sighed, his fists opening up and coming to rest on the lap of his white apron. 'We were together for a while, Charlie and I, but then we parted company. I said goodbye to Charlie at a train station in Boston. He was heading west. I don't think even he knew where he was going. It didn't matter really. I wonder about him sometimes – where he ended up. I think he might have gone and gone until he reached the western sea. He would have done a thing like that. I travelled back to France. I came here, and this is my life now.'

In the back of my mind I had always kept alive the notion that I might see my uncle Charlie again someday. But now I knew I never would, even if he was still alive. I was part of a world he had left long ago and to which he would never return. I looked from Ivan to Pankratov and then back again. 'So,' I said. 'The Levasseur Committee.'

'We want you to go home,' explained Pankratov. 'Now that the war has started.'

'But you are so stubborn!' said Ivan. 'It's like dealing with him!' – he pointed at Pankratov.

'My staying is not your responsibility,' I said. 'And whatever happens, I want to thank you for bringing me here.'

Pankratov made a 'pff' noise. 'You may not thank us later.'

'I owe you a great debt, both of you. I don't know how I'll ever repay it.'

And that was the end of it. They didn't try again to convince me, and I was left with the impression that they had convinced themselves I should stay, after all.

I went out into the main room of the café. I saw Marie-Claire and Balard sitting, half hidden in their world of whispered secrets, most of which were nowhere near as secret as they would have wished. They waved at me and Balard set his heel against an empty chair and shoved it out towards me.

'So you're really not going home?' asked Balard, once I had told them the story.

I shook my head. 'This is where I belong now,' I said.

'What happens if America does go to war and they call you up?' he asked.

'I'll think about that when it happens,' I told him. 'How about you?' I asked. 'Have you been called up?'

Balard began moving his mouth as if there was something stuck between his teeth. 'I'm not fit,' he said.

'What do you mean? You look fit to me.' I was trying to pay him a compliment.

'My heart is weak,' he explained. 'Blood pressure too high.'

'You should tell him the truth,' said Marie-Claire.

'What truth is that?' hissed Balard. His eyes were sharp.

Marie-Claire sat back as if she had been pushed. 'This is your friend. No one else is listening.'

'I said not to tell anyone,' he snapped. *'Anyone!'*

Marie-Claire pressed her hands together. 'I'm sorry, dear.' She looked as if she were about to cry.

Balard raked his fingers through his hair and moaned: 'Ay-yaah.' Then he peered at me with weary eyes. 'You can't tell a soul,' he began. 'I didn't want to do any military service and I knew from a friend how I could avoid it.'

Marie-Claire stopped looking sad. She started to tell Balard's story. 'He ate five tablespoons of salt and ran up and down the stairs in his building until he fainted. Then, when he woke up, he went to his medical exam. He failed it on the spot.'

They reminded me of a couple who had been married a long time and who had stories that they told together, each one with their separate part.

Balard nodded. 'No damned tramping about for me on that damp old Maginot concrete.'

Maginot. There was that word again. It echoed in my head, like a part of some incantation whose meaning had been lost.

Balard and Marie-Claire excused themselves after a short while. They often left early these days. Their stay at the atelier was coming to its end and they felt the sudden acceleration of time.

Five minutes later, just as I was getting ready to leave, Fleury walked in. 'I've been looking for you,' he said. He sat down at the table and shoved aside the empty cups.

'What's up?' I asked.

He brought out another bundle of money, pinned as before with a brass paperclip, and tossed it over to me. 'I sold the rest of the sketches.'

Even with his commission taken out, that meant another month of living in Paris. More if I scrimped. 'You are some kind of genius,' I told him. 'If it weren't for you selling these drawings, I'd be on my way home by now.'

'What do you think about doing some more sketches for me?' he asked. 'Same as the last lot. Similar, at any rate.'

'Shouldn't I be working on the paintings?'

'Those sketches went down very well. Let's stick with them for now. Just do them exactly as you did the last lot. Same materials. Everything.'

'Suits me,' I said. I would rather have been working on the paintings, but it was worth it to me to put things on hold for a while, if it meant staying longer in Paris. 'Why does this collector want my sketches?'

Fleury twisted his hand in the air, to show his slight exasperation. 'Not everyone can afford original works. Those who can't must make do with reproductions. They appreciate work like yours from a purely decorative standpoint. But don't get me wrong; there's nothing wrong with that. Most great artists have learned by copying the work of the masters who went before them. In time, even these copies become valuable. Until then, as long as your work gives people pleasure, you have a resource you'd be foolish not to exploit.'

I nodded.

'When can you have them ready?' asked Fleury.

'I'll get over to the Duarte tomorrow morning. I should have another batch for you in a couple of days.'

'Very good.' He rapped his knuckles on the table. 'I'll be in touch. Back to work.' He gave me a quick smile, got up and walked out.

The next day, Pankratov showed up late to class.

It had never happened before. He was so late that I even went down to the Dimitri and asked if Pankratov had been in yet.

Ivan shook his head.

I stood for a moment in the street. Windows reflected the clouds. There was no sign of him. Just as I reached the fifth floor of the atelier building, I heard a door slam down on the ground level. I listened for the footsteps and knew at once, by the heavy and relentless plod, that it was him.

When Pankratov reached the classroom, he found us sitting at our places. He was pale and hadn't shaved. The stubble made his face look as if it had gone mouldy in the night. 'I'm embarrassed to ask this of you,' he said, 'but has anybody seen Valya?'

We looked around at each other. None of us had seen Valya

in several days. We had assumed it was because Pankratov wanted us doing other assignments and that Valya wasn't needed.

'She left to see a friend. She was due back.' said Pankratov.

'Which friend?' I asked, thinking of that man I'd seen her with at the Polidor.

'She doesn't talk to me about her friends.' Pankratov went over to his sacred chair. He turned it to face the wall and then sat down. He didn't give us any work to do. The only thing on the stage was Valya's chair.

We began, one after the other, to draw the empty chair.

Ten minutes later the door boomed shut downstairs, echoing through the building. The footsteps of more than one person climbed up and up.

I waited for them to stop on one of the other floors, but they kept coming. I listened for voices, to pick up some laughter that would take away the menace that was coming with this quake of boots on each worn stair.

There was no knock. The door swung open and three policemen walked into the room. Their black uniforms each had a row of large silver buttons down the front. It was raining outside and they were wearing short dark capes made of waterproofed canvas, on which the rain still rested in beads. They had flat-topped caps with short, stiff brims. Their boots came up to their knees, criss-crossed with long leather laces. Their faces carried the expressions of men who had come to do an unpleasant job, the same look I once saw on a man who came to shoot a sick horse that belonged to our next-door neighbours.

The man who stood in front produced a piece of paper from his pocket. It was neatly folded. He shook it open. 'Artemis Balard,' he said.

We all turned to look at Balard.

The policeman only had to follow our stares to know he had come to the right place.

Balard had a pencil clamped between his teeth. It looked as if someone had pulled the plug on his heart and his blood had drained out through his shoes. He pulled the pencil slowly from his mouth. 'What do you want with me?' he asked.

'One week ago,' said the officer, holding the paper in front of him at such a distance that it was clear he needed glasses, 'you were notified to report to the barracks of the ninth arrondissement. You are to come with us now.'

The man out in front made some comment to the others, who stepped past him and walked over to Balard.

Balard stood up from his stool. 'I am exempt!' he said indignantly. 'My heart is weak.'

'Your heart is not so weak,' said one of the men.

'What is that supposed to mean?' asked Balard.

The two policemen took him by each arm. It is a strange moment when one man takes hold of another in this way. Only two things can happen. The man who's being grabbed can either fight back with all the explosive energy he possesses, and fight crazily, even knowing he will lose. Or he can submit. He can make noise and protest and pretend to struggle, but in his mind the decison has already been made to give in. And so it was with Balard. He made a fuss and swore at them horribly, which I suspected he would regret within a few minutes. He turned from one officer to the other, giving them equal doses of his rage. At last, before they hauled him out of the door, he turned to look at me. 'Why did you tell them?' he asked me, his voice gone high and wild.

'I didn't,' I told him. 'I swear.'

'I'm coming back for you!' he screamed.

The police dragged him out. When they had gone, the only sign they'd been in the room was the raindrops that had run down off their capes and sunk into the roughed-up wooden floor.

The police were having words with Balard as they carried him downstairs.

Don't talk back, I thought, as if to telegraph the words to him.

But Balard didn't know any better and he did talk back and they threw him down a flight of stairs to shut him up.

Pankratov left his chair and went over to Marie-Claire. He stood awkwardly in front of her, hands knotted behind his back, bending down slightly to look into her eyes. 'Are you all right?' he asked quietly.

Marie-Claire looked up at him and smiled weakly. 'Yes,' she said. 'I will be perfectly all right.' Her face seemed unnaturally peaceful. She glanced across at me. 'He didn't mean it, you know. What he said. He knows you didn't do him any harm.'

I knew he had meant every word of it.

Balard did not return the next day. Or the next or the next. By the fourth day, we knew he wasn't coming back.

Pankratov and I fussed over Marie-Claire, who never once lost her composure. We figured her heart must be broken, but she was refusing to admit it. We admired how bravely she took it.

When Fleury found out about Valya's disappearance, he went into a funk that lasted for days. On our way home from the Dimitri, where we often met these days, he would ask me again and again to describe that time I had seen Valya at the Polidor.

'Face it,' I said, finally. 'You're not likely to see her again. You never even mentioned to her how you felt. She has no idea you're fond of her.'

'I didn't say anything to her, because I had no idea she was Pankratov's daughter instead of his mistress! And it's not just being fond. It's more than that. I just never had the opportunity to tell her.'

'You could have made the opportunity,' I told him.

'You're no help,' he muttered.

'You ought to get over her,' I said. 'For your own sake.'

We walked through the entrance of our apartment building and stepped into the elevator cage. The humming clank of the machine surrounded us as we rode upwards, stopping at the third floor, where Fleury had his apartment. He stepped into the hallway and shut the elevator door. He looked at me through the black iron grille. 'I know you think it's insane that I should fall for a woman like that,' he said, 'but I did fall for her, and I'm always going to wonder if she might have fallen for me.'

I wondered if Fleury ever would tell Valya how he felt. I doubted it. It seemed to me he had grown comfortable with the idea that they would never be together. Perhaps he had become fixated on her for precisely that reason. He wanted her to be close by but still unreachable. Fleury preferred to live in some ecstasy of languishing. It was the languishing he loved. The pleasure of possibility.

He didn't mention her again for a long time.

It was the last day of our classes with Pankratov.

Marie-Claire left quickly, saying she was no good at farewells and that she had to pack her bags for the trip home. She shook our hands and kissed each of us on the cheek. She wrapped her arms around Pankratov's back and groaned sadly. Then she hurried away down the stairs.

'Poor woman,' said Pankratov, after Marie-Claire had gone. It was his first acknowledgement that he had known how they felt about each other. He turned to me, as an idea popped like a soap bubble in his head. 'We should see if we can find Balard. Maybe he's still in Paris. Maybe he failed the medical exam.'

'He's in perfect health,' I said, 'except for all that pencil lead he eats.' Considering that I was the one Balard blamed for his arrest, I was in no mood to track him down and have him go crazy on me again. 'Besides, if he could have come back, why didn't he?'

'That's what I'm asking.' Pankratov had adopted his usual stance, head tilted back slightly, hands in the pockets of his tattered canvas coat, weight balanced on his heels. 'You don't have to do this for Balard. Do it for Marie-Claire.'

'Why don't you go?'

'Because I would lose my temper dealing with bureaucrats.' Pankratov blinked at me, knowing he was right.

'All right,' I sighed. 'But you go tell her.'

Pankratov thumped downstairs after Marie-Claire, catching up with her on the street. At first, she told him that there was no need to go to any trouble. Then she said she might be better off not knowing. But Pankratov was insistent. He wanted to do her this favour. Finally, reluctantly, she agreed to meet us at the Dimitri later that afternoon, in case I managed to turn up some information.

I went to the barracks of the ninth arrondissement. It was a grey stone building with large windows and wide stone stairs that led up to the main door. There was a plaque on the side of the building that explained how the soldiers of the regiment of the ninth arrondissement had marched out of Paris with Napoleon at their head to take part in the battle against Russia in 1812. It was busy with men reporting for military service. Most of them arrived alone, already feeling awkward in their civilian clothes, perhaps remembering old soldier days, the heaviness of army boots and guts clenched tight behind a military belt. Men who had arrived with families climbed grimly away from wives with hands pressed to their mouths and crying children waving chubby arms.

Inside were the sounds of shouting and doors slamming and showers hissing and laughter and the smell of cigarettes and soap and that particular oily reek of military clothing. Men stepped past in scruffy uniforms with wide brown leather belts and boots that creaked with newness.

I went up to the registration desk.

'Name?' asked the clerk, without looking up. He was dressed in a khaki uniform with the sleeves of his shirt rolled up. His cap was tucked under the epaulette of his left shoulder.

'I am here for . . .' I began.

'Name?' he said again in an irritated monotone.

'David Halifax,' I said, to humour him.

He wrote down the names, misspelling Halifax. 'Papers.' The man held out his hand.

'I have no papers.' I gave him a tolerant smile.

Now he looked up. 'What?'

I thought about giving up. I'd tell the man I was sorry for bothering him and leave and report back to Pankratov that I'd had no luck. But I knew the way he'd look at me then. I knew what he would think. So now I found myself doing this not for Balard or even for Marie-Claire, but for Pankratov. There was only one thing to do if I was to get the information I needed from this soldier, and that was to pretend that I had more right to be there than he did. 'I am looking for Artemis Balard,' I told him.

He glared at me for a moment.

In ten seconds, I thought to myself, I will either have been thrown out into the street or I will have what I want. 'Look him up,' I commanded.

'Why? On what authority?'

'Has he signed in or do I have to track him down?' I asked mysteriously.

The soldier behind the desk stared at me. He was sizing me up, waiting for me to flinch.

It was at this moment that I had the inspired idea of taking out a small notebook I carried with me for sketching and drawing from its spine a tiny pencil. I licked the tip and stepped forward. 'What is *your* name?' I tilted my head back, eyebrows raised.

It worked. The soldier hesitated, assuming perhaps that I was a plain-clothes policeman or something even worse. Who else would dare to talk to him that way?

He turned in his swivelling chair and hauled a heavy book down from the shelf. The book was about eight inches thick and ragged at the corners. He heaved it open and it fell with a thump on his blotter. He flipped through some pages and ran his finger down a column. 'Balard. Artemis,' he said. Then he spun the book around and showed me the place.

Balard's scrawled signature was next to his name, as well as the date of his arrival, the same day the police had hauled him off.

'Where is he now?' I asked.

'I couldn't tell you. Once they leave here, it's out of my hands.'

'That's all I need to know.' I put away my notebook.

'At your service,' he said, with the voice of a conspirator.

I arrived back at the Café Dimitri to meet Marie-Claire.

She was sitting at our usual table, along with Pankratov and a distinguished-looking man I'd never seen before.

Pankratov look uncomfortable. As soon as he saw me, he stood sharply, sending his chair skidding back across the floor. 'Well,' he said, his voice almost falsetto with relief. 'Here he is!'

The stranger rose to his feet. He was tall and thin, with a gentle, honest face.

'This is Maxim de Boinville,' said Marie-Claire. 'My husband.' She looked at me with a rigid smile on her face.

'Oh, hello!' I said, and shook his hand wildly.

We all sat down at the table.

I said nothing about my search for Balard.

'Maxim has come to take me home,' explained Marie-Claire. 'We live in Normandy, you know.'

I thought of that day on my way back from Clignancourt, when I'd sat in the streetcar and the warm summer breezes had blown in through the open window. All the way from Normandy.

'Marie-Claire is very grateful for your friendship,' said Maxim de Boinville. He looked around, taking in the strange reek of the Macedonian tobacco favoured by the old legionnaires who haunted this place, and the coffee and mint tea. His gaze darted out into the busy street. It was all too much for him, just as it had been for me when I arrived. I knew he couldn't wait to be on the next train out of Paris as it chugged away across the fields towards the place where he could breathe the scent of apple trees and ocean-salty air.

'We have a train to catch,' said Marie-Claire.

'I am so proud of her,' said Maxim. 'The works of art that she has made.'

Marie-Claire smiled at her husband. Then she looked at me. 'Did you find who you were looking for?' she asked.

I shook my head.

'Ah,' she said quietly, and glanced down at the table.

Pankratov pretended to be busy, using his fingernail to pick at something that was stuck to the table top.

We exchanged addresses and promised to write and said it would not be long before we all met up again. Then we hailed them a cab and they headed for the train station.

Pankratov and I stood side by side.

I felt the space between us. 'Balard signed in at the barracks on the same day the police took him away,' I told him. 'That's all I could find out.'

Pankratov stared straight ahead. 'Did you ever wonder how they found him?'

'I don't know.' I shrugged. 'I guess they tracked him down.'

'I know how,' said Pankratov.

I turned to him. 'You do?' I asked.

Pankratov nodded down the road to the place where the car had disappeared. 'She turned him in.'

'No,' I shook my head. 'That's not possible.'

'She told me herself,' insisted Pankratov. 'Right before her husband arrived. She came right out and told me.'

'Why did she do it?' I asked.

'She didn't tell me but I know anyway. This way, they never have to fall out of love,' said Pankratov. 'Now it will always be the war that drove them apart. I suppose you could think of it as merciful, if you thought about it long enough.'

I recalled the strange calm on Marie-Claire's face when Balard had been dragged away, calling out obscenities through his charcoal-blackened teeth. She had known all along, despite any promises made in their long waking dream, that it could not last. But Balard had not known. She had found it necessary to show him. Now Balard would learn things the hard way.

I said goodbye to Pankratov.

He treated me with a distant formality, as if he had already said all the goodbyes he was ever going to say in his life. It was almost as if he no longer recognized me and my face had become part of the past, fragmented by time.

I was quietly miserable about leaving the atelier. In my time there, I'd persuaded myself that I knew Pankratov. Now I realized that I didn't and would never have the chance to know him better. 'I'll come spy on you at the Dimitri,' I said, trying to sound cheerful.

'I'll be waiting,' he replied. 'Same as always.'

7

I returned to my work. I was glad to be free of those long hours at the atelier, but I missed our old group and the Egyptian-mummy dryness of Pankratov's humour.

I completed another set of sketches, charcoal studies of several works by Gauguin, and handed them over to Fleury.

He had them all sold within a week.

I felt more fortunate than ever to be working with him.

We were friends now. I was comfortable around him and did not measure my words before I spoke, the way I used to do in his company.

Having put aside my worries about paying the rent, at least for now, I grew more confident about my chances of remaining in Paris without some imaginary boundary between staying and leaving. The more time I spent here, the less I thought of my old home and my mother and my brother. When we met up again, we would pick up where we left off, as we always did. But for now, the vast silences that stretched between us were proof to me of the different worlds we had come to inhabit.

Aside from Fleury, I hadn't made many friends in Paris. I missed the company of women. In the past, I had thought no good would come from beginning a relationship when I would have to break it off and disappear as soon as the Levasseur grant ran out. I didn't want to get involved simply for the feeling of being involved. When I first arrived, I had promised myself no entanglements that would take me away from my work. Keeping that promise had proved hard enough even without the distractions of a romance. I hoped all that might change from now on.

I'd been figuring this out one Saturday afternoon, when

Fleury and I had gone to see a movie at the Cinéma Coloniale on the Boulevard du Montparnasse. It had been a matinée show, and afterwards we were dazed to find ourselves back in the daylight. It had been stuffy in the theatre and I said I wanted to get some air. We walked down the Avenue de L'Observatoire to a fountain that lay in a shaded area of the Luxembourg, just in from the café called La Chaise Bleue on the Rue de Vaugirard. The stone of the fountain was damp and peppered with algae, and the statues that spat water from their mouths looked bleary-eyed and ancient, as if they too had just found their way back into the light from centuries spent underground. With each gust of wind, leaves blew down from the trees in flickering browns and reds and ambers. They settled on the surface of the fountain, skimming around like little boats in the breeze until they became water-logged and rested flattened on the surface of the water like confetti left over from a wedding.

We sat down on a bench to have a smoke. Fleury liked English tobacco, which he bought from a tobacconist in the foyer of the Hôtel Continental on the Rue de Rivoli. He smoked a brand called Craven A, which came in flat, red tins with a black cat on the front. I had brought a few packs of Chesterfields with me from the States but I didn't often smoke and the tobacco went stale before I finished it. So now I was trying the French stuff, Caporals, which took some getting used to.

I opened my mouth to ask Fleury what he had thought about the movie, but never had the chance to speak, because a voice called to us from behind.

We both turned and looked past the dappled bark of the trees.

A man stood behind some tall black railings that separated the street from the park. He was waving to us. He was tall and wore a big hat.

It seemed to me I had seen him someplace before but I couldn't recall where and his face was in the shadows.

'Monsieur Fleury!' the man called down. 'I have been meaning to speak with you.'

'Yes,' said Fleury, his voice strained. 'Call me tomorrow.'

The man laughed. 'No. I mean now. I will only be a minute.' He was already on his way.

Fleury smiled and waved and then slumped back on the bench. The smile had been sliced off his face.

'Who is it?' I asked.

Fleury cleared his throat. 'Lebel. A collector. You met him once. At that opening I took you to.'

I had some vague memory of his grizzled grey hair, sweat coming through his starched shirt and being told that he owned a cabaret. 'Why don't you want to see him?' I asked.

It was too late for Fleury to reply, because Lebel had already arrived. He had a dog on a braided leather leash, which was wrapped around his hand like knuckle straps on a boxer. The dog was a tough-looking little schnauzer with bushy eyebrows and grey fur.

Lebel and Fleury shook hands.

'This is David Halifax,' said Fleury, rising to his feet.

'Excellent,' said Lebel and stared right through me, just as he'd done the time before. He let the leash fall to the ground. The dog sniffed at my shoes with busy jerking motions of his nose.

Lebel turned back to Fleury. 'It's working out so well!' he said. 'You remind me that there is still quality work to be found. Work by the great masters that hasn't yet been gobbled up by museums or millionaires. It is out there!' – he waved his hand expansively over the pond. 'Monsieur Fleury, you have given me hope. I see in you a partner of many years.'

'Yes, well,' said Fleury, hands in pockets, looking down at his shoes. 'I'm glad it's all working out.'

I wasn't paying much attention. I stayed sitting on the bench. I bent down and scratched the dog's ears. The leash trailed behind him. The leather braid reminded me of the pattern on the back of a copperhead rattlesnake.

'Those Gauguin sketches. Such a trove,' said Lebel, wrapping his lips around the word.

For a moment, I couldn't believe what I was hearing. Looking up, I saw a sudden greyness in Fleury's cheeks as the blood left his face. Then I knew that I hadn't misunderstood. Fleury had been selling my sketches as originals. I felt suddenly nauseous.

Lebel grasped Fleury's hand and shook it violently. 'Thank you,' he exhaled. Then he turned to his dog and snapped, 'Bertillon!'

The dog gave my feet one last sniff and scuttled off, the leash slithering behind.

I didn't wait for Lebel to meet my eyes in some blind gesture of farewell. I was staring at the ground.

Fleury sat down beside me. 'That's what I love about Lebel,' he said. His voice was falsely jovial. 'When he is happy, he just can't stand the thought of keeping it to himself.'

I watched Lebel disappear across the park, his footsteps crossed by the wandering paths of others. His shape blurred among the rippling shadows of the fountain and the trees, like a cat-lick figure in the background of an Impressionist painting.

'You son of a bitch,' I said very softly. 'You lied to me.'

It was quiet for a long time.

Fleury sighed. 'Yes, I did,' he admitted.

At that moment, I was too stunned to feel anger. Instead, I sensed a rushing static all around me, sealing me off, so that Fleury's voice reached me as if down a long cardboard tube.

Fleury had his hands in front of him now, as if weighing in his palms the air that came out of his lungs. The cigarette was wedged between the first two fingers of his right hand, smouldering patiently. 'The moment I saw those sketches,' he said, 'I knew I could pass them off as originals to someone who wasn't an expert. Lebel was the first person I thought of. He lives on our street, you know. That's how I met him. Lebel may know how to run that cabaret of his, but he's not the art expert he believes himself to be. The more I praise his intelligence, the less intelligent he becomes. I knew he would buy them. At a glance, and even at a second or third glance, it would be assumed that the sketches were original Gauguins. The paper was old, and you were probably using old pencils, too, and your sketches were very good. Very fluid.' He was touching his lips with the tips of his fingers as he spoke, as if trying to stop the words from coming out.

'Where did you tell him they came from?' I asked.

He sipped at the smoke from his cigarette and stared straight ahead. 'I made up a story about how the sketches came out of the private collection of a family friend who had passed away and that the other family members were letting me buy the work rather than putting it out on the open market themselves.'

'And everything you told me about them being sold as decorative pieces . . .' As the numbness of shock wore off, anger was taking its place.

'You should take it as a compliment.' Fleury tried to find his way around the lie. 'I knew you'd never agree to it.'

'You're damned right I wouldn't,' I snapped. I was suddenly conscious of his physical frailty, in a way I never had been before. Rage glanced off my bones in coppery sparks.

'Look,' he said. 'I know I had no right . . .'

'You had no damned right at all!' I shouted. 'Do you have any idea what you've done?'

Fleury got up slowly and walked over to the edge of the water. He stood for a moment, hunched over like a man grown suddenly old. 'Do you *want* to stay in Paris?' he asked. He spoke so quietly that it was as if he were talking to his own reflection in the water.

'Of course I do,' I said.

Fleury straightened up. He spun on his heel and walked back to me. His face had lost its greyness. 'Then you ought to *thank* me!' he said. 'I did you a favour. You said yourself that if I hadn't sold those sketches, you'd be on the boat home by now. And if I'd sold them for what they're really worth, I could have bought you a week or two. A month at the most. But I knew I could get more for them, so I did. And that's the only reason you're here now.'

I stared at him in disbelief. 'But what about the risk you took with my career?'

He slapped his hand against his chest, bouncing his palm off the thick, rough tweed. 'Mine, too! I took the risk just the same as you did.'

'Yes, but you knew you were taking it! My part of that risk wasn't yours to take and you can't deny that!'

'What would you have done if I'd told you the truth?' he asked. 'Would you have let me sell those sketches as original Gauguins?'

'Of course not!'

Fleury paced in front of me, stirring the gravel with his shoes, yellow dust coating the toe-caps. 'Exactly. You're too high and mighty. You have no idea how things work. What to do when an opportunity comes along. How to balance it against the risks. And you can't just *not* take risks. I know what you want more than anything else in the world. I know, because I want the same thing. To be here. To be making a go of it and doing well for yourself. And did you honestly think you could get what you wanted without paying some kind of price?'

I didn't answer. I stood and walked past Fleury, heading for the street.

Fleury stopped pacing. His anger seemed to leave him. His hands found their way into his pockets. 'What are you going to do?' he asked.

I walked right by him and still gave no reply.

He made no move to stop me. 'You have what you want,' he said. 'Don't forget that.'

I shuffled through the fallen leaves, my mouth and eyes dried out, noticing nothing around me.

The next morning, I woke as usual to the sound of the men lining up outside the Postillon warehouse. They were mostly older men now, the younger ones having been called up for military service.

For the rest of that week, I worked on my paintings. All my confidence had gone now. I worked only out of a grim stubbornness to get the job done.

Fleury kept his distance, which took some doing, considering we both lived in the same building. I tried not to think about what had happened, but of course this didn't work. If the word got out that Fleury was selling forgeries, and that I was the one who had made them, we would both be finished in Paris. And wherever the story spread – New York, London, Rome – we'd be finished there, too. I realized that even if we seemed to have got away with it, I couldn't forgive Fleury for taking the risk.

When I thought about it that way, it all seemed clear. I would have nothing to do with Fleury from now on. If I happened to run into him, which seemed inevitable if we were both to work in Paris, I would fend him off with a deep-freeze of politeness.

Other times, it didn't seem clear at all. The other half of my brain was telling me to shut up and face the fact that the only reason I was still here was that Fleury had sold those sketches. He had been right when he said I wanted to stay here more than anything else in the world. I asked myself what I'd have done if Fleury had come to me first and asked me what I wanted him to do. Would I really have told him not to sell the sketches, and then just packed up and left Paris? I would have run out of money by now if it hadn't been for the sketches. I could only have taken on a job illegally, since I had no papers, but any job like that would have paid me so little and worked me so long that I would never have got any more painting done. I honestly didn't know what I would have said to Fleury. I didn't have the right to dismiss so easily the wrong that he had done.

These separate voices clashed so furiously inside me, warring back and forth across the tundra of my brain, that it seemed to me my sanity was fracturing in hairline cracks across my skull. I couldn't sleep, hearing the volcanic rumble of the city. The wind blew in off the rooftops, carrying the smell of baking bread and the distant clank of trains. I wondered how many others out there were like me, among the hundred thousand sleepers, hounded through their dreams by such confusions.

Late Friday evening I finished the last of the paintings.

All Saturday I sat with the canvases set up around me, trying to decide what to do.

Before it had all happened, I'd never have thought I could stay friends with someone who pulled a stunt like this. Now it didn't seem so black and white. You start out with some image of how things will need to be, clear-cut and defined, and it all seems reasonable to you at the time. But when the image gets dented and scarred, as it always does, you remember the promises you made yourself about what you would do and what you wouldn't. Maybe you never do find out what is in another person's heart, or in your own. It boils down to whether you can live with the uncertainty, and in some ways even want it, even as you fear it – just as you want and fear the few things that are certain in life.

By the end of the day, I had made up my mind.

That evening, I wrapped up each of the paintings in brown paper and string and brought them downstairs to Fleury's apartment. I had to make several trips in the elevator, and found myself hoping he didn't hear the racket I was making in his hallway.

He answered the door wearing a smoking jacket made of lurid red and black velvet. 'Ah,' he said, tilting back his head the way he always did.

I waited for him to say something else, but that was all he said. Just 'Ah'. A breeze blew in the window of his apartment and past him and into my face. I smelled soap and aftershave.

I looked into his apartment and saw how small and clean it was. I had stopped by a few times to pick him up before we headed out to the Polidor, but mostly he liked to meet in the hallway downstairs. I thought he might be a little ashamed of his place, since he liked to give the impression of living more grandly than he did. The window sills were busy with flowers in tiny white pots with designs painted on them in orange and blue. An empty red glass bowl stood on the kitchen table. His polished shoes were lined up just inside the door – one pair of black and one pair of brown – and he wore a pair of fancy slippers on his feet.

'You've brought your paintings with you,' he said.

'That's right,' I said.

His eyebrows bobbed. 'I thought you'd had enough of me.'

'I kind of thought that, too,' I said.

'I wondered if perhaps you were coming down to rough me up a bit. For my crimes and misdemeanours.'

'I didn't come here to rough you up. Look,' I told him, 'if you still want to work together, there'll be no more going behind my back.'

'Yes,' he said. 'Of course.' He scratched at the back of his neck. 'I'm sorry. I made a mistake.'

I helped him carry the paintings into his apartment. We opened them up and I told him what they were about.

'Do you think you can sell them?' I asked.

He breathed in sharply. 'I'll do my best,' he said.

I was very tired now. As I said goodbye to him, he insisted we shake hands.

I walked down the corridor and pressed the elevator button. When I turned to look back, he was still standing in the hallway. 'Where the hell did you get that jacket?' I asked.

He looked down at his chest, then back up at me. 'This is my armour,' he said.

'Armour?'

'Oh, yes,' he replied. 'It's a different kind of armour. But it is armour, all the same. And it never fails me.'

My paintings were shown at Fleury's gallery the following month. I sold eight of them during the time they hung in the show and all but one sold soon after that. They didn't go for a great deal of money and it made me realize that even if I was successful, survival in this place would not come easily.

I had, by now, taken over the rent payments on my apartment. Madame LaRoche seemed impressed. 'You've given up painting?' she asked me. 'You have taken up employment?'

'Painting is my employment,' I replied.

She blinked in slow astonishment, unable or unwilling to make the connection.

In the weeks that followed, she treated me with grudging respect, even introducing me to one of her landlady friends as 'a painter of things'. This other woman, Madame Côty, was a near-duplicate of Madame LaRoche, in her flower-patterned housecoat and thick, fleshy stockings. The two of them used to sit outside the front door in the sun, perched on rickety chairs, smoking their pipes. Their expressions reminded me of two old jack-o'-lanterns that had been left out on a doorstep after Hallowe'en. Their once-savage faces had sagged like the slowly rotting pumpkins. Now they just looked paunched and ornery, with only rudeness to chase demons and children away.

It was only after months of living here that I had begun to find myself on friendly terms with the people who lived on my floor. I rarely saw them. We seemed to live in completely different schedules, like employees of some non-stop factory, all working different shifts. On those rare moments when we did pass in the cramped hall, or rode the elevator down to the street, our greetings were so filled with awkward flinching that it seemed easier, even more humane, to pretend the other person wasn't there at all. I hated the silence in the black cage of that elevator as it seemed to close in around me like some complicated torture device, while the other person seemed to be expanding until there was no place for me to look. Eventually I took it upon myself to start conversations. To my surprise, it worked. An old man with watery eyes introduced himself as Laurent Finel. He had been invalided out of a job in a coal mine ten years earlier and had come to live in Paris with his sister. The sister had died and Finel continued to live in the apartment. He was one of the men who stood outside the Postillon warehouse every morning, more I think because he wanted something to do than because he needed the money, as he had a disability pension. From then on, I recognized him when I looked out of the window at the line each morning, the stoop of his back and the type of floppy cap he wore.

There was a young family, the Charbonniers, who had a six-month-old son named Hubert. At first, when I knew there was a baby on the floor, I had worried that the child would keep me up at night with his crying. But the little boy was so quiet that I started hoping he *would* make some noise, because I had begun to worry that there might be something wrong with him. It turned out that there wasn't. He was just fat and cheerful and quiet.

And there was a woman who worked as a dance instructor. She was originally from Norway, a little place called Krossbu, that I never could find on the map. She had flaming red hair, lots of it, and huge bright eyes that made her look, depending on whether her eyebrows were raised or lowered, as if she were in a state either of realizing something very important or of having just forgotten what it was. Her name was Madame Lindgren. She never did let me know her first name, which I took to be a signal that she didn't want to get involved. One day, in the elevator, she showed me a couple of dance steps. 'It's jazz,' she said, pronouncing it as 'tchazz'.

'Not when I'm doing it,' I told her.

From then on, whenever we bumped into each other, she would teach me new steps and I would mangle them and we would laugh about it.

With each of these people, I developed a small but consistent list of topics, which would last us the forty-five seconds it took to travel up or down in the elevator. Even if that didn't amount to much, at least I didn't find myself listening at the door to see if the hall was empty before venturing out.

All through the winter of 1939–40, I made more paintings and Fleury was able to sell them. There was a moment when Fleury joked with me about making a new series of sketches and selling them as old originals. I pretended he was joking. He got the message, and we left it at that. Sometimes I worried that the sketches would be exposed as forgeries, but as time went by, thc chance of that seemed less and less likely. After a while, I stopped worrying about it altogether. Instead, like everyone else, I worried about the war.

By the beginning of October, the Polish army had been defeated. The Germans were torpedoing ships all over the Atlantic, but lost their big battleship, the *Graf Spee*, in December. In that same month, the Russians invaded Finland. The Germans didn't attack the Maginot Line. After a while it became possible to think that they might not.

In Paris, the war still seemed a long way off, but its presence could be felt in higher prices for things like bread, bacon, butter, sugar, milk. Some foods, like baguettes, could be sold only on certain days, while croissants, for reasons I never understood, could be bought any time. Cafés could serve alcohol only three days a week. Tobacco prices went up sharply and coffee became almost extinct. Instead, the cafés began serving something called Café National, which was made of roasted acorns and chick peas. The only way it could be drunk at all was if you didn't try to pretend it was coffee. There was very little gasoline and because of this fewer cars in the street. Officially, the government was rationing all these things, but in the beginning you could still buy what you wanted. This was lucky for me since, although I was granted a ration card, mine took longer to process because I was a foreign national. I received two eggs a week, about three ounces of cooking oil and two ounces of margarine. The only food that could be found in any quantity was turnip. I boiled it, mashed it up like baby food and forced it down without thinking.

It was a very cold winter. Madame LaRoche turned down the heat so that the radiators were barely warm to the touch. She only turned them up for one hour a day, right before dawn, when the building would fill with grumbles and hisses and clanking, as if some midget were crawling through the heating pipes with tiny hobnailed boots. Some landlords turned off the heat altogether.

The snow that fell was thick and wet. It froze against the manes of horses pulling carts along the Quai d'Orsay. I saw people being towed around on skis behind cars whose tyres were wrapped with chains. The river froze on either side of the Îsle Notre Dame and bargemen hit the ice with huge hollow steel balls attached to the ends of bamboo poles. The sound they made was like the ringing of a cracked bell, echoing past the ice-bearded window sills and shop signs. Paris bums, the *clochards*, froze to death beside the Pont d'Austerlitz and the Pont de Tolbiac, where they had set up huts made from cobblestones and canvas sheeting stolen from barges moored on the banks of the Seine.

One day I noticed that Madame LaRoche's heavy, wooden family crest was missing from its perch in the front hallway. When I asked her if it had been stolen, she flapped her hand at me and frowned. 'I burned it,' she said. 'There was three days' worth of fuel in that old thing.' She tottered off towards the elevator on her stiffened legs. 'It wasn't my family crest, anyway,' she called back without turning around.

'Whose was it?' I asked. I was thinking maybe an uncle or something.

She climbed into the black cage and closed the door. 'I don't know,' she said. 'I bought it for ten francs at Clignancourt.' She laughed as the elevator rumbled her up out of sight.

There were times that winter when I wished I'd had my own fake family crest to burn. I got used to sleeping in my overcoat and with a wool blanket under the bottom sheet as well as on top of me. I wore my woolly socks until they fell apart and then I learned to darn and repair them myself.

Military uniforms were everywhere, along with rumours of soldiers abandoning their posts, less out of fear than from the crazed boredom that the French called *le cafard*. The French army took these incidents very seriously, remembering the mass desertions that had taken place in the last war. There was also widespread drunkenness among the soldiers. Each French *poilu* was issued with two litres of strong wine per day. They called it *pinard*, and would riot if the wine did not arrive. The train stations had special rooms set aside for soldiers to sleep off their hangovers before heading back to the front, where nothing seemed to be happening, except for the occasional firing of heavy guns for the benefit of visiting officials.

I made no plans to leave the city and remained optimistic about my luck. I had a stubborn faith it would not fail me.

In those harsh months, I came no closer to expanding my circle of friends. I was so close to being broke most of the time that I didn't get out to the places where I might have met people. Slowly, I grew used to the idea. I didn't get too worried about the fact that I didn't have a girlfriend, or that I wasn't invited out to parties, the way I might have been in normal times. The war had set everything off balance. There was no such thing as normal any more.

8

'Mr Halifax!'

I had just walked into my building when a voice called to me from the street.

'Mr Halifax,' said the voice again.

I turned to see a man with short-cut hair and a tweed sports jacket with a white polo-neck sweater underneath. He had the dented nose and shallow eyes of a boxer. It was a face built for taking punishment. The daylight blinked as he stepped inside the foyer.

'What can I do for you?' I asked cautiously.

'My name is Tombeau. I'm with the French police. I was wondering if I could have a word with you.'

'Go ahead,' I said, sudden worry hollowing me out inside. 'What's it about?' But I knew what it was about.

His face showed no expression. His hands stayed by his sides. 'I need you to come with me.'

'Now?' My throat had dried out so quickly that I could barely talk.

'Now,' he said. 'We're pressed for time.' He turned and looked out to the street.

I followed his gaze to a car that was waiting at the kerb, its engine still running.

For a moment, I felt panic scattering inside me, like small birds startled from their grassy hiding place. Then I felt myself giving up. I had nowhere to run. Part of me even felt a little relieved that it was over now.

Tombeau seemed to know what was going on inside my head, as if my thoughts had passed like shadows across the angles of my face. 'Come along,' he said softly. 'It won't take long.'

We climbed into the back and the car pulled out into the stream of traffic. I could smell the driver's cologne and the leather of the seats. Nobody spoke on the short ride. We pulled up outside an alleyway, at the end of which was a large green wooden gate and above it a sign which read: *Préfecture de Police. Commissariat du Quartier des Halles.* Above the sign was a French flag, hanging limply in the damp cold air. The alley was dirty and the walls that bordered it were unpainted and slapped with the tatters of old theatre bills.

Tombeau got out of the car. Then he looked in after me. 'Let's go,' he said.

As I walked up the heavy cobblestoned alley, I had a sudden urge to run. I didn't know where to. Just to bolt like a frightened animal.

Tombeau opened the gate, which led into a courtyard. The courtyard was much cleaner than the alley. It was lined with windows and doors, each of which had numbers done in blue and white enamel above the doorway. He seemed to relax as soon as we got inside the building. He walked me down three flights of stairs to a corridor with many doors. The further down we went, the more helpless I felt. Electric bulbs with green-topped glass shades lined the centre of the corridor with a harsh glare. People bustled in and out of rooms. It all looked very busy.

Tombeau showed me into a waiting room, which had a table and a bench and a standing coat rack with brass hooks in the corner. There was a door, which was closed, at the end of the room. 'Sit down,' said Tombeau. He opened the far door and ducked into another room and was talking to someone as he closed the door behind him.

In the few seconds that I spent alone in that room, my lips became chapped and even the skin on my knuckles seemed to have dried out. I wondered whether there was any chance this might not be about the sketches Fleury had sold. I wondered if there might be any point in trying to deny it. I knew that was an idea I should have fixed in my head long ago if I had any hope of it working. I had left it too late for that now. The only thing I could do was to hold on to some kind of dignity.

When Tombeau returned, he had taken off his sports jacket. The white polo-neck glowed like marble in the light of the bulb. He had with him a large cardboard folder. He sat down at the other side of the table. The toes of his shoes brushed against mine and I tucked my legs under my chair. He set the folder down and pressed his hands together, laying them flat on top of the folder. 'Well,' he said. 'Mr Halifax.'

I nodded.

He opened up the file. And there were my sketches, just as I had feared. He took one out. 'Is this yours?' he asked.

My guts twisted. I took the sketch from him and looked at it for a couple of seconds. It was a study of a fox's head which I had made of a Gauguin called *Young Girl and Fox*, which was itself a study for a painting he did called *La Perte du Pucelage*. I had done the sketch on yellow paper in charcoal and white chalk, just like the original. The fox was lying on top of the woman's naked chest the way a cat might sleep on its owner. I felt the paper soaking up sweat from my fingertips. 'I drew it,' I said, and handed back the sketch.

Then he went through a small stack of sketches. I noticed that Gauguin's signature had been added to some of the pieces, and that there were small signet-ring-sized stamps on the back, the kind that some collectors have for marking ownership.

'I didn't sign anybody's name to them and I don't know where these stamps came from, either.' I sighed. 'But I suppose I could guess.'

He grinned. 'If you guessed Fleury, you'd be right.'

I sighed and licked my dried-out lips.

When we had been through all the sketches, Tombeau closed the file. He took a packet of Caporal cigarettes from his pocket, tapped one out of the pack and lit it. Then he inhaled deeply and set it down carefully on the edge of the table, the smoke rising cobra-like towards the green-shaded light. 'You have to understand,' he said, 'that you are guilty of forgery. They're getting ready to throw you in jail. I'm here to try and prevent that.'

'I'm not a criminal.' I croaked out the words. I had no spit left to talk.

'You're a forger,' he told me, raising his voice. 'You pollute the market place and galleries and museums with everything you do. You fill minds with doubt when there should be no doubt. We happen to need you at the moment, so you have become a necessary evil. But if you don't do exactly what you're told to do in the next couple of hours, I can guarantee that you'll be put away in a French prison for three to five years. Now, whether you think you deserve that doesn't make any difference to me. You owe the people of France a debt for not locking you up. Monsieur Fleury was very understanding about this fact when we explained it to him.'

'Where is Fleury?' I asked.

'We already let him go home. You could be home soon, yourself, if you're helpful.' Tombeau got up and walked over to me, resting his hand on my shoulder. 'I want you to talk to someone,' he said. The door opened again. I heard Tombeau say, 'Three minutes! That's all. Or we do this a different way.'

The door closed and I sensed that I was no longer alone. My head stayed down. I looked at the grain of the wood and the sweat stains on the table's old polish.

'Hello, David,' said a voice. It was Pankratov.

I looked up. 'What the hell are you doing here?'

He lowered himself into the other chair. 'If you had listened to me about Fleury, you wouldn't be in this mess now.'

I just stared at him. I felt like telling Pankratov that if it wasn't for him, I wouldn't even be in Paris.

'Well, I guess it's too late for that now,' said Pankatov. 'What I don't understand is why Fleury even bothered. He sells a lot of paintings. Some major works have passed through his hands since he first opened his gallery. He didn't make a fortune off your sketches. He didn't need the money. I don't understand why he did it.'

'Because he could,' I said. 'He did it because he could.'

Pankratov shook his head and sighed, as if to show that he would never understand what went on inside the mind of Guillaume Fleury. He gestured at the door behind me. 'The people in that next room are waiting to find out whether you will agree to help. It's all or nothing, you see. If you don't co-operate, none of this is going to work and you'll both end up in prison.'

I smoothed my thumb across my lips, back and forth, feeling more helpless with every new thing Pankratov said. 'What co-operation?'

'They have asked me to explain it to you,' said Pankratov. 'They need your help.'

'Who?' I squinted at him. 'Help with what?'

Over the next few minutes, Pankratov told me that a group had been formed to deal with the safe-keeping of works of art in the event of Germany invading France. The Germans were planning to establish an 'art capital' of Europe in the Austrian city of Linz. Plans for a museum there had already been approved by Hitler. The Germans were going to remove as many works of art as they wanted from the countries they invaded and then sell off or destroy the rest. Pankratov told me they had a long list of Impressionist, Expressionist, Cubist, Futurist and Dadaist art that they considered 'degenerate'. He said arrangements had already been made by French authorities to hide as much of the art as they could within France, or to get it out of the country. 'But we won't be able to hide all of it,' explained Pankratov.

'You're talking as if the Germans are already here,' I said.

'It would be foolish for the French people not to take precautions. Don't you agree?'

'How should I know?' I rocked back on two chair legs, not wanting to listen. 'I'm an American.'

'It seems' – Pankratov drilled his pinky into his ear – 'that the American embassy has been very co-operative allowing for you to volunteer for temporary French citizenship.'

'Volunteer?'

He nodded, looking away. 'A request I suggest you follow.'

The door flew open again and Tombeau filled up the doorway. 'Get on with it, Pankratov!' he yelled. He banged two heavy fingers against his wristwatch. 'We have no time!'

'I was just finishing up,' said Pankratov, without turning to face the man.

The door banged shut.

'Why is he in such a hurry?' I asked.

'Never mind that now,' said Pankratov. 'David, they want you to make forgeries. They came to me and asked if I thought you had the skill and I told them you did. And you do, even if you don't yet believe it yourself.'

'But if the Germans are putting together one vast European art museum, they're going to rip out half the paintings in this country! You can't fake all of those and expect to get away with it.'

'We're not trying to. It's more complicated than that. Everything will be explained very soon.'

At that moment, I was positive I would be absolutely no use to them, despite what Pankratov was saying. 'What makes you think I could do it?'

'With training . . .' he began.

'And who's going to train me?' I demanded.

'I will.'

I clicked my tongue with irritation. 'Why don't you just do it all yourself, then?'

'It's one thing to know the techniques. It's another to be able to use them the way you can. You have skills I don't possess. But I have knowledge that can make those skills stronger.'

'I stayed here in order to do my own work!' I leaned across the table towards his wide and complicated face, the grey hair swept back in crooked threads. 'Not someone else's.'

'I know what's going through your head,' said Pankratov. 'You're caught up in thinking about your own career, making a living, all the little details that leave you too exhausted at the end of every day to see beyond your own small concerns.'

'They don't seem small to me!'

'I know. But they will, one day. The work that lies ahead of you now is more important than your own career, more important than any one artist's career. You might not understand this now, but in time it will become clear,' he said. 'Some people wait their whole lives for a chance like this to come along.'

'What do you mean?'

'The chance to do something at which you are a natural,' said Pankratov.

'What did they threaten you with to get you to come in here?'

'Nothing,' he said. 'They explained it to me and I volunteered.'

'And you're asking me to volunteer as well? Why the hell should I? Just because you tell me to?'

'I know you don't want to do this. We're all doing things we don't want to do, but you'll feel a lot worse about it if the Germans wipe out entire generations of art.'

'But what's the point in doing that?' I asked, frustration boiling over. 'Why is an invading army going to put so much effort into destroying the artwork of another country. They might steal it – that I can understand – I'm sure France plundered Germany in the past. But what would be the point in destroying it? Blow up the Maginot Line instead. Blow up the tanks and the guns. But paintings? That makes no sense to me.'

'They'll do it,' he said, 'whether it makes sense to you or not.'

I felt powerless to argue. If Pankratov believed it, he who seemed to care nothing about the order of the world outside the bone box of his skull, then maybe it was true.

He sat back in his chair and rubbed his eyes, as if he had not slept in a long time. 'You once said you owed me a great debt for bringing you to Paris. You said you didn't know how you'd ever repay me. Well, now you can. And you'll be doing a lot more than that. You'll see why it's so important that we work together on this.'

There was a long silence. I did owe him a debt, it was true. But it was what he said about us working together that started rattling around in my head. This would be my only chance to know him as an equal. If I didn't take this offer, I would spend the rest of my life in search of his grudging admiration. No act of logic could shake it from my skull. It wasn't something he had done to me. I had done this to myself.

I wondered if, somewhere out on the frozen tundra, he had left behind his own unwilling master.

'You're not exactly giving me a choice, are you?' I asked.

'Not exactly,' he replied.

'Then I might as well volunteer.'

Before I left, Tombeau walked me from the room and down the corridor. 'They're letting you go now because the Russian persuaded them that you wouldn't cross us. Personally, I have my doubts. If you let us down, it's going to be my job to come and get you. And when I find you, I'm going to blow your damned head off.' Tombeau smiled again, to show how insincere his smiling had been all along. 'And then I'm coming for the Russian, because I'll be holding him responsible. Until the day I say you're free, I'll be watching you. You can count on that.' He gave me one last slap on the back and walked away down the corridor, ducking the green-shaded lights.

Pankratov and I reached the street and began to walk.

I started talking immediately. 'Even if I have agreed to do the work, you know damned well I'm not skilled enough to make copies and for the fakes to go unnoticed.'

'It is precisely that kind of thinking that makes the art of forgery possible,' said Pankratov. 'We are not talking about creating a masterpiece. We are talking about creating the illusion of a masterpiece. In our work, the painting or the drawing itself is only a part of the puzzle. You are right that someone can't just pick up a paintbrush and start churning out Caravaggios. The great forgers, the proof of whose greatness is the fact that we'll never know their names, study the materials that go into the work of art and, after that, methods of ageing. I am not saying you are a forger now. But those sketches of yours are proof that you have the makings of a forger.'

I had no way of disagreeing with him.

'You won't be making direct copies,' continued Pankratov. 'That's too risky. You'll do work in the style of certain artists. Previously unknown paintings and drawings are always turning up out of private collections, or they could be works that were wrongly attributed.'

'What good will that do, anyway? How will it save the originals?'

'They'll be looking for people like Titian, Botticelli, Vermeer. They're not going to set fire to every Degas, Manet, or Van Gogh they get their hands on. Those paintings will be used for trade.'

'And we'll be giving them fakes?' I asked.

'For originals. Exactly.'

I found myself dodging cracks on the sidewalk, which I often did when I was preoccupied. 'And you think this is going to work?'

'With enough of a head start, and enough skill, yes.'

'What was the rush back there?' I asked.

'If the Germans come in,' he said, 'they'll take over the police and security services before they do anything else. Some people will get dragged off to prison camps and others will be promoted because they'll agree to collaborate with the Germans.'

That was the first time I heard the word 'collaborate'.

'That man back there,' continued Pankratov. 'Tombeau. He wanted to make sure you were brought in as part of a regular arrest. He wanted people to see that. But what happened once you got inside that room was something he didn't want anyone else to see. He doesn't know who to trust. That's why he wanted you out of there so fast.'

'But why pick me? There must be a hundred other people in Paris who could do a better job.'

'There are other people, most with criminal records. But the Germans know their names. They won't be able to make a move without the Germans knowing. They needed someone without a record. That's why they picked you.'

'And what about Fleury?'

'They picked Fleury precisely because he *is* known. He's suspected of being unscrupulous. They need someone like him because when he starts showing up with paintings that the Germans don't know about, they'll need to believe the work was stolen out of some private collection. If Fleury's the man doing the selling, they'll have no trouble believing it.'

'Who's Tombeau working for?' I asked.

'I expect you'll meet them very soon.'

'Are we the only ones?'

'No. I don't know how many others there are. We've been split up into cell groups. That way if the Germans get one group, they can't get to the others.'

'How are the Germans going to know the locations of all these paintings, anyway?'

'They sent in people as art students, all through the 1930s. They called themselves the East European Commission. They catalogued paintings in galleries. When the war started, these students all disappeared. We'll see them again, I expect, but next time they'll be wearing army uniforms. Valya fell in love with one of them. I think she left when he did. I believe she's been working for them.' He shook his head to show his helplessness.

I began to see a little more clearly why he had set aside his stubbornness.

We walked all the way to the Café Dimitri and sat down together at a table. We drank his drink, coffee with steamed milk on the side, and we each ate a medjool date to sweeten the coffee's harshness. It was real coffee, too, for a change, and the last Ivan would serve for several years to come.

My earlier cynicism was starting to fade away. We would be equals now, Pankratov and I. We would do the work, not for the reasons they gave us, not because of intimidation, but for reasons they might never understand. I thought about what Pankratov had said earlier – how sometimes you have to wait a lifetime before a chance like this comes along.

Pankratov sat back in his chair. 'Do you trust Fleury?' he asked. 'I mean, trust him completely?'

It would have been complicated for me to explain that I didn't, not completely, but that he was still my friend. Pankratov didn't force me to say it. He understood my answer by the silence.

'He could get us killed,' said Pankratov.

'We could get him killed, too,' I replied, 'if we don't get it right.'

'Yes,' admitted Pankratov. 'That much is true.'

I realized it had not occurred to me to question whether or not I could trust Pankratov. I knew instinctively that I could. It was the same qualities that made him difficult to be around as also earned my confidence in him. Pankratov could not be intimidated by the threat of physical pain. One glance at him, and anyone could tell. He could not be beaten into submission by the threat of having his possessions confiscated. He owned nothing that anyone else was likely to value. Pankratov could not be bribed with money or tokens of social acceptance. He didn't care enough about himself to be tempted. This was why I trusted Pankratov. It was why I pitied him, too.

When I returned to the apartment, Fleury was waiting outside my door. His face was pale.

We went inside and I filled two coffee cups with wine. We sat down at my kitchen table.

'Well,' he said. 'What did you tell them?'

I sipped at the wine. 'I agreed to do the work.'

Fleury's shoulders slumped with relief. 'Thank God,' he said. 'They said they'd throw us both in prison if you refused.' He set the mug against his teeth and drank. His Adam's apple bobbed twice as the wine went down his throat. 'I felt sure you'd tell them all to go to hell.'

'It was Pankratov who convinced me,' I said.

'As long as *somebody* did.' Fleury finished the wine and helped himself to some more. Then he brought out his red Craven A tin and lit one. Those were not Craven A he was smoking any more. He bought whatever he could get, and just kept using that red tin. 'I can't say I'm looking forward to working for this thug of a man Tombeau, but I'd rather do that than end up in a French prison. Strange how your life can be moving along in one direction, and you even start to take that direction for granted, and you give yourself all these little matters to worry about and then something comes along and changes everything. And it can happen.' He clapped his hands together. The ash from the cigarette floated on to the table top, like the downy feathers of a bird. 'It can happen like that.'

I walked over to my bed and lay down, hearing the old springs squawk under my weight. I rested the heels of my shoes on the bed rail and tucked my hands behind my head. The bed was right beneath the window sill, and I saw the silhouettes of pigeons on the roof of the Postillon warehouse. I was thinking that, all my life, I had been fighting against a current. Like water. Water deep under the ground that I struggled through even though I couldn't see it. I couldn't beat it and I *knew* I couldn't beat it, but I didn't know what else to do except keep struggling against it. Today was the first time that I felt as if I'd quit struggling.

Fleury pinched the burning end off his cigarette and then put the stub in his pocket. He was saving his tobacco, these days. 'Do you think we can do what they want us to do?'

'Do I think you can sell paintings to the Germans? Yes. Do I think Pankratov knows enough to teach me? If he says so, yes. But do I think I can learn it? Do I think I have enough talent to begin with?' I shook my head, feeling the pillow rustle. 'I seriously doubt that.'

'If Pankratov says you can do it,' Fleury told me, 'then you can.'

For the first time, I allowed myself to consider the possibility that Pankratov's faith in me might not have been misplaced, after all. I closed my eyes and felt the current pulling me, smooth and gently, down fast-running rivers, out towards the rolling of the jade-green sea. I did not fight it. I would not fight it again.

9

'I'm going to tell you everything I know,' said Pankratov.

We were back in the atelier. The stools were piled into a corner. The stage looked huge and empty without Valya scowling down from it.

Pankratov had set up a painting. It was very old, without a frame, the paint spider-webbed with tiny cracks. The subject was an old man with a froth of grey beard, looking up from writing in a thick book. A quill was in his right hand. His clothes were velvety red like the curtains in my apartment and a wide-brimmed red hat hung on the wall in the right-hand corner of the picture. The man looked good-natured and intelligent, but a little sad, as if growing old had caught him by surprise.

'As much as we can,' he explained, 'we'll be using old materials. For paintings, the canvas is the most important thing. It's the first place they'll look. The best kind is linen. It's easiest to work with when it comes to ageing a piece. Some canvases are made from cotton or hemp, but they aren't as good.' He picked the painting from the easel and flipped it around so that we were looking at the back. It was peppered with grey blotches. 'Canvas can be spoiled by moisture, especially at the back, where it hasn't been treated.' He scraped his fingernail across it, popping the fine threads, which sent tiny puffs of white dust into the air. 'This kind of damage devalues the work, but it also serves as proof that the materials are old. When a dealer handles a painting, he looks at the way the paint has aged. The cracking, fading, darkening. He looks at the frame. All this before he has even studied the quality of the work itself. He has a checklist in his head. It's our job to make sure he can go down that checklist without getting suspicious.'

I sat down dejectedly on the stage. It seemed too much to learn.

'Don't worry,' he said. 'That's why I'm here.' From his satchel, he pulled one of my sketches that Fleury had sold. He must have got it from Tombeau. 'And this,' he said, 'is why I need you.'

There was a noise on the stairs. Both of us tensed. We turned towards the rippled-glass pane in the door to the atelier. Seconds went by. We didn't move. There was no more sound.

Slowly, Pankratov put my sketch back in his satchel. He walked towards the door, trying not to creak the floorboards. He opened it, and peered out on to the landing. When he saw there was no danger, he turned and walked back inside.

The next day I found a note in Pankratov's handwriting at the foot of the stairs. It said: WAIT FOR ME HERE.

'What's this about?' I asked him when he showed up, the leathery smokiness of just-drunk Café National on his breath.

We climbed up four flights of stairs and then he put his arm in front of me to stop me going any further. He walked up two of the twelve steps of the fifth flight and then stopped. 'When you get here,' he said, 'I want you to count the steps. When you reach the third step, don't tread on it.'

'Why not?' I asked.

Pankratov placed his foot on the step and pressed down gently. The step collapsed, the ends folding up around his calves. 'It'll snap your leg,' he said. Pankratov had broken the board and repaired it so that the break didn't show. 'After yesterday,' he said. 'That noise on the stairs.'

'Yes,' I agreed.

'Are you afraid?' he asked.

'I guess,' I said. 'Are you?'

'It used to be the damned communists who were after me. This time it will be the damned fascists.'

We went into the studio and locked the door behind us.

'What happened when the communists came for you?' I asked. 'All I know is what Valya told me.'

Pankratov didn't answer. He busied himself with hanging up his coat.

'You said you'd tell me everything you knew.'

He paused. 'I suppose I did.' He went across to his sacred chair and sat down. His hands closed around the armrests. 'The locals had told us they were coming. There were no telephones, but news passes from village to village almost as quickly. We were just there to guard that outpost, but guard it against what I never understood. The population were mostly Laplanders, about five hundred of them. They followed the reindeer and were gone half of the year. They never gave us any trouble. When the Lapps were gone, the population of the town dropped to fewer than fifty.

'There were only two of us. I was a lieutenant because I had done one year of university. The other man was a sergeant named Rokossovsky. We had been sent to a village called Alakiemi, to act as military representatives for that region. We took over one of the little shops on the main street, which was only a hundred yards long and made of dirt. This became our headquarters. We also lived there, Rokossovsky and I. We grew our own potatoes. We had a cow and some sheep. Even before the Revolution, our wages stopped coming in, so we had to fend for ourselves. We knew there had been a revolution. We just weren't sure who had won. We heard so many different stories in the beginning that after a while we stopped believing any of them. After a while, my uniform became so ragged that I had to throw it away. After that, the only thing to show I was a soldier of the Tsar's army was this belt' – he tapped his finger against the plate of brass with its double-headed eagle – 'and that was only for holding my trousers up. After two years, Rokossovsky got married to a woman from the village. Her name was Ainu. She was half Lapp – what she called Sami – and half Finnish. She wasn't very healthy. She'd had some disease in her lungs when she was little and she wasn't suited to the migratory life of the people in the village. Her family were glad that she could stay behind. After Rokossovsky got married, he set himself up as a blacksmith, which had been his trade before he joined the army. A while later, they had a daughter. That was Valya.'

'What did you do?' I asked, seeing that Pankratov had wandered away so far into his head that soon words would fail him.

Pankratov shrugged. 'I moved across the road. Had a one-room place. Not so bad. Made my own furniture out of spruce.'

'What did you do for a job?'

'I painted,' said Pankratov. 'I painted the inside of the Alakiemi church. Top to bottom. Saints and angels and God knows what else. People came from all over to look at it. That was where I learned to paint, you know. That church was my first big project. When I finished that, I painted a mural on the wall of the headquarters. I did paintings for people in the town. I sent off for materials. Each time I sent off for things, it took two seasons to arrive. Two seasons. You couldn't even measure it in months. I used to make my own paints and my own canvases, too. I couldn't just sit around waiting. The winters. Jesus, the winters,' he said. Then he stopped talking.

'The communists,' I reminded him.

He breathed in suddenly, as if his heart had stopped and restarted. 'We knew about a week in advance that they were coming. We knew there was only one way they would approach us. They would circle around the town and strike at us from the back, across a frozen lake. It was the only way that made sense. The only direction in which they wouldn't risk an ambush. It was the middle of January when they came, the darkest and the coldest part of winter.

'It was a company of horsemen. They had a platoon of infantry as escort but the footsoldiers had been left behind about three towns back. Half the men had frostbite. They had been told there were fifty of us holding out in Alakiemi. But as they got closer, they found it was only the two of us, and that we weren't holding out. The authorities had just forgotten about us. By the time they remembered, we had become the enemy.'

'When they came for you,' I said, reminding him gently.

'They rode across the lake. Just as we thought. Some were carrying torches and the rest were waving sabres above their heads. All shouting at the tops of their lungs. This was their big moment, after all. Six weeks out of Leningrad and all for this. All for just two of us and a woman and a little girl, but they were still going to put on a show. Coming across the frozen ground, they looked like meteors bouncing along on the ice.

'What they didn't know, and what the locals didn't tell them, was that we'd had enough time to dig a trench out of the ice in the middle of the lake. We let it freeze over again, but not enough to hold any weight. The horses ran across the ice until they reached the trench and then they all fell into the water. The horses coming behind had no chance to stop. Some reared up and fell and crushed their riders. Other riders skidded on their backs, on their bellies, howling as they slid into the water in their heavy greatcoats, weighed down with swords and rifles and bandoliers of ammunition. They went under as well. Seventeen men and horses went into the lake. The torches went out one after the other. The horses and the men were screaming. The sound of those horses was the worst thing I had ever heard. I could see the heads of the horses in the water as they tried to stay afloat. In ten minutes, it had gone back to being one of those dead still winter nights when everything is frozen so solid that there is nothing for the wind to move when it comes except little whirlwinds of snow across the ice.

'Rokossovsky and I ran out on to the ice. We ran towards the place where we had dug the trench. Even at that distance, I could smell the sweat of the horses. And I could smell *makhorka* tobacco, the rough kind that Russian soldiers smoke.

The stench of it gets in your clothes and your hair and your skin, no matter how often you wash. It tattoos itself into your lungs. It was hanging in the air. Rokossovsky and I breathed it in.

'We went back to the shore and waited until morning before going out on to the lake again. We found the men frozen completely solid, some of them on their hands and knees, as if they were waiting to give some child a piggy-back ride. Even those few men who were able to climb back on to the solid ice froze to death in their waterlogged clothes before they reached the edge of the lake. And out in the middle, where the trench had been, we looked down and saw men and horses staring up at us. They hadn't sunk to the bottom. They had got stuck between the layers of broken ice and were trapped there like specimens between two microscope slides. Some of them had their mouths open as if they were trying to talk to us. That's why I don't sit facing the window. The way this old glass twists the light reminds me of looking down into the ice.' He ran his fingers through his hair.

'We knew that it would take the infantry several days before they found out what had happened and several more days before they got to Alakiemi, if they made the trip at all. At first, Rokossovsky and I decided we would have to go. But then he backed out. He believed it was only a matter of time before the Reds caught up with us, so he and his wife made up their minds not to run. Ainu was too ill to survive a future of always moving on. I still decided to leave. On the night before I was due to depart, I brought most of my home-made furniture out into the street and gave it away. Rokossovsky and his wife came to me with Valya. They asked me to take her. They knew what would be left of this place by the time the Reds were through with it, and what their own chances were. Even though Rokossovsky and Ainu were prepared to take those chances, they wanted to make sure their daughter stayed safe. I offered to take her away and bring her back in a couple of months, if I could. But Rokossovsky shook his head and said that our old way of life was over now, and that I should just take her and start again somewhere. Ainu agreed. What could I say? What kind of person would I have been if I'd refused? I brought her with me. Valya was almost two years old then. I packed up a few things of my own. I had a horse for me and Valya and another to carry my belongings. I even took my paints. And the chair of course. It comes apart. You can roll it up in a bundle.'

'The paints I understand,' I said. 'But why the chair? And why do you still wear that old belt?'

Pankratov shrugged, as if he wasn't sure. 'We all need things to remind us of who we were. Besides, so many of my memories were wound around it and around that chair, like invisible vines. Each night, when I was on the run and heading out through Finland into Sweden, I would set up my tent in the forest or out on the tundra. Then I would build a fire and I would assemble the chair and Valya and I would just sit there, she on my lap and bundled in my coat, looking out into the dark. I had no books. It was too cold to paint.

I imagined him sitting by the fire, his arms around the sleeping girl, the vastness of the night sky fanning out above him. I pictured him staring up at it, breath frozen white on his eyebrows, like some Norse god carved from of the ice of his kingdom. 'I reached Paris almost two years later,' said Pankratov. 'I started painting again.'

'I don't understand why Valya . . .'

'Why she is so bitter,' he finished my sentence. 'It's one thing to know where you come from, and to know that you were cast adrift, the way I was. But to know that your own father handed you to his friend, rather than stay with you, no matter what the risk. Well, she thinks she was abandoned.'

'But it saved her life.'

'It doesn't make any difference,' he said.

'Then she should be angry with her father, not with you.'

'It makes no difference,' Pankratov said again. He brought out a box of cigarettes and a yellow box of matches. He broke one in half, put one piece in his mouth and offered me the other.

We sat in silence, the smoke from our cigarettes curling without a shudder towards the dusty rafters.

In the weeks that followed, Pankratov put me on a schedule that obliterated my already meagre social life and had me studying with him every waking hour. But he had no complaints from me. Not under these circumstances. As the days went by, I began to refine my skills. I grew more hopeful and more confident, but never far from my thoughts was the frustration that my own work had been put on hold indefinitely.

Pankratov's teaching methods were erratic, but his lessons broke down into three basic categories. First, we studied the work of a particular artist. In the beginning, we focused entirely on the work of Lucas Cranach the Elder. This was no random choice. He had been selected by Tombeau's superiors, whom we still had not met, as an artist whose work would be in demand once the Germans arrived. The next category was study of materials – everything from brushes, to paint, to wood panels and canvas. Finally, Pankratov instructed me in the art of ageing the work.

We dodged from topic to topic according to whichever one obsessed him at the time. He was particularly manic about the mixing of paints. He showed me how to measure out the powder on a small ceramic dish. He did this with a spoon that was made of horn. The scoop was wide and shallow and the horn was almost transparent, run through with smoky veins of black and brown. It was the same kind of spoon I had seen used for eating caviar.

I loved to watch him mixing paints. I loved his precision and the way the dull brightness of the powder turned glossy when he turned it into an emulsion, as if it gave out its own light.

He liked to quiz me about what pigments had been invented when.

'Ultramarine! First used in what century?'

'Twelfth century.' I focused on the work bench behind him,

where the brilliant red, blue and white powders and copper pans and spirit lamps were laid out from the lesson.

'Wrong. Thirteenth century. Prussian blue.'

'Eighteenth century.'

'Right! Would you see Prussian blue in a painting by Goya?'

'You could.'

'Right again. Good. Cobalt blue.'

'1802.' I knew that because I had made a rhyme of it. 'Cobalt blue in 1802.'

'Titanium white.'

'1830.'

'Wrong!' he clapped his hands. '1930! Do you realize what will happen if you put titanium white in a painting by Delacroix?' When he spoke this way, he would never say 'a forgery of' or 'a painting in the style of'. He would say 'a painting by', as if somewhere in his warlocks' book of recipes was hidden the secret by which we would become the artists of our imitation. We summoned their flaked bones back into flesh and marrow and teeth and hair and eyes, then stepped into the framework of these men and wore their spirits like cloaks of hardened blood.

'All right,' he said. 'Start again. Cadmium yellow.'

'1850.'

'1851. Close enough.'

There were times when we both became so exhausted that we would sleep for an hour or two on the floor of the atelier, our coats bundled under our heads as pillows, the quiet of the room broken only by the rattle of window panes, loose in their lead frames in the glass mosaic of the great window. It was always night by the time I reached home again. Sometimes I had such skull-cracking headaches from paint fumes that it felt as if smooth river stones had lodged themselves beneath the skin of my neck.

Fleury, meanwhile, had thrown himself into his work. Now that things were out in the open, he made no attempt to keep secret from us the fact that he had been selling forgeries for years. Sometimes it seemed to me that the gods had played some kind of trick on him, to make his brilliance a crime.

The hours I spent with Pankratov were so consuming that I had no sense of what was going on beyond the walls of the atelier. On those few nights when Pankratov grew so tired that even he thought he wasn't making any sense, he might let me go a few hours early. Then I'd go and find Fleury and the two of us would head over to the Polidor. The menu was skimpy these days, and the prices much higher than before, but it was still the Polidor. Fleury became my only contact with the world outside. He told me about Finland's surrender to Russia in the second week of March, and the battles for Norway in April.

We swapped stories of this strange new life. I would find myself both disgusted and amused by the depth of Fleury's schemes for dealing with the Germans if they ever arrived, while Pankratov's recipes for paint paraded in front of my eyes like mathematical equations come to life. The war was a loud but distant prospect. It still seemed possible, even likely, that the Germans would never attack France, and that all this work would be for nothing.

By the end of March 1940, Madame LaRoche had turned the roof of her building into a garden, where she grew tomatoes, carrots, beans and cabbages. She also kept rabbits in a large chicken-wire cage. The rabbits were always escaping. We'd find them hopping around the hallway, or riding the elevator up and down. Fleury liked it when they came to visit. He left his door open and baited them in with scraps of turnip. The rabbits hopped around Fleury's apartment, while he sat in his armchair reading art history books. Every evening, Madame LaRoche would round up the bunnies. They were very tame. She scooted them down the corridor with a broom, then carried them by the scruffs of their necks back to the roof.

I was still broke half the time. That much stayed the same. I had not painted anything of my own since the arrest, so no money was coming in from that. I relied instead on rations and a small weekly stipend grudgingly paid to me by Tombeau.

One day, along with the stipend, Tombeau dropped off my new French passport. It was the same size as my American one, but red instead of blue and had *République Française* in gold-leaf writing on the front. The picture from my old passport had been removed and placed in the new one, along with several travel stamps, one from London, another from Irun on the Spanish border.

I showed it to Fleury, who flipped through the pages, noticing the stamps.

'Looks like you've been doing some travelling,' he remarked.

'I wonder if I enjoyed myself.' I tried to make a joke of it, but couldn't hide a feeling of emptiness that spread inside me when I saw my picture in that unfamiliar little book.

Pankratov came to my door at five in the morning. It was 9 May.

I stood there in my flannel nightshirt, sleep like cobwebs in each wrinkle of my brain.

He strode into the room. 'The Germans are advancing through Belgium. They're going through the Ardennes forest. Bypassing the Maginot! That whole ridiculous parade of guns and tunnels will be completely useless.'

'I thought the Maginot Line went up into Belgium,' I said.

'They hadn't finished it. They didn't want to offend the Belgians.'

'The French army,' I told him. 'They'll drive the Germans back.'

Pankratov ordered me to get dressed.

My heart was clattering behind my ribs as I pulled on my clothes and then sat down on the bed to lace up my boots. My breathing came shallow and fast. It was the same feeling I used to get when I was going out on to the football field to play a team I knew was going to beat us. I just wanted it to get started. When things were in motion, I had no sense of fear. Only before and afterwards.

We both went down to get Fleury and I stood in Fleury's apartment while Pankratov gave him the news.

Fleury stood in his lurid red smoking jacket, which apparently doubled as a dressing gown. He didn't have his glasses on, and his bright-blue eyes looked small and useless. 'The French army will stop them,' he said, confidently. 'And there's still the British Expeditionary Force. They're in Belgium.'

'The French and British armies,' said Pankratov, 'are falling back towards the sea.'

'I don't believe you,' said Fleury. He turned to me. 'You mustn't believe what he's saying.'

But I did believe it. If the Maginot Line had not stopped the Germans, nothing would. I had held on to the flimsy faith that the Maginot would simply prevent them from starting. I imagined that people all over France, all over the world, were encased in that same numbed helplessness that I felt at this moment. We had believed it wouldn't happpen. Now we would stand by in our helplessness while it did.

I had no real image of the Germans as an enemy. They had remained a vague menace. But slowly they were taking shape, a rolling thunder in the dense pine forests of the Ardennes. A human flood. Unstoppable. 'What are we going to do?' I asked Pankratov.

'I need your help,' he said. 'We are going to move some paintings to a safe place.'

'All right,' I said. 'When?'

'Now. Immediately.' Pankratov glared at Fleury. 'You, too. If you have some food, bring it along.'

Fleury shuffled off to get dressed, then laid out some food on the kitchen table – bread and apricot jam and some apples and chocolate and some *cervelas* sausage and a bottle of wine. We stuffed as much as we could into an old canvas satchel. I slung it over my shoulder, feeling the wine bottle dig into my hip.

A little white Citröen van stood parked outside the building. On its side was the logo of a bakery: GALLIMARD ET FILS. BOULANGER. PROVISANT DE PÂTISSERIES DE MAISON.

'Where'd you get that?' I asked.

Pankratov didn't answer. 'Just get in,' he said.

It was cramped with the three of us in the van. There were old chocolate-bar wrappers balled up on the dashboard. The seats were torn and shined with use, the grain of the leather worn off. The floor showed the marks of someone with large feet who had rested his heels on the same spot many times.

Pankratov crashed the gears, jolting us forward. Then he crashed them again, swearing in Russian. He clung to the steering wheel as if it were a snake with its tail in its mouth, which would slither away out of the window if he didn't keep his grip.

'Would you like me to drive?' I asked.

'Of course not!' he snapped. 'Don't be ridiculous. Stop asking questions!'

Fleury glanced at me and rolled his eyes.

Five blocks later, Pankratov had chewed up the gears a few more times. The grating, zipping sound of crunched metal made us all wince. Pankratov swore in several languages within the same sentence. Eventually, he pulled over, got out of the van and walked around to the other side. As he did this, he pounded his fist on the hood, as if it was all the van's fault. When he reached the passenger side, he hauled open the door. 'God damn all machines!' he shouted.

I drove us the rest of the way. The light was greyish-purple, the way it is before dawn on a cloudy day.

Pankratov gave me directions to the Jeu de Paumes museum. It was a long, rectangular building made of pale khaki stone. It stood at the far north-east corner of the Tuileries gardens, right where the Rue de Rivoli intersects with the Place de la Concorde. It had been built by Napoleon as some kind of indoor tennis court and had then been converted into an art museum. The front had two large letter Ns engraved on it. It was an ugly building, compared to the grandness of the Place de la Concorde and the tall houses along the Rue de Rivoli.

We joined a line of other trucks in the Place de la Concorde, at the base of a short flight of stone stairs. All the trucks were of all different types. Some were mail vans. Others were delivery trucks, with company names painted ornately on their sides. They kept their engines running. I saw a wisp of tobacco smoke seeping from the cracked-open window of the truck in front. A hand held out a cigarette, flicked ash from its tip, then retreated from the cold air.

The main doors of the Jeu de Paumes were wide open. Through a screen of trees that grew between the road and the museum I could see a table set up on the gravel outside. On the table was a storm lantern. A man with round glasses sat at the table, encased in the light of the lantern, alternately writing and then handing out sheets of paper to the drivers of the trucks, who jogged back down the steps to their vehicles. Others were carrying paintings wrapped in white sheets and stacking them in the trucks. A few men in civilian clothes stood guard at the top of the steps, shotguns slung over their shoulders. They wore heavy sweaters and the cuffs of their trousers were rolled up around their boots.

The only noise I could hear was the puttering of engines and wind shuffling through the trees of the Tuileries gardens.

One after another, the trucks were loaded up. They gunned their engines and left in different directions.

'Where are they going?' I asked Pankratov, forgetting not to ask questions.

'No idea.' He was hunched down in his seat, arms folded across his chest.

'Well, where are *we* going?' asked Fleury. 'Do you know that, at least?'

'You'll know soon enough,' he said. 'There's the signal. Drive up. Come on. Drive up.'

I pulled the truck up to the base of the stairs, riding on to the kerb, directed by hand signals from one of the shotgun men, who showed me his palms when it was time to stop.

Pankratov jumped out. Fleury and I followed.

We went up the steps to the table, footsteps crunching on the yellowy gravel. There were two men ahead of us.

In the foyer of the Jeu de Paumes I saw men and women removing paintings from frames and stacking the empty frames to one side. They sized sheets against the paintings and tied them up with balls of string. The white balls unravelled across the floor. They worked quickly, without talking. The sheets were then marked with numbers in black laundry pen. The paintings were carried past us and down the steps to our van.

The man at the table glanced up at us when it came to our turn. On his desk was a list of names of paintings and next to each name was a code number, the same numbers that were being written on the sheets. In another column was a letter. The paintings that had been sent down to our truck were all marked 'Q'. The man took off his glasses and wiped his forehead on the sleeve of his shirt. His jacket was hung over the back of his chair. Next to his left hand was a hammered brass ashtray that was filled with cigarette butts. Tiny bugs weaved around the lantern's light. He took an envelope from a box. The envelope had the letter Q marked on the front and nothing else. He tore a sheet off his notepad, on which the paintings were listed by code number only. Then he handed the envelope and the sheet to Pankratov. 'Head around the Place de la Concorde and get on the Champs Élysées. Head for the Boulevard de la Grande Armée. That will get you on the main road out of Paris to the west. Once you are out of the city, open your instructions and follow them. When you get to your destination, check the paintings against the numbers. Make sure they all get delivered. When you get back to the city, return the list to me. All clear?'

'Clear,' said Pankratov.

A woman walked out of the Jeu de Paumes and right over to us. She was the woman from the gallery opening – the one with the crowd gathered round her.

I couldn't remember her name.

'Alexander,' she said to Pankratov, raising her chin slightly as she pronounced his name.

Then she glanced at Fleury. 'Monsieur Fleury,' she said. 'Under the circumstances, I suppose I should be glad to see you here.'

Fleury smiled weakly.

'But now that I have a better understanding of your methods,' she continued, 'these are the only circumstances under which I would welcome your company.'

'The honour is to serve,' said Fleury grandly, returning her insult with one more subtle than her own.

'Madame Pontier,' said Pankratov, 'this is David Halifax. He is one of the painters we will be using.'

'Ah,' said the woman. 'You are the American.'

'Not any more,' I said, and shook her hand, which was strong and bony.

'We have high hopes for you,' she said and turned and walked back into the building.

'Who was that?' I asked Pankratov.

'That woman owns you right now' – Pankratov's voice was a hoarse whisper – 'so think nice thoughts about her.'

'Well, I know what I'll be thinking about her, anyway,' said Fleury.

When we reached the street, the last of the paintings was being loaded into our van. In the back, I could see mountings where the bread bins had been. By the thin light of a bulb in the compartment I could see traces of flour in the gridded metal floor. I wondered what the owner of the truck would do without it.

I climbed behind the wheel and pulled out into the Place de la Concorde. The buildings that we passed loomed dark and empty. The trees along the Champs Élysées were leafy and still. I saw no people in the streets.

It was cold in the truck, even with the three of us squashed in.

'That woman on the ramp,' said Pankratov, 'is Emilia Pontier, curator of the Duarte gallery. She's been put in charge of removing works from all the major galleries. She's probably the only one who knows the locations of all the paintings. She made up the lists and code numbers, found locations and contacted people who would hide the paintings. Right now, she's probably the most important person in the French art world.'

Pankratov tore open the directions. He took out a sheet of paper and a stack of fuel ration coupons. He let the envelope fall to the floor. 'Normandy,' he told us.

Again, I thought about that day in the streetcar. So much had happened since then, it was as if I'd stolen the memory from someone else's life.

'Where in Normandy?' asked Fleury.

'To the Ardennes Abbey,' he said. 'The ancestral home of the Count and Countess de Boinville.'

'De Boinville?' I asked.

'That's right.' Pankratov nodded. 'They offered to let us store some paintings there.'

'I didn't know Marie-Claire was a countess!' said Fleury. 'Why didn't you tell us before?'

'She asked me not to. What difference would it have made, anyway?'

'It might have made a difference to Balard,' I said. I wondered where Balard was now, still alive or dead up in some muddy field in Belgium.

We drove out through the flat farmlands west of Paris, the long straight roads lined with hedges and crop fields neat and geometric. After the city, it was strange to have the horizon broad and open again and to see thick groves of trees. I saw a dull red tractor ploughing a field. Mist clogged in the muddy furrows. A jumble of magpies and seagulls followed behind the hunched-down driver. A pipe jutted from his mouth.

There was no sign of war: no soldiers, tanks or guns.

Pankratov stared out of the window, steaming up the glass

with his breath and then wiping away the condensation again. He unbuttoned one of his pockets, pulled out an apple and munched at it.

'Where is this abbey?' asked Fleury.

'Near Caen,' said Pankratov.

'What are we going to do?' I asked. 'Just hang them on the wall?'

'Actually,' explained Pankratov, 'we're going to put them *in* the wall. If France falls, some German magistrate is going to be living in the abbey and the last thing he'll want is for his new house to be damaged. The paintings will be behind a few feet of plaster and paint and he'll never know they're there.'

By afternoon, we were approaching Normandy. The roads became sunken and narrow. Sometimes, all we could see was a tunnel of the thick bushes closing over us. Pankratov said this was *bocage* country. The roads were below the level of the fields because they were hundreds of years old. Over the centuries, the level of the fields had risen with each successive crop, while the road level stayed the same. I beeped the horn every time we came to a bend in the road, in case there was a car coming the other way, but after a while, I gave up slowing down. Once in a while, over the sound of our own roaring engine, we heard the goose-like honking of another horn and I jammed on the brakes. The only vehicles we passed were two milk trucks and a tractor. Once we had to stop to let a herd of black-and-white cows cross the road, pestered on by a boy who slapped their muddy flanks with a stick.

We had long since run out of conversation. Now we lived alone in our thoughts.

A fine rain was falling as we passed through Caen. The wipers jolted drunkenly across the windscreen. In the distance I could see the thin spike of a cathedral spire, jutting from a cloak of fog. We tanked up for the third time in a place called St Germain-La-Blanche-Herbe, using the fuel ration coupons. By then, we were only a few miles away. I had been driving for over ten hours. At the gas station, I could smell fuel around the pumps and the reek of grease and rubber from the repair shop. Next to the gas station was a bar café run by the same man who pumped our gas. His once-blue overalls were bleached the colour of cigar smoke.

We went into the café, where the owner served us our Café National in heavy cream-coloured mugs with a green stripe around the top. He refused to take our money. 'If you don't drink it, the Germans will, and I'll throw it away before I give it to them. Besides, they probably have real coffee, anyway.' Then he went on to tell us that he had killed a bunch of Germans in the Great War. 'And now they're coming back for more,' he said. 'I must have let a few of them get away last time.'

Pankratov sipped at his coffee. 'Better hope they don't remember your face.' Then he walked outside to stretch his legs.

The morning papers arrived while Fleury and I were sitting there. Large black headlines in *La Nation* announced the invasion of Belgium and attacks on French airfields up north. The Germans had used dive-bombers to break French strongholds along the Meuse river. The French Seventh Army, under General Giraud, was withdrawing towards the Dutch coast.

The café man stood looking out of the window, as if he expected the German tanks to come rolling down the road at any minute. 'We'll stop them,' he said. 'They'll hit the main French lines tomorrow and then we'll stop them.'

The Germans were already through the main French lines. That much was clear from the newspaper, but I didn't have the heart to tell him.

The first turn to the right out of St Germain took us on a small and arcing road out to the converted abbey, a small fortress of buildings with high walls around it and a huge wooden gate at the entrance. The entrance was set back into the abbey itself, and we had to drive down a narrow alley flanked by high stone walls. The stone was pale and sandy and looked rough, as if it would take the skin from my palms if I ran my hand across it.

There was a small door set into the gate, which opened when I pulled the car up to it. A short man in a heavy wool coat stood in the doorway.

Pankratov got out. The two men talked for a while. Fleury and I sat in the truck.

'For a while,' said Fleury, 'I actually believed none of this would ever happen.'

Before I could tell him that he hadn't been the only one, the gate was opened and Pankratov waved us in.

I pulled the van into a large courtyard, which had a fountain in the middle and plants growing in stone pots set against the walls. The courtyard was paved in loose stone, which crackled under the van's tyres. The windows of the abbey were tall and arched. There was a great silence to the place.

The man in the heavy coat had been joined by another. Both men were stocky, with broad foreheads and slightly flattened noses. They looked to be related. They wore waistcoats and had no collars on their shirts. Their thick hair was grey with dust. One had a moustache, which was so caked in grime that it looked as if it had been carved out of chalk and glued to his face. The men shook our hands but didn't smile. They looked very tired. The man with the moustache introduced himself as Tessel and the other man, who wore the heavy coat, as Cristot.

I knew those weren't their real names. They were small towns further along the road to Bayeux. I'd seen them on the map.

On Tessel's orders, I backed the truck up to the main entranceway and we all began to unload the paintings, stacking them against the side of the truck and up against the side of the house.

I counted forty paintings, the largest of which was about

two feet by three feet and the smallest maybe only one foot by eight inches.

'Where are the de Boinvilles?' asked Fleury.

'The Count and Countess,' said Tessel, clearly irritated by Fleury's familiar tone concerning their local nobility, 'have gone off to Caen for a few days. They said they didn't want to know exactly what it was we were hiding. The less they know, the better.'

We moved the paintings inside. In the front hallway was a stained-glass window. It bled watery greens and blues across white sheets that covered the canvases. We carried the paintings up a staircase made of reddish-amber mahogany.

I tried to imagine Marie-Claire in this place, drifting down the stairs in some long gown; but I couldn't do it. To me, she belonged and would always belong in the smoky air of the Dimitri, or bundled in a coat and sketching the hostile face of Valya.

There were tapestries on the walls, showing knights on horseback, stags and hounds. The place smelled of old fires and polish. We set the paintings down in the dining room, in the centre of which was a huge table of the same wood as the stairs. It must have been built in the room, because it would never have fitted through the door. The silver candlesticks and the salt dish had been placed on the sideboard.

Overshadowing all the beauty in the room was a large and ragged hole that had been dug into the wall, through the paint and mortar and stones, exposing a narrow area in between.

A housepainter's cloth had been set on the floor to catch falling debris. Two sledgehammers lay crossed on top of the stones that had been removed. Cracks radiated out from the hole all across the wall and I wondered how these two men who had made the hole would ever be able to repair it in a way that no one would notice. Even with the cloth set out, there was dust everywhere in the room.

Cristot climbed over the pile of rubble and stood in the gap between the walls. 'We figure there's enough room in here for all of them. You can grab a screwdriver or whatever you want and start taking the paintings off those frames.' He gestured to the table, where a canvas bag sagged open, loaded with tools. 'Then we can roll them up and stash them. It shouldn't take too long.'

'Wait a minute,' said Pankratov.

'What's the matter?' asked Tessel. He pulled a red handkerchief out of his pocket and began smoothing the dust from his moustache.

'You can't roll these up,' Pankratov told them.

'We'll be careful,' said Cristot. 'Now come on.' He snapped his fingers and held his hands out for the first painting.

'First of all' – Pankratov dug his hand into the canvas bag and hauled out a paint-spattered iron file – 'you can't just gouge a canvas off its stretcher with one of these. And secondly, if you want to take an old painting off its stretcher, you need to place it on a wooden roller, which you turn only six inches a month. This is a job for specialists. Nobody's taking these paintings off their stretchers.'

It seemed to grow very hot and quiet in the room. The floating dust was clogging up my lungs.

Tessel turned to Cristot. 'I told you we never should have got involved.'

'You're the one who talked me into it,' said Cristot.

'I have two children and a wife at home . . .'

'And I'm their godfather, for Christ's sake!' Cristot interrupted. 'Don't you lecture me, Jean-Paul.'

'Oh, and there you go using my real name!'

'It was only your first name.'

'Well, thanks a lot, anyway. And here I am risking my life with you of all people for a bunch of paintings that I've never seen and don't care about.' His voice rose with indignation, as he turned his attention to Pankratov. 'I don't care about your damned museums and . . .'

He was going on like this when Pankratov lifted up one of the paintings, set it on the table and, with one flip of his hand, undid the bow that held the string in place. He swept away the white sheet wrapping. The painting came into view.

It was a Vermeer. I knew that at once. The Lacemaker. *La dentellière.* It was a small painting, made on canvas laid over wood. It showed a young woman, maybe nineteen or twenty years old, in a yellow dress with a broad white collar. The woman's hair was braided at the back and curls hung down by her ears. She was hunched over her work, and it was hard to make out what she was doing. Something with pins and tiny spools of thread. Red and white silk spilled out, almost like liquid, from a soft case beside her. She looked tired and busy and the faint cheerfulness on her face seemed strained. Every time I had gone to the Louvre, I had sought out this painting just to look once more at the smile on that woman's face. Each time I saw it, the smile seemed less and less sincere, as if she were stuck in some purgatory of a job that she knew would make her blind, as many lacemakers went blind. By now, I felt I knew her from some place beyond the confines of that canvas.

To see the painting there in front of us, robbed of its beautiful pale-wood frame, beyond the safety of the Louvre, shocked us into silence. We just stared at it.

A long time passed before Cristot sighed noisily. 'Oh,' he said, the way all Frenchmen say 'oh', deep-voiced and long.

'Are they all like that?' asked Tessel. The red handkerchief dangled from his hand.

'Just give me the paintings,' said Cristot. 'We'll find a way to get them in.'

We began handing them across the pile. Cristot took each one and shuffled away out of sight, sidestepping down the gap. We heard the rustling of his movements, like a giant rat living in the space between.

It took an hour for the gap to be filled up, by which time it was dark outside.

We sat down for a break. Fleury brought in his satchel and passed out the food and wine. Pankratov went downstairs to the kitchen and brought back cold ham and bread and some

Camembert and three bottles without labels filled with what looked like muddy water.

Tessel took out a small, hook-bladed knife and carved the wax top off the bottle. Then he drew out the cork with a corkscrew attached to the other end of the knife. He ran the bottle under his nose, sniffed once and then took a short sip. He swished it around in his mouth and then swallowed, his Adam's apple bobbing.

I saw on his face the first smile I'd noticed all day. 'Calvados,' he said. '*Première distillation.*' He curled his lips around the words, as if they tasted of the drink itself.

We ate the ham and bread and the chalky-rinded cheese and drank the hard Calvados cider, passing the bottle around.

A plane droned overhead. We all stopped until the sound had faded away, as if the machine might sense our breathing while it scudded through the clouds.

Tessel picked up a piece of bread and laid a slab of ham on top. He chewed at it thoughtfully. 'It could be years before anyone comes back for these paintings,' he said. 'We might all be long gone by then.'

It was night when we finally pulled out of the Ardennes Abbey, leaving the two men to plaster up the wall, repaint it and remount the tapestry that had hung over the space.

We drove back to Paris, through towns whose streetlights had been switched off as a precaution against air raids.

I tried to imagine the paintings staying hidden, not just for years but for centuries, and what it would be like for those who found them far into the future, whether they would even know what they were, or how much the world had valued them. I wondered what precious objects in the past had been hidden by people whose civilizations were being overwhelmed. I wondered if they felt the way I felt now as they hurried their treasures into hiding, too tired to think straight, too frightened for their own lives to envision the deaths of whole nations. I thought of the great tribes that had vanished – the Minoans, the Etruscans, the Vandals and the Easter

Islanders – becoming first legends, then rumours, then finally nothing at all, while somewhere deep inside caves in the shuddering earth lay the relics of their sacred lives and the bones of those whose stories had died with them.

10

Pankratov decided to move.

From now on, he decreed, we would work at what he called his 'warehouse'. In fact, it was a cramped little space, formerly a stable, in a section of an old brick viaduct. It stood between the Père-Lachaise cemetery and the Rue des Pyrénées. The viaduct had once been used for a railway, but new tracks for the *Chemin de fer de Ceinture* had been laid down beyond it. There were dozens of these little warehouses all along the base of the viaduct. Each one had its own arched door, painted with thick coats of glossy green paint.

On Pankratov's door, in stylish orange letters, was: *A.Pankratov. RÉPARATION D'ANTIQUITÉS.* Each word was underlaid in a shadow effect with red paint.

'It's too risky at the atelier,' he told me, as he rummaged through his keys for one that would unlock the door. 'Besides, all my supplies are here.' He swung the doors wide and a smell of dank air wafted out.

The ceiling inside was high and vaulted. Several electric bulbs hung on cords from the ceiling. When Pankratov switched them on, they threw out a sinewy glare. Piles of junk clogged the shadows, consisting mostly of ruined paintings. Proud faces glared from white-flaking canvases of old portraits, as if emerging from a snowstorm. There were also frames, jars of old nails, various pots of powder for mixing paints and bottles of dirty linseed oil, bins of rags and so many jars of brushes that they looked like strange plants that had learned to grow in the damp darkness of the warehouse.

'Where do you work exactly?' I asked. The stone space echoed with my voice.

'Eh?' said Pankratov. 'Work? Well, wherever I feel like it.'

'Do you know where we are, Pankratov?' I told him. 'We're not in a warehouse. We're inside your brain. All this junk . . .'

'Stop!' he raised his hand like a traffic policeman. 'You can stop right there. From this junk, in a couple of weeks, I can conjure up a Caravaggio, all with a trick of the dust.'

'Poof!' I said, and waggled my fingers as if I were casting a spell.

'Forgery,' said Pankratov, 'isn't just about painting a good copy of something. In fact, it isn't really about copying at all.'

'Then what is it about?' A train clattered past on the tracks beyond the viaduct. It was a steady, comforting sound.

Pankratov scuttled into the gloom. His shadow lumbered after him, huge and crippled against the sloping walls. He emerged a moment later with the remnants of a frame. 'It's about this!' He held the frame in front of him as if he were a talking portrait of himself. 'Look at this frame. Come here and look at it.'

Obediently I went across. 'It smells in here,' I said.

'It's the smell of authenticity,' he replied.

I stood in front of him, the two of us on either side of the frame.

'Look here,' he said, nodding down at one corner, since he had no hands free. 'What do you see? Tiny holes peppered the wood and the old gilded plaster.

'Looks like worm holes,' I said.

'Exactly! Do you have any idea how long it takes to get worms to eat holes in wood?'

'To *get* them to?'

'Yes! It takes years and years. Which we don't have. Do you know what inexperienced forgers sometimes do to fake worm holes? They put the frame against a tree and fire buckshot at it. It makes little holes like these. The trouble is, worms don't make straight holes when they burrow, the way shotgun pellets do. Besides that, you have to dig the buckshot out again. And that's the sort of thing they'll be looking for, these experts. If you really want to fool someone, you start off with something old. You don't get new stuff and then kick it around or pour all kinds of solvents on it. You need as much authenticity as you can get.' The frame shook in Pankratov's hands as he laid out the laws of his obsession. 'Now do you understand?' he asked.

'Yes,' I said. 'Worms are my friends.'

'They are for now,' he told me.

When I woke up, on the morning of 22 May, I read in the paper that the Germans had reached the English Channel near Abbeville. Now they were driving north to cut off the ports of Boulogne and Calais. The city of Rotterdam had been surrounded and ordered to surrender, and then bombed before the surrender deadline had expired. De Gaulle's Fourth Armoured Division attacked north of Laon and was repulsed by German Stuka divebombers. The seventy-year-old French general Gamelin was fired and replaced by the even older general Marshal Pétain. The roads of northern France were jammed with refugees.

So much was happening that by the time I read about these events, new battles had already broken out. I could keep up with the general flow of information, but my ability to imagine the magnitude of suffering was becoming exhausted. I could no longer picture the dead, civilians abandoning their homes, towns that had been burned. They were now simply facts. I used to feel guilty about my lack of emotion. Then even the guilt went away. There was nothing to do but wait and see what happened when the war at last reached Paris, which by now we knew it would. I think it was like that for most people: they waited in dread for the moment when the war would come to them and they would know its full brutality first hand, no longer suffering in the abstract.

I set down the paper, and walked to the open window. The sun was gentle and warm, and the air filled with pollen from trees in the Tuileries gardens.

Down in the street I saw cars ride past with suitcases piled up on their roofs, fleeing the city.

The man with the dragoon moustache from the Postillon company was carrying out boxes. He stacked six of them, one on top of another, and then took off the tops. They were filled with documents. He brought out two bottles of what looked like brandy and poured them on top of the papers. After that, he selected a match from a little wooden box that he took out of his pocket, struck it and then flicked it at the pile.

He wasn't prepared for the force of the flames, which jumped into the air with a thumping boom. He backed away, arms in front of his eyes, swearing. Frantically, he patted his fingers against his moustache, in case it had been singed.

Soon the street was filled with smoke. Half-burned papers flicked up into the air.

Out across the rooftops was the smoke of other fires.

The Dragoon brought out a large broom and swept stray papers back towards the fire. The bristles of his broom were smouldering.

The fire burned away to ashes, leaving a large black stain on the pavement. The Dragoon swept the ashes into a large dustpan. Then he washed down the pavement with buckets of water, but some of the black stain remained. When it was all done, he leaned the broom against the wall and sat down in the sun to smoke a cigarette. After a few puffs, he stubbed it out on the sole of his shoe. Then he locked up the warehouse and pedalled away on his bicycle.

By 9 June the British Expeditionary Force had evacuated over a 100,000 troops out of Dunkirk, leaving 40,000 French troops to be captured. After this, the bulk of the French army was in full retreat, slowed down by thousands of refugees clogging the roads. German Panzer columns had advanced to the east and west of Paris.

Italy declared war on France.

On 11 June Paris was declared an open city. Billboards went up overnight, stating that there was to be no resistance offered when the Germans reached the city. These posters covered up the posters from a few months before, summoning all soldiers and reservists to their barracks. Cars with loudspeakers strapped to their roofs, like corsages of giant metal tulips, trundled through the streets advising everyone to stay inside.

Thick black tornadoes of smoke rose from burning oil-storage tanks on the outskirts of the city.

That night, there was the sound of breaking glass as looters ransacked shops whose owners had left the city.

I heard a story that hospitals were injecting Prussic acid into the hearts of patients who could not be evacuated.

I also heard that three million of the five million people who lived in Paris had gone. There was a constant line of traffic along the Boulevard St Michel, where I saw everything from cars to bicycles to farm tractors hauling people away.

The newspapers stopped coming out.

Factories shut down.

Trains shut down.

There were no taxis.

Food markets shut down.

The bars and cafés, on the other hand, stayed open twenty-four hours a day. People drank themselves stupid. Some places were giving their stock away.

At first it seemed as if everybody who stayed behind had a different reason for doing so. Some were too proud, others too poor. By now, reasons no longer mattered. The city had been divided between those who fled and those who didn't.

'Balard is dead,' said Pankratov, when Fleury and I arrived at his warehouse the next morning. Pankratov made no attempt to soften the news with any words of consolation. He blurted it out and then began to tidy up the place.

'When?' I asked.

Pankratov's head popped up from behind a pile of broken frames. 'A week ago. His parents called to tell me. They found out from a man from Balard's unit who was sent home wounded and stopped by to tell them the news. Otherwise, they probably wouldn't have found out for months.'

'Where did he die?' asked Fleury.

'Somewhere near the Meuse river,' he said. 'That's all they told me.' There was silence after that, except for Pankratov's clumsy rearranging of his junk into different but no less chaotic piles of junk.

I hadn't known Balard well enough to feel the kind of sadness I wish I could have felt. I regretted that we had argued. Somehow, the fact that he had been dead for two weeks made it seem like the very distant past. It seemed so strange that, even though I hadn't thought about him much, Balard had still taken up some space inside my head. And in this space he had continued to breathe, half-remembered but alive, until this moment when the space suddenly contracted into nothing and vanished.

Soon Balard's face and the memory of his voice became blurred and distant. As time went by, fragmented images of him would return unexpectedly, but only for a second, and then they would be gone again.

The only thing that stopped me from going crazy in those last days before the German occupation was my work with Pankratov. We still hadn't received instructions on what to paint, so all we could do was prepare.

A chill crept around me every time I walked into the warehouse. It drilled through each layer of my clothing, coiled around my bones and threaded through my joints. It clung there all day. I could never get warm in that place.

Fleury was in his own frenzy of activity. For reasons he at first declined to spell out, he had set himself the task of buying as many old art books as he could find. Many came from *bouquainistes* who sold second-hand books from green metal display cases balanced on top of the walls that overlooked the Seine. The old art books didn't have illustrations printed directly on to the pages. Instead, colour postcards were glued beside descriptions of the works. Fleury explained that he would have postcards made of our own versions of the various paintings or drawings. Then he would remove the original postcards and replace them with his own. That way he could fake the provenance of a work.

After a week, Fleury decided he had enough books and that there were no more jobs to be done. This left him at a loose end. Rather than stay at home alone, he came to the warehouse and sat in an old chair with half its stuffing gone. He wrapped himself in a red-and-grey-striped horse blanket, reading books by the light of a candle jammed into a wine bottle and starting up conversations whenever he got bored.

We tried to remain optimistic. Each of us fed off the other's fabricated nonchalance, until we had built up a kind of lie between ourselves as the only kind of barricade against the panic that might otherwise overwhelm us. The only thing I could compare it to was the autumn of 1938, when I had gone up to Narragansett to help my brother and mother board up the house before the arrival of a hurricane. We had finished the work and were sitting in the basement of the house, listening to radio broadcasts that tracked the path of the nor'easter. It was going to be a bad storm. My mother's house stood four blocks back from the sea, which had always put it clear of any storm damage, but this time we were beginning to wonder if we should have evacuated inland, along with half the neighbourhood. But my mother had been stubborn about it, and by the time I arrived on the train from New York, my brother had already started laying in supplies: bottled water, cans of food, lanterns, blankets, and a pistol in case looters came by after the storm. With several hours still to go before the hurricane was due to hit us, we had nothing left to do but sit in the basement on old lawn furniture and listen to the wind pick up. We heard the monotonous radio broadcaster, advising everyone along the coast to leave their homes, and then the station went dead. We opened up the storm door to the basement and looked up at the sky through the thrashing leaves of the oak tree in our garden. Obscenely muscled clouds bunched greyish-yellow in the north. When the storm finally arrived, it made darkness out of daylight, smashed the waterfront to pieces, threw sailboats up on to the road, hit Point Judith so hard that the place was almost removed from the map, flooded the city of Providence and tore off half my mother's roof. It was the most powerful hurricane anyone could recall, but still the worst of it was the waiting. That was exactly how it felt now.

Pankratov and I were in the process of stripping the paint off an old canvas, which we would then recover with a painting of our own. The original work was an early nineteenth-century portrait of an overweight, middle-aged man. The painting had no frame and was on a stretcher that had one spar cracked, so that the man's face sagged down, making him look simple and deformed. The man was sitting in an ornate chair with a greyhound lying at his feet. His hands, which dangled off the arms of the chair, were fat and pink like uncooked sausages.

The canvas was very dirty, but rather than just see this as the cause of the painting's ruin, I had grown to appreciate the finer points of dirt. I was now able to tell the difference between a painting that had hung in a room where there had been smoke fires, which veiled the painting in a hard, old-iron greyness, and one that had been exposed to sunlight, which lightened the colours, or still another that might have been stored away for a hundred years, whose colours would be dark and sinister.

Pankratov worked with acetone soaked in a little sea sponge. He mopped away the colours. The sausage-fingered man slowly disappeared, perhaps the only image left of him in the world. Eventually Pankratov reached the white undercoat, drawing the faintest white smudge from the canvas. At this point, he would grunt and I immediately applied a sponge soaked in turpentine, which stopped the action of the acetone. Over the past few days we had 'cleared', as Pankratov called it, over a dozen paintings in this manner, and had hung them up to dry. It was an odd sight, these blind white rectangles hugging the warehouse walls.

The fumes made us dizzy. Often we had to stagger out into the alleyway and sit there in the sun, breathing deeply while the parachutes of dandelion seeds drifted down from the old railroad tracks above.

For the first few days I didn't use rubber gloves, because I couldn't work as well in them. But now, after exposure to the chemicals, my fingers were so creased with deep and painful cracks that I had trouble doing up my shoelaces. I also had tiny black spots appearing like freckles. The sight of these frightened me into buying gloves, which I wore now whether they made me clumsy or not.

'What I don't understand,' I said, giving voice to a conversation that had been going on in my head all morning, 'is if the picture is beautiful and we enjoy it, who cares who painted it? Why should one work that was done by a famous artist be worth so many hundreds of times more than another picture which is just as beautiful?'

'Who's to judge what's beautiful?' asked Pankratov.

'What I mean is,' I said, 'if someone buys a painting because they like the look of it, then that should be their only judgement. You can call it an appreciation of beauty. You can call it an appreciation of skill. Call it whatever you like. I'm sure it has a hundred names . . .'

'So does the devil,' said Pankratov.

'And then suddenly,' I continued, 'they find out that this painting isn't by Van Gogh, after all. And immediately, they can't stand the sight of it.'

'What they can't stand,' said Pankratov, 'is being reminded how much they paid for it.'

'But that's my point!' I told him. 'My point exactly. Do they value it because of how much money they paid for it or because they are drawn to it?'

Now Fleury joined in. 'They are drawn to it,' he said, 'because of the thought that Van Gogh touched that canvas, because his muscles worked the spatulas that laid on the paint so thickly. That it was his madness making him do it. They want to touch something that has been touched by someone whose name is immortal. Because it was there when he was there. That's what they pay for. And if they find out it's a forgery, the spell is broken.'

Now Pankratov joined in. 'But the whole business of forgery is not as clear-cut as they'd like to think. Some paintings were only done in a certain style, like a Van Gogh style, or a Klimt style, or whatever. They get sold, then someone else comes along and mistakes it for an original. Or someone fakes it up a bit and then deliberately misleads the buyer.'

Fleury shifted in his chair.

Pankratov continued. 'And then there are paintings that were done in a certain school of painting. Rembrandt for example. Say Rembrandt gets a commission to paint a portrait of some wealthy aristocrat. One of his students might do all of the work except the hands and face and would leave those to Rembrandt himself. This lets Rembrandt get on with his other work. But does it mean that the portrait of the aristocrat is a fake Rembrandt? What's the difference between a painting that was done only by Rembrandt and one that was done partly by him?'

'A hell of a lot of money,' replied Fleury. 'Somewhere out there, in one of the great museums of the world, some little old man is standing in front of a painting – one of the great paintings – one people travel across continents to see and they weep over it and say how brilliant Caravaggio was, or Goya or Velázquez or whoever. And they lean forward and try to catch a breath of the sweat and the genius. But it isn't Goya's breath, or the breath of Velázquez. It's the breath of that little old man. He made that painting, and now that all the so-called experts have pronounced it to be original, even if he confessed that he'd done the work, no one would believe him. But he won't confess. We'll never know his name and he doesn't want us to know his name, because his anonymity is an expression of his art. And that man is a master forger.'

'That's what we're doing,' I said. 'With us, there is no doubt.'

'No,' Pankratov mumbled. 'There is no doubt. We are forgers. And between the three of us, given time, I imagine we could forge almost anything.'

'*Almost*,' said Fleury, drawing out the word. 'And where do you draw your line, Monsieur Pankratov?'

'At the Mona Lisa's smile,' he replied. 'It can never be duplicated. There is something unearthly about it.'

Pankratov tossed his sponge into the little ceramic bowl which was filled with dirty, grey-brown acetone. He set the bowl on the table and walked over to the door. He flung it open and afternoon light blasted in. For a moment, his silhouette stood huge and blurred in the doorway, then it was gone. He sat down heavily against the wall outside and pulled out his cigarettes. He dug his brass lighter out of his pocket and lit himself a smoke. Then he settled back against the sun-warmed brick, smoke streaming out of his mouth.

'You've been studying the techniques,' Fleury told me, 'but I've been studying you. And I say you're a pair of sorcerers.'

Maybe it was true. Pankratov and I were dabbling with spells, drawing across from a dimension just beyond our own the phantoms whose help we required.

That evening, as Fleury and I rode the elevator up to our apartments, I clung to the bars. I pressed the black iron against my cheekbones and watched the wall file past me, only a few inches away. I noticed that someone had drawn a pencil line all the way from the ground to the top floor. It had stopped when the pencil lead broke and then been continued at another time. There were many breaks and starts, and I could see how the person had become more proficient in joining up the lines as time went by. I wondered how long it had taken. I thought about this small obsession that must have filled the person's mind, watching the lead burn down as the elevator climbed from floor to floor, then starting all over again. Much of my own time painting had been spent in that same cage of fixation.

It ought to be enough, I thought, for me to risk insanity by looking inside myself. But now I would be taking on the madness of people whose madness was what made them great. If I couldn't grasp the obsessions that had propelled their creativity, I would never succeed. If I failed, there was someone even now, out there in the country built for war, who knew his own obsessions, and the pain he would inflict to see them through. That pain will be ours, I thought, if I do not get it right.

That night, when it came time to head home, I told Pankratov and Fleury that I needed to go for a walk. I had too much nervous energy swirling around in my head. We arranged to meet up later at the Dimitri, if it was still open.

The Germans were expected any day now. The streets were mostly deserted. Shop windows were boarded up or criss-crossed with white tape. Some places even had sandbags piled up against them. Scattered amongst the closed businesses, a few stubborn cafés stayed open. Their menus grew smaller by the day, inky lines slicing through the *Croque Monsieurs* and *Entrecôtes*. The only thing that never seemed to run out was the wine. It made me wonder how many millions of bottles must be stored beneath the streets, as if the whole city were precariously balanced on pyramids of glass.

An hour later, I reached the Pont Royal. It was sunset. I stood looking down at the river, which slid fast and milky green around the pillars of the bridge. I breathed and breathed until sparks weaved in front of my eyes and the numbing oiliness of turpentine fumes no longer tainted my lungs.

I set out for the Dimitri, crossing the Place de le Concorde. The obelisk of Luxor stretched its shadow down the Rue Royale. A few cars rounded the fountain, tyres pop-popping on the cobblestones. Then it grew completely quiet, except for water shushing from the mouths of the bronze fish, held in the arms of half-human sea creatures, which stood in the fountain's thigh-deep water. I wonder who had thought to keep them running. Before the war, at this time of day the Concorde would have been a zoo of bicycles and motor scooters and taxis, caped policemen whirling as they steered the honking traffic.

I was shuffling along with my hands in my pockets, when I heard a mechanical whine over the rooftops. As I raised my head, a small and flimsy-looking aeroplane appeared from the direction of the Champs Élysées. It was German, black crosses outlined in white on the undersides of its wings, with large struts attaching the wings to the body of the plane. It had fixed wheels with fat little tyres at the ends. The canopy was large and made of many segments and, as the plane passed slowly overhead, less than a hundred feet above me, I saw the pilot staring down.

The Place de la Concorde was empty.

I stopped and stared.

The plane circled and appeared to fly off. Then it banked low over the Arc de Triomphe and levelled out, heading towards me. The machine flew right along the Champs Élysées, losing altitude. Its engine burbled in a lower pitch, coming in to land between the rows of trees that grew on either side of the road. The plane bounced once, then settled. It came to a stop right where the Champs Élysées joined the Place de la Concorde, between two statues each of which showed a man trying to control a wild horse.

The canopy opened, folding back on itself like the wings of an insect. Then a man climbed out. He wore high black boots, whose hobnails crunched on the stones. He had on grey riding breeches and a green-grey jacket buttoned up to the throat. There was a small pistol holster on his leather belt, which he wore over his jacket. He had brown leather gloves and was carrying a peaked cap with a short black visor, which he immediately fitted on to his head.

Another man stayed in the plane and kept the engine running. His eyes were hidden behind small, dark goggles.

I stayed absolutely still, like a deer terrified by the glare of a car's headlights. The man walked around the plane, looking at the statues and the buildings. He turned to look back down the Champs Élysées at the Arc de Triomphe. He stared down the Rue Royale at the columned temple of the Madeleine. His hands opened and closed. He seemed to be in shock, as if he had always dreamed of landing a reconnaissance plane in the Place de la Concorde and now couldn't believe he had actually done it. Then he caught sight of me and stopped.

I did nothing. I just kept staring. I was too stunned to feel frightened or angry.

It seemed to me the German was also lost in amazement. He raised his hand to one of the large pockets on his tunic and pulled out a cigarette case. He opened it and held it out to me.

I didn't move. I could see the white sticks of the cigarettes.

The man nodded. He held the case out further.

We were like two men hallucinating each other, and the gulf of twenty paces was the distance between waking and sleep.

Slowly and hesitantly I raised my hands, showing the whiteness of my palms, as if any rapid movement would cause this vision to separate and disappear into the sky like a flock of frightened birds.

He picked a cigarette from the case, fumbling for a moment in his leather gloves. He set it down on a stone ridge at the base of one of the rearing horse statues. Then he looked at me, to make sure I had seen.

My hands were still raised.

The German officer returned to his plane, his footsteps sharp on the stones. He climbed inside and pulled the hatch shut after him. The plane's engine fired up and the machine turned until it was facing back down the Champs Élysées. The engine's roar grew louder. At last the plane lurched forward. Its gawky landing gear trailed like a heron's legs in the moment that it left the ground. It climbed steeply and was gone over the rooftops.

Still in a state of shock, I walked over to the statue, where the cigarette was lying on the stone. The man had even left me a match, one match. I left them where they were. No one else came by. The city was quieter than I'd ever heard it before. Even in the deepest part of night, there had always been the rumbling like distant thunder, but now even this had gone silent. The light faded out and the purple sky turned navy blue. The stones grew slick with dew and there was the musty smell of rain.

I had to get clear in my head the meaning of this small gesture, which I could not match against the idea of an enemy. I wondered how long it might take before our first reaction would be to shoot each other dead.

11

The Germans came quietly to the Rue Descalzi.

I woke to the sound of hoofbeats down at the far end of the street. I leaned out of my window and saw horse-drawn wagons towing small artillery pieces, the German gun crews in their sharply angled helmets and rough field-grey uniforms returning the stares of the crowd that had gathered in silence to watch them go by. I ducked back inside and ran down to Fleury's apartment.

He arrived at the door in his smoking jacket.

'They're here,' I told him.

Fleury looked calm at first, but then I noticed the tassels at the end of the jacket's silk belt. The ends were trembling, almost imperceptibly, like water in a glass when a truck drives by outside.

Fleury and I spent the day migrating back and forth from his apartment to mine, trading the unnerving stillness of one place for the stillness of the other. We heard no shooting outside – only the sound of heavy vehicles, as the Germans pulled into the city.

In the afternoon, a German truck stopped in the road. Two men got out and began putting up posters.

When the truck had left, Fleury and I went down to see what was on the posters. The street filled with people. I knew most of them only by sight. We began to exchange greetings that should have been made months ago. I'd seen the same thing happen back home, after the hurricane had ploughed through Narragansett. The threat from outside drew us all together, but what we shared that day was helplessness instead of the anger I had expected to feel.

The posters had 'PEUPLE DE PARIS' in large black letters

at the top and underneath that the declaration that German troops had occupied Paris. It went on to say that the military governor would take whatever steps he thought necessary to maintain order. Every act of sabotage, active or passive, would be severely punished. German troops had been ordered to respect the people and their property. It ended by saying that this was the best way to serve the city of Paris and its population.

Gradually, we all filtered back into our apartments, unsure about what remained of our old lives.

The next day, the foreman with the dragoon moustache arrived for work. Except for weekends, the arrival of the Germans had been the only day he'd taken off since I had arrived in France. He kicked up a fuss when he found the posters slapped up on his steel doors.

The jobless men arrived as well, having no place else to go.

The Dragoon tried to carry on with his routine. He picked his usual handful of bicyclists and the weary-looking men pedalled off with the heavy placards on their backs. The rest shambled away with their hands in their pockets.

Within two days the occupation posters had been joined by more colourful ones. These had a black oval outlined in orange and the lettering was done in several different type-faces. 'Germany Offers You Work,' it said. 'Immediate Employment. Paid Holidays. Housing. Insurance. This is the guarantee of a better future for you and your family.' Then it gave an address where people could show up for more information.

By the time the Dragoon arrived, most of the jobless regulars had showed up, read the posters and left. Some of them were running. Only Monsieur Finel from my building was still there.

The Dragoon read the posters. He swore at them quietly. Then he turned to Monsieur Finel and held open his hands with a gesture of futility. The two of them went inside the warehouse and, ten minutes later, pedalled out on the rickety bicycles, Postillon billboards on their backs.

Over the next week, life didn't exactly return to normal, but more of it returned than I had been expecting. The streetcars were running again. Schools re-opened. Bars. Municipal buildings. The post office. People who had fled into the countryside were now returning, as if they'd gone away on holiday. French gendarmes directed traffic alongside German military policemen. German guard huts, painted in chevronned candy-stripes of black, red and white, appeared at street corners on the Rue de Rivoli, at the Quai d'Orsay and in front of the Chambre des Députés. Several large hotels, like the Meurice, the Majestic and the Continental, were taken over and the area around them sealed off to non-Germans.

Soon German soldiers could be seen with cameras at all the touristy places. I got used to the sight of the officers with their riding breeches and high-peaked caps, and the soldiers with their side caps and the coarser wool of their uniforms. I saw a lot of German women in uniform. The French called them 'grey mice', on account of the colour of their dowdy skirts. Many soldiers had the wincing look of awkwardness, as if they would rather have been out in the fields, sleeping under their camouflage rain capes, with their fur-covered backpacks for pillows, instead of sightseeing in Paris.

There were rumours, which turned out to be true, that the fortress of Mont Valérien on the outskirts of the city had been turned into a political prison. Other rumours spoke of the work of the German secret police and the collaborating French militia, the *Milice*. But none of this was evident to people like me, at least not at first.

Pankratov and I returned to the Rue Descalzi atelier in order to keep alive the idea that his workshops were still running. We had no idea if anyone would be watching us, but thought we'd play it safe.

First, we lounged ostentatiously at the Dimitri, which had also received its share of German soldiers. I brought my portfolio of old sketches. Pankratov pulled them out, shook them, blew off the old charcoal dust and made loud comments, tracing his stubby finger down the line of a thigh, or across the shadow of a jaw. Most of my sketches were of Valya. It made Pankratov miserable to look at them. There had been no word from her.

As part of our act, Pankratov called over to Ivan, who obediently left the shiny copper altar of his bar. He stood by our table, nodding thoughtfully while Pankratov showed him the sketches.

The German soldiers were our real audience. They had arrived just after us, stepping cautiously into the room, as if afraid of slipping on the tiled floors in their hobnailed boots. They removed their forage caps and dragged a couple of tables together. They brought along their own coffee, *real* coffee. They had boiling water brought to the table along with the plunger-type coffee pots called *cafetières*, and made the coffee themselves. Their voices slowly grew in volume as they began to feel at ease. They set their army ration cigarettes, which came in yellow-and-red paper packets, on the table. On top of these they laid their army lighters, aluminium cylinders about as big as a man's thumb. They were not officers, these men – just three privates and a corporal, who wore a silver chevron on his upper sleeve. I had learned a little of their rank insignia from an article in the paper, which had with it a list of helpful German phrases:

IST HIER DAS VERTRETEN VERBOTEN? – Is it forbidden to go here?

WO BEFINDET SICH DIE POLIZEIPRÄSIDIUM? – Where is the police station?

MEINE PAPIERE SIND IN ORDNUNG – My papers are in order.

Now and then, the soldiers looked over in our direction. They made an effort not to stare. They broke out a pack of cards and three of them played while the fourth just sat and smoked and stared up at the ceiling.

After a while, I packed the sketches back into my portfolio. 'Enough,' I said quietly.

Pankratov seemed relieved.

The Germans watched as our chairs grumbled back across the floor. Soon they turned their backs to us again.

Pankratov and I didn't speak as we crossed the road and it was only after several flights of stairs that he found his voice again.

'All this fake politeness,' he puffed out. 'All this bogus tolerance. I'll feel better when we go back to being enemies with them again.'

'Maybe it will stay this way,' I said.

'I doubt that very much,' he replied. 'Mind the step.'

I dodged his boobytrap.

He stopped at the studio door and fished out his knot of keys. He bounced them in his hand until he found the one he wanted.

It was stuffy in the atelier and strange to think of the old days with Balard and Marie-Claire.

We mixed up some paints, setting the powder in little heaps on the wooden mixing boards and then stirring in turpentine with little sticks like chopsticks. I was always careful not to breathe the powder. Even the thought of the brilliant greens and reds sticking to my lungs was enough to make me wheeze.

'I suppose we'd better get started,' said Pankratov. He had moved his chair out to the warehouse and now looked around for a place to plant himself.

There was a sound of heavy footsteps on the stairs.

We both froze, just as we had done the time before.

I held the chopstick in my hand, poised in a puddle of cobalt blue. I heard the footsteps reach the third-floor landing and begin to climb to the fourth. I kept waiting for them to stop and go into one of the rooms lower down. By the time they got to the fourth, I knew they were coming for us. I gritted my teeth and closed my eyes.

Pankratov's trap came to life with a splintering crunch. A man cried out in pain and then a woman shrieked. There was a heavy thump as someone fell down to the fourth-floor landing. This was followed by the man swearing, loud and embarrassed, in German, and the woman running down the steps to help him, asking in a mixture of French and German if he was all right.

When she spoke, I knew it was Valya.

Pankratov stood with wide eyes fixed on the door.

Quick footsteps were followed by a shape appearing behind the blurred glass pane. Then the door flew open.

It was Valya, all right. She stamped in, furious. She was dressed in a short brown moleskin jacket. She wore a dark-blue skirt that came halfway down her calves, white socks and black shoes. Her hair was pulled back in a ponytail. She had a suntan, which contrasted with the paleness of her artists' model days. She looked prettier than I recalled. 'You!' she shouted at Pankratov. 'You idiot! You could have killed him!' She offered no explanation of where she had been or why she had left without telling Pankratov.

'I'm all right,' said the man at the bottom of the stairs. He spoke French with a German accent. There was the sound of him getting to his feet and cautious treading as he made his way up the steps.

Valya rested her fists against her hips. She turned to glare at me. 'You still here?' she shouted. 'I told you the war was coming. You should have listened to me.'

I gave her the go-to-hell smile.

The man appeared behind her. It was him: the man I'd seen at the bar. He wore a grey double-breasted suit, with a red, black and white Nazi party pin in his lapel.

Valya stepped aside to let him pass.

He nodded hello at us.

Pankratov ignored him. 'Not one word,' he said to Valya. He started walking towards her. 'Not one lousy word did I get from you while you were gone! I've been so god-damned worried I couldn't think straight.' Pankratov wrapped his arms around her and squeezed her so tightly that I heard her back cracking. He closed his eyes and pressed his lips tightly together.

Slowly, her arms reached up to his back. She patted him uncertainly, as if she lacked the strength for any more.

Suddenly, I glimpsed her as a young girl, dodging the uneven moods of this man who might have led a more contented life if he'd been born without the genius he possessed. I understood better now how difficult it must have been to live in the shadow of a man like Pankratov. He was built for always moving on, leaving no attachments to tear up his heart with regret. I wondered how many people he had left behind in his life. Even his own artwork, when he felt himself become attached to that, was fed to the flames rather than become a weakness.

The German and I glanced at each other awkwardly. He sidestepped the embracing couple and walked over to me with a confident stride. 'Thomas Dietrich,' he said.

'David Halifax,' I told him.

He jerked his head over towards Pankratov. 'His student?'

'That's right,' I replied.

'Ah,' he looked around again. 'Only you?'

'There were others, but they went away when the war started.'

'That's too bad,' he said. Then, having reached the limits of his patience for small talk, he changed the subject. 'I am with the East European Commission,' he said. 'Perhaps you have heard of us.'

I played dumb and told him no.

'It's just as well,' said Thomas Dietrich, 'because the Commission is now called the *Einsatzstab Reichsleiter Rosenberg*. It's all military now. In fact, it always was.' He tipped his head to the side and then back straight, as if fixing a crick in his neck. 'I have come to speak with Mr Pankratov. Alone, if you don't mind.'

Obediently, I went and fetched my coat.

Valya and Pankratov were talking softly, but they stopped as I walked past.

'Where are you going?' Pankratov asked me.

'They want to talk to you,' I said. 'I'll wait at the café.'

Pankratov looked at Valya. 'What's going on?' he asked.

'It's all right, Daddy,' she said, giving him a reassuring smile. 'It's just a thing in private.'

It was the first time I had heard her call him by anything other than his last name. I wondered if she was sincere, or if she was in fact the coldest-hearted thing in the world and was saying the one thing she knew he needed to hear and would do anything to hear again.

I clumped slowly down to the street, sidestepping the broken stair.

The soldiers were gone when I got to the Dimitri. They had left behind an ashtray full of cigarette butts, which the other customers were quickly grabbing up. On their table were the stacked plates to show how many drinks they'd had. Each drink came with a little dish, which had a green ring around it and the amount that the drink cost printed on the china. The glasses were taken away, but the dishes were left behind to accumulate for as long as the person stayed at the café. When they were ready to leave, the dishes were counted up to make the bill.

'Are they good customers, Ivan?' I asked, taking a seat at the bar and nodding at the stack of saucers the Germans had left behind.

Ivan puffed. 'They don't tip very well, but considering they could just as easily come in and take whatever they wanted, yes, they are good customers.' He nodded towards the atelier. 'I saw Valya,' he said.

'And the German,' I added.

'Him too.' Ivan mopped imaginary blemishes on the bar top. 'Is it bad?' he asked.

'I don't know,' I said.

'I hope Pankratov can keep his temper,' said Ivan. 'Usually he can't.'

Pankratov didn't appear for a couple of hours. I read all the papers at the Dimitri and drank too much Café National and switched to steamed milk to settle down my stomach. Just when I was starting to get worried, Pankratov walked into the café.

'You'd better come on,' he told me. 'They want to see you, too.'

As we climbed the stairs, Pankratov told me what he knew. 'This Rosenberg thing. It's an organization specifically designed for stealing art. They have a list of the paintings they want, but of course half the stuff has been hidden. Now they're scratching around trying to find people who know the locations.'

'And they think you know something?'

'Valya seems to have convinced this man Dietrich. She knows I had that part-time job at the Louvre. She doesn't know any more than that. I think she's just trying to impress him.'

'But why would she drag you into this?' I spat. 'Doesn't she understand what kind of trouble she could get you into?'

'She wouldn't do anything to hurt me,' he said quietly. 'She's impressed by what this man has to offer. It's all champagne and caviar. She has a certain blindness about who he really is.'

I stopped him there. 'If you believe that, then you're the one who's blind. You'd better see her for who she is, or it's going to cost us more than just our jobs.'

A look came over him that I had never seen before. He rolled his eyes around, as if he was about to faint. He pushed by me and kept walking up the stairs.

I realized, then, that she could make him do anything, and I knew Pankratov would rather die inside the maze of her lies than face the truth.

Dietrich and Valya were standing at the window, looking out over the city. They were holding hands and talking to each other in lowered voices. When Pankratov and I arrived at the door, they stopped holding hands and stepped apart.

'Why don't you and your father go outside for a while?' Dietrich asked her.

Valya and Pankratov stood out on the hallway.

Dietrich walked across the room and gently closed the door behind them. Then he turned to me and smiled.

'What can I do for you?' I asked.

'It's what we can do for each other,' he said. 'You and your friend Monsieur Fleury. Valya has told me all about him. You and he are just the kind of people we are looking for.'

I listened to him explain the plan for the art museum in Linz.

'One single European museum to house the best of European artists,' he said, 'as a symbol of a united Europe. To create in artistic terms a European community of the arts, instead of this scattering of museums holding on to whatever mish-mash of paintings they can scrape together.' He spoke fast and passionately. 'The property of French citizens will not be touched. All we ask is that, for safe-keeping, dealers and private collectors place their artwork under the protection of the French government. It will be put into storage at the château in Sourches. It will be more secure there than in their own homes.' As he made each point, he bent one finger back to count them off. 'What's happened is that people have panicked. They've stashed it away in half a million basements and barns all over the countryside. God knows how much of it is already damaged beyond repair.'

'You're not going to touch any of it?' I asked. 'I don't understand.'

'None that doesn't belong to us,' he said. 'We do intend to repatriate the German works of art that were looted from Germany by Napoleon during his campaigns against our country. They were stolen – simple as that. Not bought or borrowed.'

He began naming paintings. 'Breughel's *Hay Harvest*. Stolen by the French. Rembrandt's *Portrait of a Man*. Stolen by the French. Dürer's *Portrait of Erasmus*. Stolen. We are simply bringing them home. We have requested 1,800 paintings that rightfully belong to us. And do you know how many we have been able to find?' He didn't wait for my guess. 'Three hundred and fifty-nine!' He undid the top button of his shirt, as if it were choking him. 'We'll get them all in the end, of course. It's just going to be more work than I had thought.'

I imagined the paintings in their stone tomb at the Ardennes Abbey, the darkness and the stillness of the air. 'What's this got to do with me?' I asked.

'Nothing directly.' We were face to face now. Same height. Same colour hair.

'You are friends with Pankratov,' he said. 'Valya told me he worked at the Louvre. He must know where some of those works have been put. All I ask of you is that you' – he paused while he chose the right word – 'encourage him to remember. That's all.' He held out his hand for me to shake.

I didn't reach out, but he kept his own hand there, the smile plastered lopsidedly against his face. Eventually, I held out my hand.

He shook it. When I tried to let go, he kept his grip on me. 'I've been given this task,' said Dietrich. 'It is mine. Do you see?'

I stopped trying to wrench my hand away. I stood there, trading his stare for my own. I'd been waiting a long time for the war to reach me – not in rumours or things I read about or glimpsed in the distance. I had waited for some evidence that came to me alone, to tell me I was part of it now. And here it was. In this man's eyes I saw his vision of what the world would become, and all the horror it would take to make the vision real.

When I got home, I found Fleury sitting outside the door to my apartment. At his feet was a basket of food, some of which he had unpacked and was eating. He gnawed at a piece of sausage and held a bottle of champagne in his other hand. He rolled his head to face me, groggy with pleasure. 'Mr. Halifax,' he drawled. 'So good of you to come.'

'Explain this,' I said. I was in no mood to trade jokes with him. I was angry at Pankratov for his blindness about Valya, and angry at my own helplessness in front of Dietrich.

'We're going to a party,' said Fleury, his words sloppy from drink, 'and the people who invited us have also sent a gift.' He waved his hand crookedly over the basket, like an arthritic magician performing some kind of trick. 'All that you see here.'

I thought he was joking. He must have spent a fortune on some black-market deal. One glance at the contents of the basket – chocolate, cheese, two bottles of wine, another bottle of champagne – and I knew he had done something illegal to get them. It didn't surprise me that he'd got his hands on the stuff. The opportunity must have presented itself, I thought, and he was unable to resist the temptation. That was just part of Fleury's character, and there was no point getting angry about it. But I did mind him being drunk and useless, just when things were starting to get serious. I jammed the key into the lock and opened my door.

Fleury, who had been leaning against the door, fell with a tweed-muffled thump into my apartment. Champagne ran out of the bottle and over his hands, until he realized what was happening, then yelped and yanked the bottle upright, spilling even more.

I stepped over him and walked into the kitchen. I shucked off my jacket and hung it on the chair in the kitchen, the same as I always did. Then I turned on the tap and washed my face.

Fleury climbed to his feet and brought in the basket of food. He set it on the kitchen table. 'You really ought to partake,' he said.

'What did you do?' I asked. I turned off the tap and dried my face with a dish towel. 'What kind of deal did you work this time?'

'No deal at all,' he replied, raising his eyebrows. 'It was a gift, as I said.'

'All right,' I said, to play along. 'Who's it from?'

He rummaged in the basket and pulled out a card, which he then handed to me.

The card was from Dietrich. On one side were his name, Paris address and phone number, printed in blue ink. The other side had a handwritten note. '6 p.m. German embassy. Formal. Car will collect you.' I felt myself stop breathing for a moment.

'I don't even know who he is,' said Fleury.

'I do,' I told him. 'Christ, this man moves fast. I only met the guy an hour ago. I don't think we should be going to any German embassy party.'

'I thought we were supposed to collaborate,' he said, smugly. He handed me the champagne bottle. 'Look at this.'

Printed over the Veuve Clicquot label was a stamp in German and French. It read: 'Reserved for the German Armed Forces. Purchase or resale forbidden.'

The anger that was dammed inside my chest now flooded through my body. I held the bottle over the sink and flipped it upside down. The champagne poured away, hissing.

'Oh, for God's sake!' shouted Fleury.

I took the other bottle of champagne and wrenched off the little wire cage over the cork.

'Have you gone completely mad?' Fleury grabbed the bottle out of my hands and held it to his chest. If you want to prove a point, why don't you just start singing the "Marseillaise" in the middle of this embassy function tonight? That'll get their attention. But not this.' He held his hand out at my sink, where the last brassy bubbles of champagne were crackling on the white ceramic. 'Oh, why did you have to go and do that?'

I went downstairs and across the road to the payphone at the Dimitri. Shutting myself in the little box with the folding glass door, I put in a call to Pankratov.

It rang for a long time. Then there was a lot of scraping on the line and distant cursing. 'Hello? What? Hello?'

'It's me,' I said. I explained about the invitation at the embassy and the basket of food.

'Oh, yes,' said Pankratov. 'I got one, too, and an invitation to the party.'

'Are you sure that's the right thing?'

'I called Tombeau as soon as the invitation arrived. I told him about it. Tombeau said he wants me to stay out of the way, but you're to go see what they want, and then get in touch with Tombeau tomorrow to let him know what you've learned.'

I thought about Pankratov's short fuse, and it seemed to me that keeping him in the background might not be such a bad idea. 'Are you going to eat the food they sent?' I asked.

'Look, David,' said Pankratov, finally lowering his voice. 'I heard a story once about Alexander the Great. He was travelling through the desert with thousands of his men and they had no water and were dying of thirst. Then one of Alexander's men found one almost-dried-up puddle and scooped out a helmet full of water. He brought it to Alexander. Right there, in front of his troops, he lifted the helmet above his head and poured the water on to the sand. And they all loved him for it, because he wouldn't drink while his men were thirsty. But do you think he really had no water? Of course he did. He just didn't drink it in front of his men. So here's what I think. If we'd been given the food in front of a lot of hungry Parisians, then it would be smart to throw it away and make sure everybody saw us doing so. But if no one's there to see it, you haven't got much of a gesture to make, have you?'

After I hung up the phone, I went back up to see Fleury. He was still sitting at my kitchen table. He had the empty champagne bottle laid flat on the bare wood table and was rolling it back and forth under his palm. He stared at the bottle, as if hypnotized by it.

'Pankratov says you should go ahead and stuff your face,' I told him.

Slowly, Fleury raised his head. 'Did he really say that?'

I nodded.

'Well, that's more like it.' Fleury heaved out the other bottle of champagne and quickly had it open.

'Valya's back,' I said.

He had the bottle to his lips, but now he set it back down on the table, thumb over the mouth of the bottle to stop it from overflowing. 'Is she alone?' he asked.

'No,' I said. I told him about Dietrich.

Fleury looked around the room while I spoke, alternately blinking and squinting, as if he could see my words as they drifted by in the air. He picked Dietrich's card out of the basket and stared at it. Then he flipped it on to the table. When I had finished, Fleury sat there for a moment in silence. He pushed the champagne away from him, nudging the bottle with the tips of his fingers until it was as far away as he could get it. 'I seem to have lost my thirst,' he said. Then he stood up suddenly, the chair scooting back across the floor. 'Do you think it matters to her that the man is a *Nazi*? Is it *possible* she doesn't know?'

'She knows all right,' I said.

The car that came to meet us was a black Mercedes convertible, with front doors that opened from the left side and swoosh cowlings over the front wheels. It was immaculately polished. The driver wore a black uniform and a black cap. He showed no reaction to my grey flannel trousers and rumpled sports jacket or Fleury's tired-out tuxedo with its frayed lapel.

The German embassy was on the Rue de Lille. It was lit with floodlights and long, dark curtains were drawn across the windows. Two huge red banners hung down in front of the building. In the middle of the red was a white circle with a swastika inside. The car pulled up outside the building and the door was opened by an embassy staffer who wore a short blue tunic with brass buttons. People in tuxedos and evening gowns milled around the entrance.

We made jokes to shake off our nervousness.

'I insist that you walk three paces behind me and to the left,' Fleury told me. 'I can't have you spoiling my image.' He raised his eyebrows and peered at me, which made him look like an old barn owl.

'What image is that?' I asked him.

'The dashing image,' he explained. 'The raucous, devil-may-care exuberance that surrounds me like a golden halo and that ignites the passions of all who cross my path.'

The driver glanced at Fleury in the rear-view mirror.

Fleury noticed this. 'Oh, yes,' he told the man, 'I see you feel it, too.'

The driver's face remained without expression. He looked back at the road.

When we arrived, I gave our names to a man who stood at the door and showed us in. It was crowded and noisy. I heard laughter and the bee-hive hum of talk. A band played waltzes in a space between two huge staircases that curved around and joined on the second floor.

We were ushered over to a short, stocky, grey-haired man in his mid-fifties, who wore a tuxedo and a large red sash across his shoulder. He introduced himself as Otto Abetz. 'I am the ambassador,' he said, and gave a short bow.

We told him our names.

Abetz immediately turned his attention to Fleury. 'I understand you own a gallery. I've been looking for someone to serve as an appraiser for my decorations,' he said, lifting his champagne glass to indicate the walls, which were already hung with paintings.

I saw a Rembrandt whose title I knew was *Les Pèlerins d'Emmaus*. There was a self-portrait by Dürer. A portrait of a man in black clothes by Bellini, and a Caravaggio of Christ being whipped at a post. They were all in huge frames, each with elaborate plaster mouldings that had been covered in gold leaf.

'Perhaps you can stop by the embassy,' said Abetz.

'I'm sure I can.' Fleury smiled confidently. He was in his element now, and he could not be out-talked or out-charmed or out-stared if things got ugly.

There was nothing for me to do but stand back and watch him at work, because this was definitely not what I did best. Already I could feel sweat cooling as the drops inched down my side.

'Tomorrow would not be too soon,' Abetz told Fleury. He excused himself and walked over to another group of people, champagne glass locked in one hand and cigar smouldering in the other.

'That's what we came to do,' said Fleury. 'Now let's get the hell out of here.'

'I'm surprised to hear you talking about leaving a party when you've only just arrived,' I said.

'In this case,' Fleury told me, 'I'll make an exception.'

On our way out, I heard someone call my name.

It was Dietrich. He was sitting in a small room off to the side of the main door. It appeared to be some kind of library. The walls were made up of bookshelves, each inch of space jammed with volumes. The room was thick with smoke. Dietrich lounged in the middle of the room in a large red-leather chair, cradling a glass of cognac.

Sitting on the arm of Dietrich's chair was Valya. She wore a long black gown and a double band of pearls close at her throat. 'Ladies and gentlemen, the comedians have arrived!' she announced, when we walked into the room.

'Did you get that little present I sent over?' asked Dietrich.

'Yes, I did,' I replied.

'Tip of the iceberg!' he shouted. 'I can get you anything! We at the ERR . . .'

'I'm sorry,' I interrupted. 'What's the ERR?'

'Short for the Einsatzstab Reichsleiter Rosenberg. If we had to say our full name all the time, we'd be too tired to do anything except introduce ourselves.' He reached into his pocket and pulled out his cigarette case. 'Smoke?'

'Not for me, thanks,' I said.

'And you, perhaps, Mr Fleury?' He held the case out to Fleury.

He already knew who Fleury was, even though they had never met before.

I wondered how much else Dietrich knew.

'No, thank you,' replied Fleury, stiffly. He was studying Dietrich, appraising every facet of the man. Then he turned to Valya. He gave her a small, sad wave, like a tired man polishing a window. 'I've missed seeing you around,' he said.

Valya smiled at him, but it was a nameless kind of smile with no way to read what lay behind it. She seemed too caught up in being where she was, in the pleasure of it and the distance it put between herself and the shivering, naked woman I had seen when I first arrived in Paris.

Dietrich snapped the case closed and slid it back into his pocket.

Nobody else in the room seemed to notice us. They talked among themselves and filled their glasses from bottles ranged along the bookshelves.

'So, Mr Fleury, what do you think of our ambassador?' asked Dietrich.

'He serves very good champagne,' replied Fleury.

'He wants you to find him some paintings, doesn't he?'

'He didn't say that, exactly,' said Fleury.

'Oh, but that's what he wants. Trust me. If he hasn't asked you today, he will ask you tomorrow. Am I right? Did he schedule you in for tomorrow?'

'He did,' answered Fleury.

Dietrich stamped one foot and laughed. 'I knew it!'

'We ought to be going,' I said.

Dietrich slid his foot forward until the toe of his boot touched my shoe. 'Just remember,' he said. 'I got to you first.'

We decided to walk home, rather than take the car. There was a curfew, but we had been given a pass to show to any police who might stop us.

'People will see us as collaborators,' said Fleury. 'Going to embassy parties. That's why we left in such a hurry.'

'Once they found out what we were really doing,' I told him, 'that would change their minds.'

'What makes you think you'll have a chance to explain?' he asked. 'This man Tombeau, he is going to look after us, isn't he?'

'You can ask Tombeau yourself,' I replied. 'We're meeting him tomorrow.'

The way we got in touch with Tombeau was by calling a taxicab company called Moto Fabry and asking to be taken to 100 rue Voisin. There was no such address, but a cab would come along and Tombeau would be driving it.

I made the call and sat with Fleury at my kitchen table, which was the only table in my apartment. I tried to teach Fleury how to play poker. I was left with the feeling that once he'd learned it, if I were foolish enough to gamble with him, he would rob me blind.

Finally the buzzer rang. Tombeau announced himself with gruff impatience.

When Fleury and I reached the street, we were surprised to see that Tombeau's taxi was in fact only half a car, with the front seats and the engine taken out. In place of these parts of the car was a small motor scooter, which was attached to the rear by two welded metal pipes. Tombeau sat on the scooter, wildly revving its little engine. His shoes were wooden-soled, which had become a fashion of necessity now that leather was scarce.

'What is this *contraption*?' asked Fleury, his nose in the air.

Tombeau was in no mood to explain anything. 'Just get in!' he shouted over the shrill, pathetic buzzing of the engine. 'There's plenty of room.'

There was not plenty of room. Fleury and I clambered into the back, shoulders hunched to make space. The exhaust was hot and rude in our faces. We moved almost at a walking pace down the road. People stopped to watch us crawl past.

'It's sort of a motorized rickshaw,' said Fleury, trying to sound jolly, but at the same time arching his back with discomfort.

'I'll tell you what it is,' shouted Tombeau. 'It's what's left of my damned cab! I got in an accident last week and this was all they could salvage. Besides, gasoline has got too expensive. This is more economical.'

Tombeau wore a floppy cap. His big square head craned forward. One enormous fist gripped the wheel. The other yanked the gearstick around so viciously that I felt sorry for it. Tombeau was a hopeless driver, almost as bad as Pankratov, and swore almost as colourfully. His obscenities flowed together in one long incantation of rudeness. Tombeau explained that he had resigned from the French police before the Germans arrived, giving an excuse of ill health. Then he had gone to work for Moto Fabry. 'The Moto Fabry company,' he explained, 'is run by a group called Fabry-Georges. They're gangsters. They run gambling and protection rackets. Fabry-Georges have businesses all over Paris. Now that the Germans are here, they're hiring themselves out to do any dirty work the Germans don't want to do themselves.'

'So why are you doing working for them?' I asked.

'It's the safest place to be,' he shouted over the whine of the straining engine. 'Who's going to question which side I'm on now?'

Fleury asked him to explain why Dietrich and Abetz seemed to be in competition with each other for paintings.

'Dietrich works for the ERR,' said Tombeau. 'That's a completely different organization from the embassy. The ERR have already taken over the Jeu de Paumes and are stockpiling paintings there.'

I asked Tombeau where these paintings were coming from, since Dietrich had told me the Germans had promised not to raid the property of French citizens.

'It's from Jewish collections and galleries. The Rothschilds. The Wildensteins. The Jews have been designated "enemies of the German state", and anything they own is considered stolen property. They've already raided the Jacques-Seligmann gallery on the Place Vendôme.

'The ERR comes under the protection of Hermann Göring himself,' continued Tombeau. 'So far, he's made two trips to the Jeu de Paumes and has bought over sixty works of art – sketches, paintings, statues, furniture – whatever he wants.'

'Why is he bothering to buy them? Why doesn't he just take them?' I asked.

'Göring might as well be stealing them,' replied Tombeau. 'He brings in his own appraisers to the Jeu de Paumes. They undervalue whatever painting he wants. Then he knocks the price down even further. No one lifts a finger to stop Göring and Abetz wants the same kind of deal. That's why he wants you to work for him instead of Dietrich.'

'Which one should we choose?' asked Fleury.

'Choose neither,' ordered Tombeau. 'Just get them both to trade you as many paintings as you can before they get shipped off to Germany and we never see them again.'

'How long do you expect this to last?' I asked him.

He glanced at me with his big, deep-set eyes and then snapped his head back to the road. 'It depends on how good you are. A lot of German buyers are getting the artwork back to Germany as quickly as they can and stashing it away in warehouses. They don't have time to examine the pieces as thoroughly as they should.' Now we were going in circles round the Place de la République. 'Nevertheless, I hope you're as good as Pankratov says you are.'

'I'm more worried about your driving than his painting,' said Fleury.

Tombeau laughed through his clenched teeth with an intermittent hissing sound, like air being squeezed out of a ball.

We hurtled through the intersection of the Rue des Pyrénées and the Avenue Gambetta. The traffic was being directed by a caped gendarme with long white gauntlets on his hands. The gendarme stared bug-eyed as Tombeau's taxi passed by only a few inches from him. The policeman's cape wafted up in his face and by the time he had pulled it down, we were already far away. His white-gloved hands waved madly as he cursed us.

Tombeau stopped the cab at the beginning of the Rue de Lille, about ten houses down from the German embassy. The red banners hung limp in the still morning air.

It was time for our meeting with Abetz.

Tombeau turned to face us. His forehead was pebbled with sweat. 'Now go kiss some arses for the glory of France.'

An embassy staffer directed us around to a door at the side of the building.

The only signs that there had been a party the night before were black smudges on the sidewalk, where cigarettes had been stamped out.

We had our names checked at a desk by a pretty but stern-faced woman whose hair was knotted in what looked to be a painfully tight bun at the back of her head. The hammering clatter of typewriters filled the little rooms that we passed by. We were shown downstairs to a basement office, and told to wait.

Fleury sat down and closed his eyes with a cat-like smile. He didn't seem the least bit nervous.

I wanted to ask how he managed to stay so calm.

Only a few seconds had gone by when a man in military uniform stepped into the room. He looked younger than I was and had several medals on his chest. I noticed the motto on his belt buckle: GOTT MIT UNS. He sat behind the desk and drummed his fingers on the pale-green blotter as if giving himself some imaginary fanfare of introduction. 'I am Leutnant Behr,' he said. 'I am a military attaché with the embassy. I'm responsible for purchasing works of art for Ambassador Abetz.'

'What's the army got to do with art?' Fleury talked to the young man like a schoolmaster speaking to a boy who couldn't remember his lessons.

From the glazing of the soldier's eyes, it was clear that Fleury had already struck a nerve.

I found myself staring at the small eagle and swastika done in silver thread that was stitched above his right chest pocket. With each breath, it seemed to spread its wings and let them fall again.

'Before the war,' said Behr, 'I was apprenticed to Mr Hasso Dietz of the Dietz Art Gallery in Berlin.'

'The Dietz Gallery' – Fleury drawled out the word – 'oh, yes.'

'I joined the army but after the fighting in Poland they sent me here.'

'Lucky you,' said Fleury.

'Luck nothing,' replied Behr. 'That stint at the gallery was just something my uncle found for me as a summer job. I didn't give a damn about art before I started at the gallery and when I was finished, I gave even less of a damn. I signed up to fight. Not to sit here and do nothing. I'm getting out of here as soon as I can.'

'Where is the ambassador?' asked Fleury.

'The ambassador is busy,' said Behr, straightening his back. 'I will be acting as the ambassador's representative in all future dealings with you. Now' – he spun in his chair to face the noticeboard, ripped a document off the cork with one sharp motion and then spun to face us again, leaving one white triangle of paper still tacked to the board – 'here is what I would like from you.'

'Tell you what,' said Fleury. 'Let me tell you what I can do for the ambassador. That will save us all some time.'

Behr glared at Fleury for a moment. Then slowly he eased his chair away from the desk. He tilted it back on two legs, until he was resting against the wall. He flipped the document on to the blotter. Then he folded his arms across his stomach. 'Fine,' he said.

'You're looking for works by artists such as Rembrandt, Vermeer, Correggio, Hals, Titian, Dürer, Breughel. Is that right?'

'Yes, yes,' droned the young man, 'and Velázquez, Holbein, Cranach and Van Dyck. All of them.'

'And,' continued Fleury, 'you have no interest in artists such as Dufy, Sisley, Corot and the like.'

'I wouldn't even say their names out loud in here if I were you.'

'Very good,' said Fleury. 'But you have a stock of paintings by these artists. Confiscated from the Rosenberg Gallery, the Wildenstein Gallery, the Bernheim-Jeune Gallery. Am I right?'

Behr raised his chin almost imperceptibly. 'You might be.'

'For exchange perhaps.' Fleury picked Behr's pen off the desk. He turned it around in his hand.

'Possibly.' Behr watched his pen, as if he were being hypnotized.

'I'll get you the paintings you're after,' said Fleury. 'This gentleman here is my' – he paused – 'my field agent. Yes.' He liked this title he had given me and he said it again, as if to make it official. 'Field agent. His particular skills are useful in this difficult time.'

'I don't need to know where they come from,' said Behr.

'Naturally.'

'Everything will be paid for,' said Behr. 'We will open an account in your name and will make deposits in Reichsmarks. It's all here.' He tipped forward and tapped his index finger on the document. 'It will all be typed up once you have agreed.'

'Ah,' said Fleury. It was a slow and cautious word that he breathed out, to show there would be no agreement yet.

Behr looked up. 'Ah what?'

'Payments will be in gold bullion,' Fleury told him, 'or I'll take other paintings in trade.'

'I'm not authorized to give you bullion!' snapped Behr. He had gone red in the face. He picked at the Iron Cross that was pinned to his chest pocket, as if the pin had gone through to his flesh. 'Who do you think you are?'

'I'm someone who can get you a painting by Cranach. I can have it by this time next week.'

'Cranach.' Behr repeated the name quietly. Three creases crumpled the skin of his forehead. 'Lucas Cranach?'

Fleury nodded.

Behr swiped a thumb across his chin. 'Well, I'll see what I can do.'

'Why don't you see about it now?' Fleury smiled at him patiently.

Behr's shoulders slumped momentarily, as he gave up being in charge. The name of Cranach had worked on him like the trigger of some long-ago hypnosis. He left the room without a word.

I stared at Fleury in amazement, as he reached across to a wooden box on Behr's desk. He opened it and held it out to me. 'Would you like one of this little man's cigarettes?'

I declined, so Fleury lit up on his own. He puffed contentedly until Behr returned.

'All right,' said Behr. He stopped and smelled the smoke. Then he seemed to dismiss the idea that anyone could possibly have swiped one of his cigarettes. 'As long as you agree to exchanges of paintings in preference to bullion.'

'Done,' said Fleury, 'as long as you have paintings to trade.'

'Don't you worry about that.' Behr leaned across the desk. He wanted to have the last word. 'You'd better have that Cranach and it had better be the sweetest thing I've ever seen or I'll kick your pompous arse all over this city. I told you I didn't want this job and people like you are the reason why. This isn't the kind of war I should be fighting.'

Fleury's lips had gone a little crooked, as if he were trying to stop himself from laughing. 'You'll put up with me, Mr Behr,' he said, 'because I'll make your bosses happy. And they'll make you happy. Promote you out of this mausoleum of an office. Get you back to killing people, or whatever it is that you were born to do.'

'That poor little man,' said Fleury, as we made our way down the Rue de Lille. 'He'll work as hard as he can now, in the hopes that they'll reward him with a transfer back into *action*.' He said the word sarcastically. 'The trouble is that the better he does, the less likely they are to let him go. I wonder if he'll ever figure that out.'

I walked beside him in a reverential silence.

'That gold bullion bit was a nice touch,' I told him.

'It was no touch at all,' said Fleury. 'All those Reichsmarks aren't going to be worth anything if these Germans lose the war.'

'I take it you plan on getting rich,' I said, trying not to sound disgusted.

Fleury stopped and spun on his heel. He eyed me with curious amusement. 'If my own country is going to turn me into a collaborator, I intend at least to profit from the experience. Besides, they need me. *You* couldn't have done what I did in there. There's a secret to dealing in art that none of you artists ever seem to figure out. It always amazes me how you manage to get anything done without people like me to look after you. What's true or false or valuable or worthless all comes down to this' – and he pointed one finger directly at his eye – 'whether I blink before you do.'

'Where do you have that Cranach stashed away?' I asked.

'I don't have it,' he said, matter-of-factly. 'You're going to make one. You've been studying Cranach, haven't you?'

It was true. 'But in a week?' I asked. 'It can't be done so quickly! It will have to be done on wood if it's Cranach.'

'It ought to be,' he confirmed.

'Even if Pankratov has the right materials, the paint won't even be dry in a week. It will take a couple of weeks at least, and that's only if he force-dries it.'

'I know,' said Fleury.

'So why did you promise it to Behr in a week?' I demanded.

'To make him anxious,' said Fleury calmly.

'He's not the only one you're making anxious,' I told him.

Fleury smiled. 'Remember not to blink, Monsieur Halifax.'

12

Pankratov turned on the light in his warehouse. The silvery bulb filled each crack of rotten brick with shadow.

I sat down in Fleury's chair with its ripped stuffing and immediately pulled the old horse-blanket around me. 'Can't we get a fire going in here?' I asked.

Pankratov had brought along extra lights. He bolted them to spare easels, and directed them towards the middle of the room. Then from his satchel he pulled a heavy book in a black binding and handed it to me.

It was a collection of the works of Cranach. The illustrations were postcards fitted into gaps in the text, just like the ones Fleury had been collecting. Pankratov had marked a page that showed a portrait of a young girl, maybe eight years old, with fine blonde hair that trailed down to her waist. She was dressed in black. The background was black, too. She wore a white shirt with a tiny collar, which was tied with a thin black ribbon. Her hands, which lay in her lap, were chubby, like baby hands, and her nails were clearly outlined, which made them look at first a little dirty. She looked bored in the picture, with big child's eyes and a pointy chin and ears too big to be flattering. Her shoulders were slumped, which made her look spoiled, as if she didn't give a damn about being painted.

I used to wonder if the space of a couple of centuries really did produce people who looked different or whether it was just the clothing and the hairstyles that made them seem so out of place. There was no way you would not have noticed this girl if she walked by in the street. You could have dressed her up in some Catholic schoolgirl's outfit and given her a satchel and stuck a chocolate bar in her hand, and made her like ten thousand other Parisian schoolgirls on their way home after classes, but you would still have noticed the proportions of her face, the roundness of it, the paleness. You'd have thought she didn't eat well, that she didn't breathe enough fresh air. She looked like a child who didn't get enough affection. She looked as if she knew it, too.

When I looked at the text, which was only a couple of lines, I saw it was a portrait of Magdalena Luther, the daughter of Martin Luther. She had lived from 1529 to 1542. Only thirteen years. I looked at the picture again. I changed my mind about her looking spoiled. Instead, with that resigned expression on her face, she seemed to know how short her time would be. Too short to sit still and be painted. I wondered if Cranach himself might have had some inkling of her fast-approaching death, which was perhaps why he had used so much black. I thought of other portraits I'd seen, in which people had around them the trappings of their life, the things they were proud of and by which they claimed their rank in a society – fancy clothes, jewellery, hunting dogs and castles in the background. This girl had nothing, which could be some show of Lutheran purity, but it seemed to me more likely that this little girl just hadn't been around long enough to know her place was in the world, and what she valued and how she wanted to be seen.

I thought about Martin Luther and his wife. They would have known about their daughter's frailty. It must have torn them up inside. Maybe they had commissioned the painting because they knew it might soon be all they had to remember her by.

My mind always made up stories around the silence of a picture, like a ghostly second frame. I closed the book with a dusty thump, sending her back into darkness. I breathed and looked up at Pankratov. 'Why a portrait?' I asked.

'You'll see,' he said.

I stood and rubbed my hands together to drive out the chill. 'Let's get going,' I said.

Pankratov laughed. 'Not so fast. We're not copying that painting.'

'Which one are we doing then?' I was filled with nervous energy and wanted to begin.

'We're doing the portrait of Magdalena that Martin Luther himself rejected because it made her look too frivolous for the daughter of a religious man.'

I picked up the book, opened it again and started flipping through the pages. 'Well, where is it?'

'It doesn't exist yet,' he told me.

'Oh,' I said slowly, and closed the book.

Over the next few hours, we leafed through the pictures, choosing other paintings by Cranach and selecting from them certain articles of background: a tree just coming into bloom, a pale-blue sky with long, thin clouds that were flattened out at the bottom and puffy on top; a double-banded pearl necklace held close to the throat.

Pankratov went to find us some lunch. He flung open the door. The sunlight was so bright that he recoiled from it as if the whole world outside were in flames. He staggered out into the glare and closed the door.

Now that I was alone, I noticed the sound of water dripping somewhere, and the rustle of wind down the alleyway. The cold that slithered through my skin became like something alive, as if the warehouse contained memories of all the living things that had passed through it. My presence here had brought them back to life in some half-formed way, which I sensed in the dead-clamminess around me. I was glad when Pankratov returned. The ghouls slipped away on their black and wide-toed feet into the shadows where they lived.

Pankratov found me studying the postcards with a magnifying glass. 'These aren't good enough to let me gauge the texture,' I said.

'Wait ten minutes,' he said. He set down two baguettes, which he had tucked under his arm like rolled up newspapers. Then from one pocket he pulled a wedge of cheese wrapped in white greaseproof paper and from the other a bottle of hard cider with a home-made label made from cheesecloth glued to the glass and the word 'CIDRE' written on it in pencil. 'This is all they had at the shop down the road,' he said. He held the bottle up to one of the electric lights. 'I hope we don't go blind drinking it.'

'What's going to happen in ten minutes?' I asked.

Pankratov didn't have a chance to reply.

A black car with chrome fenders pulled up outside the open warehouse door. It was driven by a chauffeur with a grey cap. A woman sat in the back.

'Here she is,' said Pankratov. He walked out into the light.

The woman opened her car door. It was Emilia Pontier. She stepped out, tall and willowy.

'Madame Pontier,' said Pankratov.

'I've got what you asked for,' she said. Then she turned to me. 'Mr Halifax.'

'Hello,' I said quietly.

Pankratov and the chauffeur were fetching something out of the trunk. They seemed to know each other and there was the softness of laughter in the quiet words that passed between them.

'I'll be back in two days to collect what I've lent you. You won't see it again, so spend your time well.' She looked up and down the row of warehouse doors, at the crumbled brick up on the train tracks and at the gravel of the road beneath her feet. She shook her head, then got back in the car.

Pankratov and I watched the limousine pull away down the alley, dust already settling. When the car was gone, Pankratov turned to me. 'I once heard it said about Emilia Pontier that she has no respect for people, only for their history.'

It was only now that I noticed the painting in Pankratov's arms. It was wrapped in white sheeting and bound with hemp string. 'Is that what I think it is?' I asked.

Back inside the warehouse, Pankratov removed the covering. It was the original painting of Magdalena Luther. The piece was small, a foot by a foot and a half. It was done on a wood panel that had traces of worm holes on the back. The panel was bevelled like a mirror. Pankratov set up the easel. The strong lights encased it in a marmalade glow.

'Where have they been hiding it?' I asked.

Pankratov shrugged, chewing nervously on a thumbnail. 'Could have been in a bank vault. It could have been halfway across the country in a wine cellar. I don't know. But we have it for two days. Let's just hope that's long enough.'

We began by studying the back of the painting. We tried to match the type of wood with something from Pankratov's collection of wood panels. After rooting around for a few minutes, Pankratov did find a painted oak slab. It was slightly larger than the Cranach. There were two marks on the back of Pankratov's panel. One was an oval with a crown on the top and a J in the middle. The other was a lion's head with a zig-zag line underneath. These were the stamps of private collectors, to show that they had owned the works. Pankratov looked them up in a book. The lion was the mark of an eighteenth-century collector named Antonio Leonid, who lived in Milan around 1790. Pankratov said we should leave the stamps there, at least until Fleury told us to get rid of them.

The painting on the front was of two young girls, both in matching white dresses. They were holding hands and looked vaguely lost, as if they had stayed still for the artist because they were afraid to move. Fear showed in the blankness on their faces and in the worried pouting of their lips. The background was a curtain and a chair, drab and green. It looked like the kind some artists used to paint in advance, adding their subjects later in order to speed up the process. The girls didn't seem to belong with the rest of the painting. There was no equation between the shadows of the draping curtain and the presence of the two sad girls, whose lives had been and gone before the lives of my great-great-grandparents had even begun.

Painted in a scroll fashion across the top were the Latin words: *Sanctum in Memoriam*.

'Sacred to the memory,' I translated.

'Whoever kept those women as a sacred memory,' said Pankratov, 'has long since been reunited with them.' He poured some acetone into a small white dish.

I felt vaguely wretched as their faces smeared and vanished with the dabs of turpentine. At last the bony whiteness of the undercoat glimmered through. It left us with a blank space on which we could begin our work.

Pankratov scanned the Cranach with a magnifying glass. He stood still in front of it for a long time, as if Magdalena Luther were in fact alive beneath the minute spider's web of cracks across the paint and it was only a question of waiting to see when she would flinch. 'Here,' he said, waving me over. 'Look.'

We brought our faces close to the painting. Our breath clouded the paint and disappeared and clouded up again. This was the kind of closeness that would have had a museum guard running across a gallery and shouting at us to get back.

'You see how it's built up?' he asked. 'Here. Around her face. Around her neck. And here, the way her hands are resting' – he waved the magnifying glass over the chair and oval mirror in the background. Their images loomed up large and shrank back down again when the magnifying glass had moved on. 'With the rest of it, he was confident. But here he kept shifting her around.'

I looked at the girl's face and tried to read Cranach's frustration in the soft, pale angles of her cheekbones.

'We will do a version,' said Pankratov, turning the magnifying glass slowly by its handle, like the crystal of a miniature lighthouse. 'It will be good, but not so good that someone could not understand why Luther might have wanted something different. Do you see?'

'Yes,' I said.

'Good. Now paint.'

And suddenly, set free from the seemingly endless training, I knew I could do it. The complexity was all there in my head, too much to grasp in any single thought, but all there, bunched up and tangled; and the only way to untangle it was simply to work and not think about working, but just work.

As I began, Pankratov settled into his sacred chair. He touched his fingertips together.

When I glanced at him a moment later, he seemed to have gone into a trance.

I worked through the night, not feeling fatigue. As I blinked sweat from my eyes, the image of the girl would shimmer and dissolve. My hips hurt from standing and I rocked on the balls of my feet to keep the blood flowing. At one point I looked over at the fire and saw that it had died down. Pankratov was asleep, curled in a blanket with his coat folded up as a pillow. I left the canvas and walked over to him. I squatted down in front of the fire, reaching my hands out to the embers and feeling the heat work its way into my bones. Then I took a few more lumps of coal from the pile and stoked up the fire again. Thick clots of smoke gave way to the salt-burn blue of flames.

Cranach had painted the face with several different brushes in a very small area. I kept three brushes in my hand at the same time, each one locked between my fingers.

I made her face pale but had added a little colour, the faintest glimmer of warm blood deep beneath the wintry opaqueness of skin. I kept in her expression the tiredness of a child not wanting to sit still in one place for a long time. I kept the same angle of her head and hands and the thin reediness of her hair. I made it clear that she was still a sickly child.

Using details from other Cranach paintings, I gave her a medium-blue dress and painted her outside under a cold but cheerful sky, like a day at the end of the winter when the spring is coming but not yet there, and the fields are still muddy and the country lanes still pocked with brown-water puddles. I painted the bony branches of a tree reaching into the frame and I put those same flattened clouds in the sky.

I liked painting on the wood. The solidity of it. The way it did not give, as canvas did, against the pressure of the brush.

Over the course of the next few hours I redid her hands a little to be less spidery. I gave her a plain silver ring. I was careful to paint over the work I changed, to build up the layers of paint as Cranach had done in the original.

Pankratov woke up around six. He looked around as if he had no idea where he was. Then the daze of sleep left his eyes. 'How is it?' he croaked at me.

'Come and see,' I told him.

He shuffled in front of the painting and I stepped aside to let him look.

After a moment of silence, Pankratov started laughing very quietly. 'That old sourpuss Martin Luther saw this and gave Cranach some line about how it was undignified, but the truth was he didn't want people thinking he or anybody close to him had any thoughts on their minds but the heavy piousness of hard-core preachers like himself. I see it. I see Luther as a stingy old man. Stingy about pleasure even in the simple things.'

'That might not be the truth,' I said. 'That might be a long way from it.'

'Doesn't matter,' Pankratov stated flatly. 'What matters is that there is a story going on between these two pictures that makes sense.'

'Will it work?' I asked nervously.

'By the time I've done my part,' replied Pankratov, 'it certainly will.'

Only then did I feel tired. And suddenly I was exhausted. I walked over to the fire, spread out a blanket, lay down on it and fell asleep.

'Go away,' said Pankratov. He stood in the arched doorway of the workshop. Spiky grey stubble fanned across his unshaven face, as if he were part-porcupine.

I stood in the alley. 'You ought to come outside for a bit and stop breathing those fumes.'

'I like them,' said Pankratov.

'I could pretend to be surprised,' I replied, 'but I won't.'

'Tell Fleury he can have it in a week.' He closed the door behind him.

Rain fell softly on the city as I made my way to the Gallery Fleury, darkening the sidewalks and making the rooftops glimmmer like polished nickel. The Rue des Archives was filled with people carrying umbrellas.

I climbed a narrow, iron-banistered staircase to Fleury's office on the fourth floor. Along the way, I looked into his show spaces. They were lit by large skylights and had leather couches set back to back in the middle of the open, airy rooms. Oriental rugs padded the floors.The walls were a dull beige brown. Fleury had told me that this was to highlight the paintings, of which there were many. At first glance, the arrangement seemed haphazard: a painting of the Rialto Bridge alongside a pen-and-ink drawing of the rooftops at Arles. Fleury had explained that he didn't like to group works by era, school or subject. Instead, he found some subtle theme that linked the pieces. This theme might not be immediately apparent, but the buyer would sense a certain harmony. Fleury said that the best buyers bought on instinct, rather than by following the latest market trends. It was the dealer's job to draw out these unexplained but positive feelings for a work, which often had as much to do with the painting's surroundings as with the painting itself. To the untrained eye, Fleury's gallery embraced a kind of chaos. But Fleury left nothing to chance. Calculations lay behind every gesture he made and every detail of his business. Even his location on the Rue des Archives, away from the main drag of galleries on the Avenue Matignon, showed that he considered himself apart from other Parisian dealers, and did not need a choice location in order to draw in his clients.

Fleury's tiny office was crammed with loose documents. The walls were scaled with receipts held up by small steel pins. Most of these bore his elaborate many-looped signature.

The only window looked out over a series of grey-slated rooftops. The window was open and rain slipped in molten bars from the edge. Fleury's coat was hanging from a peg and his hat was on top, making it seem as if there were another person in the room.

'It's going perfectly,' said Fleury. 'Behr has called several times. He's a sweet boy, really. Anxious to please his masters. But he has absolutely no business sense. Every time he calls' – Fleury jerked his thumb at the ceiling – 'the price goes up.'

'How long can you hold him off?' I asked.

'How long do you need?' replied Fleury, thin eyebrows rib-boning his forehead with the question.

'Pankratov needs another week,' I told him.

'A week,' said Fleury, 'but no longer.'

That night I heard car brakes squeak to a stop down the street. Before the war a sound like that would never have woken me, even if it was three in the morning. But now, with the curfew, the sound of any vehicle at night was rare, especially on the Rue Descalzi.

I opened my eyes and just lay there, breathing very lightly, waiting to see what happened next. I wasn't afraid. If the car had stopped outside my building, I might have thought a little more about it. I assumed it belonged to someone who was working for the Germans and had permission to be out after curfew.

I heard two doors clunk shut and then nothing for a while. I was almost falling back asleep when I heard a window being dragged open and the sound of men shouting. I heard a dog bark and then another sound. It was exactly the same as if I had taken a head of cabbage and thrown it down hard on the ground. After that came the noise of running, of men speaking harshly in German, the doors of the car closing and the rising, clunking rumble of a car moving swiftly through its gears as it sped away.

I went to the window, which was open. Up and down the street, windows were being raised, French doors swung quietly open. I saw people standing on their little balconies, like ghosts in their pale nightshirts. Urgent whispers passed between them

There was nothing in the street, and nobody left their buildings to investigate.

One after the other, people vanished back inside their apartments, drawing the curtains, closing the windows again.

The next morning, as I stepped into the street on my way to the Metro stop, I saw a crowd of people gathered outside the apartment building where the car had pulled up. It was Madame Côty's place. As curious as everybody else, I made my way over. I saw a large spray of blood on the cobblestones.

Madame LaRoche was there. She already had the whole story from her friend Madame Côty. 'It was a man, Lebel. He ran the . . .'

'Cabaret,' I said. He was the one who had bought my sketches off Fleury. It shocked me to think that I had met the man who had died.

'Yes, the Metropole Cabaret,' said Madame LaRoche. 'You know, my friend Madame Côty was once a dancer there. In the old days. The *very* old days. It was very nice. Very racy. At least it was. Last month, the Germans decided to shut it down. They said it was too shocking. The costumes. The music. The whole thing. I don't know. But the next week, they turned the place into a rest-home for German soldiers. That was the real reason. Everybody knows. They just wanted the building and wanted an excuse to get him out of there. As if they even needed one. They take whatever they want, these people. But Lebel must not have known that. He was making trouble. Protesting. Demanding to be paid. He should have shut up and then he might still have been alive. But he was very full of himself, this man Lebel. He thought he was an expert on everything. But he wasn't an expert on knowing what the Germans would do because they came for him last night. They always come in the dark. Once they show up at your door, it doesn't matter what you have done or not done. You might as well just shoot yourself. Except Lebel didn't have a gun. So he jumped out of the window. Head first. And took his dog with him.'

We were outside our building now. Madame LaRoche was still talking. I had a feeling she would have gone on all day if I hadn't excused myself and dashed to catch the Metro. I had to run back up the street, past the crowd, which had thinned out. Madame Côty was down on her hands and knees, scrubbing the blood from the cobblestones. She had on a pair of black rubber boots and a brown kerchief tied around her hair. She dipped the brush in a tin bucket of soapy water and scratched away the blackened mess. The suds turned pink. Rosy bubbles rested on the cobblestones, refracting the gleam of the sun, then vanished and joined the silky froth as it made its way down to the gutter. Madame Côty's face was grim with the effort of scrubbing. She looked more resentful than appalled, as if she had done this before and was cursing her bad luck that this had all happened on her doorstep, so she had to be the one to clean it up.

A week later, a sign appeared on the front door of Madame Côty's building, advertising an apartment for rent. It was snatched up straight away and the sign was taken down.

There had been no public outcry against Lebel's death – not even much said in private. Instead, there seemed to be a kind of quiet resignation. The rules of the old days were gone. The new rules were clear enough, as were the penalties for making trouble.

Seeing that blood on the pavement brought about a change in me. Now I was afraid all the time. I had been fending it off, with sarcasm and indignation and the quiet simmering of anger meshed like barbed wire entanglements inside my brain. The sight of the blood washed them away. From then on, there was never a moment when I felt safe. I learned to live with the fear, the way a person might learn to live with the pain of an illness. My body and my mind became a kind of house in which the fear had taken residence. Fear became like a white noise, a rushing static that filled my ears so constantly that it even began to feel normal. It stopped me from thinking about the future. From then on I did my best to live purely in the present, taking pleasure in the smallest things to stop this fear from driving me mad.

It was early Sunday morning.

Pankratov arrived at my apartment. 'What are all these rabbits doing in the hallway?' he asked, nudging one away with his toe after it had begun to nibble on his bootlaces.

'They belong to the landlady,' I explained.

'They'd make good sandwiches,' he said.

I waited for him to explain why he had come.

'Get dressed,' ordered Pankratov. 'We're going to church.'

I was too tired to ask why, and knew how little good it would do for me to argue. I hauled on my one set of good clothes and walked with Pankratov to the 7 a.m. service at Notre Dame. Pankratov waited until we all knelt to pray, then took out a small penknife and began inspecting the pew. From the underside of the bench, he scraped the grime and waxy residue of wood-polish into his palm. Carefully he emptied it into his pocket.

'What are you *doing*?' I whispered.

An old lady was watching us. She frowned and looked away.

'Dust,' he explained.

Then he set to work raking the blade of the penknife across the kneeling cushion until he had another palmful of grey. He kept at this through most of the service, kneeling long after the rest of us had gone back to sitting. 'Right,' he said. 'Let's go.'

'You can't leave now,' I hissed. 'We're in the middle of the service!'

Pankratov looked around, frowning with annoyance.

The old lady glared at him, her twig-bony hands folded in prayer.

Pankratov heaved himself on to the bench and sat back with a noisy sigh.

Afterwards we filed out into the quiet streets. Eventually, we came to the corner of the Rue du Rambuteau and Rue du Temple. A large pillar had been set up, with thick white arrows pointing off in different directions. They were coded with the locations of German headquarters and with long words like: HEERESBEKLEIDUNGSLAGER-PARIS, FRONTTEILSTELLE, FELDGENDARMERIEKASERNE and STAATLICHE-KRIMINALPOLIZEIBEAMTE.

'What now?' I asked.

'Now,' said Pankratov, 'you are going to learn something.'

We took the Metro out to Gambetta, the stop nearest his warehouse, and walked the rest of the way. As we strolled down the alleyway, several of the warehouse doors were open. The weekends were the only time we ever ran into people out here. Inside the warehouses were cars that had been set up on blocks for the duration of the war. The owners were tinkering with engines or polishing chrome with large chamois rags. Others had workshops as ramshackle as Pankratov's. One space seemed to be entirely filled with electric fans, and a man in blue overalls was taking them apart one by one. Pankratov nodded hello and waved and smiled, like a county squire greeting his tenants.

'It's not finished yet,' Pankratov explained as he unlocked his warehouse door. 'You mustn't expect too much.' He didn't turn on the lights until he had the door closed behind him. For a second, we stood in the darkness, blind, smelling the damp.

When the bulbs popped on, I saw our Cranach held in a glow as if suspended by the light. I barely recognized it. The original brightness of its colours had been replaced by a dark, yellowy light, which seemed to come from deep beneath the surface of the paint. The young girl had receded into the shadows of centuries that Pankratov had laid across the wood.

'How did you do it?' I asked, walking closer.

'With this,' he explained. He held out a white dish in which lay a greyish sludge. 'This is time,' he said. 'This is the essence of it.'

'What's it made of?' I asked.

Pankratov shrugged. 'It varies, depending on where you want the work to come from. This piece, I decided, might have been in a church for a while, maybe later in a dining room. So I used some wood ash and a few grains of incense. I cooked some bacon fat and while it was burning, I held a silver spoon in the smoke until it was blackened and used it to stir the mix. I thought it needed more dust. That's why we went to Notre Dame.'

'But couldn't you get dust from anywhere?'

'I could have, but you never know how it will come out. What you want,' he explained, 'is for whoever is buying it to have held in his or her hands a piece that has hung in a church, and for them to have committed to memory, perhaps even without knowing it, the smell and the exact way in which the dust has settled on the painting. Then, when they look at this, they'll get the same feeling. It's just a sensation that everything is right. It happens in the first few seconds of holding the work, or it doesn't happen at all. Then a different process begins. Suspicions take over. Some people, if they decide they really want the piece, can persuade themselves to overlook their instincts. But others, the real professionals, will put it down and walk away, no matter how badly they want it, if their instincts warn them at all.'

There was that word again: instinct. I was beginning to see that Pankratov and Fleury's work had the same task, to put the buyers at ease without letting them know exactly why.

Pankratov spread a clean handkerchief on his worktable and emptied out the dust from Notre Dame. He lifted some of the grey flecks with the tip of his knife and carefully worked them into cracks on the side of the painting. When the crack was filled, he tipped his little finger into the grey sludge and dabbed it over the crack, sealing in the dust.

'I can't wait to show this to Fleury,' I said.

Pankratov picked up the painting and held it out at arm's length, studying his work. 'Tomorrow we'll give it to Fleury. Then he can sell it to Abetz.'

'I'd buy it myself if I didn't know any better. It's perfect.'

'There's no such thing as perfect,' said Pankratov. 'The best it can be is persuasive.' Whenever someone paid Pankratov a compliment, he would find some way to deflect it.

I sighed and looked around. 'Who'd have guessed we'd end up doing this?'

'The mission always changes,' said Pankratov.

'And what does that mean?' I asked.

Pankratov made no reply. He was lost someplace inside his head, long in the past, out on the frozen lake, in the darkness of the Arctic winter night.

13

I wrapped the painting in brown paper and brought it to Fleury's gallery. He had told me to come by at four o'clock, and kept me waiting while he closed the doors downstairs. I unwrapped the Cranach and placed it on an easel. I sat down to wait on Fleury's leather couch. It felt cold and rubbery. My earlier confidence had begun to fail me in the formality of these surroundings. My lips and my knuckles dried out with worry. I jerked the knot of my tie back and forth. Then I got up and covered the painting with a brown cloth that I'd found slung over the easel. I was too nervous to look at it.

I heard him climb the stairs, slow and light-footed. His steps made a swishing sound like someone sanding a piece of wood. He appeared in the doorway, wearing a blue suit, with a red silk cravat bunched at his throat. 'Ah,' he said, looking at the brown cloth. 'You've gone for the dramatic moment.'

'The what?' I asked.

'It's what we call "The Dramatic Moment" when you cover a painting and unveil it before the buyer's eyes. It only works with a certain kind of client. You have to know which ones.'

I tugged off the brown cloth.

Fleury's eyes narrowed. 'This is some kind of sorcery,' he said, after a moment of silence.

'Will it do?' I asked.

'It will,' he said. 'It will do very nicely.'

I couldn't help smiling.

Fleury walked right past me and up to the canvas. He pulled a kind of monocle from his shirt pocket and peered at the painting through the lens. 'Layering,' he said. 'Good. Patina. Good. Frame. Period. Worm holes. Nice touch. The right amount of dirt. *Craquelure*. Yes. Good.' Then he came very close to the painting and breathed in through his hawk's-beak nose, which made a tiny whistling sound. 'Oh, yes. Oh, yes, that's just right.' He walked around behind it. 'Leonid,' he said. His head popped up. 'Did you do this?'

'It was there when we began. We can lose it if you want.'

'No need,' he said cheerfully, and disappeared back behind the painting.

I felt the muscles of my shoulders and at the base of my skull unclenching with relief. I went back to the couch and sat down.

'All right!' announced Fleury. He walked up to me, wag-gling the monocle absent-mindedly in one hand. 'You look like you could use a holiday.'

'I expect I could,' I replied.

'Unfortunately you can't have one just yet, because now that you've given me this painting, I want you to steal it back.'

I waited for an explanation.

'I want you to take it to Behr and tell him you've recovered the painting from a private collection. That's the word I want you to use: recovered. He won't ask too many questions. He'll think you've stolen it and have chosen to cut me out of the deal. Tell him I wasn't paying you enough. Tell him we had an argument and that you decided to go into business for yourselves. Tell him you don't want money. You want to trade this for some modernist works, which you then intend to sell out of the country. If he asks, you can tell him you have a buyer in Switzerland.'

'And why am I doing this?' I asked.

'Because if Behr thinks he can get a better deal from you, he'll take it. Besides, the more disorganized we seem to be, the more he'll feel like he's in charge.'

'You've done this before,' I said.

'I've done just about everything,' replied Fleury. He handed me a list of paintings. On it were two Picassos, one a charcoal of the head of a man with a pipe, the other a pen-and-ink wash of a couple at a bar. There was a Matisse entitled *La Danse*, a découpage done in ink and watercolour. A Redon charcoal of a skull on brown paper. A Monet pastel of the cliffs at Étretat. 'I happen to know that these paintings have been acquired by Abetz.'

'Are you the only dealer Abetz is working with?' I asked.

He laughed. 'A good number of dealers in Paris are squabbling over those great Jewish collections. Some are making deals with the Germans to let them know where the hidden paintings can be found. The Parisian art world is too small for keeping secrets and some dealers are too greedy to let a bargain pass them by. If this war lasts ten years, there'll be another fifty years of people denying what they've done.'

I met Pankratov at the Dimitri and told him what Fleury had said.

Pankratov showed no emotion. He sat with arms folded, Café National steaming in front of him. When I finished talking, he rubbed his hands across his face and sighed. 'That bastard,' he said.

'Why's he a bastard?' I asked. 'It sounds like a fairly good plan.'

'What he's doing,' explained Pankratov, 'is covering himself in case something goes wrong. If the Germans don't believe it's genuine, Fleury can say he never saw the painting up close. He can say, quite rightly, that he wasn't the one who sold it . He can load all the blame on you.'

'You don't know that,' I said. I didn't want to believe it.

'Valya came to see me today,' he said. 'Valya and Dietrich. They came to where I live.'

'What did they want?' I asked.

'Dietrich wants us to work for him, too,' said Pankratov. 'She says he can convince us, whatever that means.'

'Doesn't it bother you that Valya is with that Nazi?' I asked.

Pankratov was picking at his teeth with his thumbnail, staring off down the street. 'Valya's never had beautiful clothes,' he said, 'never been to black-tie parties. No one ever bought her pearl necklaces. This is a fairytale for her. Why should she worry about the suffering of others when no one seems to care about what she's lived through?' He paused then, perhaps to let me agree.

But I had no answer for him.

The next day, following Fleury's instructions, I went to see Leutnant Behr.

He sat in his windowless underground office. The clicking hammer of typewriters sounded from other rooms. 'Where's Fleury?' he asked.

'Not here,' I said. I told Behr the story. 'It will work out better for all of us.'

Behr sat back. 'What makes you think I won't just call up Fleury right now and get you arrested?'

I shrugged. 'You wouldn't get the painting.'

He laughed a thin, wheezy laugh. 'We'd get it. Believe me.'

'All right, then,' I told him, 'for argument's sake, let's say you did get it. But that's all you'd get, instead of a chance at some paintings that you could buy more cheaply from me than from Fleury.'

Behr was scratching the back of his neck. 'What am I supposed to tell him?' Behr was hooked. Fleury had read him correctly.

'Don't tell him anything,' I said.

Behr stood and began to pace back and forth behind his desk. 'You said I could get this Cranach more cheaply from you than from Fleury.'

I nodded.

'How do I know that?' asked Behr.

'Simple. Ask him what he wants for it.'

Behr had begun to nod his head in rhythm with my words. 'Have you got the painting?'

'Yes.'

'Here?'

'It's in a safe place.' I pulled out the list Fleury had given me. 'These are the paintings I would like in exchange.'

Behr snatched the list and read it. 'What makes you think we have these?'

I didn't answer him.

'How the hell did you know?' he asked.

'Call Fleury,' I said, 'and ask what he wants for the Cranach.'

'All right,' Behr mumbled. 'I'll call him. Come back tomorrow – 9 a.m.' With great care, he folded the piece of paper, lining up the corners and sliding his thumbnail down the middle to make the crease. He seemed to have forgotten I was there.

I slipped out of Behr's office and up the concrete stairway to the street, breathing the cool air outside.

The next day I was back at Behr's office.

'The ambassador agrees,' he said. 'We'll meet you at midday today.'

I gave him the address of Pankratov's atelier.

'You will have brought the painting,' he told me.

I nodded and left.

They were on time.

I was alone in the atelier. Fleury had wanted it that way. I sat on Valya's chair, gripping the seat as if the legs had rockets tied to them and I was about to be blasted into the sky. I hoped to hell Pankratov had fixed that board the way I had asked him to. From the drunken window of the atelier I watched an unmarked limousine and a small delivery van pull up outside the building. The paintings, covered in paper, were unloaded by two men in blue boilersuits.

Then came footsteps up the stairs.

The first person through the door was Ambassador Abetz. He had on a black coat with a velvet collar and carried his gloves in one hand. All he said by way of greeting was, 'I don't have much time.' He walked over to the easel, which was covered with a clean tablecloth.

'For a man like Abetz,' Fleury had instructed me, 'you will definitely need the dramatic moment.'

After Abetz came Behr. He looked up at the rafters, as if searching for snipers.

I went over to the easel and drew back the cloth. My life is in the balance, I thought to myself. The words repeated in my head like some insane chorus. Life in the balance. In the balance. Balance.

Abetz rolled his gloves into a bundle and put them in the pocket of his coat. Then he moved up to the painting, his feet seeming to glide across the floor. He lifted the panel off the easel and walked over to the window with it. He tilted it in the light and turned it over. Next he brought his face close to it, just as Fleury had done, and breathed in the smell of the wood. Moisture on Abetz's forehead glimmered under the weak ceiling lights of the atelier, whose bulbs hung like drops of liquid just about to fall from the white and rust-bubbled shades.

'Has Dietrich been in touch with you again?' asked Abetz casually, not taking his eyes off the painting.

'He's been in touch,' I replied.

'He likes to think of himself as a generous man.'

I shrugged. 'He is pretty generous.'

'Dietrich is a man of limited means,' said Abetz. 'He does not have the same resources at his disposal as a man in my position. If you happen to come across any more paintings, as I'm sure you will, and if Mr Dietrich happens to find out about it, as I'm sure he will, then you must always make sure to wait for my offer.' Now he looked at me. 'I can also be generous. And I don't just mean the odd basket of goodies.' He turned his attention back to the painting. 'It's a portrait of the daughter of Martin Luther,' said Abetz. 'It has on it the marking of the Italian collector Leonid. I haven't seen it before.'

I went over to a shelf and pulled out a book of prints. 'Here,' I said, opening the page to the place where a portrait of Magdalena Luther had been. A postcard of our painting had been made by Fleury, replacing the old print.

'Well,' said Abetz. 'It's certainly a Cranach.' He rose up on his toes and settled back again. 'Everything appears to be in order. Some buyers require authenticators, you know. Dietrich, for example. You'll notice that I don't need one.'

I nodded.

'I can even tell you,' continued Abetz, 'where it has been hanging, even if I do not know the exact location. It has spent some time in a church or more likely in the antechamber of a private chapel. I'm sure I can smell sandalwood. No detail is too small for me, you see. I am a connoisseur even of smoke!' Abetz turned to the men in boilersuits, who were waiting outside in the hall. 'Bring them in. Take off the covers.'

The paintings were brought in and the paper wrappings removed. The room seemed to fill with light as the Picassos, the Matisse, Redon and Monet came into view.

I made a show of examining them one after the other. When I reached the last one, I looked up at Abetz and said, 'Done.'

'Good!' Abetz clapped his hands together. 'You can contact Leutnant Behr when another situation arises. And you may count on my discretion.' He wheeled about and started off down the stairs, followed by the men in boilersuits.

Then it was only Behr and me. 'Are you happy?' I asked him.

'Abetz is happy. It's all that matters. I wanted to thank you . . .' he began.

Abetz's voice rose from far below, echoing up the flights of stairs. 'For God's sake, Behr! What's keeping you?'

When they were gone, I went over to Pankratov's chair and sat down, too nervous to think straight. I was still sitting there when Pankratov appeared in the doorway half an hour later.

'Would you mind telling me what you're doing?' he asked, indignantly.

'I'm sitting in your god-damned sacred chair is what I'm doing,' I replied.

Pankratov opened his mouth, left it hanging open for a moment as he hunted for something to say. Then he closed his mouth again, teeth clacking together.

'I could use a drink,' I said.

Pankratov nodded gravely. 'Me, too.' He looked at the paintings that Abetz had left. 'Bastards,' he muttered.

We covered the paintings under a tarpaulin and went downstairs. As the two of us walked into the Dimitri, Ivan strode up to us and blocked our way. He looked very troubled. The tips of his fingers were shaking.

'What's the matter?' asked Pankratov.

Ivan answered him in Russian.

Pankratov grew very pale. He faltered out a reply, then turned to me. 'Let's go,' he said.

I followed him out to the street.

Pankratov struggled to light a cigarette.

'What's the matter?' I asked.

'Ivan says we can't go there any more.'

'Why not?'

'People have noticed that we're friendly with the Germans,' explained Pankratov. 'Some of Ivan's customers saw that limousine outside my atelier. They think we must be collaborating. Ivan says he can't force us to leave and that he'll serve us if we go in, but he wants us to know that we've been labelled as sympathizers.'

'This was bound to happen,' I said. 'I just didn't think it would happen so soon.'

Pankratov puffed viciously at his cigarette. Then suddenly he shouted, 'God damn it!' He threw the cigarette down on to the sidewalk and stormed back into the Dimitri.

A few minutes later Pankratov emerged with Ivan. Ivan was protesting, still in the process of removing his apron. Pankratov drowned out his complaints in a flurry of Russian.

Ivan looked at me. 'Can you tell this mad man that I have a café to run?'

'You have waiters,' said Pankratov.

'But they don't know how to make a proper cup of coffee!'

'These days,' Pankratov told him, 'neither do you.' He ushered Ivan across the road and into the atelier. 'Upstairs!' he commanded. 'Go on!'

Now I understood. 'Are you sure about this?' I asked.

'Positive,' said Pankratov.

'What are you going to do?' asked Ivan.

'Just keep moving,' said Pankratov.

Inside the atelier we sat Ivan down on the stage where Valya used to pose. Then we locked the door.

'Blindfold him,' ordered Pankratov.

'Sorry about this,' I told Ivan, as I tied a painter's apron across his eyes.

'You're all completely crazy,' he said. 'And I'm crazy for sitting here and letting you do this to me. Are you collaborating or aren't you? It's a simple question. Why can't you give me a simple answer?'

Pankratov brought out the paintings from under the tarpaulin and set them up along the wall.

Ivan sat patiently, hands resting on his knees.

'Ivan!' said Pankratov.

'Yes?'

'Welcome to your first art show.'

Pankratov explained everything.

Ivan looked at each of us in turn, his eyes fix-focused with surprise. 'Tcha,' he kept saying and shaking his head. 'Tcha.'

I wasn't worried about Ivan. I understood why Pankratov had to tell him. They came from a world that no longer existed and all they had of their past and the codes by which they had lived was each other. It was more than Pankratov could bear to think that Ivan considered him a traitor.

Pankratov told Ivan the story of each painting and talked about the lives of the artists who had made them.

'I have never seen such . . .' said Ivan. Then, a moment later, 'I have often wondered . . .' He began several sentences and did not finish them, his thoughts extinguished by new ideas that jumped into his mind.

After the tour, Pankratov told Ivan that we would steer

clear of the Dimitri from now on. Fleury too. 'We don't want to cause you any trouble.'

'I'm sorry,' Ivan told us. 'I don't know what to do.'

'I don't want you to do anything,' said Pankratov. 'I only wanted you to know the truth.'

The next afternoon, I bumped into Fleury on my way into the apartment building. He had spent the day at his gallery and I had been out at the warehouse.

We stopped in the doorway of Madame LaRoche's building and looked across the street at the Dimitri. Its awning shone brightly in the sun. Out on the pavement, three German soldiers sat at a table, counting out little zinc coins from their change purses while Ivan stood by with a long-suffering face.

Fleury and I exchanged gloomy looks.

When Ivan saw us, he began to wave. 'Hello, David! Hello, Guillaume!' He gathered the Germans' change and emptied it into the pocket on his apron. Then he plodded towards us with the slow gait of someone who could never run fast. The money jangled in his apron.

'What is it, Ivan?' asked Fleury.

'Come to the café,' he said, smiling and wheezing.

'Ivan,' I said softly, 'you don't want us in there.'

'Yes, I do. I've been thinking it over. I'm either going to close down or I'm just going to serve whoever wants to be served. It's got to be one or the other. So come to the café. Come now.'

I glanced at Fleury.

'Don't look at him,' said Ivan. 'Look at me! And what do you see?'

'A sweaty Imperial Russian.'

'Yes, well, besides that. Do I look afraid? Do I look like I'm in any doubt?' He set his hands against our backs and shoved us towards the Dimitri.

I tried not to meet anyone's stare as we walked in. The place was full. It was past quitting time and this was the first wave of café people, both French and German, settling their bones after the working day.

Ivan gave us a table near to the bar. If somebody wanted to give us grief, they would have to do it with Ivan standing there.

I felt sick with worry.

Fleury fumbled with his chair, smiling nervously as he glanced around the room.

While Ivan went to fetch us drinks, I sat with my hands on the cold table top, while sweat ran from my armpits and down over my ribs.

Fleury pulled out his Craven A tin. His hand began to shake. He dropped the tin on the floor. It clattered open and three hand-rolled cigarettes fell out. Fleury scrambled to gather them up, while people glanced over to see what the fuss was about. By the time he had sat up again, his cheeks were red and his glasses hung lopsided on his face.

Ivan set two heavy white cups down in front of us. They were filled with an oily black liquid that rocked against its sides. Bubbles of fat showed pearly at the surface. 'I'm sorry about this,' he said. 'It's bouillon – all we have today. I promise, you do get used to it.'

I was just raising the cup to my lips when I caught the eye of a man sitting diagonally across from us.

He was one of the old Legion types, red-faced and square-headed and tough. He looked out of place in his brown civilian clothes. They were all mud-brown, all different shades, as if he had tried to make a uniform of his street clothes, even though he was no longer a soldier. He sat with his hands under the table, a cigarette in the corner of his mouth, watching us with narrowed eyes.

'Here we go,' I muttered.

'What?' asked Fleury. 'What is it?' He turned sharply in his chair to see who was staring at us.

The man did not avert his gaze. He seemed to be staring

straight through us. Then suddenly he shouted, 'Konovalchik!' summoning Ivan by his last name. The cigarette wagged in his mouth.

'What is it, Monsieur Le Goff?' Ivan did not raise his head. He was drying glasses with a white towel behind the bar.

'I thought you weren't going to allow collaborators into the bar!'

That got everyone's attention. The conversation ebbed, rose hesitantly and then stopped altogether.

I heard Ivan sigh and then swallow. He raised his head, to meet the mudman's gaze. 'Collaborators?' he asked.

Le Goff jerked his head in our direction. 'Those two. Those friends of the Boche.'

I stopped looking at Le Goff and started looking at the Germans. They said nothing – only watched. They seemed to have drawn closer together, as if waiting for some sign of agreement between them, before they threw the old man through the window.

'We're all collaborators,' said Ivan. He said it so that everyone could hear.

'I'm no god-damned collaborator!' boomed Le Goff.

'You drink my coffee,' said Ivan.

'So?'

'Where do you think I get it? From a company that has a permit to sell coffee from the German authorities in Paris.'

'Well, no more coffee for me!' Le Goff looked around, the cigarette burning close to his lips, though he didn't seem to notice.

'And bread? And milk? And the hot water in your house and the food you buy at the market? Everything you do and buy and the cigarette in that grubby mouth of yours is with the permission of the German government. France is a defeated nation. We are *occupied*. And you sitting there ranting about two people who are just getting on with their lives is' – he seemed to stumble with his words – 'is not' – in his frustration, Ivan banged his fist down on the copper counter so hard it left a dent – 'is not welcome here!'

Nobody moved or spoke. The silence lasted for ever.

Slowly Le Goff raised his arms from under the table, but where his arms should have been were shiny metal clips, with which he took the cigarette from his mouth and dropped it in the ashtray. 'Mot de Cambronne,' he croaked out.

The whole room seemed to sigh.

Just then, no one had much to say about Ivan's speech, but over the next couple of weeks, the Dimitri became the most popular bar in the neighbourhood: soldiers and people who hated the soldiers and women with babies and more Legion men than before. Le Goff still showed up and minded his own business, never looking our way, as if we were a moving blind spot in his eye. Even a few German officers, Knight's Crosses at their throats and the badges of close combat on their chests, poked their heads in to see what was so special about this place.

I became what I had once taken for granted, but never would again: a regular at the Café Dimitri.

14

I hadn't seen Fleury for three days. I assumed he was busy at the gallery. I was just starting to wonder what had happened to him when Madame LaRoche appeared at my door, telling me he had not been home these last two nights. Then I knew something was wrong.

I went straight over to his gallery. It was a Saturday morning. As I rounded the corner of the Rue des Archives, I saw immediately that the place was closed. The windows had steel curtains pulled down in front of them. The accordion gate was drawn across the door and padlocked.

I wondered if he had run away. I didn't know whether to feel bad for thinking it, or foolish for not having thought of it sooner. I walked up to the gate and took hold of the padlock. It was heavy bronze with a metal slide that covered the keyhole. I turned the lock over and saw, hammered deep into the orangey-green bronze, a circle in which were the letters RZM. Next to it, more deeply impressed, were SS lightning bolts.

The mug of tea I'd had before I left home now spilled into the back of my throat. I turned around and stared into the street. It was empty. Sunlight reflected off closed windows as if they were blinking at me.

I ran to the German embassy. I didn't think I was in any danger from them. If they had wanted to pick me up, they would have done it by now. I ran down the concrete steps to Behr's office and found him sitting at his typewriter, pecking the keys with his index fingers. 'I just stopped by Fleury's gallery,' I gasped out. 'It was all closed up.'

'Yes,' he answered. 'I thought you'd know about that by now.'

'Know what?' I asked.

'He's been taken away.'

'Taken where?'

'Off to Drancy,' said Behr.

'What's Drancy?' I asked.

'It's a railway junction on the outskirts of Paris. Where they take all the Jews before shipping them out of the country.' Behr eyed me. 'I thought you'd be pleased about this.'

'Why the hell would I be pleased? And what makes you think he's Jewish?'

'I thought you wanted Fleury out of the way, so we could deal directly with you. When I mentioned it to Abetz, he said he thought it might be a good idea. He was pleased with the Cranach you brought him. He wanted to find a way to get rid of Fleury. So he asked me if the name Fleury had something to do with flowers. I mean, I didn't know what he was talking about at first. But then Abetz said that the German for flower is *Blume* and that Blum is a Jewish name, and *fleur* is French for flower, so Fleury was probably Jewish. Then he asked me if I thought that was correct. I had no idea, so I didn't say anything either way. The next thing I know, I get a call from Abetz to have the SS pick up Fleury at his gallery. I have no idea whether Fleury is Jewish or not, but if it's Abetz's word against Fleury's, the SS aren't going to care what Fleury has to say for himself.'

'Get him back,' I blurted out. 'I said *some* of the paintings, not *all* of them! If you want to see any more stuff, get him back now.'

'But Abetz was doing you a favour . . .' he began.

I grabbed the phone receiver off its cradle and stuck it in Behr's face. 'Call Drancy,' I said. 'Get him off the train.'

Behr seemed frozen at first, as if the request was so strange that he could not comprehend it. Then slowly he took hold of the receiver. 'I want you to know I'm only doing this because Abetz says I have to keep you happy.'

'Hallo?' someone was saying at the other end. *'Hallo?'*

'Drancy,' said Behr. He rolled the 'r' in his throat and pronounced it Drantsy. 'Bahnhof Drantsy,' he said. He spoke for a while in German, sitting back in his chair, the receiver tucked under his chin. He wrote something on his blotter with a freshly sharpened pencil. 'Dreizehn Uhr. Verstanden. Danke.' Then he hung up. He looked at his watch. 'The transport leaves in one hour.'

I lunged for the door.

'Wait!' Behr called after me. 'You can't just walk up and take him off the train. He's a prisoner, for God's sake. The SS have him now. You can't get anywhere with them.'

'Well, what can I do?' I asked. 'Please, you've got to do something to help.'

'I suppose I could type something up,' said Behr, hesitantly. 'But look, you've only got an hour. Less than that now. You can't get out to Drancy in an hour.'

'Get me a car,' I said. I was standing by the door. I had to stop myself from running out of the building and trying to sprint all the way to Drancy. It would have done no good, but I couldn't stand here doing nothing for much longer.

'I couldn't get you a car,' replied Behr, 'even if I wanted to. I haven't got the authority.'

'Type up a note,' I told him. 'Please.'

Behr turned slowly towards the machine. 'Abetz is not going to like this.' He cranked out the document he had been typing. He pulled a fresh sheet from a drawer and rolled it in. Then he sat back and scratched at his chin. 'I don't even know what to say.'

'Say anything!' I shouted. 'Just do it now.'

In the rooms down the hall, the typing stopped. Then, after a moment, it started up again.

Clumsily, Behr began tapping out a document. He mumbled out the words as he typed them. 'There,' he said. 'That should do it.'

I reached over and tore it out of the machine. I held it up. 'But this isn't on embassy stationery,' I said. 'I could have done this at home. How are they supposed to know it's official when I show it to them?'

'That part I can fix.' Behr reached out for the paper. He picked up a heavy stamp from the desk, banged it on an ink pad and brought it crashing down on the bottom of the page. When he lifted the stamp, I saw a slightly smudged eagle and swastika with some German writing underneath. 'These days,' said Behr, 'Jesus Christ himself couldn't get anywhere without papers.'

I took the paper and dashed up the steps to the corner. I went into a café and called Dietrich, using the number on the card he had sent with his invitation to the embassy party. I got transferred three times and finally Dietrich was on the other end. I explained to him what had happened.

'And you want me to get him off the transport?' asked Dietrich.

'Yes,' I said.

'I'll have to pull some strings,' he said.

'Can you do it?' I asked.

'Yes, I think so,' he said.

I saw a streetcar coming. It flashed blue sparks along its overhead rails.

'I have to go,' I told him and hung up.

The streetcar was heading north, which the conductor said was in the right direction for Drancy, so I got on it. At the Gare du Nord I changed to a bus. It was crowded and I had to stand, holding on to a bar above my head. It was raining outside. When the bus stopped to let people on and off, the smell of the damp came into the bus. The windows fogged up. The windshield wipers clunked back and forth in front of the driver.

I looked at my watch every minute and was making myself crazy, so I took it off and put it in my pocket.

At last, I came within sight of the great corrugated-iron rooftops of the Drancy marshalling yards. Rails ran alongside the road, twisting over each other and curving away towards the station.

At the next stop, I jumped off the bus.

I could see the station in the distance, past a huge expanse of tracks and then the long concrete platform with a green-painted roof, slick and glowing in the rain. There was a locomotive pulled up at the platform, with three cars behind it. Separating the road from the tracks was a high fence with barbed wire at the top.

I started climbing the fence. I wasn't thinking. I just climbed. I reached the barbed wire and clambered over the top of it, tearing my jacket, and dropped to the gravel on the other side.

I ran towards the station house. Rain was coming down hard. I slipped on the oily wooden spacers that separated the tracks. The tops of the rails were shiny from use. I was already out of breath and soaked.

The train began to pull out of the station, engine chugging, steam rising from its smokestack. I pulled Behr's piece of paper out of my pocket and started waving it over my head. I kept running in the direction of the platform.

Someone was moving towards me from the station house. He waved his arm. He had a sub-machine gun slung over his shoulder. Through my sweat and the rain, I could make out shin-length black boots and a helmet.

I ran towards him, waving the paper and shouting for him to stop the train.

The wagon's wheels clunked from one set of tracks to another as it headed out.

The soldier unshouldered his gun. He was shouting. Keeping the gun at waist height, he levelled it at me and kept walking.

I'd never had a gun pointed at me before. I could see the black eye of the end of the barrel. I flinched and a second later, I tripped over a rail and fell hard on the track spacers. Over my own breathing, I could hear the soldier but had no idea what he was saying.

I lay there gasping, face down, holding up the piece of paper, which sagged over my fingers. I could smell the creosote that coated the spacers. The rust on the rails smeared against my clothes. Smears of blood and oil mixed with the torn-up skin of my palms.

The soldier's boots crunched over the gravel, coming closer. He stopped right in front of me. 'Betreten verboten,' he said. That was what he had been shouting the whole time.

I raised my head and saw the leather of his boots and the bumps of hobnails on the soles. I held up the soggy piece of paper.

He crouched down slowly. The black sub-machine gun rested on his knees. It had a long, straight magazine and a folding stock. He took the paper from my hand, unfolded it and read it. The grey-green steel of his helmet hid his eyes. I looked at the rough wool of his uniform and the pebbly finish on his uniform buttons. Only now did I feel pain in my knees from where I had fallen against a rail.

'Transport Vier,' he said. Then he spoke to me in French. 'Transport number four left yesterday,' he said.

Exhausted, I let my head fall forward. 'I thought it was leaving today.'

'Transport five left today. About an hour ago. Whoever wrote this got the number wrong.'

'What was that train at the station?'

'A work crew. Going out to fix the rails. That's all. Just a work crew.'

I rose up to my knees, then sat back on my haunches.

The soldier tilted his helmet back on his head. He had a thin face and pale-blue eyes. His uniform was a little too big for him and he carried the Schmeisser like someone not used to carrying a gun.

We sat there on our haunches in the middle of all those rails and in the pouring rain.

I had a strange feeling of standing far above myself. I was looking down from a great height at the maze of rails and the rain and the overflowing gutters of the station platform roof. I saw the two small figures that were me and the soldier. Then, just as suddenly, I was back inside myself again and looking through my tired, sweat-salted eyes.

He handed me back the piece of paper.

I balled it up in my fist and squeezed until drops of black-tinted water from the ink dripped out on to the tracks.

We got to our feet.

'You have to go,' he said. 'It is forbidden.' Then he turned and walked away unhurriedly, lugging the burden of his gun, his long legs stepping carefully over the polished tracks.

I got back to the fence, climbed up over the barbed wire and dropped down to the street, jarring my knees. I stood waiting for the bus, with no idea when it would come again. My thoughts swung between anger and fear with the movement of a pendulum. The rain came down in sheets. There was no place to hide from it. No point in even trying.

By the time I reached my apartment I felt sure I would never see Fleury again. I was exhausted, but knew I had to get out to the warehouse and tell Pankratov what had happened. I changed into some dry clothes and put my soaked wool coat back on, since it was the only coat I had.

I opened the door and was shocked to see Fleury standing there right in front of me. His clothes were dirty and torn and his hair was a mess. His shoes were gone and his socks were wet from walking through the rain. He smelled of sweat and piss. 'Can I come in?' he asked.

He sat at my kitchen table and wept while he told me what had happened.

Two plain-clothes SS men had come for him at his gallery. They would not explain why they were arresting him, or even if this was an arrest. He was driven straight to Mont Valérien and put in a large cell with about fifty other people. There were men and women mixed together. There was not enough room for everyone to lie down, so people took turns. There was a bucket in the corner, which had overflowed long before Fleury arrived. He was able to piece together that some of the prisoners were Jews, others former members of the Communist Party, and people with records of petty crime. The first night, half the people in the room had their names called out and left. The only people remaining were Jews. Fleury told me he wasn't Jewish, and nor was he a member of any political party, but he could think of any number of petty crimes of which he had been accused and never convicted. He didn't know whether to stay where he was or to summon a guard and explain the mistake. He decided to wait. The next night, without having been fed, Fleury and the remaining people in the room were hustled down into the courtyard and searchlights were shone in their faces as their names were read off and they were piled into trucks. It was then that he had approached a guard, who had told him to shut up and pushed him on towards the truck.

They had been taken to Drancy and put straight into red military wagons, which had barbed wire over the air vents. The cars were already overcrowded when they arrived. Fleury and the Mont Valérien Jews were crammed in with the rest. He said he had expected the train to start moving immediately, but instead they were left there all night.

In the morning, the door had been opened and his name was called out. He was driven back to Mont Valérien and returned to the room, which by now had a new set of people waiting inside.

He had been called out of the room six hours later and found Dietrich's driver, a man named Grimm, waiting for him down in the courtyard. Fleury had been driven back to the Rue Descalzi and arrived home only a few minutes after I had.

I boiled some water and cooked a turnip I had been saving for a meal. I mashed it up and then used the water to make a drink. Fleury ate some and I ate what he left.

I told Fleury about Abetz's decision to have him arrested and about my call to Dietrich.

'It's my own fault,' he said. 'I underestimated them. And I think, now that I've been to Mont Valérien, that we have all underestimated them.' Then he just sat there at the table, eventually falling asleep with his head on his folded arms.

I put a blanket over him and went to bed. When I woke up, just before dawn, he was gone, back to his own place, and the blanket was neatly folded on the chair.

Tombeau called for me the next day. I met him on a walkway by the Seine, where old men in berets fished for carp with long bamboo poles.

Tombeau walked with his hands in the pockets of his jacket, wooden-soled shoes knocking the stones. Already the heels were worn down.

I told him about what had happened to Fleury.

'Is he going to crack up on us?' asked Tombeau.

'Is that all you care about?' I fired back.

'It's important,' said Tombeau.

'If he hasn't cracked by now,' I said, trying to remain calm, 'I don't suppose he will.'

'He'd better not,' replied Tombeau. 'There's too much riding on this now.'

A breeze blew down the Seine, rattling the branches of the trees.

I stopped walking. Words had been taking shape inside my head, ever since I saw Fleury standing at my door, terrified and filthy. The anger and the outrage that had eluded me before was here now, sifting like grit through my blood. 'I can't do this any more,' I said.

Tombeau stood back, as if to size me up for a fight. 'What do you mean?' he asked.

'Give me a gun. Teach me how to blow up a bridge. Let me do something that helps. Painting is not enough.'

'How about I just throw you in prison?' asked Tombeau.

'You don't have a prison to throw me in any more,' I told him. 'Let me fight.'

'What do you know about fighting?' he barked. 'Not a damned thing.'

'Just tell me what to do. I can't sit around and watch this kind of thing happen.'

'You aren't just sitting around' said Tombeau.

He took off his cap and scratched his head and set his cap back on his head. 'You *are* fighting,' he said quietly. He raised his head and fixed me with his grey-green eyes. For the first time, he did not look angry. He seemed confused, as if unsure how to behave when deprived of his rage. 'If you want to know the truth, I envy you,' he told me. 'I know how you feel now, but I also know how you'll feel after you've stuck a knife through some spotty-faced teenage soldier. Any killing we do now is purely symbolic. It shows the Germans that we haven't given up. But you, with your paintings – you can make a difference.' He breathed out slowly. 'My job is only to hate. To hate more and hate longer and to kill because of hating. But your job means being hated by the same people whose culture you are fighting to save. When this is all over, if you survive it, you'll have done more good than I could ever do.' Then Tombeau was gone, vanished in the side streets of the city.

When I told Fleury about my conversation with Tombeau, he exploded.

Fleury grabbed my arm. 'Have you gone insane?'

We were standing in the lobby of the apartment building, waiting for the elevator to come down.

I shook loose from him. 'What are you talking about? And for Christ's sake, lower your voice.'

'You listen to me,' said Fleury, his voice as loud as ever. 'If you just want to throw your life away because you're too furious to think straight, then go ahead. Go down to the Hôtel de Ville and knife one of the German guards. But you can damn well do it by yourself. After what I've seen, I intend to survive, however bad it gets. And if you had any brains, you would too.'

The elevator cage arrived, clanking into place.

'It's precisely because of what you saw that you should stop just thinking about yourself,' I told him.

Fleury slid back the door to the cage and stepped inside. When he turned around, his face was twisted with anger. 'I'm going to live through this, no matter what it takes.' He slammed the cage door shut and jabbed his thumb over and over at the button for his floor.

'If it takes you going behind my back again . . .' I told him – but never had the chance to finish, as the elevator dragged him upwards out of sight.

I could no longer stand the half-measures of trust by which our acquaintance was defined. Too much was at stake. From now on, he was going to have to show that he had changed, not only to Pankratov and me but to himself as well, I thought. There was nothing for him to do now but wait for a chance to present itself. Until then, there would always be this strange uncertainty between us.

In the coming weeks, Pankratov and I set about enlarging our repertoire.

I quickly learned that I couldn't just choose any painting and begin making works in that style. Many more artists lay beyond my reach than within it. I attempted paintings in the manner of Correggio and Hals, but never succeeded in making a passable copy. There was no set scale of technical difficulty from one artist to another. It was more a question of matching my own skills against the particular specialities of the painter whose style I wanted to copy. Because of this, I never even tried the styles of Rubens, Titian, Rembrandt or Boucher.

These days, I knew exactly what I was doing when I went out to Rocco's, and a number of other places, to buy up more supplies. When I chose the subject matter, I did so with an eye to what might please the buyer, rather than what would challenge me most in the drawing.

For our first large sale to Abetz, we made two drawings. One was a brown ink drawing of a Greek warrior holding a spear and shield, which we attributed to Giovanni Barbieri and dated around 1660. We also made a Tiepolo of a centaur cuddling up to a half-goat/half-woman, which Fleury informed us was called a satyress. It was done in brown ink and grey wash over black chalk. We signed this one, using the correct signature for Tiepolo at the time: *dom. Tiepolo f.*

Pankratov aged these by watering down the ink before I used it. This gave the sketches a faded look even as I drew them. He put wear on the edges by laying the ends on a table and scraping them with a blunted straight-edge razor. After this, he used the fluffy white insides of a baguette to rub down the paper on which the sketches had been made. This blurred the lines without smearing them too much. It also laid down the nap of the paper slightly, giving it the look of an older drawing that had been handled many times.

Pankratov wanted to make the drawings look as if they had been stolen from somebody's collection, so he glued the sketches carefully into the blank pages of an old album. Then he cut out the pages with a penknife. Finally, he put his hand inside a wool sock and rubbed down the picture and the borders of the page.

He finished up by sandwiching the pages between sheets of damp and rotten paper and leaving them for a couple of days. This gave the sketches the right musty smell and faintly blotchy look of having been kept in a damp place. If the sketches had been stolen, he explained, it was more than likely that the thieves would have mishandled them.

The only painting we offered Abetz was of three musicians sitting around a table. It was a muted canvas, with creamy browns and washed-out blues for the musicians' clothing and an unhealthy pallor in their faces. We deliberately mistook the painter as a man named J. Lopez-Rey, who was a student of Velázquez. We hoped that Abetz would recognize this as a variant of a known Velázquez, not something done by a student, and would believe that the work was done by Velázquez himself, making it worth thirty times what we were asking. One of the devices we used was to work in several pale green-brown stripes in the top left-hand corner of the canvas, which was otherwise blank, dark-painted space. Velázquez used to clean his brushes on the canvas while he worked. He would then paint on top of the marks but, over time, the smudges of his dirty brush marks would come through. This was one of the accidental personal touches that earmarked a Velázquez.

When Pankratov decided the paint was dry, he removed the canvas from its stretcher, drawing each nail carefully from its hole and setting them on a clean white sheet of paper in the exact order that he had withdrawn them. He laid the canvas out on his worktable and slowly rolled it up. Then he unrolled it and rolled it up again. He rolled it in different directions and, by the time he was done, the painting had across it a fine web of cracking, which we called a *craquelure*.

When we were ready, we called up Abetz and told him what we had.

He made an appointment that same day.

Fleury and I waited for him at Pankratov's atelier. Pankratov stayed away, as he had done the time before.

Abetz brought with him several canvases for trade, but he kept them wrapped. He said he didn't want to show us what they were until he knew we had something to trade. He paced back and forth in front of the works, pale hands knotted behind his black coat. He put his glasses on and then took them off again.

While I sat on the stage, Fleury and Abetz conferred in hushed voices. Fleury let Abetz do the talking. Abetz couldn't help giving a lecture on the artists and their painting techniques. Even though Fleury knew all this, he followed Abetz around, mumbling in theatrical amazement. The more amazed Fleury pretended to be, the more confident Abetz became, raising his voice so that I could partake of his knowledge. In the course of Abetz's speech, Fleury learned that the man had spent time at Oxford University. As soon as Abetz paused for breath, Fleury let slip that he had also been to Oxford. What he didn't say, but told me later, was that he had only been there for two days while touring England with his parents years ago. Abetz jumped to the conclusion that Fleury had studied at the university and Fleury said nothing to dissuade him of this. Abetz became very nostalgic as he reminisced about his evenings at a place called the Turf Tavern and tea at the Randolph Hotel.

In the end, Abetz didn't question any of our works. 'I'll take them all,' he said.

He removed the wrappings from the paintings he had brought, revealing a study by Ingres for the figure of Stratonice, an oil on canvas by Manet of a woman in a blue dress sitting in a rocking chair, another pastel – this one by Millet – of a man sowing grain in a field, and a Degas pastel of a ballerina in a white dress doing a kick step, which Abetz called a *pas battu*.

While Fleury inspected the work that Abetz had brought, Abetz sat down beside me on the stage. He smoked a small cigar through a black holder. From his pocket, he took a small silver dish, which he balanced on his knee and used as an ashtray.

'I hear you didn't like my arrangement,' said Abetz.

I knew he was talking about what had happened to Fleury. 'I think this way will work out better for everyone,' I told him.

He jerked his chin at the work we had for sale. 'You've been doing well for yourselves.'

'There are a few things out there,' I said, 'if you know where to find them.'

Abetz nodded. 'I'm sure there are many families who have fallen on hard times.'

'Times are hard for all of us,' I said.

Abetz gave a quiet laugh at this. 'Really,' he said. 'I expect that there are some families who have even gone into hiding.'

'I expect so,' I replied, not really knowing what he meant.

'And I'd imagine they'd do anything to stay in hiding,

including parting with their works of art.' He tapped ash from his cigarette. 'Just postulating.'

Abetz got up and walked over to Fleury. He left his silver dish beside me, as if daring me to steal it. In the course of an hour of bargaining, Fleury managed to acquire everything Abetz had brought. After he had left, Fleury sat down beside me and lit himself a cigarette. 'What are you looking so gloomy about?' he asked.

'Why haven't we been caught yet?' I asked him. 'We may be good, but it's just as Pankratov said: there's no such thing as perfection.'

Fleury sipped at the smoke, then breathed it out through his nose in two grey streams. 'For a start, Abetz isn't as much of an expert as he thinks he is. And secondly, from what I've seen, he's in too much of a hurry to check the work as thoroughly as he could. Almost everything he gets from France is immediately crated up, sent back to Germany and put in warehouses. He doesn't have time to do X-rays and so on.'

'I hate having to let Abetz think we strong-arm our stuff off Jewish families. It's bad enough that people at the Dimitri think we're collaborators.'

'Let Abetz think whatever he wants,' said Fleury. 'The worst thing would be for him not to know, or not to think he knows, where our material comes from.'

I sat back and sighed. 'I was hoping we could avoid being total sons of bitches.'

'Safest thing to be,' he told me.

That evening, the paintings from Abetz were handed over to Madame Pontier.

15

Two days later, on a brilliant early summer day, Dietrich's limousine rumbled up to the kerb outside our apartment building.

I had been sorting through some old art catalogues, trying to figure out what pieces to do next. I knew the car just from the sound of the engine. I went over to the open window and looked down. I thought to myself, Here comes the competition. I had guessed correctly that Abetz wouldn't be able to keep from bragging about his latest acquisitions.

It wasn't Dietrich who showed up at the door, just his driver, Grimm, whom Dietrich had acquired after firing a series of French chauffeurs. Grimm was a tall man with a big jaw and a sleepy expression. He wore the black uniform of an Allgemeine SS man. 'Mr Dietrich would like to see you,' he said, uncomfortable and stiff-backed as he stood in the doorway.

'Where?' I asked.

'Mr Dietrich would like to keep it a surprise,' said Grimm. His feet in heavy hobnailed boots stirred nervously on the bare wood floor, as if he were standing on a sheet of glass.

On the way downstairs we picked up Fleury, who appeared, as usual, in his red smoking jacket. 'Is this another black-tie party for me to show off my threadbare tuxedo?' he asked.

'No,' said Grimm. 'No, sir.' The sight of Fleury's garish clothes appeared to unsettle Grimm. He straightened the already-straight cap on his head. He seemed determined to deny himself any of the minute deviations from regulation dress by which a soldier can claim his individuality.

Dietrich wasn't in the limousine. Instinctively I slouched down on the smooth leather seats, since the car drew as many stares as Tombeau's ridiculous scooter. When I realized we were heading out of the city, I leaned forward and asked Grimm, 'Are you stopping for Pankratov?'

'Only you, sir, and Monsieur Fleury,' said Grimm. He held up a piece of paper, on which his orders had been typed. Dietrich's signature was at the bottom, the letters jagged like a scribble of a mountain range.

Grimm brought us to the warehouse of the Schneider Transport Company. The place had high brick walls around it and a large iron gate at the front.

Dietrich was there to meet us. He was standing outside the main office building, a small wooden structure dwarfed by the huge warehouse that rose up behind it. Dietrich was wearing a long brown leather coat. It was raining, and he stood outside without an umbrella. Droplets beaded down the length of his coat. He flashed us a confident smile. 'Thank you for coming, gentlemen,' he said. The rain plipped on his leathered back. He turned to Fleury. 'I trust you have recovered from your ordeal.'

'Yes,' said Fleury. 'I am quite fine.'

'Well, you know who to blame for your discomfort,' Dietrich told him.

'Yes,' said Fleury. 'I do.'

'And I trust you know who to thank for your release.'

'I know,' replied Fleury, 'and I am grateful.'

'Indeed,' said Dietrich. He motioned for us to follow him and strode towards the warehouse, whose large doors were open. A stony-faced man in a dark three-piece suit was waiting there, hands folded in front of his waist and a signet ring baubled on his pinky.

We reached the entrance to the warehouse. Inside it was cool. The summer heat hadn't yet forced itself through the brick walls and arching roof.

'This is Monsieur Touchard.' Dietrich nodded to the slope-shouldered man in the suit. 'He is the French art appraiser for the ERR. Let's have the lights on, Touchard.'

Touchard obeyed without a word. There was a series of

clunks as he hit the switches and the lights came on, one row after another.

The place was even bigger than I had imagined. Every foot of it, apart from a walkway down the middle, was crowded with antiques. There were statues of all types. Hands rose in the air, some holding bunches of grapes, others reaching their pale marble fingers towards bare bulbs that hung from the ceiling. I saw furniture – tables and chairs with plush red seats and cabinets with impossibly ornate carvings coiled like snakes around the legs. There were shelves of crystal, books, mirrors, candlesticks, cigar boxes and splintery wooden crates that had been nailed shut and had large red crosses painted on the sides.

Dietrich held up his hands, like the ringmaster of a circus. 'We used to have a little storage space in a garage on the Rue Richelieu. But that became a little too small for our collection.'

I heard Touchard snuffle out a laugh behind me.

Fleury and I said nothing. The scale of it, the rows and rows, and the vastness of creativity and wealth crammed into this warehouse defied any possible comment.

It made Dietrich happy to see our amazement. He swaggered over to a table and picked up a heavy silver candlestick. 'I am inviting you along on a shopping trip,' he said. 'You see, these things belong to various French people. They have been confiscated, but they are still technically under the protection of the French government. The German government has established an organization called the *Kunstschutz*. It means, the "Art Protection Agency". It's run by Count Franz Wolff-Metternich. He makes sure that all of these treasures don't simply disappear in acts of looting. However, if the French government should opt to sell them, in the best interests of their owners, it is our duty to make sure that a fair price has been paid and that the necessary paperwork has been filled out.' He flashed a smile at Touchard.

'Around here,' Touchard snuffled again, 'I am the French government.'

'Exactly,' Dietrich confirmed. 'A price for these items is established by the French government, represented here by Monsieur Touchard, and we agree on the amount. That way Count Wolff-Metternich can't complain. For example' – he spun on his heel – 'today I have been instructed by Reichsmarschall Göring to buy this statue.' He held his hand out towards a small statue, about two feet tall, of a man with long hair and a beard, with a cape slung over his shoulder and striding forward, arms held out to his side, as if clearing his way through a crowd. His face was young and fierce. His hands were strong but slightly effeminate. They reminded me of Valya's. The statue was made of reddish marble or some other stone, almost brick-coloured, and its surface was dull. 'What would you say this is worth, Monsieur Fleury?' asked Dietrich.

'I don't know,' said Fleury. He brought his face close to it, raising his glasses. 'It looks very fine.'

'Oh, it is. Would it help you if I told you it was made by the Italian sculptor Camillo Rusioni around 1720. It is St Jaque Le Majeur and is a study for a much larger statue in the basilica of St Jean de Latra or something like that. Anyway, the statue is in Rome and it is very big and important.'

'Well,' said Fleury, his voice drifting with uncertainty, 'I saw an early eighteenth-century Italian statue go at Christie's the other year for what would be about 400,000 francs.'

Touchard pursed his lips and nodded. 'Close,' he said. 'Very close.'

Dietrich, too, was nodding. 'Fair,' he said. 'And under normal circumstances, I'd say this might be worth about half as much again.'

'Normal circumstances,' repeated Touchard.

'But these are not normal circumstances, are they, Monsieur Touchard?'

'No, Herr Dietrich,' came the reply.

'So, Monsieur Touchard, what would be your best price on the Rusioni sculpture?'

Touchard walked up to it. He reached one finger out and touched it against the statue's upper lip, as if the man had been about to break from his dusty red shell and speak and declare his own worth, and Touchard committed him again to silence. 'Perhaps a hundred thousand?' He asked it; he did not say it.

Even I who had no idea what this statue was worth knew that Dietrich would not pay this price if the man deciding it had spoken so hesitantly.

'It's worth more than a hundred thousand!' said Fleury. His protest vanished into the huge space of the warehouse.

'I might pay 50,000,' said Dietrich casually.

'Done,' barked Touchard.

Fleury turned on him, 'What do you mean "done"? You know damn well it's worth ten times that!'

Touchard shrugged. 'I am the government,' he said.

'Who else can make offers on all this?' demanded Fleury. 'Is it open to the public?'

'No,' said Touchard. 'Only Mr Dietrich.'

'But look here!' Dietrich called out. 'The sculpture is damaged.'

The three of us stepped forward to see where this damage might be.

'Where?' asked Fleury. 'I can't see any damage.'

Then we all watched as Dietrich raised the candlestick over his shoulder and brought it down hard across one of the statue's delicate hands. He smashed off the fingers. Fragments cartwheeled through the air and rattled to the floor, breaking into even more pieces. 'There,' said Dietrich. The candlestick hung heavy in his grip.

Even Touchard looked shocked at this.

'You're insane,' said Fleury.

Dietrich chose to ignore this. 'It's not worth much of anything now,' he said with mock sadness.

'No, sir.' Touchard's voice was choked.

'I couldn't pay more than five thousand francs now.'

'Done,' said Touchard.

'There might even be more damage.' Dietrich's knuckles grew white as he clenched his fists around the candlestick.

'No!' Touchard called out, raising his hands out to the statue.

Dietrich lowered the candlestick, grinning.

'I'll draw up the paperwork now.' Touchard set off towards the office.

Dietrich bent down and picked up the fragments of the fingers. Then he put them in the pocket of his coat and stood to face us. 'I'll have this repaired. You'd never know the difference. I brought you here,' he said, 'because I have a particular interest in you. You're both young, capable. That's what I need. New faces for a new market place.'

We walked back out into the rain, heading for the office, where Touchard would be typing up the documents of sale.

Over and over in my mind I saw the statue's delicate fingers shattering on the concrete floor of the warehouse.

'What I would like,' said Dietrich, 'is for you both to work exclusively for me from now on. I saw that Cranach you found for Abetz. He gloated about it for an entire week. Cranach happens to be a particular favourite of the Reichsmarschall. You obviously have the means to satisfy a discerning palate.' He set his hand on Fleury's shoulder and squeezed. 'This is your great opportunity. You should take it. Besides, considering what Abetz tried to do with you, and considering that I am the only reason you're still here, I'd have thought you might show me a little consideration for my trouble.'

'And what would you have us do about Abetz?' asked Fleury.

'I'm glad you asked about Abetz. He can be very persuasive in a bullying sort of way. He's an ambitious man. This is the greatest moment of his diplomatic career and he's chosen to add to his laurels a collection of the finest art in France. But it's really just a hobby for him. He's got too much else on his plate. He has to run the embassy, after all. And what with Hitler's visit to Paris in June and other dignitaries flooding in, it's all he can do to get any sleep at night. That's why he's palmed you off with that man Behr, who shouldn't even be on the embassy staff.'

'Well, why is he there?' I asked.

'His mother had an affair with a man who is now one of the regional governors of Austria. A *Gauleiter*. I expect she reminded him of their past, and probably offered to remind everyone else as well, unless her son found himself out of harm's way. Of course, Behr has no idea about this. He just thinks it's all some bureaucratic foul-up.'

We had reached the office. Dietrich opened the door for us and we filed in.

Inside, Touchard was typing out the documents. His glasses were balanced on the tip of his hooked, Roman nose and his lips moved as he spelled out the words.

'Aren't you ready yet?' Dietrich asked.

'Almost.' Touchard did not look up from his typing.

In the room adjacent to Touchard's office was a man with short dark hair combed straight back on his head. He had his back to us and was brandishing an antique sword around a coat stand, on which hung a gaberdine raincoat and a soft hat. The man was pretending to sword-fight with the coat, flicking up the arms with the end of the sword. He shuffled around on his feet as if the empty coat were fighting back and he was dodging sword thrusts.

'Hey!' Touchard called out. 'Be careful with my coat!'

The young man turned and grinned.

My eyes widened with surprise. It was Tombeau. 'Oh,' I said.

He caught my eye, warning me. Then he looked away.

'What is it?' asked Dietrich.

I choked a little before I came up with a reply. 'That sword he's playing with. It's an antique, isn't it?'

'Christ almighty! So it is. You!' bellowed Dietrich, his shout boxing our ears in the cramped space of the office.

Tombeau stopped duelling with the coat. 'It's just a blade,' he said.

Dietrich strode across the space between them. He snatched the sword out of Tombeau's hand and turned to us, smiling. 'This is one of my associates. From the firm of Fabry and Georges.'

Tombeau made a short, sarcastic bow.

I remembered what Pankratov had said about the Fabry-Georges hiring themselves out for any dirty jobs that paid good money. It made perfect sense to me that Dietrich and the Fabry-Georges would find themselves working together.

Dietrich turned back to Tombeau. 'Do you know what this is?' He held the sword blade up between them and glared past the damascened iron at Tombeau's insolent smile.

'Of course I know,' replied Tombeau.

'No, you don't,' Dietrich snapped. 'This is a seventeenth-century French sabre, made by Ferdinand de Thézy for the Comte de Barzilay. It's worth a lot of money, and I don't want you chipping the blade.'

'Sorry,' said Tombeau, without sincerity.

'Besides,' said Dietrich. 'If you're going to use the thing, use it properly.' Dietrich balanced himself in a swordsman's pose. Then with a movement so fast and precise that I barely saw it, he sliced off one of the sleeves of Touchard's coat. The sleeve fell to the floor and lay there in a heap.

'My coat!' shouted Touchard.

Dietrich handed the sword back to Tombeau, who peered at the blade with new respect.

'What about my coat?' asked Touchard, his voice high-pitched with frustration.

'Get a new one,' said Dietrich. 'Or lose an arm. Or something.'

Touchard shook his head slowly and went back to his typing. He jabbed at the keys with his bony fingers, muttering to himself.

'I want that sculpture on the train to Germany tonight,' said Dietrich.

Touchard stopped typing. His face twitched. 'Tonight? There's no one here but me. How am I supposed to crate it up and get it to the station?'

'Make some calls. Get some Fabry-Georges people to do it. They don't mind hard work.'

'You'd trust one of those thugs with that statue?' asked Touchard.

'It's already broken,' said Dietrich. Then he turned to me and Fleury. 'The car will take you home.'

The car was out there in the rain, Grimm at the wheel, engine running, exhaust leaking silver from its tail pipe.

'What are we supposed to do when Abetz calls?' I asked. 'Because he is going to call, sooner or later.'

'If he gives you any trouble,' said Dietrich, 'just let me know. You'll only have to do it once, I guarantee.'

On the ride back, I was afraid to say anything to Fleury because I worried that Grimm would eavesdrop. I asked Grimm to drop us off a block away from the apartment, so that no one would see it pull up in front of our place. Grimm nodded at my request, no expression on his face, the way a person does who has made a life's work out of following orders.

When I reached my apartment, I found Pankratov sitting at my kitchen table. He was hunched like an old circus bear over a loaf of bread, a slab of white-flecked salami and the remains of a bottle of red wine.

'How did you get in here?' I asked, 'and where did you get all that stuff to eat?'

Pankratov's mouth was too full to talk. He held something up between his thumb and first two fingers. It was a straightened-out paperclip. Then he dropped the clip, picked up the bottle, the muscles in his neck straining as he forced a mouthful down his throat. He shook his head and finally spoke. 'Valya. Came to see me. Brought food.'

I walked to the window and looked at the windows of the Postillon. These days, I always had the feeling I was being watched.

'There's no one out there,' said Pankratov, forcing down a mouthful of sausage, bread and cheese that he had stacked one on top of the other and then compressed with the flat of his hand before packing it into his mouth.

'I don't understand why they don't follow us everywhere we go,' I said

'So they could find out our sources and grab them for themselves?' he asked.

'Exactly.' I leaned forward and breathed on the glass, fogging it with condensation.

Pankratov knocked back some wine, swished it through his teeth, then swallowed. 'Because there is no single source. At least not as far as they know. Half of the great paintings in France are tucked away in root cellars, chicken coops, and behind walls three feet thick. The Germans know perfectly well that they'd have no hope of tracking them down. Sure, they could grab us and dig out whatever little treasure trove we happened to be raiding, but what about the thousand other hiding places? They know that the best thing for them is to leave us be. As long as we keep handing them paintings, and since they're trading what they don't want for what they do, how can they lose?'

'They can lose because what we're giving them is a lie.'

Pankratov held up one finger, commanding me to silence. 'It's not a lie if they don't think it's a lie. Besides, I've persuaded Madame Pontier to part with some originals to make us more credible,' he said. 'I told her she owed us that much.'

The following week, Madame Pontier delivered to us an original drawing of a kneeling angel by Gianfrancesco Penni.

'Take it,' she said, her teeth gritted, 'and don't expect me do to this very often.'

Each time I met her, I became more convinced that she

wouldn't lift a finger to help us if we were caught. In everything she did, the way she looked and spoke and in the doll's-eye flatness of her gaze, she was the coldest person I had ever met.

That same day we brought the drawing to Dietrich.

Dietrich was no great lover of art. He had been chosen for this job because he was a businessman. He was not particularly pleased with the drawing. The irony of this did not escape me, seeing as it was original. Penni, who worked in the late fifteenth and early sixteenth century, was not high on Dietrich's procurement list. Dietrich knew as well as we did that if the artist was not a huge name, the subject matter needed, at least, to be appealing. An angel was not as choice as a picture of a young woman, or of a cat or a dog, or a classical Greek or Roman location, all of which moved very quickly through Dietrich's warehouse on the outskirts of Paris. The main problem with this angel was that the drawing had been perforated, or 'pounced', along most of the lines. This was so that the drawing could be laid out over a blank piece of paper and, if sprinkled with charcoal dust, would provide the layout of an identical drawing underneath. After several uses, the original drawing would start to get a little dirty. The one we gave Dietrich had been used several times.

The next day, a call came through to the atelier, where Pankratov and I were mixing paints. Fleury was there, too. He lay flat on his back on the stage, silently puffing a corn-silk cigarette. He let the smoke leak from his mouth. It wound in grey ribbons up towards the rafters.

Pankratov picked up the receiver.

I could hear someone shouting over the phone.

Pankratov's eyes were wide with surprise. He held the receiver away from his ear.

When the person on the other end paused for breath, Pankratov tried to speak. 'But,' he said, 'how were we to know . . .?'

The shouting started up again, this time even louder.

Pankratov looked at Fleury and me. He shook his head wearily. 'Yes,' he said to the receiver. 'Yes, I understand.' Then he hung up. He stood there in silence, still dazed from the barrage of insults. 'That was Abetz. He's furious that we let Dietrich have the Penni drawing. He says we promised him all Italian drawings.'

'No, we didn't,' said Fleury. These were the first words he had spoken in almost an hour.

Pankratov and I looked at each other and shrugged. Neither of us had made that promise, either.

'He just wants an excuse to get mad at us,' I said.

'He has demanded that one of you meet him at a restaurant in Montmartre tonight,' said Pankratov. 'It's a place called La Mère Catherine. It's up on the Place du Tertre in the old part of town.'

I walked over to the phone. 'I'm calling Dietrich,' I said.

'Why?' asked Fleury, still staring at the ceiling.

'He told us to ring him if Abetz ever gave us any trouble. Personally, I don't feel like going up against Abetz, when the man's worked himself into a frenzy.' There was no protest from Fleury or Pankratov, so I dialled Dietrich's number.

'Moment.' It was Grimm's voice.

Then I heard Dietrich's brassy voice. I explained about Abetz. When I gave the name of the restaurant, I heard Dietrich snap his fingers at someone in the room and then I heard the scrabble of him writing down the information. 'We never did agree to give him old Italian drawings,' I told him.

'Of course not.' Dietrich's voice was soothing and comradely. 'The man's out of his mind. Listen, I want you to go to the meeting. Be as friendly as you can. Tell him what he wants to hear. If he wants you to promise him Italian drawings, then make the promise. Do you follow me?'

'Yes,' I said, uncertainly.

'No harm will come to you,' said Dietrich. 'You're going to have to trust me. David, I will not let you down.' This was the first time he called me by my Christian name. I didn't know what to make of it.

Afterwards, I explained to the others what Dietrich had said.

By now, Fleury had lit himself another cigarette. He remained on his back, staring at the ceiling as if in a trance. The only movement was the regular sweep of his hand to his mouth and then down to his side. Lately, he was often like this.

I thought it would probably have been a better idea if Fleury went to the meeting. He would do a better job of sweet-talking Abetz than I ever could, and sending Pankratov to make small talk was out of the question. But Fleury didn't offer to go, and in the shape he was in just then, I didn't want to ask.

La Mère Catherine was in a little park, at the top of the Rue Norvin. The park lay in the shadow of the church of Sacré Coeur and little tables were set out among the trees. Each tree was girdled by tall metal railings. The tables were busy, and tended by waiters from a café called Au Cadet de Gascogne, which had musicians playing inside. La Mère Catherine was a few buildings down the cobbled street, with a few of its own tables set out on the sidewalk. The front of the building was glossy black and lace curtains hung in the lower half of the two front windows. The ceiling inside was hammered tin and painted white and the walls were painted red. It was a lively place, and I wished I'd known about it before the price of a good meal had gone through the roof.

I looked through the window for Abetz, but couldn't see him. Then I felt a hand against my arm.

It was Leutnant Behr. He was sitting at one of the outside tables, wearing civilian clothes. 'I saved us a place,' he said.

There were two more chairs at the small table, and three places set for dinner.

I told him about Fleury not being able to make it. Behr

shrugged to show it didn't matter. 'Where's Abetz?' I asked.

'He'll come for a drink in an hour or so. I'm afraid you're stuck with me.' He seemed genuinely apologetic about this.

'I guess you're stuck with me, too,' I said.

'Not for long.' He grinned and looked like a kid. 'I got a transfer. I've been putting in for one practically every month. I think I must have worn them down. Or maybe they felt bad for me that my mother died a few weeks ago.'

'I'm sorry about that,' I said. But then I knew why he had got his transfer, and I was happy and sad for him at the same time.

'I'm going to be part of the Sixth Army,' he said.

The waiter appeared, long apron and short black jacket and the seriousness of a man expecting a big tip.

'Do you like coffee?' Behr asked me.

'Monsieur,' said the waiter with a slight bow, 'there is only Café National.'

'I like real coffee,' said Behr. 'And I like it at the beginning of a meal. It's a strange habit, I know.'

'Monsieur . . .' said the waiter. He was about to explain again that there was no real coffee, when Behr pulled a screw-cap Bakelite box from his pocket. It was round and about an inch tall, just small enough to fit into my outstretched hand, and the Bakelite was orangey yellow

When he unscrewed the cap, I could smell the coffee inside.

The waiter was watching him. There was a gentleness behind his deep-set eyes and frowning, dark moustache.

'Bring us two cafetières of boiling water,' he said to the waiter.

The waiter disappeared back through the crowded restaurant into the kitchen. People shuffled by in the dark, silhouettes trailing cigarette smoke.

'Mr Abetz thought you might appreciate not being in the stuffy surroundings where you normally meet him. He can be un-stuffy, too.'

'What did you want to talk about?' I asked.

'First of all, Ambassador Abetz would like to apologize for his outburst earlier today. He would like you to know that he can match any favourable treatment you are receiving from Dietrich. Abetz means what he says, too.' Behr spoke as if he had memorized what he was going to say. 'You could be a great asset to him, you and Monsieur Fleury, and believe me, a German ambassador is a good friend to have these . . .'

At that moment, everything seemed to stop moving. A huge crashing explosion surrounded me. Muscles clenched in bands across my chest. It sounded as if a truck had smashed into the restaurant directly behind me. I heard breaking glass. Then the explosion was gone. In its place came a ringing that blanketed all other sounds. It flashed through my head that I might be having a heart attack. I seemed to be falling over. Then I realized that it was Behr who was falling.

He tipped against the window. His head struck the glass so hard that the pane broke in bright lightning bolts up into the shiny black frame. His chair collapsed underneath him. He rolled on to the sidewalk.

The place where his head had struck the glass was bloody. Blood in the silver lines. There was more blood on the tablecloth and on the cutlery and the glasses.

I couldn't understand where it had come from. I looked down at my chest, expecting to see some great gaping wound, but there was nothing except flecks of red on my white shirt.

People inside the restaurant were looking out into the dark, to see where the noise had come from. A woman pointed to the broken glass where Behr's head had struck. Her husband jumped up, his chair flipping over. He grabbed the woman and pushed her down on the floor, then got down on the floor himself. Somebody shouted. Then somebody screamed.

I turned around to see a man standing in the street, almost on top of me.

It was Tombeau. His eyes were wild. He was holding a large revolver. Smoke drifted from the barrel and the chamber of the gun.

Only now did I realize that he had shot Behr.

Tombeau looked down at me. The gun was aimed right in my face.

I just sat there, staring back at him, too confused to be terrified.

'Courtesy of Mr Dietrich.' Tombeau's voice was thick and slow. 'You'd better get out of here, before the police arrive.' He turned around and walked away into the dark, across the little park, right by the tables where people were eating their dinner. The gun was still in his hand and he made no move to put it away. No one tried to stop him. Some people dived under their tables. One man put his hands in front of his eyes. Others sat there in shock, watching him go by.

I stood, feeling shaky, and stepped around to the other side of the table.

Behr lay on his side. His mouth and eyes were half-open and his head was wreathed in shadow. Beside him lay a white ashtray, which must have fallen off the table.

The waiter pushed his way through the crowd that had begun to gather at the door. He stepped carefully over Behr's body. 'Who did this?' he asked.

I didn't answer. I had just realized that the ashtray was not an ashtray, but the top of Behr's skull. In the lamplight by the door, it looked strange and pink and rippled, like the inside of an oyster shell. Blood spread out thick and dark as tar from under his body. It fanned out across the pavement, as if it knew where it was going.

The restaurant customers piled into the street. Others came over from the park. They all stared down at the body. A man in a bow tie caught sight of the Bakelite box of coffee, still open on the table. He leaned past me, avoiding my glance, carefully screwed the top back on the box, put it in his pocket and walked away down the street.

I ran. I sprinted down the Rue Berthe and crossed over on to the Rue des Trois Frères and across the Boulevard Rochechouart and after that, I had no idea what streets I took except that it was almost an hour later when I reached the river at the Pont Neuf. I stopped running then. My throat was raw and my shirt was stuck to my back with sweat. I forced myself to walk across the bridge on to the Îsle de la Cité. Then I went down to the point that juts out into the Seine, the Square du Vert Galant, which in the daytime was usually crowded with people fishing. The place was deserted now. My watch had steamed up and stopped. I had no idea what time it was, except that it was long after curfew. I sat down by the water. I wrapped my arms around my knees and started shaking, and when I finished shaking I wept for the first time in as long as I could remember.

I didn't know if I was crying for Behr, or for myself, or the breaking strain of always wondering whether the paintings I did were good enough, trying not to think about what would happen if we were caught, and how if we were caught it would be my fault and Madame Pontier with her crumpled, unsmiling lips would say she had known all along that I would fail them. Fleury and Pankratov and I were just as likely to be killed by the French for doing our job well as we were likely to be killed by the Germans for not doing it well enough. Until this moment, I had thought I had it all safely battened down inside me: the weight and measurement of risk. But I was wrong.

I remembered the dream I'd had of how Paris would be before I arrived. The picture-postcard views, soft-focused with the hope of what my time here would bring me. I glimpsed and felt it all suddenly and clearly, like remembering a dream from the night before as you fall asleep.

'Look at you now,' I said to myself.

The blood-dark river rushed by. The water seemed to pulse against the pale stone banks, as if threatening to flood and drown the city in its endless arterial flow.

In the news two days later was a report about the shooting of Leutnant Albrecht Behr, aged twenty-two, holder of the Iron

Cross, First Class. The blame was laid on a communist group called the Front Populaire. In reprisal, twenty suspected communists were shot up at Mont Valérien.

A bottle of champagne arrived from Dietrich, along with a note telling us not to worry.

There was nothing to do but get on with the work.

We never did hear from Abetz again.

16

From then on, we dealt only with Dietrich.

When he brought along Touchard to authenticate, it seemed to be more for the amusement Dietrich could get out of the slippery little man than for the skill Touchard had to offer. I was left with the impression that Dietrich only used Touchard because he had been ordered to do so, and that he would rather have taken our word over the authenticator's. Touchard was no expert, anyway. Often, he had no idea who was supposed to have done the painting, let alone whether or not it was authentic. Dietrich confided in us that Touchard had been forced upon him by the directors of the ERR, since Touchard was the brother of a prominent director of the *Milice* in the city of Lille, who had pulled strings to get him the post.

When it came to ridiculing Touchard, Dietrich couldn't help himself. The two men disliked each other instinctively. Dietrich was tall and solid and jovial, while Touchard was frail and long-suffering. He returned Dietrich's mockery with a martyred silence that made Dietrich like him even less.

'Come along, Sniffles,' Dietrich would say, since Touchard always seemed to be suffering from a cold that rosied his nose.

Dietrich's legs were much longer than Touchard's and Dietrich had a habit of striding quickly everywhere he went. This left Touchard trotting along behind, glaring hatefully at Dietrich's back as he struggled to keep up.

By contrast, Touchard had grown very attached to Fleury. Fleury, too, seemed to find in Touchard a kindred spirit. It wasn't hard to imagine the experiences they had in common. Both men were physically unimpressive. They had doubtless suffered the fate of all non-athletic boys in school, immediately reduced to second-class citizens, and too intelligent not to be insulted by the unfairness of it. I could see the same loathing on Touchard's face when he spoke to Dietrich as I had seen on Fleury's when he had to deal with Tombeau. Both men looked lonely, not just alone. They had built for themselves fortresses of arrogance from whose ramparts they could hawk and spit on the rest of the world that ignored them.

The result of this was that Touchard gave Fleury outrageously favourable terms whenever it came time to negotiate for paintings. All Fleury had to do was treat him with formality and respect, which left Touchard dizzy with gratitude.

'Why are you so hard on him?' I asked Dietrich one time when we stood on the landing outside Pankratov's studio, while Fleury and Touchard were sorting out the details of another painting exchange.

'I don't know, really,' said Dietrich. Then he waved his hand dismissively at the frosted-glass door, behind which Touchard's thin voice could be heard. 'He doesn't deserve the job. I don't tolerate whining from myself, and I'm damned if I'll tolerate it from him.' Dietrich was losing his patience as he spoke, revealing that Touchard annoyed him far more than he ever liked to show.

Valya often came along to these meetings. She made a point of having nothing to do with Fleury and me. I used to wonder why she bothered to come if she couldn't stand the sight of us, until I figured out how important it was to her that we felt so completely ignored.

I kept waiting for some kind of admission from Fleury that he'd made a mistake in falling for her. But Fleury appeared to have an infinite patience for Valya, no matter what she said or did.

It was Pankratov who bore the brunt of Valya's taunts. She flaunted how different her life had become. Pankratov endured it, never losing his temper. He knew that if he did blow up, she would tell him he no longer had the right. She would make Pankratov see the distance she had put between herself and him. That was why Pankratov stayed silent, refusing to part with the past, which only served to fuel Valya's bitterness.

'What about you?' Valya asked me one day at the atelier, forgetting to ignore me.

'What about me?' I replied.

'Whatever happened to the days when you were going to be a great artist?' She pretended to look around the atelier. 'I don't see any great art being done here. How far you are from all your dreams, Monsieur Halifax.'

I brought my mouth close to her ear and whispered, 'I'd rather live in a world where my dreams don't come true than in a world where yours do.'

She slapped me in the face for that. Hard. My left ear buzzed and stung.

Dietrich saw this and laughed.

Valya turned on him. 'You think that's funny?' she shouted. 'You don't care what happens to me at all, do you?'

By now, Dietrich's laughter subsided into a smile. 'You don't believe that,' he told her. 'Not for a moment.'

Valya and Dietrich were always raging at each other, the anger subsiding as suddenly as it appeared. They lived in a world as bloated with luxury as it was with confrontations. From what I had seen of the two of them, I knew that Dietrich loved Valya, in spite or even because of the fact that she didn't treat him well. She found fault with almost everything he did, at least in public. This didn't stop him from lavishing on her all the luxuries he could find. Valya loved him, too, in her own strange way. She seemed to have convinced herself that any show of real affection would cause Dietrich to lose interest. Every gesture of her love was made with sarcasm or followed quickly by the announcement of some petty grievance. The two of them had grown so used to their peculiar balance that they seemed to have forgotten what life was like before chaos had brought them together. Now they could no longer live without it. They even seemed to look with pity on the rest of us, at the same time as we were pitying them. They believed they were somehow more fortunate, somehow more alive, even in the midst of their fighting.

As the war dragged on, and hardship seeped into every facet of life, Fleury and I did not go hungry. Following a new set of instructions from Tombeau, designed to make sure we were seen more publicly as collaborators – *collabos* the French called us – we drank real coffee and ate profiteroles stuffed with cream and topped with Belgian chocolate at the Soldatenkaffee Madeleine on the Rue St Honoré, sitting among the iron-crossed officers and their too-loud-laughing girlfriends. We were regulars at the cramped space of Ladurée on the Rue Royale, with its green walls, elaborate sconces and gilt-edged fresco of fat-baby angels on the ceiling. We went to the Gaumont Palace Cinema, and watched Jeanne Hériard perform at the Scheherezade cabaret on the Rue de Liège. Fleury and I were expected to take what Dietrich offered us and to continue the charade. To refuse him would have aroused suspicion.

We also had to give the outward impression of wealth, in order to convince Dietrich that we were selling the paintings we received from him in exchange. There were plenty of avenues for moving these works overseas and fortunes to be made in doing so. The reality, of course, was that every painting went straight to Madame Pontier and into hiding. We lived off the allowance given to us by Tombeau, who also allotted us special funds to buy clothes. He told me to set up an account on the Boulevard des Capucines at the Heereskleiderkasse, which used to be called 'Old England' until the Germans renamed it.

We accepted the special passes Dietrich had made for us, which the Germans called *Sonderausweise*. They allowed us to violate curfew, which a lot of people did anyway: they took off their shoes and walked home in their socks so as to make less noise. The punishment for violating curfew was not in itself very severe, but if you were brought in on a night that a German soldier was murdered by the Resistance, you might get yourself shot as one of the dozens they would execute as a reprisal.

If we needed to go some place, Dietrich would have his private staff car sent over. He had upgraded his old Mercedes to a Horch convertible, which had two sets of front-facing rear seats and hooded 'black-out' lights mounted next to the regular lights and extra horns and the same swooshing front cowlings as on the Mercedes. It was, Dietrich told us, an even better car than was being driven by the military governor of Paris and a hell of a lot better than what Abetz was puttering around in. Grand as this Horch was, Dietrich seemed to flaunt its grandness even more by refusing to have it cleaned. So the black sides and the chromed front grille were powdery grey with dust and showed the streaks where hands had touched the paint while opening the door.

None of this applied to Pankratov. Dietrich himself showed little interest in the old Russian. As far as he was concerned, Pankratov was a bad-tempered, unclean old man who hung around with us because he had no place else to go. But anyone who could have seen Pankratov in his workshop, consulting his notes on the properties of canvas, paint and paper would have known there was a genius at work.

Dietrich never brought us to 54 avenue d'Iena, the headquarters of the ERR, in whose basement was rumoured to be a torture chamber whose walls had been soundproofed with asbestos. Nor had we ever met Alfred Rosenberg, the head of the ERR. At first, I used to think that this was because we weren't worth the bother. Later, I blamed it on Dietrich's selfishness, taking all the credit for the paintings for himself and keeping the people who worked for him hidden safely in the shadows. Eventually, I realized that Dietrich kept us out of the way for our own protection. He knew how dangerous his own people could be. He made it clear to us that if we were ever harassed, by French or Germans, one phone call to him would bring down the whole heavy-handed brutality of the Fabry-Georges boys. The reputation of Fabry-Georges, and Dietrich's ability to summon them like genies from a bottle, seemed enough to deter anyone who wished to do us harm.

I used to ask myself whether there was ever a time when I enjoyed these luxuries, despite everything they had come to represent. The answer was always the same: how could I enjoy myself when I knew that someone was watching me, all the time, obsessed with vengeance? Sometimes I would see these people and clear in their eyes was a simmering fury as they watched me eat and dance and walk in my warm coat, a grotesque kabuki mask of pleasure bolted to my face.

A part of me was resigned to the idea that we would all be caught, sooner or later. I tried not to think about the luck we'd had so far. Instead, I thought about the work. We churned out a steady stream of paintings and sketches, feathered in amongst the real paintings grudgingly supplied to us by Madame Pontier. Day after day, I painted and drew in that damp space below the old viaduct. I distilled my life down to the simple equation of the job. I saw the forgeries go out and I watched the original paintings that Fleury brought back – the masterworks of generations, which might otherwise have been destroyed.

When a German officer was shot at the Barbes subway station in mid-August of 1941, I became convinced that Germany would win. Some people saw this as the exact opposite – the beginning of serious resistance – but to me it had about as much effect as the barking of a chained-up dog.

The Germans arrested dozens of suspected communists, hauled them off to Mont Valérien and shot them ten at a time. The gunfire echoed out of those stone courtyards. All those dead in exchange for one German soldier. Collaborationist newspapers like *Je Suis Partout* went into full gear, making it sound as if the Germans didn't have a choice but to kill off that many people.

When America entered the war in December 1941, I was

surprised at how little I felt. The event should perhaps have simplified my thoughts about the violence that was going on around me. It should have swept from my mind all doubts about the outcome of the conflict. But it didn't. Maybe I had begun to believe what was written in that fake identity card that Tombeau had given to me – that I was no longer American. But it wasn't as simple as that. I was caught up, as many people were, in the small details of life from day to day. I couldn't stand back far enough to see the bigger picture.

Later on, when Germans were shot on train platforms or knifed while they were taking a piss in some restaurant urinal or beaten over the head and thrown in the river, the Germans did what they always did: rounded up hundreds of people, who were then tortured by the *Milice* or the Gestapo in chambers beneath the Rue des Saussaies. Even when the Resistance blew up the German language bookshop on the Place de la Sorbonne, and the street was filled with glass and smoke and thousands of pages of torn-apart books, these efforts seemed hopeless to me.

I had been dealing with the German authorities for several years now. I knew that they would pay back every strike against them with such efficient heavy-handedness that they would make the original act of violence look pathetically small. They would do this until not one Frenchman was left alive in France. They would not quit, if only to avoid the shame of quitting.

That all changed in early February of 1943, with the fall of Stalingrad. The German army had been cut off and over 100,000 troops had surrendered. This had been the Sixth Army, the same one that had marched in a victory parade down the Champs Élysées after the fall of France and the same one to which Behr was to have been transferred. At Christmastime there had been a broadcast from troops in all the various places where the Germans were fighting, including Stalingrad. I remembered that part of the broadcast, and now that I was speaking a little German, I even understood what they were saying.

'Attention. Attention,' said the radio announcer. 'I am calling Stalingrad.'

'This is Stalingrad,' came the scratchy reply. 'The Front on the Volga.'

Afterwards I heard rumours that the broadcast had been faked, and that the last German messages out of Stalingrad had ceased a week before. While the fake broadcast had claimed a victory, stories circulated across the whisper-dampened table tops of the Dimitri that Germans were being killed in Stalingrad at the rate of one every seven seconds.

For the first time, people began to speak seriously of the Germans losing the war.

The acts of sabotage that took place all around Paris had not convinced me. But Stalingrad did. The whole unimaginable slaughter of it made even the German reprisals against the French Resistance seem like nothing. I understood, finally, that they could be defeated – that they *would* be. From now on, it was only a matter of time.

I started to notice a change in the appearance of the German soldiers in Paris, particularly among the lower ranks. Most of them no longer wore the heavy jackboots. Instead, they had ankleboots now, and these were often made of rough and mottled leather. They tucked their trouser legs into canvas gaiters. The clothing changed, too. You could tell that the quality of wool was going down. Particularly in bright sunlight, the dyeing of their field-grey wool tunics seemed patchy, as if the wool had been recycled. I noticed a lot more young-looking soldiers, and a lot more older ones, too. But maybe none of that mattered, because they were still carrying the same Mauser rifles, and the same Schmeisser burp guns and the officers still had the same pistol holsters on their belts.

For us, the greatest change of all was that the market for trade in modernist paintings had begun to dry up. Apparently, Hitler himself had heard about collections of unapproved art being compiled by high-ranking German army officials, such as Foreign Minister Ribbentrop. The existence of abstract, constructionist and Expressionist works had been tolerated up until now because it was assumed that they were only being used as trade items. But in late July of 1943, as a response to the collecting, the SS took a number of paintings by Miro, Ernst, Picasso, Léger, Picabia and Klee, among others, and burned them in the garden of the Jeu de Paumes.

Business tailed off sharply. Tombeau urged us to sell paintings to Dietrich for gold bullion. He said the Resistance needed the money. But Pankratov and I refused, despite Fleury's reasoning that it was time we started looking out for ourselves a little. I told Tombeau I wasn't taking these kinds of risks for gold. With Pankratov supporting me, Tombeau and Fleury had no choice but to agree.

I used the free time to do some of my own pieces, the first I'd made in years. I did a sketch of Fleury one morning as he was sitting in his chair at the warehouse, reading the Sunday paper by the light of a candle.

Fleury didn't care for sitting still. 'I didn't realize this was so difficult,' he said.

'It's just difficult for you,' I told him.

I did a drawing of the candy-striped German sentry box at the Quai d'Orsay. I drew the line of Velo-Taxis outside Les Halles. There were hardly any motorized taxis now. Instead, they were small, two-wheeled carriages pulled along by bicyclists. I did a series of drawings of German soldiers relaxing in the Tuileries gardens. The one I liked best was of a general who had fallen asleep on a bench, while his deputy stood by, shading the man with an umbrella. The deputy grinned at me as I made the sketch, knowing how silly he looked with that umbrella. It felt good to be working for myself again, even just to be staring at the canvas, the way I often did before I began a painting, knowing that the painting would come from me, not cribbed from the mind of a stranger.

In the middle of the night, I heard the car brakes squeak again. I knew from the sound that the car had stopped right outside our building.

I went to the window and had to lean out dangerously far to see the car and the two men who banged on the door until Madame LaRoche came to open it.

At that moment, I knew that everyone on the Rue Descalzi was awake and holding their breath. Without thinking, I put on my clothes and my shoes. I fetched my coat from the peg behind the door and then I sat on my bed, hands sweating. It was easier than lying down and trying to pretend they weren't coming for me.

I heard the whirring of the elevator. Heard it stop. Start again. The men bundled someone out into their car.

I put my hands to my face and felt the sting of salty liquid on my cheeks. 'Oh, my God,' I said to myself. 'Oh, that was close.' I got off the bed, my knees gone shaky, and hung up my coat on the peg.

That was when I heard the elevator start again.

I stayed frozen by the door, waiting for the machine to stop, but it kept going, right up to my floor. I felt bile splash into my throat as the accordion door creaked open. I saw the shadows of the men in a gap between my door and the floorboards. There was some muttering and then a knock on my door.

I lifted my coat off the peg. The weight of it was suddenly almost too much for me. I didn't make them knock twice. I opened the door, and saw the two men in knee-length leather coats, one black, one brown. Under their coats they wore drab grey civilian suits. The man in the black coat held out his hand and in the palm was a bronze oval disc, on which were the words 'Staatliche Kriminalpolizei'. Under the words was a serial number. They didn't seem surprised to find me already dressed.

'You have thirty seconds to be ready,' said the man in the brown coat. In his hand he carried a thing like a small looped pair of tongs.

'I don't need thirty seconds,' I said, and stepped out into the hall.

They didn't speak to me as we rode down to the level of the street. As we slid from floor to floor, I thought about the others in their rooms and the relief they must be feeling that they had been left alone. This was the first time in my life that I got so scared I had to stop myself from throwing up.

I had forgotten about the other person. Under the circumstances, I was not surprised to find Fleury waiting in the back seat, while the driver of the car stood outside, in his shirt-sleeves, smoking a cigarette. A gun in a shoulder holster bunched under his armpit. There was nothing to say. We had both lived through this nightmare so many times in our heads that both of us now felt locked inside the same bad dream.

The man in the brown coat sat between me and Fleury. The man in black sat in the front with the driver. We set off through the empty streets. The headlights of the car had been hooded so that the beams were reduced to horizontal slits, appearing solid in the misty air.

The man who sat between Fleury and me still held the strange pair of tongs.

'What?' I asked, but then my tongue got stuck to the roof of my mouth and I had to start again. 'What is that?'

'Hold out your hand,' he said.

I did.

He clamped the tongs on to my wrist. Then he turned his fist slightly.

Pain shot up my arm and halfway down my back. I realized he could have broken my wrist with hardly any pressure at all.

We pulled up outside 54 avenue d'Iena.

'We are friends of Mr Dietrich,' said Fleury, out of breath with worry, but still trying to cram some measure of authority into his voice.

'Apparently not any more,' said the man who sat between us.

We were brought up the white steps, past two guards in black uniforms with sub-machine guns. I saw the SS lightning bolts on their collars. We went inside. There was a large foyer with a desk on which were three telephones. At the desk sat Grimm, staring at the phones as if daring them to ring. We were made to sign our names in a book. Then Fleury and I were led towards a staircase that ran up the right side of the wall and curved at the top. Before we reached it, however, a door was opened and we were ushered down a narrow stone staircase, which spiralled into the earth, like the path of all my nightmares, trodden down with repetition.

At the bottom of the stairs was another door, painted cream and made of steel. It was opened and we were led into a room with a brick-red linoleum floor and low ceilings, from which hung very strong unshielded lightbulbs, as well as a series of iron railings that were suspended horizontally about a foot below the level of the ceiling. The walls were dull white and made of a substance like pasteboard. The place smelled of disinfectant. In the middle of the room stood Dietrich and behind him, as if trying to hide, was Touchard. Touchard was holding the first original piece of work we had given to Dietrich as an exchange. It was the drawing of the kneeling angel by Gianfrancesco Penni.

I realized now that we were in the torture chamber. I'd heard so many rumours about this place that I had begun to wonder if it really did exist. I was surprised at the bareness of it – at how clean it appeared to be, and at the way these pasty walls seemed to drink the sound out of our voices.

Fleury was shaking. He looked as if he might collapse. His head hung down, as if he lacked the strength to raise it.

Touchard peered out from behind Dietrich's broad shoulders. He looked as frightened as we must have done.

Dietrich stepped to one side. 'Tell them,' he ordered.

Touchard was left standing with the Penni drawing, holding it against his chest as if to use it as a shield. 'It's a fake,' he said. He glanced at Fleury. 'I'm so sorry,' he whispered. 'We just found out.'

Fleury raised his head sharply. 'That's an original!' He held out his hand, like a man introducing a distinguished guest who has just entered a room. 'That is a Gianfrancesco Penni.'

'Fake!' bellowed Dietrich and his shout left no echo in the room. 'What the hell kind of game do you think you are playing?' He began to pace up and down in front of us, hands knotted into fists at his side. 'Are you trying to make me look foolish? Is that it?'

'Of course not,' said Fleury.

'This is your doing,' continued Dietrich, twisting his head, almost cobra-like, to glare into Fleury's eyes. 'This is your fault.' Now Dietrich stepped over to me.

I had just noticed the impressions of hands pressed into the soft, sound-drinking asbestos walls. For a moment, I couldn't understand how they had got there. Then I realized that these marks must be from the people who had been tortured here. I began to shake. It seemed to me that these walls had swallowed so many terrible sounds that some residue of the horror still remained, threaded in the fibres of asbestos, which might at any moment be released in a deafening chorus of screams. I felt a kind of resignation settling in me, heavy and thick, as if my heart had stopped and blood was already clotting in my veins.

'It's not you I blame,' Dietrich told me. 'No, you're not the expert. He is.' Dietrich's arm shot out, finger pointing at Fleury. He returned to Fleury. 'I want those paintings back. The ones I gave you for this piece of junk.' Then his rage overtook him again. He snatched the drawing out of Touchard's hands and tore it to pieces.

A dry rush of air passed down my throat.

Dietrich threw the pieces of the sketch into the air and let them flutter down around Fleury's head.

'You don't know what you've done,' said Fleury.

'It's you who doesn't know,' shouted Dietrich. 'I swear, if

you ever, *ever*, bring me another fake, I will show you what misery happens here. You owe me, Mr Fleury. I saved your life and in return you have insulted me and I will not let that go away. I will not forget it. There will be a reckoning between us.' Spit was flying from his mouth. His neck bulged against the clean white collar of his shirt.

For the first time, Fleury looked Dietrich in the eye. Suddenly he did not seem afraid. Instead, he looked as if he had gone away far inside himself, where nothing could touch him, and only the shell of his body stood there now, hollowly speaking these words. 'You may have your paintings back,' he said. 'You may always have your paintings back, if there is any doubt.'

When Dietrich heard this, he seemed to lose some of his anger. 'Well, that's good,' he said. 'That's a step in the right direction.' He walked over to the far wall, as if trying to extinguish the last reservoirs of his anger. Carelessly he fitted his hand into one of the handprints on the wall. 'You can go now,' he said, without turning around.

Touchard stepped towards Fleury. 'Monsieur,' he said, 'I beg you to believe that this was not . . .'

'Touchard!' shouted Dietrich.

Touchard shuddered and fell silent.

Back out in the street, it was still very dark. The cool air chilled my sweat. I hadn't realized how hot it had been down in that room. The car that had brought us was gone. I went back inside and persuaded Grimm to write us passes to get home, since neither Fleury nor I had brought our *Sonderausweise* with us, and we didn't want to get arrested for breaking curfew without permission.

On the way back, I wanted to burrow in the ground someplace and hide. 'It's all right,' I said, more to myself than to Fleury, who paced in silence beside me. 'It was just a foul-up. Just a temporary setback.' I didn't believe any of what I was saying. I was hoping that Fleury would take up the chant and we would convince ourselves with lie upon lie, the way we had done in the old days.

We were passing a set of shoulder-high black iron railings that fenced in the front of a large house at the end of the Avenue d'Iena.

Fleury turned suddenly and took hold of the tops of two railings, which were forged in the shape of blunted spear-heads. He tried to shake the railings, heaving his body savagely against them. He swung his body back and forth, growling and thrashing, until he had run out of strength. Then he staggered back into the street.

'Fleury,' I said quietly.

'Get away!' He glared at me as if he no longer knew who I was. Then he ran off down the road.

I didn't try to follow. There could be no reasoning with him now. I wandered home in a daze, returning again and again in my thoughts to the emptiness of the room in which we had met Dietrich. It was as if the emptiness itself created pain.

At six in the morning I was woken by the rattle of a key in the latch.

I rolled out of bed and hit the floor. Not again, I was thinking. I started to crawl under the bed, confused by half-sleep and helplessness.

'Monsieur Halifax!' It was Madame LaRoche. She stood with a bucket and a broom, silhouetted in the doorway.

I got to my feet, still shaky in my knees.

'They took you away,' she said, astonished to find me here. 'And Monsieur Fleury, too. I thought you were both gone. I had come to clean out your room.'

'Is Fleury all right?' I asked. 'Have you seen him?'

'He is here,' replied Madame LaRoche. 'He is himself.' She dropped the broom and bucket, which fell with a clatter. She marched into the apartment and wrapped her arms around me. 'My poor boy,' she said.

I put my arms around her and squeezed gently. It was like hugging a giant, ripe plum.

'Poor boy,' she said again.

At that moment, I heard a sigh, like the swoop of a bird's wing. When I looked up, I saw that the open doorway was filled with people. Everyone from my floor had gathered to welcome me back. There was Madame Lindgren, the dance instructor, with her slept-on red hair flowing down over her shoulders like molten lava. And Mr Finel, the Postillon bicycle man, his naked, hairy legs planted in a worn-out pair of workboots. And the Charbonniers and their son Hubert. They were all smiling at me, as if I had been gone for years.

I walked over to them and they put their arms around me and slapped me on the back and kissed me on both cheeks.

'Thank you,' I said. 'Thank you. Thank you.'

Later that morning I knocked on Fleury's door.

He emerged in his smoking jacket. 'Have you been embraced by Madame LaRoche?' he asked.

'I believe I have,' I replied.

'Quite something.'

I nodded. 'It certainly was.'

Fleury looked around, as if tracking the flight of an invisible insect. 'I got a bit carried away last night,' he said.

'Can't say I blame you,' I replied. I leaned against the doorframe with my hands in my pockets. 'All that stuff Dietrich said about paying you back – about you owing him – it was all just talk. You know that.'

'Do I?' he asked. 'Do *you*?'

Conscious that someone might be listening, I stepped into his apartment. Morning sunlight filled the space. The bed was neatly made and the air smelled of the sweet-dryness of the soap he used. I could see through to his tiny bathroom, the shaving soap and mug and bristle brush all laid out on a towel, the way he liked to keep them.

'Well,' he asked again, 'do you think it's just talk?'

'If he'd wanted us dead, we'd be dead by now.' I clicked my tongue. 'The one time we give him an original, Touchard gets it wrong.'

'I wonder if Touchard is really that much of a fool,' said Fleury. 'I think perhaps he's not.'

We set up a meeting with Madame Pontier at Pankratov's warehouse for later that day.

Pankratov, Fleury and I had been waiting several hours when we at last heard a car pull into the alleyway. When the engine quit, I heard Madame Pontier swearing and the low murmur of Tombeau as he offered up excuses about his driving.

Pankratov swung the doors wide. Magnesium sunlight flared across the sloping walls of the warehouse.

Fleury and I shrank back from it, shielding our eyes.

Pankratov showed them inside.

Fleury explained the situation to her, while Pankratov switched on the electric lights. Tombeau and I hung back in the shadows. I kept thinking of him standing by the table at La Mère Catherine, the gun in his hand. We had not spoken about it. I doubted if we ever would.

Madame Pontier stared hard at Fleury while she listened. She kept her arms folded, as if she felt the damp in this cramped space.

Fleury handed her a sheet of paper with the names of the two works we had received in trade for the Penni drawing.

I hadn't seen the list or the works. All I had seen was the Penni, and each time I thought of it, I saw the shredded paper twitching in the air as it fell from Dietrich's fingers.

Madame Pontier looked at the list. She seemed to be spending a very long time reading it. Then she raised her head suddenly and folded the paper in half. 'These are valuable works,' she said. 'They've already cost us that Penni drawing.'

'There are bound to be some losses,' said Fleury, his voice gentle and reasoning.

'I can't just give back the works,' she told him. 'It makes no sense.'

I felt my heart jump when she said this.

'You can, Madame Pontier,' replied Fleury. 'It makes all the sense in the world.'

'No.' She shook her head. 'I simply can't. What I will do is give you some other paintings. Some things we are more able to spare. You'll just have to make Mr Dietrich happy with that. I'm sure he will be, given the right explanation.'

Fleury pressed his hands to his face, then slowly dragged his fingers down his cheeks. 'You hand back those works this instant,' he said quietly, 'and I'll pretend I never heard what you just said.'

'That's it!' she snapped. 'Come along, Tombeau. We're leaving.' She took three paces towards the door, then stopped.

Tombeau was not following.

'Tombeau,' she said, without turning around.

'Madame,' said Tombeau.

I felt his breath brush by my face in the still air.

'You must return the works to Monsieur Fleury,' said Tombeau. 'I know this man Dietrich. I know what he is like. It isn't the work he cares about. He feels that Fleury has insulted him. If Fleury tries to give Dietrich something different in return, it will only make the insult worse. You know what will happen then. We have already seen it happen several times.'

This was the first I'd heard about other cells being broken.

'Madame Pontier,' continued Tombeau, his voice stiff with formality, 'in having to give back these works, I know you also feel as if perhaps you are being taken advantage of. But Madame Pontier, you will give them back, because you see more clearly than he does what is really at stake and what the consequences would be to you.'

She spun around. 'What consequences are those?'

Tombeau did not reply. His eyes were gleaming in the sharp-shadowed lights.

'Choose your words carefully, Monsieur Tombeau,' she said. 'They might be misinterpreted.' She walked out and kicked the door shut.

The slam of the huge timbered door boxed our ears.

After a few seconds, Tombeau followed her out. He didn't say goodbye to us. It was as if he'd been leaving an empty room.

In the silence that followed, Fleury fished out a cigarette from his old tin, the image of the Craven A black cat almost chipped away now by the coins he carried in his pockets. While he smoked, he polished his glasses with the end of his tie. He polished the lenses beyond the point where they would be clean. The strain was breaking him. He knew his job was the hardest. He had to do the lying and not blink. If anything went wrong, he would be the first to find himself in that basement on the Avenue d'Iena.

The next day, Tombeau returned with the works. The drawings were both by Lautrec. One was of a black man in a cap dancing in a café, done in pen and watercolour. Fleury said the man had been a popular dancer named Chocolat. The other was also a café scene – a heavy-set bartender with a handlebar moustache. This one had a tag on the back, which gave the title as *La Caissière Chlorotique*. As with most of the other works we received in trade from Dietrich, these showed ERR inventory marks, along with the small swastika inside a black circle.

'She didn't understand about Dietrich,' said Tombeau. 'About what kind of man he is. I explained it to her. It's all been straightened out.'

'I wouldn't mind hearing an apology from her,' I said.

'The fact that you have the drawings back *is* her apology.'

'Thank you for helping us,' I told him.

'It was not personal,' replied Tombeau.

I breathed out and looked away, wondering why I had bothered. But when I looked back, I saw Tombeau smiling. It was the first genuine smile I had seen from him. It creased his face like a sliver of new moon.

Fleury gave the works back to Dietrich, and all his anger seemed forgotten.

Two weeks later, after another exchange, Madame Pontier had the Lautrec drawings once again.

17

In the last week of May 1944 I received a call from Dietrich. There was a phone at the end of the hall on my floor, and somehow he had got the number, even though I never gave it to him. He said he would pick me up at the apartment in one hour. 'We're going to lunch,' he said. 'Can you make sure Fleury and Pankratov are there, too?'

'Pankratov?' I asked, uncertainly. 'All right.'

'Valya's idea of a joke,' he explained. Then he hung up, saving me the awkwardness of trying to think of something else to say.

Dietrich arrived in his magnificent but dusty Horch, Grimm at the wheel as usual. Dietrich had on a plain grey suit with a red tie and his small round Nazi party badge on his lapel. Valya was there, with white gloves and a salmon-pink dress that buttoned at her throat.

Once we were inside, the Horch set off fast through the streets. We sat facing each other, Dietrich and Valya on one side and me, Pankratov and Fleury on the other.

'So what's this all about?' asked Fleury.

Valya giggled. 'We've been drinking champagne,' she said.

There was an open bottle of Clicquot on the seat between them.

'*You've* been drinking champagne,' Dietrich corrected her. He smelled of aftershave. 'I'm taking you three to meet the boss,' he said. 'Your presence has been requested.'

'Which boss?' asked Pankratov.

'Göring,' said Valya, in between her giggles. 'Hermann Göring wants to see you. Originally he only wanted to see Fleury and Halifax, but then I put in a call and made sure you were invited, too, Daddy. I think that's so funny. I can't believe it! The Reichsmarschall is having lunch with Alexander Pankratov.'

'I'll try not to embarrass you,' said Pankratov in a monotone.

'Oh, I'm sure you'll *try*!' laughed Valya.

Dietrich glanced at us apologetically.

'Why does he want to see us?' I asked.

'To be honest,' replied Dietrich, 'I don't know.'

Valya puffed up her cheeks and swayed her body from side to side, in her imitation of a fat man walking down the street. 'Bring me this painting!' she said in a low voice. 'Bring me that painting!' Then she swung her arms up and down in an awkward imitation of marching.

'That's enough,' said Dietrich again, not looking at her. 'Some things we do not joke about.'

'I'll do whatever I want, you old Nazi.'

Dietrich's lips grew pale.

I clenched my jaw, waiting.

'I know what you are behind that suit.' She flicked at him with the tips of her fingers.

'Grimm,' said Dietrich, 'pull over.'

Grimm pulled fast and hard towards the kerb, as if he'd been expecting the command.

'Get out,' Dietrich told her quietly.

'I will not!' she shouted. 'I'm coming to this party and when I get there . . .'

'Valya!' boomed Pankratov.

His voice stunned everyone in the car. Even the immovable Grimm flinched.

Valya stopped. She turned towards Pankratov, eyes blazing. For a moment, it looked as if she were about to attack him. Then, slowly and shakily, she opened the door and got out.

Dietrich reached across and shut the door.

Grimm didn't wait for the order to drive on. We sped off down the street.

I looked back at Valya. She stood on the pavement, hands covering her face.

We drove the rest of the way without speaking, looking anywhere but at each other, eyes craning awkwardly around in their sockets.

It seemed to me that Dietrich and Valya were determined to destroy what they had together, to see how much they could take before love inverted into hate. They would never have anything in between. It would always be one extreme or another. I wondered if they'd gone too far this time.

The Horch pulled up outside the Hôtel Continental on the Rue Castiglione. On one side was a long covered walkway, separated from the street by pillared arches. A globe light hung from each arch. The entire hotel had long ago been taken over by the Germans and their flags hung out front.

Grimm opened the door for us.

Inside the Continental, footsteps echoed on the marble floors. Dietrich shepherded us towards an elevator and we rode up to the third floor. We walked down the pale-green-carpeted hallway to a set of doors at the end, in front of which stood a guard in airforce uniform. He had a sub-machine gun slung across his chest.

When we got to within a couple of paces of the guard, he smacked his heels together and opened the door.

The room inside was a small waiting chamber, with another set of doors at the far end. These doors were closed. Dietrich walked up to them and raised his hand as if to knock, but then thought better of it. He turned to us. 'Maybe we're a little early,' he said.

While we waited, Dietrich stood and smoked a cigarette. He looked nervous.

Fleury and I sat down on an overstuffed crushed velvet couch, done in the same pale green as the hallway.

Pankratov tried to make himself comfortable in a chair with ornately carved wooden arms. But the cushion was too puffy and he stood up again.

Dietrich sucked the smoke hard into his lungs. There was no ashtray, so he tapped the ash into his palm and then put it in his coat pocket.

We waited for half an hour in the airless, windowless space.

Nobody mentioned Valya.

Dietrich puffed down half a dozen cigarettes. The room was tinted grey with smoke.

Then the door into the rest of the suite opened and a short, elderly man in a white coat and black trousers poked his head in. He looked very patient and dignified, with watery blue eyes and thin hair sharply parted down the middle.

'Finally,' muttered Dietrich.

'The Reichsmarschall is sleeping,' said the old man.

Dietrich looked at his watch, which was a black-faced Hanhart chronograph. 'We have an appointment for one o'clock. It's almost two now.'

'The Reichsmarschall is sleeping,' said the old man again, as if perhaps Dietrich hadn't understood the first time. He ducked back inside and closed the door again.

Another half-hour of waiting.

'Jesus Christ,' said Dietrich, quietly. He slumped down next to us on the couch.

Pankratov stayed on his feet, picking at the wallpaper with his thumbnail.

When the door opened again, Dietrich jumped up. 'All right,' he said.

'Still sleeping,' said the old man.

'Look,' snapped Dietrich, 'we had a one o'clock appointment.'

The old man sighed.

'One o'clock,' repeated Dietrich.

'You would ask me to wake the Reichsmarschall?'

Dietrich fell silent.

'I didn't think so,' said the old man.

At this, Dietrich lost his temper. 'You thought *wrong*,' he snapped. 'I am a Sturmbannführer of the SS and I didn't get to be one by waiting around in hotels. Now wake him up and tell him Thomas Dietrich is at his door.'

'At my door,' said a voice. The door swung wide and there stood Hermann Göring. He was smiling the smile of a man with limited patience. He had a broad, severe face. He was a little under six feet tall, and badly overweight. His big barrel gut was hidden under a double-breasted tunic, which was grey like the feathers of a dove except for the lapels, which were white. He wore a white shirt with a pointy collar and a blue-and-gold cross, which I knew was a Blue Max, at his throat. Then, tacked on to his left side were more medals, another cross and a circular wreath with an eagle in the middle. His trousers had two wide white lines running down the seams.

Behind him was a view out to the Tuileries gardens. In the distance stood the Eiffel Tower. The room was carpeted in pale green and there were several doors leading off into other rooms. In the centre of the room behind Göring was a table set with a white cloth and silver cutlery. A bottle of white wine was chilling in a bucket beside the table.

Dietrich straightened his back in a fast and almost violent gesture, as if an electric current had rushed painfully down the length of his spine. He cracked the heels of his boots together in one precise movement.

'Thomas.' Göring's voice was deep and slightly drawling. He shook Dietrich's hand, placing his left hand over their hands when they were shaking. 'You are as obnoxious as ever. Can't I even take a nap?'

'Yes, Herr Reichsmarschall. Of course.'

I waited for Göring to tell Dietrich to call him something else – Hermann or something. But Göring seemed to like calling Dietrich by his first name and being called 'Herr Reichsmarschall' in return.

'These are the people you wanted,' said Dietrich, and stepped aside to give Göring a clear view of us.

Göring nodded at me and at Fleury, but when his eyes came to Pankratov Göring raised his head slightly and did not seem to know what to make of him.

Pankratov returned the same confused stare.

'Are you an old soldier?' asked Göring.

'Yes, sir,' said Pankratov. 'Cavalry of the Tsar.'

Göring nodded. 'And were you an officer?'

'Yes, sir,' said Pankratov, 'as a matter of fact.'

'I knew it,' said Göring. Then he turned to the rest of us. 'Old soldiers get like this.' He held his hand out to Pankratov, who stood there in his ratty canvas coat. 'They spend half their lives dressing up for people and then, when they are done with the army, they refuse to smarten up for anyone. Ever. Not even for me.'

'That is exactly right,' said Pankratov. 'I have tried to explain it . . .'

Göring brushed aside the idea with a sweep of his hand. 'Only an old soldier would understand.' He insisted that Pankratov sit beside him. The two of them walked off towards the window, speaking in lowered voices. Göring made some expansive gesture at the skyline and, when he heard Pankratov's mumbled reply, burst out laughing so loudly that it made the rest of us flinch. Göring pounded Pankratov on the back with the flat of his hand, as if he were trying to save him from choking. A small puff of dust rose up from the place where Göring's hand made contact with Pankratov's jacket. It caught Göring by surprise at first, but then he laughed even louder.

Dietrich stared at this in disbelief. The rest of us stood by our places at the table. Place cards had been made for us, which the old man in the short double-breasted jacket had immediately shuffled around when Göring changed his mind about Pankratov. Now, instead of the choice seat, Dietrich was placed at the other end of the table.

The old man opened the wine. Even though he appeared to be concentrating on the task, the corners of his mouth were turned up, enjoying Dietrich's discomfort. Göring and Pankratov reached the table, sat down and then we sat down. Soup dishes with one thin blue line around the rim were set in front of us. The old man served us lobster bisque, with bread still warm from the ovens and a huge block of real butter on a bed of ice, which he set down in a glass dish on the table.

Göring stabbed a chunk of butter off the block and set it on to a piece of bread, folded the bread around it in an envelope and ate it.

When the wine was poured, it beaded condensation on the glasses.

Göring raised his glass to toast us. 'I would like to thank all of you,' he said, 'for allowing me to share in your success.'

We drank to that and then Dietrich made some toast in return and we drank to that, too, and then Göring decided that we ought to be drinking vodka to remind Pankratov of the good old days, whatever they were.

The plates were slipped away from under us and the next course was wheeled in on a trolley. It was a whole leg of roast lamb with a crust of rosemary, and new potatoes and baby carrots and asparagus. The roast was carved by the old man. Göring watched the process carefully, then gestured towards the pieces that he wanted.

Göring did not say one word to Fleury or Dietrich or me through the appetizer, or the main course or the fresh strawberries, which were served with Chantilly cream, or the coffee – and not until we were drinking brandy and the old man was walking around to each of us with a box of cigars. Through all this time, he had grilled Pankratov about his old days in the Tsar's army, as if he had been starved for too long of talking about anything that really interested him.

At one point, Göring raised his hand above his head, grasping a spoon. Then he lowered his straightened arm in one slow gesture, recalling some great cavalry charge. 'Mit Volldampf Voraus!' he shouted.

This was followed by a roar of laughter from Göring. When

the laughter had died down, he sat back, arms folded across his belly, face serious, shaking his head. Later, his hands began to twist and turn in front of him, as he described some moment of air combat.

'Ah,' said Pankratov, nodding to show he understood. Throughout the dinner, he had remained quiet and observant.

Dietrich could not take his eyes off any of this. He reminded me of a young boy witnessing for the first time conclusive proof that his father was not perfect.

When the brandy was served, I noticed that Göring was given brandy different from ours. It was discreetly poured for him at the side table out of a crystal decanter, which had its own leather travelling case.

Göring talked in a hushed voice to the old man in the white waiter's tunic.

The man nodded and left the room. He returned a few seconds later with a leather folder. He handed this to Göring and then set about clearing the last of the plates. He pulled something that looked like a straight-edge razor from his pocket and scraped the breadcrumbs off the tablecloth.

Göring opened the folder and took out a photograph. He held it out for us to see. 'Have you seen this painting before?' he asked us.

'Yes,' said Fleury at once. 'It is Vermeer's *Geographer*. One of a set of two.'

'Exactly,' said Göring. 'It was purchased from the Charles Sedelmeyer gallery, here in Paris, in 1885, by the Frankfurter Kunstverein. It's still in Frankfurt, at the Staedelsches Kunstinstitut.' He flipped the photo around to look at it himself. 'The irony is not lost on me that if we had waited fifty years or so we could have got it for free.' He put the painting back inside the folder and took out another. When he showed it to us, Fleury didn't wait to be asked.

'*The Astronomer*. The second painting in the set.'

'Yes,' said Göring. 'In 1886 this painting was bought in London by the Baron Alphonse de Rothschild. It was last known to have been hanging in the home of Baron Edouard de Rothschild, in France. But it, and several other very valuable works, have managed to disappear.' He set the painting down on the tablecloth, then picked up his brandy snifter with both hands, rocked it in his cupped palms, breathing the fumes, but did not drink. 'Despite his enquiries – very forceful enquiries – Mr Dietrich, a Hauptsurmführer of the SS . . .'

'Sturmbannführer,' Dietrich attempted to correct him. 'I am a Sturmbannführer.'

Göring ignored him. '. . . has turned up nothing.'

Dietrich went red in the face. 'With respect, Herr Reichsmarschall,' he said.

'With respect,' replied Göring, 'I am talking.' Then he set his little finger on the photo of *The Astronomer*, as if to stop it from blowing away in the breath of his words. 'I want this painting,' he said, 'and have what I think will be an interesting offer. Thomas tells me that you specialize in exchanges. Modernist paintings in particular.'

Fleury nodded slowly, eyes masked behind the light reflecting off his glasses.

'Have you heard of the Gottheim collection?' asked Göring.

'I have,' said Fleury. 'It was the property of Albrecht Gottheim, a Berlin art dealer in the 1930s. The collection was confiscated in January of 1939 and in March of that year it was burned in public as a protest against *entartete Kunst*.'

Göring shook his head. 'Not true.'

'Indeed they were, Herr Reichsmarschall,' Dietrich interrupted. 'I saw those paintings burn with my own eyes.'

Göring shook his head again and smiled. 'We had copies made. The burning was carried out at night and no one was looking too closely. We didn't have to burn the originals to make our point. I have the actual works in storage. I will give you the entire inventory, over sixty paintings and drawings, if you will bring me *The Astronomer*.'

'But we don't know where it is,' said Fleury.

Göring stood up wearily. He rested his knuckles on the

table top. 'No,' he said. 'I don't think you do, or you'd have offered it to Dietrich by now. But I think you can find it. Thomas tells me if anyone can turn it up, you can.'

There was total quiet in the room.

'The truth is,' said Göring, after a moment, 'that I would like to make a gift of it. I will be candid with you. I would like to give this painting to Adolf Hitler, and as soon as possible. The fall of Stalingrad has caused a rift in our ability to understand each other. I made certain implications about the capacity of the Luftwaffe to supply the troops within the city.' He rolled his hand in front of him, as if to shape the words as they came out of his mouth. 'These implications led to expectations that were sadly not fulfilled. There was blame. There is a need to make amends. Hitler has become – I think I can say this – mildly obsessed with the missing Vermeer. He has cleared a space for it on the wall of Berghof and has declared that it will stand empty until *The Astronomer* hangs on his wall. And I think it would be a good idea for me to be the one who puts it there.'

The sunlight had gone now. The room felt cold.

'Thank you,' said Göring.

I wondered why he was thanking us but, as Dietrich got to his feet, I understood that this was the signal to depart.

We said our goodbyes; Göring looked impatient, as if wondering whether he had wasted his time with us. The only time a smile returned to his face was when he said goodbye to Pankratov. 'I hope there will be other times,' he said.

Out in the street, the Horch was there to meet us.

Back inside the car, Dietrich opened up his silver cigarette case and offered us each a smoke. 'The big man took a shine to you,' he told Pankratov, still unable to mask his amazement.

Pankratov didn't answer.

Dietrich lit our cigarettes with his clunky lighter and the car soon filled with smoke. 'You've got to find that painting,' he told us. 'If there's anything you need from me, just name it. I'd put a Panzer division at your disposal if I knew it would help.'

'Could you get me a list of the Gottheim paintings?' asked Pankratov.

'Done,' said Dietrich.

No more was said about it. Dietrich dropped us off at the far end of the Rue Descalzi. Pankratov came, too.

'What did Göring talk to you about?' Fleury asked him as we walked towards our building.

'The glory days,' said Pankratov.

'Am I supposed to know what that means?' asked Fleury.

'No,' said Pankratov, 'but I can tell you that is the most dangerous man I have ever met. He has set his mind on that painting and whether we want the job or not, he expects us to find it for him.'

We reached my apartment and put the water on to boil for tea. It wasn't really tea, but a mixture of camomile and mint that I grew in my windowbox. When the drink was ready, we sat at the bare wood table, cradling the cups in silence. Outside the streets were quiet except for wind rattling padlocks on the Postillon warehouse doors, like the ghost of the old Dragoon come to check that all was well.

'Gentlemen,' said Fleury, 'in case you were thinking about it, a forgery is out of the question.'

But of course that was exactly what Pankratov and I had been thinking about.

'If we used a period canvas,' Pankratov thought aloud. 'Period frame.'

'No!' Fleury cut him off. 'This isn't going into some warehouse. This is going up on the wall of Hitler's bedroom! He'll be showing it off to every art connoisseur he can drag in there.' Steam rippled across the lenses of Fleury's glasses. 'Even if Vermeer himself were painting your canvases, you still couldn't do it without having the original in front of you. We don't know where that original is. The forgery would have to be perfect and you said yourself that there is no such thing. Let's face it, we could never make it work.'

Pankratov set his mug down on the table. 'Yes, we could,' he said.

It was the day after our meeting with Göring. I'd just returned from the warehouse, where Pankratov and I had been talking all morning. We thought we had worked out a plan.

'You're mad!' shouted Fleury, throwing his hands in the air and walking off to the far end of the apartment, only to come pounding back a second later. 'Completely mad!'

'Will you just meet with Pankratov and listen to what he has to say?' I asked.

Fleury shook his head. 'It's crazy. The whole thing.'

I tried to reason with him. 'Pankratov says Madame Pontier might be able to get the painting for us. Then we can do the forgery.'

Fleury pressed the heels of his palms against his temples and groaned with frustration. 'No you *can't*! Who the hell do you think you are? Are you so obsessed with the challenge that you just can't turn it down? You've lost touch with reality working in that warehouse all the time. Do you remember what Pankratov said about the Mona Lisa's smile? About how it could never be forged? Do you remember?'

'Yes,' I said quietly, to offset his shouting.

'Well, there's a good reason for that and it doesn't have to do with anything unearthly about the painting. The reason it can't be forged is that no one would be foolish enough to try. It's too well known. And the same goes for the Vermeer. You would have to *become* Vermeer!' Fleury shook his head. 'You no longer understand your limitations.'

I sat there in silence. I knew that nothing Fleury could say was going to change my mind, no matter how much sense he made. I understood what he was telling me. I saw the logic in it. But my mind had raced ahead of his words. I kept thinking of the moment when Pankratov had said we would be able to make the forgery. I trusted his judgement of my skills more than I trusted my own. Fleury was right that I didn't know my limitations. Only Pankratov did. Over the years, he had become an almost supernatural presence for me, as if he were the creation of a spell, drifting in and out of human shape. And yet for all my faith in his mysterious powers, a warning image of that Mona Lisa smile flickered half-alive inside my brain, like a death's head moth in the darkness.

'I'll go to Madame Pontier. Get her to find us *The Astronomer*. Then, when I finish the work, if you don't think it's good enough, we won't give it to Dietrich.'

Fleury was quiet for a moment. His eyes closed slowly and then opened again. 'I'm telling you now, if it doesn't look right . . .'

I sighed. 'Thank you.'

'Don't thank me yet,' said Fleury.

Madame Pontier agreed to meet me on the Pont Royal. She told me to come alone. It would look less suspicious that way.

We stood on a part of the walkway that jutted out over the river and had stone seats built into it. It was a cool day. Hard wind blew down the Seine into our faces.

A silk scarf over her hair, she kept her hands in the pockets of her loden coat.

I told her about Göring's offer and our plan.

Before I'd even finished, she told me it was out of the question.

'But we can't reproduce the Vermeer if we don't have it in front of us,' I said, exasperated. 'You've understood that with other works. Why not with this?'

'You must let it go,' she said. 'For everything else you have done, I am grateful to you. The people of France are grateful . . .'

'I'm not doing this for the people of France,' I told her angrily.

'Then the artists themselves, whether they're alive or not, would all be grateful . . .'

'I'm not doing it for them either, Madame Pontier.'

She watched me for a long time, as if waiting for me to flinch. 'I have never cared about your motives,' she said, 'only your results. The answer is no, Mr Halifax.' She turned to leave.

'Why do you hate us so much?' I asked.

She stopped and turned around. 'Do you really believe that I hate you?' She gave me no chance to reply. 'If you try to do this Vermeer, you will fail. And if you fail, you will end up dead. The forgery cannot be done.' The condensation of her breath made it seem as if her lungs were smouldering. 'The painting is too well known. Hitler appointed a man named Dr Hans Posse to be in charge of selecting paintings for the museum he hopes to build in Linz. Dr Posse died two years ago, and the man who took his place is Hermann Voss. Voss is far too busy to check every painting being shipped into the Reich. He's too busy at the moment even to unpack most of them. But the Vermeer he will examine. And you might be able to fool Dietrich, or Göring or even Hitler, but you will not fool Hermann Voss. He's studied the original. It's not going to be like those others you've made.' She paused for a moment, blinking in the freezing air. 'I am saving your life, Monsieur Halifax. I know the stories people tell about me – that I care more for paintings than I do for people. I know how it must look to you. I am what I need to be. And I am looking out for you.' She was already walking away. When she reached the end of the bridge, a man who had been standing under a lamp-post smoking a cigarette fell in step with her and they crossed the road together. It was Tombeau. He had kept his distance, not showing himself to add to Madame Pontier's threat. But the fact that he stayed out of sight showed me they were beyond the point of making threats. She may have been looking out for me, but if I went ahead and put her in danger, or the paintings in danger, she would have me killed. It would not be personal, as Tombeau had told me before.

But I wondered if I had misjudged her all along.

That evening, Pankratov came to my apartment, where Fleury and I were once again eating mashed turnip for dinner. I told them what she'd said.

'There,' said Fleury, laying down his spoon. 'It's over with.'

Pankratov reached into his pocket and pulled out a sheet of paper. He laid it on the table, smoothing out its creases with the heel of his palm. 'This is a list of the paintings in the Gottheim collection. I picked it up from Dietrich earlier today.' He slid the page across the table towards me.

I checked down the list of names, feeling vaguely sick at the thought of these paintings fading back into irretrievable darkness. Corot, Klee, Sisley, Picasso, Picabia, Munch, Dufy, Braque, Léger, Masson. Then, jabbing at my sight as if something were rising off the page, I read the name Pankratov. There was one painting, titled *Valya*. Confusion twisted inside me. 'I don't understand,' I said.

Pankratov was clearly upset. With shaking hands, he brought out his halved cigarettes and shook one out of the packet. He put it in his mouth but couldn't get a match lit. The sticks kept breaking on the box. Eventually he gave up, forced a deep breath down his throat and put the cigarette down on the table. He spoke in a wavering voice. 'In 1938 a gallery here in Paris decided to have a retrospective of all my paintings. The gallery managed to persuade all the various owners to lend them for the show. We stored them at my studio. I had all except one, and that was Gottheim's. The National Socialists were in power and Gottheim didn't think he could transport the paintings safely out of the country. So he refused. One year later, the Nazis turned his whole collection into their sacrificial lamb.' Pankratov picked up the cigarette again and this time succeeded in lighting it.

'Why didn't you say anything to us earlier?' I asked.

'I wanted to be sure,' said Pankratov.

'But what would you have done with the painting, anyway?' asked Fleury. 'Burned it like the others?'

Pankratov shook his head. 'I burned them for reasons that made sense to me at the time. Now I look at paintings differently than I used to. I see them as separate from the people who made them. The way a child is separate once it is born. Once I made them, they became separate from me. I had no more business setting fire to them than I would have setting fire to someone else's work.' He scratched his fingers down his forehead, streaking the skin violent red. 'Things are different now,' he said.

Fleury folded the list along its original creases. He handed it back to Pankratov. 'Without the original,' he said, and left it at that.

Fleury was right: the Gottheim collection, and everything it had come to stand for in my head, now seemed completely out of reach.

Pankratov had been staring at the table for a few seconds. Now he glanced up at us. 'It's in Normandy,' he said.

'What?' I asked.

'How do you know?' Fleury's voice was sharp and accusing. 'Only Madame Pontier has that information.'

'When we stopped at that café on the way to the Ardennes Abbey, and I went out to stretch my legs, I looked under the wrappings of every single painting in the truck.' Pankratov shrugged. 'I couldn't help myself.'

'But how could we get it now?' I asked. 'We don't even know if the de Boinvilles live there any more.'

'They do,' said Pankratov. 'I called Marie-Claire this afternoon.'

'Did you tell her about the Vermeer?' asked Fleury

'I couldn't tell her exactly. I hinted at it.'

'Do you think she understood?' I asked, knowing that what Pankratov called a hint might make no sense to anyone else on the planet.

'I guess we'd know if we showed up at her door,' said Pankratov. 'The question is whether we should go.'

Fleury sighed. He took off his glasses, put them in the

pocket of his jacket and gently patted the pocket to make sure they were in place. Then he walked over to the sink, pushing aside the red curtain that separated the living room from the kitchen. He turned on the tap and washed his face, letting droplets run through his fingers. 'What if Madame Pontier finds out what we're doing?' he asked through the cage of his hands.

'She might not have to know,' said Pankratov, as he stood up to leave. 'You two need to talk it over. Whatever you decide, we will do.'

Fleury smoothed one hand down the length of his face. 'I have already made up my mind,' he told Pankratov, 'but if I don't like the look of your forgery, the whole business ends there.'

We told him that was fair enough.

Fleury smiled, which was rare for him these days. It was a smile from the old days, before we knew how lucky we had been.

18

The following morning, 6 June, Allied troops landed on the French beaches.

I didn't learn about it until the evening. I spent the whole day tidying up Pankratov's repair shop, cleaning out the fireplace, scrubbing down the work surfaces with soap and water and a wire brush. I swept months of dust from the floor. I had given myself the job mostly because I was too nervous to do anything else. I had been carried along, first by the whole idea of saving the Gottheim collection, and then by the thought of saving Pankratov's last surviving painting. Only now was I beginning to see how unlikely it would be for me to produce a passable forgery. I could only guess at the depth of Pankratov's disappointment when Fleury refused to accept my work. I knew I wouldn't blame Fleury if that happened. I was glad he had made us promise to give him the final say. It was true that Pankratov and I had allowed our minds to become clouded. Fleury had understood this before we could grasp it ourselves.

I didn't leave the repair shop until after dark, sliding the heavy padlock into place, knocking it shut with the heel of my palm and then trudging off down the unlit alleyway, feet crunching on the gravel, hands in pockets, heading for home.

The first time I noticed anything out of the ordinary was when I stepped inside the Dimitri. There were no Germans tonight. The only customer besides myself was Le Goff, wedged behind his usual table. His piggy eyes were dull behind pasty, folded cheeks.

'Hello,' said Ivan cheerfully. He stood behind the bar, wiping out glasses with a cloth.

I took off my coat and hung it on a peg. 'Quiet tonight.'

'It's the invasion,' he said.

My whole body went numb. 'Is it certain?' I asked.

'Oh, yes,' said Ivan. 'It's for sure.'

'Where was it?'

'Normandy,' said Le Goff, butting in. 'Those Germans you've been kissing up to for the past four years won't be around much longer, will they?' He puckered up his fish-pale lips and made sloppy sounds.

I tried to ignore him.

But Le Goff wasn't finished with me yet. 'Your deeds have not gone unnoticed. Your friendships with the enemy.'

'That's enough, Le Goff,' said Ivan. 'The truth may be different from what you think.'

'I doubt it.' Le Goff coughed up a laugh like a man hawking phlegm. 'Some heads are going to roll before too long and I expect Mr Halifax's will be one of them.'

I glanced back at him.

'You know what you are?' asked Le Goff. 'You are a son of a bitch. If I was any younger . . .'

'But you aren't younger,' I said, cutting him off. 'You're old and slow. You're a dead man who's forgotten to lie down.'

Le Goff slumped back in his seat. He filled the air with obscenities.

I took the opportunity to leave.

I went straight home and knocked on Fleury's door.

He had heard the news, and all the rumours, too. German radio reported that the landings had failed, but the military in Paris had been put on full alert. Rumours were that German divisions were now, after a delay of many hours, advancing towards the coast. At first, the German High Command had been convinced that Normandy was a decoy with the real thrust coming at the Pas de Calais. 'I wonder how long it will be before the Allies get to Paris.' Fleury was tying and untying the black silk belt of his smoking jacket. 'I hope we get a chance to explain what we've been doing for the past few years.'

'Old Le Goff down at the Dimitri took a few pot-shots at me just now. He didn't seem too interested in anything I had to say.'

'Pot-shots with words I don't mind,' said Fleury.

'Maybe the Vermeer deal is off,' I thought out loud.

'You'll find out tomorrow,' answered Fleury. 'Dietrich's coming by first thing in the morning. If the deal's still on, we'd better get hold of that painting as quickly as we can, before some artillery barrage flattens the Ardennes Abbey and everything in it.'

Fleury and I had planned to meet Dietrich on our usual street corner at the far end of the Rue Descalzi. But either Fleury got the time wrong or Dietrich decided to come early. He showed up when I was still getting dressed.

Dietrich had never been inside the building before. When he arrived at my door, swathed in his double-breasted leather coat, he couldn't hide his surprise that my place was so small and the furnishings so Spartan. 'But this is even worse than Fleury's!' he said loudly. 'He was wearing some bizarre red coat when he came to the door!'

'That's a smoking jacket,' I explained. 'It's his armour.'

Dietrich started to laugh, but realizing that I had not meant it to be a joke, he stopped. 'Well, I made him take it off before I sent him down to the car.' Dietrich continued to look around the room, baffled by what he saw. 'So what do you two do with all the money from those paintings?' he asked. 'I thought you'd be rich by now.' He turned a slow circle in my living room, his fingers dragging past the old red curtains. 'What's going on?'

My mind spun like a roulette wheel. I knew I'd have to offer some excuse. 'We put our money in the same Swiss banks as Hermann Göring,' I announced. 'There's no sense flaunting it here.' Then I stood very still, waiting to see what would happen next.

Dietrich nodded slowly. 'Good thinking.' Satisfied, he changed the subject. 'Did you hear about the invasion?'

'Of course,' I answered, the wheel in my brain slowly clattering back to its normal speed.

'God knows what will happen to us now,' said Dietrich.

It felt strange to hear him grouping his own destiny with mine. 'How are things with Valya?' I asked.

Dietrich's features softened at the mention of her name. He unbuttoned his coat and sat down at the kitchen table. He looked like some large machine collapsing in slow motion, his bones folding in on themselves. 'It used to be that we always had time to make up, but now I don't know any more, the way things are going. We will have to leave.'

'Where to?' I asked.

'It won't be back to Germany, that's for sure.' He straightened up, as if suddenly ashamed of his dilapidated state. 'I have in mind a little town in Mexico I've read about called San Cristobal de las Casas. I think that might be far enough away. The Fabry-Georges boys are getting restless. They're thinking they might have backed the wrong side. There's about ten of them I promised I'd have shot if they ever turned on me. The irony is that it's the Fabry-Georges people who used to do all the shooting. Do you suppose I could pay them to commit suicide?' He smiled weakly.

'What about that man who shot Behr?' I asked, and felt my jaw muscles twitch, as they did every time I thought back to Tombeau's face on the night that Behr had died.

'Tombeau. He's the worst of the lot,' said Dietrich. 'Always stirring things up. He's the first one I'll finish if I have to do any killing myself.' He breathed out slowly. Then he turned to business. 'Do you have that Vermeer yet?'

'Does Göring still need it?' I asked. 'Even now?'

Dietrich nodded. 'He calls me almost every day. I tell you, we're all dead if you can't turn up that painting.'

'Why does Hitler want it so badly?'

'Who knows? Who dares to ask?' said Dietrich. 'It's an astronomer – a man pondering the mysteries of the universe. That's how Hitler sees himself, I suppose.'

'We need you to get us some fuel,' I said. 'A truck, too.'

'Done,' he said quickly. 'We'll do that right now.'

I had the feeling he would have given us just about anything to get the job done. I saw on his face the same intensity as I had seen in Göring when he mentioned *The Astronomer*, blind with the need to possess it.

Dietrich stood up to leave. 'I won't ask where you're going, but if you're heading towards the fighting, you ought to leave soon. Allied planes are shooting everything that moves along any road within a hundred kilometres of the front line.'

'So let's go,' I told him. I hauled on my coat and headed for the door.

What Dietrich found for us was a military ambulance, which he kept at the Schneider warehouse. 'The best I could do at such short notice,' he said, when we arrived, having picked up Pankratov from the Dimitri.

The ambulance was a requisitioned Citröen delivery van. The whole machine was painted dull field-grey, except for the tyres, and these were mismatched and almost worn out. On the sides and on the roof were neat white squares with a red cross painted inside. The headlights had been fitted with dampeners, which made them look like a pair of squinting eyes. Five jerrycans of fuel were lashed on to the roof. 'We often use it to transport works of art around the city,' Dietrich explained. 'No one stops an ambulance, least of all a military one.'

In the office, Dietrich filled out passes that allowed us to travel by any roads we chose and to requisition fuel anywhere we could find it. He signed it himself, then pounded the pages with numerous eagle-and-swastika stamps. It would be enough, Dietrich said, to scare off any military policeman who might flag us down. He also had yellow armbands for each of us, on which was written in black Gothic letters: IM DIENST DES DEUTSCHEN HEERES – In the service of the German military.

Just as the four of us were walking out towards the ambulance, there was a flicker in the light around us, as if the sun had blinked. We looked up and saw the first of what looked to be hundreds of planes crossing the path of the sun. The planes were high, throwing the chalkiness of contrails behind them. If I looked closely, I could see they were four-engined, the streams of vapour merging into two, which merged with the other condensation paths until the whole sky looked like glass that had been scratched with a handful of diamonds. They were American bombers, coming over from England and heading deep into Germany. These days, the sky was never empty of contrails. Even at night, they stretched across the cloudless sky, lit up by the moon.

Dietrich stood with his neck craned back, tendons strained, his eyes almost shut against the brightness of the afternoon sun. 'You'd better get going,' he said.

I drove Fleury and Pankratov out of Paris along boulevards as deserted as the ones we'd travelled four years ago, on our way to Normandy.

I kept to myself on the ride out.

Pankratov's and Fleury's conversations drifted in and out of my head. One time they were talking about food, and Pankratov was going on about some Finnish recipe for marinading raw salmon in vodka, dill and rock salt. Another time Pankratov was wondering who had painted the forgeries of his work in the Gottheim collection and if the forger had done a good job. Later, when I heard them discussing what they would do after the war was over, I realized that I had done almost no thinking on the subject.

I was just opening my mouth to say something about it, when we came over the ridge of a small hill and saw the wreckage of two German army trucks. I remembered what Dietrich had said about air attacks. One of the trucks was flipped on its side in the ditch and another was standing out in a field, just off the road. The one in the ditch had burned out completely and the still-smoking metal was dirty orange from incinerated paint. The windows had melted out. The tyres were bubbled and smeared all over the wheelwells. Only the steel-tube frame remained of the canvas-covered roof. The truck out in the field had been blown almost in half, the cab fallen forward from the rest of the truck, making it look strangely beheaded. All around the truck were pieces of soldiers' equipment: German helmets, some with chicken wire bent around the rims for holding camouflage, unravelled white bandages, leather belts, mess tins and felt-covered canteens so twisted and torn that it looked as if they had been wrenched off their owners' backs by a tornado. I saw white chips in the tarmac where bullets had struck the road.

We were now on the outskirts of Caen. The city was burning. Four separate pyres of smoke rose from the city and merged, dirty and black-brown against the sky. I could smell the smoke, even though it looked to be about a mile away. It tangled with heat off the fields, the smell of the warm earth, pink foxgloves and the tiny white blooms of elderflowers in the thick *bocage* hedgerows.

It was here that we met our first roadblock, but it was only a traffic diversion. Two military policemen, one of them standing on top of a fifty-gallon oil drum, pointed us down to the south. They wore half-moon chained breastplates across their chests and aimed the way for us with long-stemmed lollipop markers. They both wore camouflage jackets and had camouflage paint on their helmets. Beyond them, on the road, lay more burned-out vehicles.

The detour took us down through a village called St André-sur-Orne, then crossed over the river Orne and up through the towns of Maltot, Verson and Carpiquet. By that time, we had overshot the Ardennes Abbey by a couple of miles and had to double back.

Most of the old houses had their rickety, paint-peeled shutters closed up. There were very few people moving around in the little towns, and no vehicles at all. Nor were there any traces of German troops, except in the fields, where marks of recent encampments could be seen as fade-marks in the grass and deep gouges of tank tracks across the muddied ground. They had all gone forward to the front.

I pulled into the shade of some large trees that grew across the road from the Ardennes Abbey. Then I cut the engine. For the first time in many hours, I took my hands from the wheel. I clenched my hands, working the blood back into my knuckles.

Pankratov ran across the road to the gate. It opened before he reached it.

Marie-Claire came out to meet him. She looked as pretty as I had remembered. She gave Pankratov a big hug and then pointed back into the courtyard.

Pankratov stepped back from the hug, rested his hands on Marie-Claire's shoulders and spoke to her.

She nodded.

Pankratov kissed her on the forehead and went inside the abbey.

Seeing Marie-Claire again brought back to me the almost-forgotten lightness in my chest of being a stranger in Paris.

Marie-Claire walked across to where Fleury and I stood stretching our legs after so many hours of being cramped up in the ambulance. Her small feet crunched on the khaki gravel of the driveway. Above her, a warm breeze rustled the tops of the trees. 'How are you, my darlings?' she asked, embracing each of us in turn.

I said how good it was to see her again. Then I asked if Pankratov had explained why we were here.

'My husband has already opened up the wall.'

'Has Madame Pontier called you?' I asked nervously.

'Pankratov swore us to secrecy,' she replied. 'She can call all she wants. She won't learn anything from us.'

'Thank you,' I breathed out. 'I'll go help with the painting.'

She shook her head. 'There's nothing for you to do. You must rest now.' She didn't need to ask me twice.

I eased myself down beside the truck and let my head fall

back against its chevronned engine grille. 'I think it's been about a million years since I sat in the grass and did nothing,' I said.

'Has it been terribly difficult for you in the city?' asked Marie-Claire. 'I hear the most awful stories. The only thing that happened to us was that we had to move out because a German officer came to live here. His name was Generaloberst von der Schulenberg.' She made no attempt to pronounce the words correctly. 'After a few months, he got bored out here in the country and took our apartment in Caen instead. That was in 1941. We've been back ever since.' She looked off down the shady road. 'Wasn't it sad about Artemis?' she asked.

'It was,' said Fleury.

I thought back to the day we found out he'd been killed. I wondered if Marie-Claire had convinced herself it wasn't her fault – that he would have been conscripted anyway, that he would have been killed in the fighting.

She breathed in suddenly. 'It'll all be over soon. I just hope they don't wreck this place on their way through.'

'All be over soon.' The words repeated in my head. I closed my eyes and felt the warm breeze coming off the fields.

Marie-Claire's hand brushed softly against my face. 'Why don't you stay?' she asked.

'Stay?' My eyes opened wide.

'Yes,' she said. 'The Allies aren't far away. The whole of Normandy will be liberated soon.'

I said nothing. The idea had put me into shock.

'My God,' said Marie-Claire. 'You didn't consider this, did you?'

'There's more work to do,' I mumbled. 'It's more complicated than you think.'

She turned to Fleury. 'What about you?'

Fleury just stared at her.

It was the first time I had ever seen him at a loss for words.

Marie-Claire pointed down the shady road. 'In about a week, the Allied armies will be driving their tanks down this little road, and they may blow a few holes in our house before they get here, but I don't care, because I'll be free. But God knows how long it's going to take them to get to Paris. And who's to say the Germans won't destroy the city before they leave it? You don't want to be stuck in the middle of that.'

Just then, Pankratov emerged from the gate. He was carrying the painting, still wrapped in its white cloth.

'It's not too late,' said Marie-Claire, her voice an urgent whisper.

Fleury was looking off down the road, as if to see Allied soldiers advancing through the dappled shadows of leaves upon the shady road. Then he glanced at me.

'It's all right,' I said. 'You stay.'

'What about you?' he asked.

I shook my head. 'Got to try,' I told him.

One more time, Fleury looked down the road. Then he got back in the ambulance. He rolled up the window, and the dirty glass rose around him like floodwater. He sat very still.

'You're leaving, aren't you?' asked Marie-Claire.

I stepped over to the door of the ambulance and opened it.

Fleury sat with his Craven A tin on his lap. He was down to his last cigarette, which was often the case. He seemed to be debating with himself about whether or not to smoke it.

I opened the door and leaned down to him.

'Look,' I said, 'stay if you want.'

Fleury smiled. He took hold of the door and pulled it shut. A moment later, a wisp of smoke rose up around his head.

Marie-Claire took hold of my arm. 'What's happened to you people?'

Pankratov reached the ambulance, carrying the painting. He got down on his haunches, back against the door of the Citröen. He tore off the painting's white cloth cover and wrapped it around his neck like a scarf. The painting was small. He held it at arm's length, gripping the honey-brown frame.

I sat down next to him. We stared at The Astronomer, in his

blue robe, long hair down around his shoulders. One hand touched a globe. The other gripped a table, as if the shock and vastness of whatever knowlege was about to reach him might throw his body back across the room. A tapestry bunched on the table. Yellowy light through the window lit up the brilliance of the threads. It was the first time I'd seen the actual painting. Now I understood how someone could become obsessed with it.

The Count de Boinville appeared at the entrance. He was lugging two watering cans made of tin with brass spouts. As he came close, I could smell that they were filled with gasoline. 'I've been hoarding fuel for months,' he said. 'I thought you'd need some now.' He glanced at the painting and looked unimpressed. 'All this work for that?' he asked.

'All this,' said Pankratov.

The count shook his head, and smiled wearily, as if Pankratov had just told him a joke he'd heard before. 'I tell you, I'd trade that thing for fifty litres of petrol, and so would almost everybody else around here.'

Marie-Claire slapped him on the arm. 'Max,' she said, 'you talk such rubbish.'

'No, I don't,' he insisted. 'I meant it. I think you're all insane to be taking such risks.'

'And what do *you* value?' asked Pankratov.

'Peace of mind,' said the count, without hesitation.

Pankratov opened up the two doors at the back and stashed the Vermeer under a pile of blankets that were folded and strapped to a stretcher.

I wondered what it must be like to see *The Astronomer* through the eyes of the Comte de Boinville – just canvas, wood and paint.

Marie-Claire hugged me goodbye. As she stepped back, she let her hands trail down my arms until they reached my fingertips.

It was dusk as we drove the long way around Caen and on to the main road back to Paris. The moon was out and lit up the fields. We saw the silhouettes of tanks and guns lined up, preparing to advance. German soldiers passed us on the narrow roads, their helmets wet with dew. Whenever we came to a roadblock, where trench-coated military police held up lollipop signs that said 'HALT', we handed them our papers and they waved us on our way.

At one point in the drive, while Pankratov was snoring in the corner, I noticed that Fleury was awake. 'I wanted to thank you,' I said.

'Thank me for what?' he asked.

'For coming back with us. You didn't have to do that.'

'Yes, I did,' he told me. 'I wanted to. I know you've found it difficult to trust me. I don't say it should have been any different. The best I could do was to show I trusted you.'

We reached the outskirts of Paris by two in the morning.

Five hours later, at Pankratov's warehouse, I began work on the forgery.

19

In the weeks that followed, I started and stopped and restarted so often that I no longer had any idea of which version I was working on. I ruined three canvases simply by working on them and then scraping them down too many times.

Pankratov never told me to quit, but I knew he was thinking about it.

Fleury was also patient. He fended off calls from Dietrich and told him we were still trying to get hold of the painting.

Dietrich's old confidence was gone now. Things were falling apart at the ERR. Most of the staff had departed for Germany, leaving Dietrich in charge. The Fabry-Georges were looking to be paid off, but Dietrich had nothing to give them because almost all the ERR funds had been transfered back to Germany. Even Touchard had become insolent and was making demands that he be evacuated to Spain with enough gold bullion to start a new life. It was all Dietrich could do not to shoot the man himself. Now that things seemed finally to have fallen apart with him and Valya, the only thing keeping Dietrich in Paris was the chance of that Vermeer.

My days ran together. I lost track of time. I worked alone all day. I had a sense of things moving too quickly around me, as if all of us in the city were trapped in some whirlpool of anxiety that had become a separate living thing, swirling through the streets.

There were times, towards the end of the day, when my mind was exhausted but my body still hummed with nervous energy, that I had the sensation of standing half outside my own body. I felt like an image seen through a pair of misaligned binoculars.

I felt myself trespass in the mind of Vermeer himself. It

made no difference that he had been dead for centuries. His thoughts were still alive, and I moved like a burglar through the dark rooms of his mind. Afterwards, when these brief but overpowering visions had passed, I could not tell whether I had truly glimpsed the genius of the artist or had wandered out instead into the lake of madness.

In the evenings, I'd take the subway to the Rue Descalzi and stagger into the Café Dimitri. It was here that I heard the names of resistance groups spoken out loud for the first time, as people grew bolder in their talk of liberation. By eavesdropping, I was able to learn about the different groups that were competing for control: Le Front National, Ceux de la Résistance, the Parti Communiste Français, the Liberation Organization, the Parti Socialiste, the Union des Femmes Françaises and the Mouvement de la Libération Nationale. They all had their abbreviations – CNR, CPL, CGT, CFTC and so on. Some groups seemed to be advocating a general insurrection before the arrival of the Allies, who by now were through the city of Rennes and making for Alençon. Others were trying to prevent any uprising, convinced that the Germans would flatten the city. A rumour began to circulate that a special cannon was being brought in by rail that could destroy an entire city block with just one shell.

One day, in the second week of July, there was a parade of British and American prisoners of war through the streets of Paris. I hadn't known it was going to take place and only saw it because the parade passed by on the route I took to work. The streetcar stopped to let the lines of shuffling men go by. At the front of the parade was a German staff car with a megaphone bolted to the roof. The loudspeaker announced that these men were criminals who had been released from prison to fight against the Werhmacht. The soldiers were still in their combat clothes. Some had greasepaint on their faces. They looked very scruffy and tired. Some men tried to keep step and march in military order, but it seemed to me that the German guards who flanked them made sure they kept falling out of step. I saw German soldiers take out cigarettes, light them and take just one puff. Then they threw the smouldering cigarettes among the soldiers, some of whom scrambled to pick up the smoke. Other soldiers, realizing that this was being done to humiliate them, stepped on the hands of those who grovelled for the tobacco.

Crowds gathered on the street corners to watch the men go by. I saw a few French people, mostly women, shouting and spitting at the Allied soldiers. The soldiers looked astonished at this display of hostility. One woman darted into the crowd and began screaming at a man who had a small American flag sewn on the left arm of his tunic. The man tried to ignore her. She slapped him in the head. Then she spat in his face. The man spat right back at her. A German soldier pulled the woman out of the ranks.

I wondered if some of those people who shouted at the Allied soldiers had been put there specially by the Germans, but when the parade had passed, these same people went back into their houses and shops. The nasal hum of the loudspeakers faded away down the road.

When I saw those soldiers degraded like that, I felt the same rage as I had seen in the eyes of people who stared at me when I emerged from fancy restaurants or the opera, living the life of a collaborator.

There was nothing to do about it, except get on with the work.

My turpentine-fogged brain turned into a maze of technical complications concerning *The Astronomer*. Like most Vermeers, of which there weren't that many, it was a complicated work. This was particularly true in Vermeer's use of shadows. They were not merely shadows but incorporated all the colours of the objects – the wall, the armoire, the astronomer's robe, the book being consulted by the astronomer; Metius's *Astronomicae & Geographicae*. There was more to this complexity than any nameable sum of its parts. The painting, to a greater degree than any other work I'd studied, contained something overwhelming and mysterious. I became fixated on one thin line of white that showed on the astronomer's left forearm, where his shirt peeked out from under the robe. I made myself dizzy thinking about the repetition of circles in the painting: in the globe and the astronomer's head and the curve of his shoulder and the chart on the wall and the stained glass in the window. Sometimes I could hold all these ideas inside my head in some fragile scaffolding of thought. Other times, the whole structure would crash down around me and I would be left staring at the frosted windows of the Dimitri, too dazed even to talk. I thought about Hitler's art expert, Hermann Voss. I had imaginary conversations with him. I dreamed about him, and in those dreams he took on the face of the man in the painting.

On one of these nights, I heard voices. First I thought it was people in the adjoining apartments. Then I thought it was people out in the street. I wondered if I might be dreaming. But I was wide awake. Listening to them was like the times I had talked on the telephone and heard conversations on other lines. I couldn't make out the words, just the voices. They didn't seem to be aware of me. I felt as if I had come up against some kind of veil that lay between us. It was as if the voices themselves made up the fabric of this veil. They seemed to come from more than one place. I had no sense of where they belonged in space or time. I thought there must be some trick to pushing past this veil, but I couldn't grasp it. Each time I reached for it, even in my thoughts, the veil would disappear.

I'd had the same sensation as I worked on *The Astronomer*. It was an overwhelming feeling of being in the presence of something whose complete meaning I could not comprehend. Even to try would open up a vastness that could not be contained within the flinty casing of my skull.

After a while the voices faded away. In their place was the familiar rumble of the sleeping city.

Finally, after six weeks of work, I was close to completing a version that I believed might be successful if Pankratov could age the canvas properly. In all this time, there had been no word from Tombeau or Madame Pontier.

By then it was the beginning of August. The situation in Paris had become precarious. A new German military governor named von Choltitz was installed at the end of the first week. There were rumours that he planned to destroy the entire city, after engineers had been seen attaching explosive charges to all the bridges over the Seine.

There was a transport strike. It looked as if I was going to have to get out to the warehouse by bicycle, which would have added hours to each working day. But Pankratov told me not to bother. He said it was time for him to take over. It would take him at least a week to complete his own work. He told us to let Dietrich know he could have the painting in ten days.

'Dietrich will never be able to get the Gottheim collection to Paris in time,' said Fleury. 'The city could be liberated any day now.'

I put in a call to Dietrich and asked him if he could still get the Gottheim collection.

He laughed. 'It's already here in the city. How soon can you get me my painting?'

'Ten days,' I told him.

'You haven't got ten days!' he shouted. 'Neither have I! I need it sooner.'

I paused. The sound of static was like water rushing through my head. 'I'll do the best I can,' I told him.

'David,' he said, 'you've got to bring me that painting. I will give you until the twenty-third. After that, you stand to lose more than just the Gottheim collection. Do you understand?'

On 15 August, the Paris police went on strike.

French officials of the collaborationist government fled the city.

The German radio station, Radio Paris, stopped broadcasting.

On the morning of the eighteenth, the postal workers went on strike, followed by most other services later in the day.

I was sitting in the Dimitri that evening, when two men burst in carrying rifles. 'Ferdinand Le Goff,' they said.

Out of reflex, everyone looked at Le Goff, who was sitting at his regular table, in his usual mud-brown clothes and smoking a cigarette pinched between one of his hooks.

One of the men dragged him out into the street and bundled him into a car.

Le Goff shrieked and wept and flailed his chrome-clawed hands.

The other man stayed in the café. 'The traitor Le Goff,' he announced, 'is responsible for the deaths of thirty-four members of the CPL, executed by Germans in the Bois de Boulogne the day before yesterday. He gave up their names for a thousand francs apiece,' he said, before ducking back out into the street.

The car sped away.

It had happened so quickly that we only looked at each other in confusion, knowing that Le Goff was as good as dead. We could do nothing about it. Our emotions had long ago been overtaxed. There was nothing left to feel for him. I could find neither pity at the certainty of his inevitable execution, nor anger at his betrayal of the resistance fighters, nor even fear that I might be the next to get dragged off. Like so many things in those days, it became simply a fact, to be filed away and worked through at some later date, as other facts piled up inside my head.

Slowly, inevitably, we turned back to our drinking. A woman came in and sat in Le Goff's place. She ordered a drink, and Ivan served her.

Posters appeared on the morning of the nineteenth, announcing that the Comité Parisien de la Libération had taken control of the Mayor's office and were promising to restore services as soon as possible. At the bottom of the posters, in block capitals, was: VIVE LA REPUBLIQUE! VIVE LE XIV ARRONDISSEMENT! VIVE PARIS! VIVE LA FRANCE! VIVE LES ALLIES ANGLO-SOVIETO-AMERICAINS!

In the afternoon Germans troops attacked the Prefecture of Police, but agreed to a cease fire, which lasted through most of the twentieth. By then, the Town Hall was also in the hands of the Resistance.

Early in the morning on the twenty-first, a German truck that had been stolen by a member of the French communist resistance blew a tyre while it was racing down the Rue Descalzi. The driver lost control and crashed through the front of the Café Dimitri. The café wasn't open yet, but Ivan was still sleeping on the bar top. The room filled with dust and broken glass and the first thing Ivan saw when he opened his eyes was the front of the truck and the face of the astonished driver, who turned out to be a regular customer. The driver got out of the truck and looked around at the wreckage of the café. He was dazed and bleeding from a cut on his chin. 'It's all right,' he told Ivan. 'It's only me.' Then he ran away before the Germans arrived.

Later, when the truck had been towed off, the café floor swept and the damaged chairs and tables thrown away, Ivan hung a sign in the place where the window used to be. The sign said: MORE OPEN THAN USUAL.

On the twenty-second, Resistance fighters patrolled the streets in cars. They carried bird-hunting shotguns and ancient pistols and swords. Men clung to the running boards and sat on the roofs and the cowlings. They wore armbands painted with the double cross of Lorraine and the letters FFI beneath, the letters of the Resistance movement. Others became stretcher-bearers, carrying the wounded to makeshift hospitals set up in pharmacies or restaurants. All across the city, people who had been forced into apathy by the years of occupation at last found themselves able to act. Even the smallest gestures became things I would never forget, like a woman I saw who lowered a pot of soup down from her window and left it hanging a few feet above the ground for anyone passing by who might be hungry. I knew also that scores were being settled. Before the Allies reached Paris, Parisians would die at the hands of other Parisians, payback for the years of collaboration. I had no doubt that we were on somebody's list – probably on a good many lists – and that we would have no chance to explain before their vengeance overtook us.

'Pankratov asked for my help at the warehouse tonight,' I said to Fleury when we met that afternoon at the Dimitri. We had a table in the corner, where we could talk without being overheard, as long as we kept our voices down. 'We're almost done.'

'Good,' said Fleury. 'I can't stand much more waiting. I sit around the apartment . . .'

'In your armour.'

'Yes, indeed, but I tell you it is straining the image a bit to wear a smoking jacket when one has nothing left to smoke.'

'I don't know what you'll think of the painting,' I said.

'What do *you* think of it?' he asked.

I shook my head. 'The damned thing has filled up so much of my brain that I can't even picture it as a complete image. It's as if I can see it through a magnifying glass – pieces of it, the tiniest detail. But the whole thing . . .' I shook my head again. 'I just . . . I don't know.'

Public transport had pretty much shut down. I had to borrow a bicycle from Madame LaRoche. It was a ridiculously heavy thing with brakepads made of wood since the rubber had worn out. She told me to wear my oldest pair of shoes, because the wooden pads sometimes failed, in which case I would have to stop the bike by dragging my heels on the road. I didn't get very far, anyway. Barricades had appeared on street corners all over Paris. The tarmac on the roads was peeled up and the old cobblestones beneath used to make walls. Some barricades were made of downed trees, others of beds and mattresses and chairs. It took me over three hours of detours to get to the warehouse. Some streets were wide open and empty. At others, we were flagged down by men and women in civilian clothes waving pistols and told that German snipers had staked out the road ahead. At some barricades, there were more spectators than Resistance fighters, and it was hard to tell which was which, since everybody who could find a helmet or an old gun was taking to the streets.

That night, with the sweat from bicycling still cooling in my soaked clothes, I helped Pankratov switch the frame from the original to our forgery. By morning, we were finished. It was 23 August, the last day Dietrich had given us to deliver the painting.

I was tired and shaking with cold, because I'd had no chance to change my wet clothes and we hadn't lit a fire. The only thing keeping me awake now was adrenalin. I sat down in Pankratov's chair and looked at *The Astronomer*. 'Voss,' I said, as if to summon the demon who had lived inside my skull these past two months. Every time I managed to persuade myself that the forgery was fine, the spectre of this man would rear up and destroy my confidence.

'Hermann Voss is not in Paris,' said Pankratov, 'and even if he can tell the difference, there won't be anybody like him waiting at Dietrich's office. Anyone with that kind of expertise is smart enough to have left by now.'

Using scraps of wood, we built a small crate around it and attached two canvas straps so we could take turns carrying the painting on our backs. I tried to call Fleury but the phone line in Madame LaRoche's building was dead. Then I tried the Dimitri, and that line was dead, too.

'We should go straight to Dietrich,' said Pankratov. 'This is our last chance. It might already be too late. There's no time to check with Fleury.'

'We promised him,' I said. 'We have to.'

Pankratov looked down at his boots. He scratched at the back of his neck. Then he nodded slowly.

We set off through the streets, Pankratov shouldering the crate. As we made our way to the Rue Descalzi, we saw the first Allied tanks to enter Paris. They were surrounded by men and women waving bottles of wine and throwing flowers on to the armour-plating. The tanks were painted with French names like *Romily* and *Champaubert* and each machine had a small white map of France painted in a white circle on its side. Behind them came armoured cars and French troops. The crowds screamed and danced in front of the soldiers. I wondered where those people were now who had spat and jeered at the Allied prisoners of war as they had straggled through these streets only a few weeks before.

I began to feel the exhilaration of the crowd. It hummed in me like an electric current. I had the strange feeling that everything going on around me was inevitable, as if I had lived it before, like an event whose happening had been predicted far in the past. The whole of history was pivoting on this one place. Nobody who was here today would ever forget it.

Pankratov weaved dangerously close to me on his bike. My wooden brakepads smoked against the rims. The heels were almost worn off my shoes. At one point, Pankratov stopped, his head bowed over the handlebars of his bicycle. The exertion of the past weeks had finally caught up with him. I made him unshoulder the crate. The wood was damp with his sweat and his old canvas coat was shredded where the splinters had dug into his back. I heaved the crate on to my own back and we kept going. By the time we reached the Rue Descalzi, I was coated with sweat and dust. My shoulder blades were raw from the sharp edges of the wood. We found the street blocked by a barricade made of two park benches, some old suitcases and Madame LaRoche, along with her friend, Madame Côty. Madame LaRoche had found herself a German helmet that was too big for her. Madame Côty was carrying two German stick grenades in her apron. As usual, both were wearing their housedresses. Behind the barricade, they had set up their chairs and were sitting on them when we arrived. A dozen rabbits were hopping about on the road.

Pankratov and I stopped just in front of the barricade. It was like this all over Paris. In one street, people were celebrating. In another, snipers were doing battle on the rooftops.

Outside the Postillon warehouse, I noticed a man sitting by himself on an upturned wine crate. He had a bottle of red wine open beside him and was drinking from it thoughtfully. He raised his head to feel the sun against his face and the threads of grey in his moustache were lit up in the afternoon brightness. I recognized him now. It was the old Dragoon. Crouched beside him was Monsieur Finel. The two men were speaking in voices too low to pick up. Now and then, one of them would nod thoughtfully, and this would set the other nodding, too.

I also noticed Madame Lindgren and the Charbonniers. Madame Lindgren was giving an impromptu dance lesson to their son Hubert, who stared at her in amazement as she held his arms and swung them back and forth.

Madame LaRoche walked up to me. She tilted her head back until she could see out from under her helmet. 'Oh, it's you, Monsieur Halifax,' she said.

'They shall not pass!' shouted Madame Côty, and waved one of her grenades.

'Have you seen Fleury?' I asked.

'He's gone,' replied Madame LaRoche. 'A man came to see him and they both left several hours ago.'

'What did the man look like?' I asked.

Under the iron hood of her helmet, Madame LaRoche's face crumpled with the effort of thinking. 'He was wearing a suit. He had shiny shoes. At first I thought it was you.'

Then I knew it must be Dietrich. 'Did they say where they were going?' I asked.

Madame LaRoche shook her head. 'They didn't seem to be in any hurry. They walked that way.' She gestured down the street.

I turned to Pankratov. 'That's towards the Avenue d'Iena.'

'Be careful with those grenades,' Pankratov told Madame Côty. 'Do you know how they work?'

'You throw them!' shouted Madame Côty.

'Madame LaRoche,' I said. 'Your rabbits.'

'I have liberated them!' she shouted.

By the time we left, Madame LaRoche was dancing with the Dragoon to an Edith Piaf song being played on a gramophone out of someone's window far above us. The two of them rose up on their toes, holding hands and sawing back and forth and singing. Madame Lindgren was sidestepping around them, holding up her hands, fingertips pinched together, and saying 'One, two, three, four. Very good. Very good.'

We set off for the Avenue d'Iena. Even if Dietrich and Fleury weren't there, someone at that place would know where to find them. By now, gunfire was coming from all directions, and with it the revving of big engines, shouted commands and the sound of breaking glass. We managed to avoid streets where there was fighting. Blocking one avenue was a Sherman tank. It was one of the tanks I had seen earlier, a large number 34 painted on its turret, which had been flipped upside down by an explosion. It was still garlanded with flowers from its entry into the city. The olive paint was blistered by fire. Oily smoke billowed from its hatches. One of the crew lay face down on the cobblestones beside it. Someone had scattered flower petals across the dead man's back.

We kept moving, through the heat and dust. I tried to block out the pain in my cramped leg muscles from pedalling the bike. We raced along the streets. Sunlight flickered off the windows of buildings high above us, splashing into my eyes and blinding me.

Half an hour later we were standing in front of the ruins of what had been ERR headquarters. The street was covered with sand from spilled sandbags. The road surface was patched with the starburst marks of exploded grenades. The windows had all been shot out and chunks of stone were gouged from the window frames. The marble steps that led up to the main door were smeared with blood and littered with bullet cartridges. The huge doors had been blown off their hinges. Smoke seeped from one room. The curtains had burned and the little wooden rings that had once held the curtains were smouldering. A black streak, like the path of a comet, showed across the wall inside where a Molotov cocktail had blazed.

The Avenue d'Iena looked empty now. I looked up at the buildings on either side of me. A few of the windows were broken, but otherwise they looked untouched.

'We're too late,' said Pankratov. He set his bike against the iron railing that ran in front of the ERR building. The rails had been pierced by bullets and curved up like crooked fingers.

I walked up the steps, kicking aside brass cartridges, which jangled over the bloody marble. As I stepped inside the foyer, the first thing I saw was the reception desk, where Grimm had manned the phones when he wasn't driving for Dietrich. The front of the desk had been chopped to splinters by a burst of machine-gun fire. Grimm lay behind the desk, spread-eagled on the floor next to the chair in which he had been sitting. He had been hit several times in the chest and legs. There was very little blood, only spatters of it around where the bullets had gone through his clothes. His eyes were open and patient, the way I remembered them in life. The holster for his pistol was open and the pistol was missing. His pockets had been turned inside out and the lightning-bolt insignia cut from his collar.

The foyer had been stripped of furnishings. There were no tapestries or pictures on the wall, and the bullet marks in the plaster reminded me of a map of some constellation of stars.

The staircase that led up to Dietrich's office was charred by more Molotovs. Wine bottles that had held liquid for the home-made bombs lay in melted shards on the steps. There was more blood on the wall at the top of the stairs, where it looked as if someone had been shot and had fallen back down the staircase.

It was quiet, except for the rustle of my feet over the sand-gritty floorboards. 'Dietrich?' I shouted, hearing my voice bounce back. 'Thomas Dietrich? It's David Halifax. I'm here with Pankratov.'

After another moment of silence, I heard footsteps upstairs.

'Hello?' I called out.

'Is that you, David?' It was Dietrich.

'Stay there!' I raced up the stairs, the crate bouncing against my back, its makeshift shoulder-straps numbing my hands and elbows as it cut off the flow of blood.

Dietrich stood on the landing outside his office. He was holding a Schmeisser, the folding stock tucked up into the armpit of his grey suit, which was torn at the knees. The red, black and white enamel Nazi party badge was still in his buttonhole. His hair was scorched and his face smudged black with smoke.

'We brought you the Vermeer,' I told him.

'I thought you weren't coming,' he said. 'I was sure you had let me down.'

At his feet, just outside his study door, was the body of a man, in a short leather jacket, lying face down on fragments of broken glass.

'What the hell happened?' I asked. 'Are you all right?'

He looked around, as if seeing the damage for the first time. 'They only left about ten minutes ago. They'll be back. I think they just ran out of ammunition.'

'Who?' I asked.

'The Fabry-Georges.' He jabbed one of the dead men with his toe. 'I expect they thought if they could bring the Resistance my head on a plate, it might make up for everything else.' He rubbed his forehead against his sleeve. 'I've spent the last half-hour trying to change their minds.'

'Where's Fleury?' I asked. 'You were with him, weren't you?'

'Yes,' replied Dietrich, 'but he's not here now.'

'He must have gone back to the apartment,' I said. I was thinking how angry he would be that we had brought the painting to Dietrich without letting him see it first. But it was too late now.

'Did you see Grimm down there?' asked Dietrich.

'Yes,' I said. 'I'm afraid I did.'

Dietrich leaned back against the doorframe. 'I was hoping he might have got out.'

Pankratov appeared at the top of the stairs. 'Holy Christ,' he said, when he saw the body and the bullet cases.

I unshouldered the crate.

With a stag-handled pocket-knife, Pankratov pried off one of the slats and pulled out the painting.

Dietrich lowered the Schmeisser, never taking his eyes off the canvas, which Pankratov slowly turned around so he could see the painting. With one reddened, gun-smoked hand, Dietrich took the painting from Pankratov's outstretched arms. He glanced at it for a couple of seconds before he turned his face towards us. He was smiling.

Pankratov and I watched him carefully, for any trace of doubt to cloud his face.

Dietrich turned back towards his office. 'Come out!'

I glanced at Pankratov.

Pankratov shrugged and shook his head.

There was a muffled moan from somewhere in Dietrich's office.

'Out you come,' commanded Dietrich impatiently.

'Has the shooting stopped?' asked a nasal, terrfied voice. 'My ears are still ringing.'

'Of course the damned shooting has stopped!' barked Dietrich. 'Now come out of that damned closet and do your job and then you can go home. Come along, Sniffles.'

Then I knew it was Touchard who had been hiding in the closet. I felt the familiar out-of-control pounding in my chest.

Touchard appeared in the doorway. His suit was crumpled. One of the sleeves was torn at the elbow. 'But I don't want to go home!' wailed Touchard. 'I want to go to Spain! And I expect it's too late now, anyway! You've never treated me fairly!'

'Stop blathering.' Dietrich gave him a shove with the barrel of the Schmeisser. 'Just get on with it.'

Touchard caught sight of the dead Fabry-Georges man on

the landing. He cried out and stepped back into Dietrich, who pushed him forward again.

'Tell me if it's right,' said Dietrich, handing out the painting to Touchard. Then he looked at us and smiled. 'Just a formality, you understand.'

Touchard stepped forward to take it, bony hands held out. It was the first time he acknowleged our presence in the room.

Dietrich leaned against the doorframe. The Schmeisser dangled in his hand. The black tip of the barrel with its covered gunsight swung like a pendulum just above the level of the floor.

I didn't look at Pankratov. I kept my eyes on Touchard.

Touchard squinted at *The Astronomer*. He held it close to his face and then held it out again. His eyes were narrowed. Then he looked up from the painting and right into my eyes.

It was the first time he had acknowledged our presence in the room, and in that moment, I knew he had seen through the forgery.

'What's the matter?' asked Dietrich. His face seemed to change, as if his body would at any moment crack like glass, and something terrible would step from the brittle shell: what he really was; what I'd known all along in my heart. He would kill everyone. Me, Touchard, Pankratov. His rage would overtake him.

'What is it, Touchard?' he asked.

I tried to breathe in but couldn't.

'Nothing,' blurted Touchard. 'There's nothing wrong with it. I've just never seen it so close up before.' A nervous laugh slithered out of his mouth.

I looked down at my shoes. My eyes had dried out from staring.

Pankratov cleared his throat. He looked around the room, blinking as if he had just woken up.

Dietrich took the painting and propped it against the wall.

Touchard wiped his nose, which had started to run. 'Can I go now?' he asked.

'Not yet,' said Dietrich. 'Hold out your hands.'

Hesitantly, Touchard held out his cupped hands, as if he expected Dietrich to cut them off at the wrists. 'What is it?' he asked in a whisper.

I thought of the statue back at the warehouse. The one Dietrich had smashed. I imagined Touchard's brittle fingers rattling to the floor.

Dietrich reached into his pocket and pulled out a fistful of coins. They were gold. He set them in Touchard's hands. The heavy sovereigns clunked as they settled in Touchard's palms. 'Now you can go,' said Dietrich.

Touchard pushed past us, avoiding our glances. At the head of the stairs, he turned to Pankratov and me. 'I have always been . . .' he began.

'Go!' shouted Dietrich.

Touchard ran down the stairs and out into the street. His footsteps faded away.

I wondered then whether Touchard might have seen through more than just this one painting. Perhaps there had been many that he let slip through. The little man had paid back Dietrich after all, for five long years of ridicule.

Holding *The Astronomer* with one hand, Dietrich reached into his other pocket and pulled out an old iron key. He chucked it to Pankratov, who caught it as it slapped into his palm. 'There you go, gentlemen. The Gottheim collection is in the basement. It's all there. I'll be leaving now. Perhaps you'd be kind enough to see me off.'

Pankratov and Dietrich fitted the painting back into its crate. They tapped the nails back in place with the butt of the Schmeisser. Then Dietrich shouldered the crate. He rolled his shoulders, settling the splintered wood against his spine. He tucked the Schmeisser under his arm. Then from his pocket he pulled a white armband. On its band was a poorly drawn cross of Lorraine and the letters FFI. He tugged the band up his sleeve until it rested over his biceps. 'About time I joined the Resistance,' he said. 'In the last twenty-four hours, everybody else has.' He plucked the party badge from his lapel. He lifted the dead man by the hair and hooked the needle clasp of the badge right through the dead man's lips. Then Dietrich let him go again. The head thumped back on to the floor.

We followed him downstairs. On our way out of the building, Dietrich stopped to look down at the body of Grimm. Then he kept walking, out to a metal storage shed in the courtyard at the back. Inside was a large Zundapp motorcycle. He rolled it off its kickstand and out into the courtyard. Then he straddled it and fired up the motor, revving hard.

'Where's Valya?' Pankratov shouted over the rumble of the engine.

'She left me two days ago,' he said. 'I expect she'll turn up at your place before long.' Dietrich smiled his old confident smile. 'I never should have doubted you. I'm ashamed to say that I did. My mistake,' he said. 'Gentlemen, I will see you on the other side.' He gunned the Zundapp's engine, roared out into the street and sped away.

When the sound of his engine had become indistinguishable among the other sounds of the city, I turned to Pankratov. 'What did he mean when he said he'd see us on the other side?' I asked.

'I don't know,' said Pankratov.

'I thought we were finished,' I told him.

Pankratov breathed out, composing himself. He held up the key. 'Shall we take a look?'

The narrow stone staircase spiralled down to the basement. High, gloss-white walls rose up on either side of us. The stairs ended abruptly at a door, which had a large bolt drawn across it, held in place by a bronze padlock. Pankratov fumbled with the key, then opened the padlock and slid back the bolt. He set his shoulder against the door and pushed it open.

The first thing I saw when the door swung wide was Fleury. He was hanging from a hemp-rope noose, his feet only a few inches above the floor. The rope was attached to the iron railings that spanned the ceiling. A chair lay on its side underneath him. Fleury's head was slumped over on to one shoulder. His lips were blue and his eyelids puffy and red. He wore the armour of his smoking jacket.

I ran across the room and grabbed his legs, holding him up, while Pankratov set up the chair, climbed up on to it and cut through the rope with his penknife. By the time we got him down to the floor, I already knew he was dead.

It was only then that I took in the walls of the room. Filling almost every inch of space were the paintings of the Gottheim collection. My eyes fixed on one small painting on the back wall. It showed a little girl in a dark-blue dress, holding a basket of flowers. It was Pankratov's painting of Valya.

I sat down beside Fleury. Everything around me slipped in and out of focus. The colours of the paintings seemed to shimmer.

Fleury's glasses were in his top pocket, where he always put them. I took them out and held them.

Pankratov was standing over me. He was looking down at Fleury. His eyes were filled with tears.

I thought about what Dietrich had said – that he had been sure we weren't coming. This was Fleury's punishment for having failed him. I knew he would have done the same to me and Pankratov if we had been there at the time.

Pankratov went over to his painting and took it off the wall, where it had been hung on a nail. He held it close to his face. Behind where the picture had hung, on a nail driven into the soft wall, were the same ghostly handprints I had seen the time before.

We were startled by the sound of footsteps and shouting up at street level. Then someone came running down the stairs.

We stayed frozen. There was no place to go.

The man was so shocked when he saw us that he fell over backwards in an attempt to get out of the way. He was also carrying a Schmeisser, and the gun fell back hard against his chest. The man pressed himself against the wall, but there was no cover.

I recognized him. It was Tombeau.

His teeth were bared and his heavy leather coat was torn from the fall. He aimed the gun into the room. It was a second before he realized it was us. 'Where's Dietrich?' he shouted.

'Gone,' I said.

'How long ago?'

'Ten minutes,' I told him.

'On foot?'

'Motorcycle.'

Tombeau gritted his teeth, then kicked a hole in the wall. 'Damn!' he shouted. Then he noticed Fleury. He walked over to the body, bent down and took Fleury's jaw in his hand. The rope was still around Fleury's neck. Tombeau turned Fleury's head from side to side, then let him go and rose back to his feet. 'Madame Pontier just found out what you did with *The Astronomer*. You'd better know exactly where it is or you're all going to end up like your friend here.'

'*The Astronomer*,' said Pankratov slowly, 'is in my warehouse. Dietrich left with a forgery.'

Tombeau paused. 'You actually forged it?'

'We did,' Pankratov told him.

'Well, I'll be damned,' he said. 'Madame Pontier said you didn't have the guts.'

There was the sound of footsteps. Someone was coming down the stairs.

Tombeau walked over to Pankratov. He jerked his head at the stairs. 'You're coming with me to the warehouse, and the original had damn well better be there.'

'Fine,' replied Pankratov.

Another man appeared in the doorway. He was tall, with a beer-belly and a scrub-brush moustache. He wore a leather coat like Tombeau and carried a Luger. He glanced at us, then turned to Tombeau. 'No sign of Dietrich.'

'Doesn't matter now,' said Tombeau.

The man scanned the walls and whistled through his teeth.

'Not bad,' he said. 'This should make up for some of the money we're owed.'

'I expect it will,' replied Tombeau.

The man jerked his head towards us. 'What are you going to do with this lot?'

'Do what I have to,' said Tombeau.

The man looked at us for a second, then nodded and looked away.

'Go tell the others what's down here,' Tombeau told the man. Then he waved a hand at us. 'Move!' he shouted.

'What about Fleury?' I asked, still not getting up. I couldn't stand to leave him here.

Tombeau crouched down beside me and whispered, his lips so close to my ear I could feel them touching me. 'If we don't leave immediately, these people are going to find out who you are. And if they do, you'll never get out of here. Do you understand?'

'David,' said Pankratov.

His voice knocked me out of my shock. I got up and shuffled towards the door.

Pankratov was carrying his painting of Valya.

'You leave that,' said the man at the door. 'That's ours.'

Pankratov hesitated.

'Leave it!' shouted Tombeau and his voice sank dull and echoless into the torture chamber walls.

Pankratov put down the painting and we filed up the stairs with Tombeau, just as a dozen Fabry-Georges were walking down. Each of us pressed our backs to the walls to make room. The men held their guns to their chests. We eyed each other curiously. I smelled tobacco, alcohol and sweat.

Out in the street, two black Renault cars belonging to the Fabry-Georges were pulled up on the kerb. One had bullet holes in the windshield. Tombeau glanced back to see if any of the Fabry-Georges were behind him. Then he turned to us. 'You,' he said to me, 'you have to get out of here. Out of Paris.

There's about five hundred people who'll shoot you on sight, until I can clear up this mess.'

'What about me?' asked Pankratov.

'You're staying with me until we get the Vermeer. When Madame Pontier gets that back, you'll be all right with her.'

'What about the Gottheim paintings?' I asked.

'As soon as I get back here, I'll take care of them.' Tombeau set his hand on my shoulder. 'I told you I'd set you free one day and now you are free. Get out of here while you still can.'

I looked at Pankratov.

'Do as he says,' said Pankratov.

I shook Pankratov's hand.

'No time for this,' hissed Tombeau and bundled Pankratov into one of the Renaults. He flicked his hand at the other car, the one with the holes in its windshield. 'Take it,' he said to me. 'The keys are inside. There are two cans of fuel in the back.' Then Tombeau climbed behind the wheel of his car. He started the engine, clanking it into gear, and sped off down the road. Pankratov watched me through the rear window until they turned sharply at the corner, tyres squealing, and disappeared.

I found myself suddenly alone on the Avenue d'Iena. The smell of extinguished fires blew lazily into the street from the charred window frames of Dietrich's building.

I got in the car and drove.

One hour later I was heading through fields west of the city. Flowers were stuck under my windshield wipers from a street party I had passed through on my way out. My eyes watered from wind blowing in through the holes in the windshield. The August sun was hot on my knuckles as they gripped the steering wheel. Convoys of American trucks passed us, heading in the other direction. Large white stars were painted on their hoods.

I didn't know where I was going. I just kept heading west. Late in the day, I was stopped at a military checkpoint near Carpiquet. An American military policeman walked over to my car and leaned in. The green paint on the rim of his helmet had been worn away, showing the bare steel underneath. Behind him an old farmhouse was burning by the side of the road. Milky smoke poured like an inverted waterfall from the upstairs windows. 'Taking a road trip?'

'Yes, I am,' I answered him in English.

He raised his eyebrows when he heard my accent. 'Where you from?' he asked.

'Paris,' I told him.

'No,' he laughed quietly. 'Where you from really?'

We talked for a few minutes. Then he told me I was free to go.

I continued on through the twilight and into the night, towards the coast of Normandy. Across the moonlit fields I saw the lights of distant towns out in the dark, where street-lamps pooled their glow on empty roads.

That was more than half a century ago.

I returned to America on a hospital ship in September of 1944.

In 1946 I took a job teaching art at a school in Narragansett, just down the road from where I grew up. I taught for the next thirty years. In 1950 I got married to a woman named Catherine, who was another teacher at the school. Over the next five years we had two children. I continued to paint, and if my life's work was more complicated than those around me knew, I kept it to myself.

The only souvenir I had from my time in Paris was Fleury's glasses. Sometimes, when no one was looking, I would put them on and feel the pull in my eyes as they tried to focus into Fleury's blurry world.

I never found out what happened to the forgery. I often wondered where it was and what had become of Thomas Dietrich.

Madame Pontier became a national hero in France. For many years after the war I often saw her still-unsmiling face in the grey haze of newspaper pictures.

I kept in touch with Pankratov. I last saw him in Paris in the late 1950s. He and Valya were still running his atelier, although Valya didn't model any more. They used to joke that they were the only people who could put up with each other, and they were probably right. Valya managed the books and made sure he didn't chase away all his students by acting crazy. He still went down to Ivan's every morning, and the two of them carried on much as they had done before the war. Pankratov and Ivan both passed away in 1960, within a few months of each other.

The Gottheim collection never surfaced. By the time Tombeau returned from Pankratov's warehouse with the

Vermeer, the Fabry-Georges had taken everything and disappeared. Over the years, a few of the works appeared at auctions, their sources listed as anonymous. The authenticity of the paintings was often disputed, since few people believed that the Gottheim collection had in fact survived.

Last year, I saw Pankratov's painting of Valya pictured in a Christie's auction catalogue. It was unsigned and the catalogue listed the painter as unknown. I attended the auction, bid on the painting and acquired it. The bidding went high. I found myself in competition with one other unidentified bidder who participated in the auction by closed-circuit TV. During the auction, I turned to look at a camera through which this bidder was viewing the proceedings. Immediately afterwards, the other person dropped out. At the end of the sale, I enquired as to whether I might be able to know the name of the other bidder, but was told that would not be possible. I think it was Dietrich. I remembered what he said about seeing me on the other side and thought how, in a strange way, he might have been right after all.

Until the auction, I'd never had a chance to study the work up close. In it, Valya was sitting on a plain wooden bench in a room with white-painted walls, wearing a blue dress. Her red-brown hair was ponytailed and her little buckle shoes had geometric patterns cut into the leather of the toes. The colours were bright, seeming almost to vibrate. It was strange to see such beauty from a man as gruff and coarse as Pankratov.

My wife and I donated the painting to the Musée Duarte, with a plaque on the frame that read: VALYA, BY ALEXANDER PANKRATOV. IN MEMORY OF GUILLAUME FLEURY. We had a very small ceremony at the Duarte, with the museum director, Valya, Cath and me.

'I never really knew Fleury,' Valya said to Cath. 'He was always just that funny little man.' She had brought along Pankratov's canvas chair. The museum director allowed it to be placed beside a viewing bench that faced Pankratov's painting.

As we left, I watched a group of students fanning out through the museum, paper in hand, ready to draw their assignments. A young woman settled into Pankratov's chair and began a sketch of Valya.

We said our goodbyes.

That evening, I took a walk alone in the honeyed sunset light. I went as far as the Gare St Lazare and stood at the end of the main platform, watching the trains pull in and out. I felt the hot breath of the engines passing by.

I won't be coming back again. Until this day, those few years I spent in Paris had always been my great unfinished business, scattered among unconsummated loves and half-grasped revelations. I have lived in quiet, patient hope for the moment to arrive that would mark the end and the beginning of this dream I had when I was young.

Now it is time to go home.

Notes

Notes are based on texts studied in the preparation of this book and may be only partially complete.

The Astronomer, painted by Vermeer *c.* 1668. Became part of the collection of the Baron Alphonse de Rothschild in 1907. At the time of the German invasion, the painting was in the collection of Baron Edouard de Rothschild in France, where it was seized by the ERR. It was taken to the Jeu de Paumes, declared to be property of the Third Reich and was then transported by train to Germany in a crate marked H13, indicating that it was designated to be part of Hitler's private collection. On 13 November 1940, Rosenberg, head of the ERR, wrote a letter to Martin Bormann, Hitler's financial secretary, announcing the find and mentioning Hitler's special interest in the painting. The painting was returned to France at the end of the war and was exhibited in the 'Exhibition of Masterpieces from French Collections recovered from Germany', held at the Orangerie in Paris in 1946.

SOURCES:

The Lost Museum, by Hector Feliciano, HarperCollins/Basic Books, 1997.
Johannes Vermeer, Gemalde Gesamtausgabe, Ludwig Goldscheider, Phaidon Verlag, Koln, 1958.

Portrait of a Young Girl, painted by Lucas Cranach possibly as early as 1520. Collection Paris, Louvre, acquired in 1910. Although it is widely believed to be a painting of the daughter of Martin Luther, who was born in 1529, the style of the painting is closer to Cranach's work in the early 1520s, so the identity of the subject remains in question.

SOURCE:

Lucas Cranach, by Max Friedlander and Jakob Rosenberg, Tabard Press, NY, 1978.

Although many of the other paintings mentioned in this text do exist, their roles in this novel are entirely fictitious and any correspondence with their actual history during the time period of the novel is accidental and unintentional.